ONCE UPON A TIME

Other Books by John Barth

ONCE UPON A TIME

A Floating Opera

JOHN BARTH

LITTLE, BROWN AND COMPANY

BOSTON   NEW YORK   TORONTO   LONDON

First Paperback Edition

This novel is a work of fiction. Names, characters,
places, and incidents are either the product of the author's
imagination or, if real, are used fictitiously.

Portions of this book have appeared, in somewhat different form,
in the *Mississippi Review*, *New York Times Book Review*, and *Paris Review*.

Library of Congress Cataloging-in-Publication Data

Barth, John.
 Once upon a time : a floating opera / John Barth.
  p. cm.
 ISBN 0-316-08262-7 (hc) 0-316-082589 (pb)
  1. Novelists, American — 20th century — Fiction. I. Title.
 PS3552.A75O53 1994
 813'.54 — dc20   93-31456

10 9 8 7 6 5 4 3 2 1

MV-NY

*Published simultaneously in Canada
by Little, Brown & Company (Canada) Limited*

Printed in the United States of America

for Shelly

PROGRAM NOTE

❧ ❧

Once Upon a Time — a memoir bottled in a novel and here floated off to whom it may concern — is not the story of my life, but it is most certainly *a* story thereof. Its theme is Vocation. The better to sing it, I have passed over or scarcely sounded other themes, and have reorchestrated freely to my purpose. Of my children, for example, as of real friends and colleagues past and current, there is scarcely a mention. My twin sister makes a fictionalized cameo appearance. My ship- and lifemate, this opera's dedicatee, takes a larger role, likewise fictionalized, in its opening and closing scenes. My thanks to both for their permission to be thus imagined. I have been careful of all hands' privacy except my own, and even that has scarcely been trespassed upon. Every life has a Scheherazadesworth of stories.

—Langford Creek and Baltimore,
12 October 1990 –12 October 1992

PROGRAM

OVERTURE
"Gone"

"GONE."

What?

"Century."

Ah.

It was no dream, then. Our creekside windows have been open through an Indian-summer night, and in our predawn sleep we've registered a sound as of muffled horn: three fading calls that melded, in mid-October earliest light, with cries of geese and swan moving down from Canada. They melded too, on my side of our bed at least, with confused warm dreams of things past . . . and now reforgotten.

You've slipped from me — bare bedmate, my Reality Principle — to stand handsome with the house binoculars in the pewter light of a water-facing bedside window. My head not right, quite, I make my way around the king-size square to embrace you from behind, peer over your shoulder.

"I'm not done sleeping yet," you let me know: part info item, part request, part warning. You unhand my left hand, press into it the seven-by-fifties, and duck deftly back undersheet. "Look. Not a sign."

From the Bahamas or thereabouts, a mild damp air moves through the American South to Maryland and Chesapeake Bay, up the wide and placid Chester River and our fork of Langford Creek, across our lawn, and sweetly over my skin. A touch groggy still, I refocus from your correction to mine, admiring first my summoner (until you draw the bedsheet up and over your head) and then, through the magnifying, light-collecting lenses, the gray but cloudless dawn of what bids to be a fine Delmarva* day.

Aria: "Our pool is winter-covered"

Our pool is winter-covered, its furniture stashed, its concrete deck brown-soaked with a heavy dew that silvers our driftwood trophies and all the grass as well. Along its perimeter, our birches are shedding early over everything. My mate's planters in that neighborhood are firing last rounds of petunia, geranium, impatiens, portulaca. One variety of day lily, even, still flowers down by the creek bulkheading. In the garden proper, where chrysanthemums are in full fettle, our black-eyed Susans are all but done; our tea roses are leggy now, but still producing; marigolds and begonias go strong yet around the emptied, scoured, inverted birdbath, and will till our first hard frost — maybe next week, maybe not before December in these mild latitudes. Dull by New England autumn standards, our maples, crab apples, and cherries are doing their mid-Atlantic post-equinoctial best; the hollies, yews, ivy, and pyrocantha, trimmed once already in September, will need another pruning before they pack it in. Our chestnuts are all harvested. Over by our treasured patch of tidemarsh, where mallows still blossom daily, our tomato vines are cleared out; firewood's stacked on the slab nearby; the "martin house," summer-tenanted by redwinged blackbirds, is stowed against winter gales. My fiftieth-birthday flagpole, blown slightly out of plumb southeastward by a dozen years' northwest storms, awaits its daily banner from our supply.

At the dock, low tide. "Our" mallards — a communal family of year-round residents whose newest generation, born last spring in our marsh, we cannot now distinguish from their parents — quackdabble around the pilings and ladders and the breakwater paralleling the pier. Except for them, our little flotilla is mostly

*The Delmarva Peninsula, between Chesapeake Bay and the Atlantic Ocean, is so named for its comprising the entire state of Delaware plus portions of Maryland and Virginia. [*Author's note, first of a series*]

hauled and stored: The old canoe and Sunfish I've block-and-tack-led up into the rafters of the garage; under them, our even older outboard runabout sits trailered, covered, winterized, and up on jack stands. Even our sailboat tender, normally secured bottom-up on the dock at the bowsprit of the boat it tends, is garaged this time of year; likewise crab traps and other dockside summer par-aphernalia, against Harvest Moon flood tides and the odd late hurricane that might yet brush by while we're at work over in Baltimore or off lecture-traveling. Only our flagship remains in commission till Halloween, hard frost, and Standard Time: a beamy, sturdy, shoal-draft cutter, *US* — aground in its slip just now, as usual at low water, but cradled snugly in the trough that its keel has molded in the mud over eight summersworth of tides. As I do every morning that we and it are both in residence (though seldom so early), I give it a remote once-over from the window: shipshape, ready for a wrap-up weekend cruise or two, a few end-of-season daysails at least, before we deliver it to the boatyard for decommissioning and winter storage.

Beyond *US*, the float of our deeper-water mooring I've replaced with a painted "winter spar," invulnerable to ice; its angle tells me that the tide has turned. Wild geese are rafted by the hundreds out there; vociferous with flyway tidings, new arrivals glide in like miniature Concordes to join them, droop-snooted on final wind-ward approach, flaps down and landing gear extended. And beyond the geese, across our fork of Langford, off "Potamock Point," on "Potamock Island" . . .

On with the overture:

Sure enough: a boatless dock at the Scribner/Duer cottage, hid-den in the rusty oaks over there, where through yesterday's Happy Hour I toasted uncertain bon voyage to Jay Scribner aboard his aging ketch, *American Century*. Those calls, then, will have been my old and problematical friend's sounding usward, over his tran-som, the conch of Departure After All: three lonesome, resonating farewells as he (and, presumably, his lawyer wife, Beth Duer, not at home when I visited) backed out of their slip and away from their dock, away from their secluded island seat — away from their country, even, and their lives thus far — in pursuit of (knowing "Jay Wordsworth Scribner") I know not quite what. They have, I observe, retrieved old *Century*'s docklines from pier and mooring piles, as we shall do some weeks hence when we lay *US* up till spring. But if the fellow means really to go forward with his retrograde, off-again, on-again adventure — retracing Columbus's first voyage in reverse, from New World back to Old, and his own voyage "back to the womb and beyond" — we won't be seeing those lines put out again with ours next spring.

In your direction I report that there *is* a sign, after all. On their dock. But I can't read it until there's light enough to wake me up.

"Come back here before that happens."

Done, and gratefully: *I wake to sleep*, the poet Theodore Roethke sings. But yours truly is a-fidget now, by those conch-calls put in mind of a golden trumpet in the late 1940s, the Fifties and the Sixties, even the early Seventies, with "Jay Scribner" on its business end. And before that trumpet, a dented bugle wherewith, in World War Twotime, Star Scout "Jerome Schreiber" of East Cambridge, Maryland, sounded across our dew-drenched scout-camp parade grounds, at the head of the Chesapeake, sunset retreats and lights-out taps that started tears in my thirteen-year-old eyes. Jerome/Jerry/Jay; Schreiber/Scribner: homegrown last-trump Gabriel! Puissant Joshua at the walls of adolescence! Self-shattering Roland!

And before even that bugle . . .

But let's take our waking slow.

Now we're up, having redozed fitfully after all and made languid Saturday-A.M. love in the full fine light of Columbus Day 1992. Breakfast done, we have withdrawn to separate studies for an hour's work before addressing whatever next weekend chore or pleasure. But I'm not myself this morning: head not quite right, whatever — a touch too much bon voyaging, perhaps. From the windows of my creekside study, where I draw out sentences like these, I re-scan Potamock with the big binocs. A half-dozen "sunbirds," en route down the Intracoastal Waterway from New England and points north toward Florida and points south, are getting under way now from their overnight anchorage behind the island: sloops, cutters, ketches, most of them crewed by middle-aged couples like ourselves, secure anchors and raise sail as they file out of Langford Creek into Chester River for their day's southing down the Bay. At Norfolk, where the bridge-tunnel between the Virginia Capes marks the ocean's threshold, they'll turn off into sheltered canals that lead Carolinaward; once safely below the Outer Banks, from Beaufort or Morehead City the more adventurous will sail "outside" down the coast, standing watches until they reach Florida waters, while the others motor leisurely "inside" to Miami, the Keys, the Gulf Coast, without ever venturing into open water. A monarch butterfly, sunwarmed now, leaves our garden and flutters across my field of view to follow them. Beth and Jay, like the ruby-throated hummingbirds whose empty feeder we've not yet fetched in, have gone before. They, too, if they're really doing it, will in all likelihood take the Dismal Swamp Canal route from Norfolk to Morehead, but will then turn salty old *Century* directly for the Bahamas and — Jay likely thenceforth solo — across to the Azores, Spain, Italy, Greece, Israel, Egypt . . . up the Nile, past the Giza Pyramids, to the limits of navigation.

"Overland, then, somehow," lately vowed my counterself. "Shuck the damn boat, everything. Naked in the Olduvai Gorge, you know? The effing primal rift. Shuck Jay Scribner; shuck Jerry Schreiber. This carcass, too, serviceable old thing: shuck it like old *Century* and dear Beth. *Resorb*, man. You follow me?"

I focus again on their dock, that signboard.

For Sale, I let you know by intercom. Wasn't there last evening. Can't quite make out the realtor's name, but the logo seems bad news: the golden globe of Eldorado Developers.

"So they're actually going the whole way."

Have gone, it would appear.

"Now it's just us, really."

Well.

"Solipsism à deux?"

Better à deux than solo, we agree, and click off. I set aside the binoculars and return to the passage suspended under my pen. But the edge is gone, flow distracted, momentum stalled. Against my own shop rules, I swivel bemused from worktable back to window. They're somewhere out there: my doughty, prickly, more or less apocalyptic, ex-academic more-or-less friend and his more or less steadfast, lately affluent legal-eagle spouse. On *Century*'s weathered decks, the dew's still drying as they beat down-bay through this splendid morning against gentle tide, mild southerly, and normal middle-age restraints.

I'm not alone in half envying them; against *your* shop rules, you call back presently to report that instead of attending your deskwork you've checked with the realtor who sold us this house thirteen years ago and whose notice no local land transaction escapes. Eldorado it is indeed on that sign over there, and Doris herself wouldn't take the property as a gift: so *isolated* (Well, yes, you've pointed out to her: from Latin *insula*, meaning Doris-knows-what), inconveniently reachable only by boat from Pota-mock Point — which, however, goes with the package — and old Pot o' Muck Island itself dissolving apace for want of some serious erosion-stopper, say a hundred thousand bucksworth of heavy stone riprap right around. But she would kill for the listing, Doris allows: romantic island hideaway on scenic Langford Creek near historic Chestertown on tidewater Maryland's unspoiled Eastern Shore, complete with rustic mansionette, pool/spa/tennis court, deepwater dock — worth a million plus, easy, as is, to some Reagan-era richo from D.C. or Main Line Philly.

Rustic mansionette?

"Quoth Doris," you reply: "We have *our* tech-talk; she has hers." Eldorado Developers of Silver Spring MD, however (Doris needn't have pointed out to you, but did) — one of Beth Duer's clients from across the Bay — is a high-powered outfit not known to go in for single-family rustic mansionettes.

"Condos," you worry.

Would Beth and Jay do that to us? Never mind *us*: They'd never do it to Langford Creek. Would they?

"You know your old buddy better than I. Anyhow, Doris thinks we might want to consider selling before that happens."

Well, that's Doris. Her professional foreboding, however — neither unreasonable on the one hand nor disinterested on the other — takes the shine off our morning and the weekend before us, which we thought to spend either sailing ourselves if the forecast is right or bicycling some autumn back roads if it isn't. Even without the Eldorado factor, that sale-signed empty slip across the way is unignorable: half mild challenge, half mild reproach. For "Beth Duer" and "Jay Scribner" — whether or not Beth jumps ship in Freeport as forethreatened and flies home to their Bethesda house to await reunion in Lisbon or Palos ("if he gets that far") while Jay singlehands *Century* back to Square One — a momentous next chapter of their life-story has begun.

Duet of sorts: "Becalmed, plateaued, suspended"
    Ours, by contrast, might be said to be becalmed, plateaued, suspended like my morning's passage or like sturdy *US* out there at ebb tide: a satisfyingly solid, reasonably elevated plateau by any but the most gilded standard, but a plateau all the same. Aware enough, after a score-and-more years together, of our separate and joint shortcomings, we nonetheless prize each other wholeheartedly, as many couples do not. Unlike most of the world's population, we are comfortably well off. Our health, by and large, is as of this sentence sound. We enjoy our callings and practice them with success. If we happen in recent years to have no particularly close friends, neither have we any known enemies; our professional lives afford us ample cordial acquaintance, and we enjoy large doses of each other's company. We maintain an agreeable small house in the city as well as this year-round rural waterfront retreat, where we spend long weekends and entire summers. I would call us fairly well traveled: Three or four times annually we manage short trips, usually outside the country and sometimes expense-paid, if a lecture or professional conference is the occasion; these over and above our sailboat cruises on the Chesapeake and my overnight lecture-junkets around the country. We have thus far lost to accident or disease none of our siblings, my grown children, or our grandchildren, and our relations with them are affectionate. In short, while no strangers to adversity or pretenders to perfection, we know our life together to have been privileged — even extraordinarily so, I would say.

"Who's complaining?" I hear my comrade complain when she reads this complaint: the protesting-too-much, the trace of a whine between the lines.

Not a whine, I would protest: merely a fidget. A bravura new chapter of our lengthening life-story: Maybe we're past that? Maybe who needs one? Unspeakably fortunate, in each other et cetera, yet beginning the typical midlife process (late midlife for me) of contraction and simplification: of our enterprises, our capacities, even our interests. As our get-up-and-go shows signs of going, B & J have gotten up and gone. Autumn's upon us, and here we sit, soaking up the late warmth while waiting for the frost; *they*'re kicking over the traces, Jay especially: throwing fortune to the literal winds, following the sun south, and then . . .

Well, we could do that, my shipmate and I. We've got the requisite boat, the saved-up bucks. My kids aren't kids; my parents are dead, hers not yet infirm. Our other commitments — my writing and lecturing, our part-time teaching (she's on academic leave just now) — can be managed, rearranged, whatever. But we don't *want* to do a Beth-and-Jay, do we? We simply feel, don't we, some wist their way? For me at least, vis-à-vis "Jay Wordsworth Scribner" at least, a not-unprecedented feeling.

"Mm."

Back to it, more or less:

Sixes and sevens then till ten, not quite myself. I check the weather radio: Forecast's fine — indeed, ideal, for days ahead, despite a late tropical depression somewhere off Bermuda, not to worry. Dew's dry out there, sun's bright, day's warming toward shorts and T-shirts. Wind's holding at a sweet eight knots straight up the pipe from Sunbirdland, spreading full the Maryland motley that I ran up our skewed pole at second-coffee time. One last go at that suspended passage of some pages back:

Extended aria: "Suspended passage"
    Author speaking:
    However autobiographical in manner and trappings, this "overture" and any opera following it are in fact fiction: *a story*

of my life, by no means *the*. Chesapeake Bay is real enough, Maryland's Eastern Shore, the Chester River and the creek making off it where Mr. and Mrs. Narrator abide. But there is no "Potamock Island" on any of those, no "Potamock Point." Nothing in our literal life and tidewater neighborhood corresponds to the portentously named "Jerome Schreiber/Jay Wordsworth Scribner," his companion Beth Duer, their erstwhile "eco-ketch"* *American Century*, and its skipper's remarkable project of resailing in reverse Columbus's first voyage's first half, not to mention his improbable extension of that retracement into the eastern Mediterranean, up the Nile, and overland into the African Rift Valley. All fiction.

Fiction most of all, this, in that I draw its sentences in late 1990, two years before the imaginary events recounted and the quincentenary of Columbus's landing in the West Indies. The project of commemorating that first historic confrontation of America and Europe, and their consequent reciprocal loss of innocence, is at this writing well advanced. My track record with the muse — three to four years between books, on average, and this one scarcely begun — makes me confident that by the time these words see print, those festivities will be history. But this overture's imagining that on Columbus Day 1992 "my wife" and "I" will still be among the able living and in the approximate circumstances described, while not unreasonable, is no more than a knock-on-wood projection from our situation as of Columbus Day 1990.

This has been (*that was*, by when you read this page) a year in which it happened that a number of things in my life and work more or less wound up in relatively quick succession. Through its first half, I finished final-editing a new novel — my eleventh book, tenth volume of fiction, eighth novel — with the terminal-sounding title *The Last Voyage of Somebody the Sailor*: a comedy whose dark muse is, in fact, that figure called by Scheherazade "the Destroyer of Delights, Severer of Societies, and Desolator of Dwelling-Places" — lethal Time. Near midyear I turned sixty and,

---

*I.e., still ketch-rigged, but no longer deployed as erst it was to propagandize for cleaning up the Chesapeake estuarine system. See footnote to future recitative "On with the lights" in *Between Acts: Light*. [*Author's retrospective note*]

per personal program, retired on that birthday from my full-time professorship at the Johns Hopkins University, across the Bay, in Baltimore: "early-early phased retirement" by the university's standards and in the language of its benefits administration office, but I had been teaching for nearly forty years, the last seventeen of them at my alma mater. I swapped my endowed chair for emeritus rank and reduced my academic responsibilities to one graduate-level seminar, fall semester only — this out of my attachment to university life, the pleasures of coaching a small group of selected advanced apprentices, and the practical benefits of a campus office and secretarial privileges, although I work mostly at home.

This/that same year, making random notes toward whatever next major writing project might follow *The Last Voyage*, I turned and filled the final page of a spiral-bound stenographic notepad reserved for that purpose. I had begun that notepad twenty-three years, or seven books, earlier, in 1967 — a world ago. It is the third such that I've filled in my professional lifetime; the other two, though of the same size, span a mere seven years each. I have delayed finding a new, fourth steno-pad to cover *1991–*____ , whether because there are still in Pad Three notes toward enough possible projects to fill out my remaining creative lifetime or because, as I enter my seventh decade, that blank space after *1991–* looks disagreeably gravelike.

In another sort of notebook (I keep all kinds: travel logs, ship's logs, house logs, even fish-tank maintenance logs) — this a small black one for the registration of what are, occasionally, small black thoughts — I noted that just as I had filled Page Last of Steno-Pad Three and entered *1990* after *1967–*, I had in September turned the last blank leaf of my old academic roll-book, also numbered Three: *Johns Hopkins, 1973–*____ . Time now to fill that blank, too, with eventful *1990* — but as of this writing, although the semester is well advanced and the calendar year winding up, I've not yet done so. Nor have I bought a fresh roll-book for autumns to come, although I intend to maintain for a while my attenuated connection with the university.

Bear with me.

Roll-Books One and Two I must have mislaid in our last house-move, and I miss them: The three together would name every student I've taught since 1951, from my maiden graduate-teaching-assistant class, through my through-the-ranks years at Penn State, Buffalo, and Boston, to my current handful of Hopkins hotshots. Those students must number several thousand, for while in recent years I've taught only small seminars, for decades before that I carried a full load of lecture-courses as well. The record-keeper in me craves the precise numbers on which his pleased fatigue is based; the academic burnout wants the stats of the fire.

Among that missing myriad would be found the maiden name of my wife, here more or less fictionalized together with her narrator husband: I met and taught her at Penn State in the mid-1960s and serendipitously re-met her in Boston some years later, as shall be sung, just when my two-decade first marriage was closing down. In the final days of 1990, having wound up my circa-five-thousandth published page, my sixth decade of life, my full-time academic career, and my third musely steno-pad and student roll-book, I'll be celebrating with her our twentieth wedding anniversary: not the end of anything, happily for us, except the second decade of a graced connection, but we'll toast the milestone with feelings beyond reciprocal gratitude. Ours will be, as of that date, each's longest-standing intimacy: Duly time-tested, it is a bond we're confident is breakable only by death — and we know that break to be exactly twenty years nearer than it was in December 1970.

L'Chaim.

Outside our house, meanwhile, the Cold War thawed, Germany reunited, the French and British Chunnel-diggers shook hands under the Channel, the new Persian Gulf crisis bade equally (as of this writing) to midwife a new world order or to abort it, and, depending on one's way of counting, either the 1980s ended or the Nineties began. Of such equivocal calendrics, more to come.

There it is. Absent fatal accident, by when this extended aria is published its singer's marriage will be well into its third blessed decade. With so few students now to keep track of, I may not bother with a new roll-book for my emeritus seasons, but no doubt I'll get around to picking up Steno-Pad Four: *1991–*____, and no doubt I'll find seeds to sow in it for possible future cultivation. Although the muse's pause this time has been somewhat longer than usual, experience leads me to expect that by the time *The Last Voyage* officially hits the stands in early '91, I'll be scribbling away on the Next: something "new," suggested by yet another reinspection of those aging bits in Pad Three: *1967–1990.**

The decades have taught me patience with my muse. Before she'll sit in my lap and sing, she visits me less like one of Zeus's daughters by Mnemosyne than like one of those vintage Hollywood monsters, almost human, whose inchoate grunts and rumbles move the heroine to declare, "I think it's trying to *tell* us something." Always, in the past, in her own good time, she has cleared her throat, refound her voice — which is to say, mine. But she won't be hurried; overtures to her must be made sidewise, left-handed.

For poets and short-story writers the case is doubtless different, and I've known novelists who work on several projects at once. But my sort of congenital, one-thing-at-a-time novelist confronts this empty interval between imagination's exhaustion and replenishment, between delivery and reimpregnation, only once every several years. I've learned to use the well-filling intermission to write an essay or two, often of a stock-taking or position-fixing character, while monitoring my new and old jottings like those radio astronomers listening for intelligent extraterrestrial signals against the low buzz of the expanding universe — except that these are *my* signals, my mutterings; it's *me* I'm waiting for word

---

*Just now, e.g., I'm re-regarding this entry, dated 26 April '86: *A Voyage from Maryland, or, The Doomsday Factor. An anti-Candide, his "garden" cultivated to exhaustion, puts his "estate" behind him (sells out to "El Dorado Developers": condos, marinas, shopping plazas, pollution). Au revoir to realism and New World; sets out for Old: mythic, fantastic. . . .*

from, whose garbled transmissions I'm trying to decipher.* King Kong and Fay Wray both; my muse, c'est moi.

Dum dee dum.

Well, it *has* gone past the norm, this particular repollenative pause. What pause doesn't lengthen for gents my age? Not a season this time, but a virtual cycle; not an essay or two, but three or four, amid *Voyage*'s copyedits and galley proofs, lecture and vacation travel, seminars and family and business matters and houseguests and housework and play — the background noise of one's personal universe, whether expanding or contracting, against which one listens, listens for the Signal; life's busywork, which lets the muse sidle up as if idly, like your secret lover at a public party, to murmur (with the gestures and expression of one commenting on the canapés) exactly what you've been waiting to hear.

Scratch that adulterous trope. Other folks' muses may wear designer duds and carry on like that, but mine's some combination of E.T.'s avatars aforenoted and Sindbad the Sailor's magic isle of Serendib, with its peculiar navigational aspect of being unreachable by direct intention. To get to Serendib, one must plot one's course in good faith elsewhere and then lose one's bearings — serendipitously. No problem for old Sindbad up through Voyage Six, when he first attained that fortunate isle: He was in good faith headed elsewhere; hadn't known the place existed. But how to hack Voyage Seven, the caliph's explicit commission to sail straight for Serendib? My muse is Serendib-like, a low-magnitude star that disappears when gandered frontally. She's like that slippery Christian grace unattainable by ardent direct pursuit, which taints her pursuer with the sin of pride.

Dum dee dee.

Kenosis, the Greeks called this emptying of the spirit's vessel in preparation for a refill. Early Christian theology picked up the

---

*Steno-Pad Three, 18 Jan '90: *We set out: down Bay, farther than ever before; hang a left at the Capes and aim for Portugal, toward end of decade, century, millennium, our able lives. And then ... However ... But scarcely had we ... [on w. story].*

term to describe Christ's relinquishment of godhood to take human form and die. See, e.g., Philippians 2:5–8.

Dee diddly die.

Because you know, don't you, singer of this extended aria, that beyond a writer's untimely demise (Italo Calvino's, Raymond Carver's, Donald Barthelme's) lies the prospect of his/her *not*-so-untimely demise (old Sophocles's, old Thomas Mann's, old Jorge Luis Borges's) — if not in this decade, then in the next, at latest the one after — and that these musely recovery times are as likely to lengthen as one's other recovery times, until comes the intermission that no next act follows. You're in robust health, I assure myself (*for your age*, the put-down parentheses add), but you're not age-proof. Your knack for slaloming on one water ski behind that old runabout upped and vanished some summers back and hasn't been heard from since. You can't jog the four flights from your university office up to the seminar room as erst you could and still speak sentences when you get there. They gave you a twenty-one-geared beaut of a mountain bike at last spring's retirement party, and you've used all twenty-one on Maryland's near-flat Eastern Shore. Where'd you put Roll-Books One and Two, by the way?

John Keats sonnetized his youthful fears that he might cease to be before his pen had "glean'd [his] teeming brain," and not long thereafter joined the ranks of the illustrious Untimelies. 'Twould be no picnic (you permit yourself in passing to counterfear) to go on being and being and being *after* your pen has glean'd etc. Or say you're Scheherazade — Who isn't? — and you took your maiden deep narrative breath all those nights ago, and now it's this many plots and characters and themes and situations later, foreshadowings and reprises and twists and pace-changes and even Weltanschauung-evolvements, for pity's sake, and here you've just wound up yet another longish yarn, neatly denouemented if you do say so yourself, and maybe the king's wowed and maybe not (What does *he* know about storytelling?), but anyhow he's not offing your head, and so now it's time to launch your thousand-and-whatevereth before the muezzin cries from the minaret that prayer is better than sleep, and let's just see now, maybe the one about — Nope, you used that on Night 602 or thereabouts, so maybe work up instead the bit you tucked away in midst of the Sindbad series, wasn't it, that bit about what was it now, had a sort of spin to it, charm to it, color, tippy-tip of your tongue, dum dee dum dum, and there's His Highness restless already for his royal next; you know well enough that little sniff and twitch of his. . . .

Scheherazade, c'est moi. King, too. That muezzin, even, whom ever at my back I hear while with some third ear listening, listening —

What was that?

A story, perhaps, perhaps in progress:

You've shut down your desk already and fetched out sea- and tote bags for filling. Seems we're going for a sail.

Overnight?

"Whatever."

Mm.

"Monday's free and Tuesday's negotiable." You check our checkout list. "Whole week's negotiable, on my end. Rest of the school year, actually. Good old academic leave."

Rest of our lives, come to that, we suppose — of which today is, as they say, Day One. That fancy grows upon us as we go about our familiar prep for a one- or two-nighter: Top off the cutter's water tanks, start up its fridge on shore power, ungarage and launch its tender, open boat and close house per each's checklist. It is no problem to keep things flexible, provisionwise: two days' fridge and freezer stuff from the house, enough canned staples and liquids aboard already for at least two more, further supplies available from any number of marinas and harbor towns out there — We know the Chesapeake's upper two-thirds by heart. Calendar commitments we can feasibly reschedule by radiophone or shoreside booth, should we find ourselves inclined to stay out past the holiday. Even mail and newspaper delivery we can stop by phone from wherever we might find ourselves. The sticking point would

seem to be clothes; in this variable season especially, we need some
idea how long a voyage we're packing for. Two days? Four?

Two weeks, I hear myself propose.

"Get serious."

Aria: "Why not?"

But there's some *Why not?* in my shipmate's tone. Watch-stand-
ing blue-water passages, really extended living aboard — they're
not our style, we guess. I would miss my missing muse, who,
though movable, is not portable (But just now she's missing anyhow, no?). My partner, ever readier than I for travel, would ordinarily miss her schoolteaching (But she's on leave these days, no?).
We both would miss our big bed and other dry-land comforts.
Every mid-June for the past many, as it happens, we have set out
down-bay from Langford Creek and cruised as far south as the
water turns out to be swimmable that year, returning north when
we reach sea-nettle country. *Chrysaora quinquecirrha*, the stinging
Medusa jellyfish that typically infests the lower Chesapeake by the
time its waters warm, has thus far set our southern limit at Point
Lookout, the mouth of the great Potomac — and that far down
only once in twenty Junes, when record spring rainfall held the
pest at bay, so to speak. More usually, the summer solstice brings
US and Chrysaora together no farther south than the Patuxent,
the Little or Great Choptank, sometimes even the Miles and the
Wye, just a day's sail out. In one rare droughty period (whence
dates our swimming pool) even Langford Creek was infested come
school-graduation time, and our sail that spring had to be all
north, headwaterward: more crowded and less various cruising
ground. Ten to twelve days, on average, these mini-odysseys,
which we still look annually forward to. But in the sixty-plus wide
miles between Point Lookout and the Virginia Capes — what we
call the Chesapeake Triangle — there is much mare incognitum,
river after river on both sides of the Bay: Pocomoke, Rappahan-
nock, York, James — Algonquin country, John Smith/Pocahontas
country, right down to the ocean's doorstep, and we have yet to
sail it. What better time than now? Water still warm, but air too

cool for swimming and thus Chrysaora no large frustration; foliage at its peak; anchorages uncrowded even on the weekends. Why not sail clear down to Capes Henry and Charles; wet our keel just once, if only for an hour, in the bona fide North Atlantic, nothing over there till Portugal; then home in time for Halloween haul-out, general Thanksgiving, Hanukkah/Christmas, hibernation — Why not?

Duet: "Let's do it"

"Let's do it."

At least let's try it? Start down open-ended, bag it anytime we want? Really, why not?

"You don't like open-ended."

True, by and large. Thus Halloween, latest: follow old *Century* as far as the Threshold, put one foot over, then come home to our life.

"While those Scribner/Duers *leave* home with theirs."

Well: with their separate *lives*, we suspect. Separately. Ours is one. Us. Do it?

"Why not."

Semi-explicatory aria: "Weak Chaos"

As I was saying back in 1990, in that suspended passage: No doubt the coinciding of those several "close-outs" aforesung with the turn of the decade — itself an imminent foreshadow of the impending turns of century and millennium — accounts for the restless air of this overture, in which one hears as well some strain of the valedictory. It accounts too, obviously, for my dreaming up a special sort-of-friend, Jay W. Scribner/Jerry Schreiber, together with his mate, to set out upon an epical voyage that I myself can imagine with interest but would never attempt; further, for my imagining ourselves — *"US"* — setting out in their wake on a different sort of voyage, more modest in its objective but perhaps, in its way, as consequential for the voyagers.

As a rule, reader, I am a thorough planner of my fictions. Although experience has taught me that some things (and what sort of things) can be left for subsequent inspiration, I don't normally begin a story without a clear idea where it's going and by what waypoints it means to get there. To this unexceptionable rule, *Once Upon a Time* I project as a deliberate exception.* Just as in fact I'm only supposing and earnestly hoping that my wife and I will be alive and able on Langford Creek come 12 October 1992, I honestly don't know — having imagined "us" setting out aboard *US* on that date upon a wistful end-of-season cruise to the bottom of the Chesapeake, so to speak — whether we'll get there, what we'll see and do along the way, whether we'll return on schedule or at all, and — Question of questions! — what "our" voyaging is *about.*

Despite that fair-weather forecast, I rather imagine a very considerable *storm* as an early complication of our plot, once that plot's stakes have been determined and established. No point in worrying my mate in advance, but what voyage-tale's complete without tempest or equivalent? Loss of way (On the Chesapeake?), loss of ship (We're insured; anyhow, you can bet that no actual boat of ours bears a hokey name like *US*), loss of shipmates (Heaven forfend!), loss of identity, even; encounters with symbol-fraught obstacles, temptations, adversaries, tasks, enchanted islands — all these old standbys are standing by, of the voyage-tale genre as worked both by myself in novels past and by my innumerable predecessors over four thousand years of written literature and the untold millennia of the oral narrative tradition.† But as to what, which, when, and wherefore in "our" case, muse sayeth naught, yet. Clear enough by now that I'm improvising this overture expressly to discover what opera will follow, as one might say "Once upon a time" in order to hear what that magical invocation might invoke.

Not only fiction, then, this, but in its peculiar way futuristic, time-travel fiction: a journey into the unknown like all our jour-

---

*Its title, for example, just now occurred to me; I've gone back and made a title page.
†One of the world's earliest written narratives is an Egyptian papyrus known as "The Shipwrecked Sailor."

neys, from Sindbad's and Columbus's to every airline- and com-
muter-train passenger's, every Now-I-lay-me-down-to-sleeper's,
every next-step-taker's, next-breath-breather's. E.g. (true story): As
of my opening this aria, a much-loved member of our extended
family — respected and prosperous physician in his forties, rock-
solid husband and father and citizen, a high-vitality, life-enhanc-
ing, good, good man — has been ominously missing for more than
a week. Car found untouched in parking lot of hospital where he'd
gone to make routine night rounds; jacket and empty wallet found
in alley across town a few days later. Police and private investi-
gators baffled; family traumatized and fearful of the worst, our
American cities being what they have become. Then, between this
paragraph and the one before it — last night of Hanukkah 1990,
as it happens, all nine menorah candles burning bright — comes
news the fellow's been found, mirabile dictu, alive and physically
intact though head-bumped and more or less amnesic, in another
hospital in another state — twenty-five hundred miles from where
he vanished ten days earlier! Nes gadol hayah sham: "A great miracle happened there" — its story still unclear and, in the nature of
the case, likely to remain so forever. A Johns Hopkins colleague
apprises me that similar flights into the unknown — unpremedi-
tated, unforeshadowed, "out of the blue" and into it, involving
loss of prior identity, boundary-crossings literal and figurative to
"other states," eventual amnesic or more or less transfigured return
to original state, and resumption of "normal" life (my chap is
reported to be his old self again already and vigorously back at his
healing profession) — are classic enough to have a charming text-
book name: *fugue*. Unlike the musical kind — but quite like Odysseus's, Aeneas's, and Dante's descents into the otherworld — these
mysterious real-life fugues are almost never repeated.

As for ours: Fiction, says Aristotle, should prefer the plausible-
though-in-fact-impossible to the possible-but-implausible, if push
comes to shove. To give my vagrant muse elbowroom, I'm setting
our story two years down the road from the drafting of its overture, but strictly speaking the interval could as well be two days
or two minutes. My medical relative didn't know, two hours

before his fugue, that his prosaic nightly round was about to turn into a quasi-mythic "night-sea journey" (launched, it now turns out, by a violent mugging). I didn't know, two sentences ago, that I'd be writing this particular sentence just now, or two words ago this word, but there it is.

There it is. Inasmuch as ink flows like time but less swiftly, it does not escape me that just as that word *word* is history now as I write *this*, so the point must come in "our" adventures when the writing present overtakes the written present and leaves it behind. I anticipate at that point something like a narrative Doppler-shift, but cannot now imagine its character: neither the *eeee-whoo!* of fast-passing vehicles, I should think (language doesn't go at such a clip), nor the one-way "red shift" of receding galaxies proportional to their distance from the observer, who passes none nor is approached by any. Of a friend's death, Samuel Beckett is said to have said, "He has changed tense." Something like that, I imagine, might be in order down the line.

"Controlled indeterminacy," "self-organized criticality," "weak chaos" — such paradigmatic notions come to mind. They go some way toward describing how our real lives are really lived, as well as a way of telling our life-stories. Sings the earlier-quoted Roethke, "I learn by going where I have to go," and like prudent navigators we may reckon our course by deducing where we are from our running plot of where we've been. Getting there, however, nonetheless involves continuous improvisation, together with what some aria to come may sing as "coaxial esemplasy": the ongoing, reciprocal shaping of our story (in this case, a story of our life) by our imagination, and of our imagination by our story thus far. On this reading, Roethke's line means "By going, we learn where we have to go." But it may also be said to say, "By going where we have to go, we learn."

Learn what? Why, perhaps the answer to our first and final question: Why? What's it all about? Come to that, Who are we?

On with the inquiry:

Au revoir, suspended passage. I cap my immortal pen (adjective to be explained presently, but no vanity involved or metonymy intended), close my venerable three-ring looseleaf binder — sacred, in fact, like the pen, though to no one except myself — and unplug our middle-aged Macintosh lest it be fried by thunderbolts in our absence. Creepy as this may sound to younger souls in particular, as is our habit before setting out together on extended journeys we each then put in plain view on his/her desktop a sealed envelope, normally drawered, addressed *To My Executors* — not so much *lest* common disaster befall us as by way of propitiatory magical insurance that it not. That little black notebook mentioned in "Aria: 'Suspended passage'" now goes into my seabag along with Steno-Pad Four: 1991– ____ , its first pages already filled with notes toward this project. If I'm to learn by going etc., I'll need wherewithal to inscribe my lessons elsewhere than in the log of *US*, which is for sailing data only. We have ballpoints aplenty on board for such inscription, but as I bid good-bye now to my creekside study, I'm moved to consider the unprecedented: taking with me on our uncertain voyage said venerable three-ring looseleaf binder and immortal pen.

Extended aria: "This old binder. This old pen"

This old binder — *Trussel Press-'lo 76CX Made in USA*, I can just make out on its once evenly blue-stippled inside front cover — antedates the writer who pens this sentence in it, though not the penman. This old binder has been mine and in near-daily use for forty-five years: I bought it new in the university bookstore during freshman orientation week in September 1947, when I was seventeen. Its stiff cloth-covered cardboard covers were a clean light gray-blue then, JOHNS HOPKINS UNIVERSITY printed on a dark diagonal across the front. Through my student years, this binder went with me in every Baltimore weather to every lecture and seminar, its looseleaf pages duly apportioned among my courses of study, semester after semester. Just another school-supplies item then; not meant to outlast the usual term of such items, it was given no special consideration. On its outside front cover, like faint ring-nebulae, are condensation stains from Truman-era cups of student union coffee and cans of National Bohemian beer. The margins of the inside covers I evidently made use of to start balky pens: Beneath a brown patina of . . . thumb oil, I suppose, from countless openings and closings, is a hatched underpainting of short straight ink-lines and blotted drops, the whole surface worn away by so many *more* openings and closings that the once-rectangular cover is worn well out of square into a sloping curve that meets the bottom outboard page-corner a full two inches short of its original dimension. The missing material, like my professional life, has been invisibly distributed, fiber by fiber, through the rooms I've lived and worked in over four and a half decades — but a reassuring margin remains. The exterior cloth hinges meant to join its covers to its spine are entirely gone, and the spine itself is half exposed, but the inside hinges still do the job. The cover fabric, ring nebulae and all, is rubbed to a mottled gray-black glaze by continual light friction against the tops of a long series of desks and worktables; correspondingly, the front-central top surfaces of my writing tables, both here on the creek and over in the city, are chafed through their varnish to bare wood by my endless tiny shiftings of this old binder as I write. Of those alabaster saints in medieval churches, their toes worn away by the kisses of the faithful, Jay Wordsworth Scribner once wondered to me in Rome: If lips can do that to stone, what must stone do to lips? The example of my old binder leads me to hope that the attrition is gently reciprocal, more a polishing than an ablation.

The three metal rings of this old binder, their open/close levers and other hardware, are uniformly corroded from their original shiny chrome but still functioning, as is the binder itself and its user: We spend all of nearly every weekday morning together in light but steady physical contact, as we have done right through my adult life. Not long after my freshman undergraduate year, I began filling one of those dividered sections with my first student attempts at fiction, while in the others duly annotating my courses in history, philosophy, literature, foreign languages, the social and natural sciences. Through graduate-school days, almost the whole binder came to be filled with apprentice fiction-in-progress, although it still went with me to doctoral seminars in this and that. Thereafter, it withdrew with its owner, M.A.'d but Ph.D.less, from formal academic study into aspiring writerhood; while I made my

living as a professor of composition, of English, of creative writing, my looseleaf binder stayed home, wherever home was,
eschewed all things academic, and to my frequent envy devoted
itself exclusively to the practice of literature. Like my muse, of
which it is an aspect and a totem, it became movable but not portable. It does not travel everywhere I travel, but it has lived everywhere I've lived: Maryland, Pennsylvania, Andalusia, New York,
Massachusetts, California, Maryland. I have first-drafted in it
every page that I've ever published and many that I've not, from
that undergraduate apprentice-work to this piece in progress:
more than ten thousand manuscript pages, I estimate. It still has a
few vintage-1940s dividers in it, their tabs long since worn off.
The fat first section, half an inch or so of fresh white looseleaf
paper on the right, a growing sheaf of black-scribbled pages on the
left, is for work in progress — just now, *Once Upon a Time*. When
this overture is drafted, out it will go into a younger binder already
labeled *OUT* and waiting, to free up this one for the first draft of
(I suppose) Act One, while the Overture moves through its several
word-processed drafts to come. A second division, emptied last
year at *The Last Voyage*'s close but steadily refilling now, is for
worknotes on this project, expanded from the germinal jottings in
Steno-Pads Three and Four. This division I expect will grow with
the project until it fills a binder of its own, for over the years my
black ballpoint "notes" have become more and more a kind of
surreptitious proto-draft: a halfway house between the true notes
of steno-pad and small black notebook on the one hand and the
actual first-drafted sentences of this old binder. Under pretext of
expanding these notes on the chapter or aria in hand, I often give
its sentences their first trial form and sequence, in prose less
responsible than this, in less responsible ink on less responsible
paper — less responsible and therefore freer to take tentative
shape.

Just as in both my city and my country workrooms there are
separate areas for Creation (a large writing table), Production (a
computer workstation), and Business (a big old glass-topped office
desk), so in this old binder a final divider divides art from accounting — more accurately, my accounts with my muse from the

archives of my accounting with my publishers. In that latter are the faithfully kept entries of every penny I've ever received for my writing since Day One of my professional career — 12 March '56 [a day that very consequentially changed my life, when this old binder was already ending its first decade]: *Advance on* The Floating Opera, *Appleton-Century-Crofts. Gross $750. Agent's commission $75. Net $675 —* with running annual subtotals thereafter down to the present. By the standards of successful commercial novelists or even of more commercially successful "literary" novelists, those subtotals are unimpressive. Given the nature of what I write, however, and the largely aliterary culture in which I write it, I find them as gratifying in their way as the circumstance that that first novel — turned down by eight or nine publishers before *Appleton-Century-Crofts* took an entry-level flyer on it — is, unlike its first publisher, still afloat. That one's books, at least most of them, not disappear before their author does: For a "serious" writer in late-twentieth-century America, that is success aplenty. Anything beyond it is a welcome bonus, and Division Three of my old binder records the thirty-six years of such bonuses that, added to my wife's contributions and to a university salary itself correlative to the books' "success," have paid for the rooms in which I write and the houses housing them, for my grown children's school tuitions in years gone by, and, in years since, for such luxuries as *US* and our winter-covered swimming pool — all which we guiltlessly enjoy after lean times past.

The numbers gratify me too for an aesthetic reason. I honor those excellent writers whose difficulty or "specialness" limits their readership to a knowledgeable few among the 10 percent of adult Americans, say,* who still read "serious" literature for pleasure at all; I have often been assigned to that category of writers myself, with and without the complimentary adjective. As a professional novelist, however, I honor also my art form's roots in the popular culture before the advent of Modernism exacerbated the division between high art and commercial "prolefeed," polar-

*So says the *New York Times*: "The Lost Book Generation," 6 January 1991.

izing novelists into James Joyces on the one hand and James Mich-
eners on the other. As a confessed Postmodernist, I have a special
admiration for first-class literary artists who in some measure
bridge that chasm. To see a Gabriel García Márquez rise to the
top of that egregious *New York Times* best-seller list I find as
cheering and about as rare as to see a truly principled human being
win a popular political election. When my novel *Giles Goat-Boy*
spent some weeks on that list a quarter-century ago, I welcomed
not only the unaccustomed royalties and notice, but as well the
phenomenon of a novel so long, unusual, and intricated holding
its own among the "bodice-rippers," the spy and detective and
techno-thrillers, the steamy pseudo-exposés and fast-lane "shop-
and-fuckers" that keep our fiction market going.

This old binder: I move it reluctantly these days, even just
across the Chesapeake on Thursdays and Sundays, when through
normal academic seasons we shift from city to country, country to
city. Indeed, when materials for the novel-in-progress reach a certain bulk, I leave it all behind in Baltimore and spend those Fridays
doing essays or lectures, for which I have another, less venerable
binder at Langford Creek — as much to spare this old binder the
slight and unnecessary extra wear and tear (as distinct from usual
and necessary wear and tear, which I have no intention of sparing
it until it disintegrates altogether) as to refresh my muse with
another sort of sentence-making. In the same spirit, I have recently
quit downhill skiing (and slalom waterskiing, as aforenoted, has
quit me), but I still exercise my aging body at least as regularly as
I exercise this old binder.

Which will fail first, I sometimes bemuse myself by asking, this
faithful, still quite serviceable old binder, this even older but likewise serviceable body, or the high-mileage imagination that links
the two? By and large, they seem to me to be reasonably in synch
in their leisurely passage toward oblivion. From time to time, however, one or another will show signs of taking the lead, obliging
me to hope (if that's the right word) that Imagination will be the
last to go.

*　　　*　　　*

From this unhurried race, I exclude the three contenders' literal link: this old pen of mine, which effortlessly draws in this old binder's pages whatever words this aging imagination directs this aging body's right hand to inscribe, and as effortlessly draws through them — adds, amends, transposes, substitutes, or deletes with appropriate strokes and squiggles. Whatever the quality-curve of my production, my penmanship has deteriorated over the decades like my old binder; nowadays none except myself can make ready sense of it, and even I must occasionally scratch my head and guess from context what I've scribbled. But this old pen — younger, admittedly, than binder or body — will, barring accident, outlast both them and all the pages I've penned with it.

I say "barring accident" because this old pen is not the original of my writing life or the coeval of this old binder. Its predecessor — a black-barreled, gold-capped Sheaffer, origin forgotten but most likely an off-to-college gift from the family or an early present from my early wife — wrote all those college course-notes from 1947 through 1953, all that apprentice fiction, the notes and syllabi for every course I taught from 1951 through 1962 and every critical comment on the thousands of student papers I graded in those years, plus all my personal correspondence, innumerable bank checks, even grocery lists (ballpoints weren't really around yet in the early part of this period, and I resisted using them for years after they were), and the notes and manuscript drafts of *The Floating Opera*, *The End of the Road*, *The Sot-Weed Factor*, and the front end of *Giles Goat-Boy* — my first three and a half novels. I was much attached to that pen — must have been almost physically so, I imagine when I review that catalogue of its pennings — although I don't remember being as superstitious about it as I am about its successor. It went with me carelessly everywhere: to classroom and grocery store, on camping trips with the family, aboard ocean- and airliners (until I learned that changes in cabin altitude can discharge a fountain pen into one's shirt pocket and switched to ballpoints for portable pennery) — and that's how it met its end:

In the front half of 1963, I took my first sabbatical leave from teaching (at Penn State by then) and made with my young family our maiden expedition outside the USA: winter in the south of Spain, where I fretted away at *Giles Goat-Boy* with that old pen in this old binder, and then a long, low-budget spring reconnaissance of the rest of western Europe, the five of us camping in a Volkswagen Microbus. A momentous season, of bittersweet memory: Fictionalized versions of it, substantially removed from the facts, have crept into more than one of my novels; yet another may well creep into this opera. To our point now is simply that through that springtime odyssey from Andalusia and Portugal to Helsingör and the Scottish Highlands, while this old binder and that young goat-boy were stowed safely in some cranny of the Microbus, my Sheaffer rode as always in shirt pocket and travel notebook, logging my impressions of Europe, our campgrounds and pensions, and the small adventures and misadventures of young American innocents abroad en famille, until some random bodily movement — in France, Italy, Austria, Germany, Belgium, Holland, or Denmark (I'm going to say Denmark: the battlements of Hamlet's castle, our northmost penetration before crossing to Britain and home) — pressed my shirt pocket between my chest and something solid, and cracked the Sheaffer's barrel quite in half.

I doubt that I wept; we Kraut-extracted WASPs can be stoical to the point of stolidity. But I felt like weeping and ought to have done so, not only because, as Virgil says, sunt lacrimae rerum — "Such things are what tears are for" — but also because... Never mind, just now.

Well, we would find me a new one. Using, I suppose, a pickup ballpoint for the travelog, we withdrew from Elsinore, crossed on the car ferry from Calais to Dover, and camped through the south of England and over toward East Anglia. There — in Rochester, in a stationer's that advertised itself as the original of "Mr. Pumblechook's premises" in *Great Expectations* — in honor of Mother English and that greatest of her novelists, I bought brand-new this now twenty-seven-year-old pen. Nothing fancy about it: a no-nonsense, British-made Parker, burgundy plastic barrel, brushed steel cap with arrow-shaped clip and some sort of polished gray stone let into the top, point neatly cowled by the lower barrel in a clean Modernist style, nib alloyed of platinum and iridium for hardness and corrosion resistance. But I was impressed by the manufacturer's recommendation that the pen be used exclusively by its owner, since over time the nib shapes itself to its user's penmanship and thus writes ever more smoothly.

I pressed it into service at once to log the circumstances of its purchase, the sights of England and Scotland, and our stressful "night-sea journey" home, from which I date the real beginning of the end of my first marriage. Once back in the States, I ceased to carry my "good" pen about with me; I took to using black and red ballpoints for student paper-grading, travelogs, and household business, leaving the Parker clipped to the center ring of this old binder between uses. But until my penmanship became virtually a private code, I wrote all my personal correspondence with this pen, and the manuscript drafts of the rest of *Giles Goat-Boy* and all the books thereafter, down to and including this. For subsequent revision, rearrangement, and editing, I've come to rely absolutely on the word processor into which, at every work-morning's end, I type the day's sentences from this old binder. But for first-drafting those sentences and rough-polishing them as they unfold, I still prefer, depend upon, even love the smooth muscular cursive of jet black Skrip flowing from this old pen across the blue-ruled lines of three-ring paper in this old binder. True to its advertising, the Parker's nib quickly shaped itself to my autography; its scratch against the paper, minimal to begin with, all but disappeared during the first season's use, and for more than a quarter-century I've been no more conscious of effort against resistance in the physical act of penning than in the physical act of breathing. The one comes as naturally as the other.

Each normal workday morning, after breakfast, the agreeable ritual follows of withdrawing to city or country study, thermal coffee mug topped up and in hand. I tuck in the Flents ear stopples (first massaging them to malleability) that I required for concentration in years gone by, when my children were young and at home and my academic course-load constrained my writing to late afternoons and early evenings, and that I cannot now concentrate without, even alone in the house in the quiet countryside. I polish my eyeglasses and blow my nose a number of times — a morning sinus drip inherited from my father, and a salute to his memory. I disassemble and feed this old pen its daily drink, reassemble its barrel, fix its cap on the butt as designed for perfect balance. When I take the readied instrument in hand, it rests lightly against the callosities of four decades of authorship. I warm up by reviewing yesterday's production in its first printout (seldom more and often fewer than two or three double-spaced pages), hand-editing the sentences as I go, until I reach the latest of them and, carried by its momentum, take up its longhand version in this old binder and draw the next with this old pen. I'm scarcely aware of writing English; I'm writing writing. Indeed, unless I happen to be writing *about* writing as I'm doing just now, and that's not often, I am no more than half aware that what I'm doing is *writing*, and I'm altogether unconscious of the complex sub-routines of orthography, punctuation, and penmanship. Even diction, grammar, and syntax are little more than higher sub-routines (carried out, however, meticulously, like the mechanics); my conscious mind attends mainly to navigation and boat-handling, so to speak: choosing and steering moment by moment the verbal course to the next narrative waypoint (as approximated from the last and course-corrected en route) to my dramaturgical destination (ditto).

Some three hours of this, interrupted by breathers to refill the coffee mug, bid good-bye to my wife if she's off to teach or do errands, make or take a phone call or two if necessary, stretch my legs, take a leak. Then — ideally when the going's good, in mid-passage, even mid-sentence, like Scheherazade — I halt, date the day's drafting in parentheses (*18 Jan '91* already, this one; time flies), cap this old pen, pop the earplugs, open for the how-many-thousandth time the rings of this old binder, and take the morning's pages from Creation to Production for Macintoshing before lunch.

When we imagine Heaven, Miguel de Unamuno remarks, "the immortality that we crave . . . is the continuation of this present life" — minus its irritations, disappointments, and miseries and plus a few goodies that we've thus far hankered after in vain. I am confident that no heaven of mine would be heavenly without this present volume's dedicator and dedicatee conjoined in the pleasurable exercise of mind and body and the registration of life-experience into language — not excluding imagined experience (such as the afterlife), the experience of imagining, and the experience of language — into this old binder, with this old pen, amen.

Back to it:

I think better of taking with us on *US* this brace of totems, in hopes of goosing my muse to the completion of that suspended passage and on to the project *Once Upon a Time* — but not better enough, as events that I'm just now imagining will later prove. This old binder, no: A couple of foul-weather pitchings from chart table to cabin sole would be the end of it. My pen, however — not breast-pocketed, for sure, but stowed securely below while we're under way. . . . Given the special nature of this voyage (just a feeling in our morning's air, you understand, by no means so clear yet to the voyagers in the story as to its author), it might be truly helpful, even essential, to write it as it goes, go it as it writes, Roethkewise: coaxial esemplasy. No Macintosh required, although PCs with navigational software are increasingly common on sailboats the size of ours; yellow notepads will do, or better yet an unsanctified binder from the anonymous several in our supply closet. But it won't be real writing if it isn't penned with —

And so I do it; do it, moreover, surreptitiously, altogether out of my character: I pop the precious Parker into the rings of, as it happens, my "Friday essay" binder, scarcely half a dozen years old and as free of battle scars as this one was in 1947, so cloistered has been its nonfictional life. If it gives to my suspended passage, to this overture and whatever therefollows, an essayistic flavor, so be it; I shift that passage from this old binder into that new one — click-click, click-click — where a brace of Friday-pieces in progress wait to miscegenate with it in the snug darkness of my seabag, among oiled-wool sweater, hooded sweatshirt, thermal undies, spare deck moccasins. . . .

End of checkout checklist.

"How's your head?"

On straight, I hope.

"What's up? You're acting funny."

Beloved Reality Principle, sine qua non and osprey-keen, who sniffeth the Fishy instanter from yea far: It's out of character I'm acting, for that I fain would sneak my Pumblechook Parker aboard *US*, antiprudently and huggermugger. Don't ask.

"You're talking funny."

But you *don't* ask, and beyond a reflexive teacherly minimum you won't scold (as I know from ample past experience of my lesser antiprudencies) if and when the regrettable occurs. My esteem for you enlarges by yet another quantum; I quit talking funny, for the present. Let's go.

House secured, *US*'s diesel warmed, shore power disconnected, docklines singled up; small Maryland flag run up to the starboard main spreader, all-purpose rainbow flag to the port, as our destination is uncertain;* the usual mild liftoff adrenaline rush as you slug Handel's *Water Music* into the portable cassette player, take your seat at the helm, check the dinghy's position astern, and release the steering-wheel brake, while from dockside I undo the remaining lines, signal you to reverse, guide the hull backward a few steps by the portside shrouds until its not-very-maneuverable sternway is established, and at the last moment swing easily up and aboard to sound over Handel our own conch of departure.

And then . . . However . . . But scarcely had we . . .

In fact — as on the ship's conch (snorkeled up from the Mexican Caribbean, off Yucatán), less sonorously than Jay Scribner I honk three honks officially to signal "Watch out: We're backing down" but actually to celebrate with our indifferent but watchful only witnesses, the nearby geese, one more nautical setting out — you click off George Friedrich's hornpipe and say "What's that, up by our marsh?"

Like all boats with "right-hand" propellers (clockwise for forward, viewed from astern), and sailboats in particular, which don't

---

*In the Caribbean, where just a few days' cruising may carry one's vessel into several "countries," nautical etiquette permits a rainbow flag to serve for the assorted national banners. The crew of *US* have imported this usage to the Chesapeake for when our port of call is undecided at flags-up time.

like to go backward, *US* has declined a straight reverse exit from its slip in favor of its customary arc, the stern pushed portward by the anticlockwise wheel of the reversing prop despite your corrective helming. We have therefore swung, as usual, broadside to our patch of tidemarsh, our stern aimed up-creek a couple hundred feet offshore and our bowsprit conveniently outbound. Cancún-conch in hand, I follow your point. You've already throttled down, shifted into neutral, and unracked the ship's binoculars from a teak drink-holder on the binnacle guard.

Uncompleted aria: "Our marsh, our marsh"
   Our marsh, our marsh.
   The modest Eastern-Shore-of-Maryland retreat whereof I sing is a two-acre parcel of what from colonial times until the 1960s had been a near-flat hundred-acre mix of scrubby woods and cornfields, bounded on its south side by the creek and to east and west by coves making off it, with tidemarsh along the lower stretches of waterfront. To our north, it's mostly woods and cornfield still; the developers' plans for Langford Bay Estates (the name sets our teeth on edge) seem happily not quite to have flown. The realtor's plat shows it scarily subdivided into scores, even hundreds of quarter-acre parcels, accessed by an airstrip and numerous byroads off the main circular drive. Thirty years later, however, it remains a string of modest houses — no more than two dozen, many of them prefabs and do-it-yourselfers owned by local working folk and pensioners — along the circle drive only (no airstrip, no byroads), especially its waterfront stretch. A few new ones of that sort have gone up in our thirteen years' residency, but a combination of factors lucky for us has thus far inhibited large-scale development: Under pressure from affluent Baltimoreans, Washingtonians, Wilmingtonians, and Philadelphians, Maryland waterfront real-estate values have so escalated that those homely, often cheek-by-jowl stock items may list for half a million, with proportionate annual taxes, and people with that kind of money to spend on a vacation or retirement place don't want, as a rule, a homely subdivision in a scalped cornfield.
   All which suits us just fine: We're comfortable with our neigh-

bors, mostly home-growners like myself. We bought what we could afford in 1979, at what seemed a ruinous price then and seems a bargain now, even when adjusted for inflation. The house, built in Lyndon Johnson days, was no more remarkable than its neighbors when we bought it, and it remains an off-the-shelf design, although over the years we've remodeled and relandscaped within our budget: It's a stock late-Fifties-style brick-and-clapboard rancher complete with period picture windows, rose-ramblered split-rail fence, goose-decorated fiberglass mailbox, and lots of young trees but no old ones, spread over five or six of those mini-parcels, three of them "high" ground (i.e., ten or twelve feet above mean high tide but classified by the Corps of Engineers as Floodplain; a real hurricane surge could take us out) and the others low — whence our marsh and this aria.

We chose this place because, after years of searching, we judged it least unsuited to our desires, requirements, and budget constraints. I prefer an open-water view, for example, my wife a sheltered; from porch, pool, or pier she can look up-creek, scarcely a house in sight along the tree-lined fork from that perspective, while I look straight down the twin forks' confluence, past "Potamock Island" into the broad Chester — no land visible on the southern horizon out there. We both are aquatic mammals who much prefer the natural element to pool or spa, and salt water to fresh; it is a peculiarity of Langford Creek that its normal salinity, as aforesung, remains just below the threshold for Chrysaora quinquecirrha until summer's end, even when the river itself is infested all the way to Chestertown. Moreover, we prize privacy, for swimming and in general, and a fortuitous combination of circumstances and evergreen plantings affords us a gratifying measure of that. Our nearest neighbors, to the north and east, happen seldom to use their waterfront or even their yards; for weeks at a time we may not see them, and the cordial hemlock screen between us grows annually. To our south is the creek, nearly half a mile wide; to our west, those lower-lying (pine-screened) parcels and . . .

Our marsh, maybe sixty feet "deep" and three times that length, must at one time have extended for a quarter-mile or so along the shoreline westward from our front yard. To eastward, the ground gently rises to thirty-foot bluffs at Horner Cove; the floodplain begins at our property's high end, where the house and pool are, and soon sinks to a mere foot or two above mean high water. The lots down there don't "percolate" to the state's requirement for septic systems; indeed, spring tides flood them partway to the road, and so our westward privacy extends well past our boundary-pines. The happy net effect is that we have both the security of reliable neighbors (no small matter, as we're often not at home) and, except on busy weekends in the boating season, near-total privacy. Right through the subtropical Maryland summers we can let our skin breathe; cover-ups are for driving into town for supplies. Like swimsuits for swimming, the central air-conditioning is for the comfort of houseguests less acclimatized, the sort who wear shoes and socks in the daytime and pajamas at night. We prefer to open every pore and window to the prevailing warm damp southerlies pumped up from the Caribbean by Bermuda Highs parked off the coast; we do our summer's work in swimsuits and as much as possible of our summer's play in birthday suits: a middle-aged, uninnocent Eve and Adam pottering happily in their subdeveloped garden . . . whereof the real centerpiece is not the house, the pool, the "high" lawn sloping down to its southern bulkhead, or the literal flower garden, but the wide creek itself with wooded "Potamock Point" across the way, the waterfront with our dock and *US*, and, in no small measure, our marsh.

My wife is a city girl who likes keeping one foot rural; I'm a small-town boy who likes keeping one foot urban. More than half of my native Eastern Shore county — Dorchester, the state's largest, three counties down from here — is sub-sea-level: fresh marsh and salt marsh. For millennia, the Indians fished, trapped, and hunted there, growing a little corn and tobacco in upland clearings; the seafood was limitless and the waters were clear, filtered by the woods and marshes and by literal reefs of oysters. Their less ecologically harmonious displacers over the past three centuries — from Lord Baltimore's original Catholic colonists in the seventeenth century and flocks of English and Scotch-Irish Methodists in the eighteenth and nineteenth to German immigrant farmers in the early twentieth, many "brought over" by my father's father — drained tens of thousands of acres of those wetlands for farming (and cleared the woods and silted the water and vastly depleted the fishery) before recent conservationism slowed such progress. Yet even today, once you're south of their labors, the marshes down there seem endless, horizon-wide in all directions: a low labyrinth of sinuous creeklets making off the shallow wider waterways to thread for miles through spartina and isolated stands of loblolly pine. I grew up not exactly *in* those mosquito-rich fenlands, but never far from them: a landscape of such ubiquitous horizontality that (as I've written elsewhere, probably more than once) any vertical in it — a lone pine, a vintage New Deal firewatch tower, a day beacon topped with osprey nest, a blue heron stalking minnows — arrests the eye, is ipso facto interesting. One of my high-school classmates from down there (not "Jerry Schreiber") was for eight out of ten years the muskrat-skinning champion of the world; the competition used to be held annually in my hometown armory, and Dorchester County's only serious challenger was Cameron Parish, in the bayous of Louisiana. Elihu Abbott cut the championship time for the standard five-rat skinning event from three or four minutes down to less than two. His best official record was five marsh-rats in one minute 3.6 seconds, cleanly skinned without damage to the pelt: one every 12.7 seconds.

Neither dry land nor sea, as the Chesapeake is neither salt nor fresh; emblematic equally of stagnation and regeneration, of death and new life — these inbetweenlands are my imagination's mise-en-scène. I understood that, I believe, before I understood myself to be a storyteller, and I doubt the authority of any story of mine in which they do not figure, one way or another. It alarms me to reflect that we might have bought the Langford Creek place without its bonus patch of tidemarsh; given our reservations about "Langford Bay Estates" and the then-characterless dwelling-house, I would rather imagine that that bonus was what tipped the scales. In any case, we treasure it, our bit of marsh, and were

appalled to learn that our upstream neighbor (dock and equipment shed, but no house) had illegally mowed and filled his share
of it — a fine thick stand of wall-to-wall spartina, now reduced to
scruffy lawn — to the end of turning his marshfront into beachfront. That disruption on its low side, together no doubt with our
(legal) bulkheading on its high side and nature's general restless-
ness, has altered the character of our marsh even in the brief
decade-plus of our residency. What our first proud photographs
show to have been all-but-solid spartina, taller than myself, is giving way to mixed high-marsh growth: mallows, briars, mimosa
saplings and other weed trees, mint, Virginia creeper, poison ivy,
wiregrass, ground ivy. Before very long (though not, we hope, in
our lifetime) our marsh will be no marsh at all, just upland scrub.

But then, before very long in geological time the melting polar
caps will drown our floodplain altogether, reconfigure the Chesapeake, rearrange the whole East Coastscape. Meanwhile, praise
be, the coast is the coast, Bay Bay, creek creek, and our marsh is
marsh, which we prize not least for the wealth of stuff we have
found in it and along its margins. There are the fauna, to be sure:
mallard ducks both migratory and year-round, Canada geese,
snow geese and swan, mockingbirds and red-winged blackbirds,
small green and great blue herons, the occasional egret, osprey, and
turkey buzzard, seagulls scavenging and kvetching round about;
rabbits, raccoons, woodchucks, box turtles, assorted toads, the
odd bold browsing deer or cruising otter, the neighbors' cats and
dogs on the prowl; along its creek side, harmless water snakes
and the washed-up aquatic dead: blue and horseshoe crabs, young
turtles strangled on promotional or party balloons, sunfish, blue-
fish, white and yellow perch, rockfish, spot, croaked croakers,
giant carp, stranded Chrysaorae and moon and winter jellies, clam
and oyster and mussel shells. I pass over the insecta, out of ento-
mological ignorance. In a week's visit, our brace of grandchildren
can assemble on the bulkhead a virtual museum of tidewater natural history; their grandparents find at least as fascinating the miscellaneous man-made dreck. Observes one of Samuel Beckett's
derelict beachwalkers, "I never needed a board but there it was, I

had only to stoop and pick it up." We have a basement hoard of perfectly usable lumber salvaged from our marsh after storms, flood tides, or extended absences; a bin of nylon and polypropylene lashings chafed through at one end but otherwise sound; a shelf of Styrofoam floats and buoys come loose from crab traps and eel pots out by the channel and beyond.

More than once, the boards we've saved have been our own: In September 1979, e.g., within a month of our first moving in, while we were off teaching in the city, an extraordinary high tide with pounding waves from a southerly gale unspiked every one of the heavy cap-timbers from our bulkheading and floated them away. Gone with the wind, we assumed, and prepared to add a large unbudgeted item to our moving-in expenses. A closer look, however, revealed two of those heavy timbers washed up in a weedy aisle between lawn and marsh; a reconnoitering stroll up-beach disclosed two or three more in the marsh itself, snagged by the tall spartina. We were prepared at that point to scout the whole West Fork with motorboat and binoculars, but further marsh-exploration turned up every one of our missing planks: some dozen massive two-by-twelves, heavily creosoted, which we were just able to lug back into place ourselves and refasten.

With the more considerable of other folks' jetsam, our policy is a week's display at the end of our dock to give the loser claim-time. Thereafter, it's finders keepers: a hefty wooden dock ladder (we needed another to add to our two, and pressed it into service when the statute ran), a collapsible aluminum boat boarding ladder, a floating boathook, a telescoping awning pole, sundry boat cushions and personal flotation devices, a dozen or more goose and duck decoys adrift from their moorings, a fisherman's fine wicker creel — all rescued like infant Moses from the bulrushes and put to subsequent use, though not invariably to their intended purpose. Our largest single find to date: an *entire poured-concrete boat launching ramp*, ten feet wide and maybe thirty long — not floated in, certainly, but laid down we presume by our house's original owner and storm-buried under silt and sand before our tenancy. We had wondered why only low marsh grass and creepers grew in that aisle aforementioned between the high-lawn bulk-heading and the spartina, where we found those first cap-timbers; after a winter gale uncovered the beachmost slabs, a bit of archaeology on our part revealed the rest of the ramp, humped and pitched under its cover of light soil and dense weed. As there is a public ramp not far up-creek for springtime launch and fall retrieval of our old runabout, and as the rest of our flotilla is either manageable from the beach or requires a boatyard lift, we gladly left the ruins unexcavated, an extension of our marsh.

Have I sung the mere litter that periodically we must pick? The discarded beverage cans and bottles, plastic jugs and bags, Styrofoam scrap, deflated helium balloons fortunately missed by turtles, crabbers' busted baskets, single socks and shoes, used condoms? I here sing it. Our own contributions: runaway baseballs, softballs, badminton shuttlecocks (the lower lawn is our sports field), some retrieved, some not; dead birds and other small former animals found about the premises, which we prefer to recycle through the marsh than consign to plastic garbage bags? Sung. We like to suppose that these wetland pleasures and responsibilities are shared by most folks lucky enough to "access" a tidemarsh; I know for a fact that Jay Scribner and Beth Duer take the same delight — used to, anyhow — in the reedy east side of their Potamock Island, for it is there, on just such a routine winter marshcombing sortie, that my counterself made a find more remarkable by far than our whole catalogue together: what he soberly claims to be the lost log of Columbus's first voyage, known to have been transcribed by the Admiral of the Ocean Sea during a life-threatening storm off the Azores on 15 February 1493* — when it appeared likely that his two remaining caravels might go down before they brought news of their momentous discovery back to Spain — and by him wrapped in oilskins, sealed in a cask, and posted overside with a prayer like the archetypal message in a bottle. *Pinta* and *Niña* survived; the cask was never found, until —

---

*See, e.g., Salvador de Madariaga's *Christopher Columbus* (NY: Macmillan, 1940).

Story:

"I don't believe it: your pal's cockamamie cask." First clause delivered binocs-to-eye, second as you hand them to me for close-up of what I've already espied and can't credit either. Whole initial notion too preposterous: Cask tossed off Azores on 15 Feb 1493 floats 499 years and at least 3,300 miles (as the crow flies; 330,000 as the cask floats?) to wash ashore in Langford Creek, Maryland, on 15 Feb 1992. Secondary hypotheses not much more plausible: that having claimed to find something that he represents to be said cask (we've never seen it; alleged finder declined even to show it, not to mention proclaim his find publicly), Jay Scribner or anyone else would actually *return it to the waters.*

"Nobody else would, for sure."

And coincidence of *two* such casks in our creek, authentic or not, too astronomical for words, at least for our words. Ditto odds against cask's happening to float squarely to our marsh even if, say, it accidentally fell off the gunwale of *American Century* (But who would ever perch it so precariously?) as Beth and Jay put our world behind them this A.M., or if — a more Scribnerish tease — he for some reason deliberately creeked the thing usward when by dawn's early light they shifted from reverse into forward, as *we* were just about to do now. No: If that algae-grown, that barnacled, that by-god cask on which I now refocus the seven-by-fifties is indeed "Columbus's" (I mean of course Jay's, whatever it was, *if* it was) — and that seems not entirely improbable, for how many by-god *casks* does one come upon these days, outside of one's local winery? — then our cross-creek neighbor, before he conched good-bye, must have gone to some trouble to plant it there for us to find.

You'll idle *US* in neutral, we quickly decide, while I dinghy ashore and retrieve the thing. You do; I do, and find it to be . . . a sturdy, by-god cask — Casklet? Caskette? — maybe twelve inches long by eight in equatorial diameter, its neatly coopered staves tapering to six-inch-diameter ends and snugly hooped and rimmed with wide rusting iron bands. Varnish long gone. Green trailing beard of sandy seaweed, encrusted with tiny mussels and alive

with copepods that wriggle out like marine dandruff when I lift
the thing from the reeds. A by-god cask, just bigger than the classic
St. Bernard's. It comes up lightly: no Napoleonic brandy or
antique sherry in there; no seawater, either, by the sloshless sound
of my shaking it. More sand and sealife rain from its still-wet whis-
kers. Ergo, it's either still watertight or else has been marsh-
stranded long enough for whatever leaked in to leak back out.

Cask.

I leave its sea-beard in place for effect, but recycle most of the
fauna with a vigorous dunking in the creek, not to smell up our
larger vessel with this smaller; then I dinghy it back to *US*'s tran-
som and hold it up for your inspection.

"A gen-you-wine cask."

A cask it is.

"Quote/unquote Jay Scribner's?"

Who knows. Columbus's?

"We're too old for that."

Old enough, indeed, separately and together, and veteran shipmates sufficiently unanimous to know without saying when
enough is enough, for the present. You accept the prize and stow
it in the cockpit while I secure the dinghy and reboard. Then you
reshift *US* into forward and the plot of our story into neutral, we
having wordlessly decided to get on downriver while there's air
and light and warmth enough for pleasant sailing, and to set aside
the minor marvel of the cask, the minor mystery of its contents,
till this evening's anchorage. Certain things are on our common
mind: motifs, associations closer to home than Beth Duer and Jay
Scribner, not to mention Christopher Columbus. We're bemused,
but have learned to savor certain deferred gratifications, curiosity
among them. Had it been a magnum of chilled Dom Perignon in
our marsh instead of this cask, we would wait likewise till hook-
down time to toast, with our find, our find.

This floating opera is not meant to be a sailing story; let's get to
anchor. Cask snugged in the cockpit foot-well, we motor straight
into the southerly and out of Langford Creek into the wide Chester

as we've done happy hundreds of times before, you steering while
I stow sail covers and raise all plain sail. Then we shut down the
engine and tack downriver against breeze and tide, neither very
strong, through what remains of the short afternoon, swapping the
helm at each tack to give each other a chance to stretch muscles,
look around, and do odd jobs as we cross and recross from one
perfectly familiar shore to the other. No music on the tape player;
not much conversation, but plenty of communication. We observe
the geese and gulls and ospreys at their work, the oystermen and
clammers at theirs; also our sail trim, depth sounder, and knotmeter, and the afternoon already cooling down by half past four.
"How about it?" we say as the river-depth shoals from twenty feet
to fifteen to nine point seven, point six, point five. "Around we
go." Or we remark and account for some fellow sailor's progress
or want thereof. By our own we know, have known since our setting out, that our first night's anchorage will be Queenstown
Creek, nine miles downriver as the crow flies but twice that as the
sailboat tacks in these conditions: the last snug outbound stop on
the Chester before one enters Chesapeake Bay, and more often
than not therefore either the first or the final anchorage of our
sailing cruises.

Thither we sedately sail, then motor through the narrow inlet
to its snug but ample interior. We putter past the sunbirds,
anchored just inside to get an early jump on the morning, and park
in entire privacy in a pet bight of ours far upcreek: as familiar a
tranquil pleasure as settling down together with a glass of light
wine after a good day's work or play. We do that, too, the wine
and hors d'oeuvres — champagne, in fact, though by no means
Dom Perignon, to wash down hummus and pita chips and to
salute yet one more modest voyage's first day's end — once the
boat has been tucked in for the night and a drop poured over the
transom to Poseidon. To safe passage, certainly, but above all to
life and health, which run apace, and to love, sine qua non for the
likes of us. One l'Chaim will serve for all: "To life."

Et cetera. Now we're watch-capped, sea-sweatered, stretched
out in the cool last light of wooded Queenstown Creek. Dew's

forming already on decks and cushions; one raccoon and two great blue herons stalk the mudline. There's a farmer tractoring late on fields invisible behind the near woods. Farther off yet, traffic buzzes on U.S. 301, headed to and from the Chesapeake Bay Bridge. No insects. I make these anchorage-notes in standard ballpoint in *US*'s log — on the penultimate page of this current volume of it, I remark. If our mild adventure goes beyond the weekend, there'll be one more old book to close and new to open. To life, then: hors d'oeuvres, gentle aging, love, champagne, and handsome Queenstown Creek. No rush to start dinner. No rush to do anything. Right?

"Open it."

Right.

A floating aria: "Water-messages"

To the aria "Our marsh, our marsh" and the catalogue of its fruits, I might have added *water-messages*, but the espial of this cask (which I now duly take up and examine with an eye to opening) — presumably the latest and possibly the unlikeliest in an intermittent, lifelong series of seaborne communications — suggested that they merit an aria of their own.

My native street — Aurora, in East Cambridge, Maryland — runs its five small-town blocks from what used to be the East Cambridge Elementary School at its head down to what very much still is the Great Choptank River at its foot. My parents' house was #301 through my childhood (fourth block down from the school) but became #107 when either the Post Office or the City Council sensibly bethought itself that renumbering inland from the river would leave room for future expansion — a future yet to arrive as of this writing. In either case, we were but one mapled, clapboarded block from the tidal Choptank, nearly two miles wide at that point, whose bush-grown banks and pebbly brown beaches called like the Hamelin piper to East Cambridge children as soon as we were old enough to range afield. We played endlessly down there in every season; alone, in pairs, in troupes; at games and amusements innumerable, most innocent, some not:

Indians and war, tag and Tarzan, desert isle and fright-fraught jungle. We threw oystershells and makeshift spears at neutral targets and at one another; we fished for perch with bamboo poles, wrestled, sneaked cigarettes and firecrackers, masturbated, killed innocent sparrows and floating booze bottles with Daisy BB-guns and, later, innocent rats and floating booze bottles with single-shot .22 "cat" rifles.

Those booze bottles, that weaponry — these were the pre-environmentalist Thirties, the wartime Forties. At the foot of Aurora Street were the county hospital and the "nurses' home" for young women trainees, with a fine grassy embankment for us kids to roll down and leap off, and a crumbling concrete seawall for angling and crevasse-jumping. Just downstream was a considerable lumber mill, strictly off-limits but rich in the illicit thrills of trespass, where we climbed the fragrant, splintery stacks of drying pine boards and sprang like Superman (or Tarzan's Cheetah) from stack to stack. Upstream, however, was the heart of mystery, adventure, and treasure: a scruffy, becreepered "jungle" — so we called it — of briars and honey locusts perched atop an eroding twelve-foot bank, cornfield behind and stone-strewn beach before, crisscrossed with footpaths, embowered with honeysuckle and trumpet vine, and terminating on its upstream end in a splendid unofficial trash dump. Here were the rats and tin cans and bottles and jars for shooting (every male East Cantabrigian had an air rifle from about age ten till thirteen or fourteen and a .22 after his voice changed) or for floating off and bombarding with beach stones and "brickbats," whereof the supply was inexhaustible; it was said that they, like the granite riprap in front of the seawall, were rubble hauled over from the great Baltimore fire of 1904. And in less Western or warlike humors, especially among the more dreamy of us and most especially on my solitary beach-prowls, here was the prime place for posting, perhaps even for receipt of, water-messages.

A note in a bottle: staple of desert-island cartoons to the present day and motif in fiction back to the eighteenth century at least, from Edgar Burroughs's *Land That Time Forgot* through Edgar Poe's "MS Found in a Bottle" to . . . Sterne, Defoe, whomever. Before them, Rabelais in the sixteenth century gives us the inverse, a bottle-in-a-message: the flask-shaped "Ode to a Bottle" in Book Five of *Gargantua and Pantagruel*, 1532 — precursor of the Absolut Vodka ad-series in the American 1990s. Earlier yet, in Scheherazade's tales, it is not messages but fearsome messengers who pop out of seaborne containers and must be tricked back thereinto. In historical fact, pastime of children on tidal shorelines and of shipboard passengers amused to post real greetings, fake urgencies, and hopeful invitations to response from the finder. In historical fact too, desperate plea and/or last testament of who knows how many hapless sinkers, drifters, strandees — or those in imminent peril of so becoming — for as long as there have been written messages, vessels to sink or strand or shatter, and smaller vessels to float word off in, Christopher Columbus's first-voyage log included.*

Nowadays, their high-tech equivalents are the EPIRBs: Emergency Position Indicating Radio Beacons, standard equipment for offshore cruisers, which in distress broadcast a locator signal receivable by satellites as well as by passing ships or aircraft; also those transmitters set afloat by oceanographers to drift with the Gulf Stream, say, and mark its chaotic eddies between the Straits of Florida and the British Isles (I do not even mention our Voyager

---

*A letter to the editors of *The Sciences* (Jan/Feb '93), signed by seven oceanographers, reports that Taiwanese sympathizers with the Chinese political prisoner Wei Jingsheng have campaigned for his release by floating bottled pamphlets on his behalf from the islands of Quemoy and Matsu. One such bottled plea was fortuitously found in June 1990 on the shores of Vancouver Island, British Columbia, by the oceanographer Richard Stricker, of the University of Washington; computer simulation of the relevant ocean currents suggests that perhaps 50 percent of the pro-Wei water-messages reached their intended destination, mainland China, and that fewer than 1 percent would have reached the northwest coast of America, 10,000 kilometers away. Petitioning Deng Xiaoping for Mr. Wei's release, the oceanographers cite a passage from the Japanese legend "The Tale of the Heike": In the year 1177, the priest Yasuyori was exiled for political subversion to an offshore island, from which he subsequently set adrift 1,000 stupas (thin wooden prayer-boards usually offered as graveside memorials), each bearing his name, the date, and two poems. Against odds, one of those stupas was found by a fellow priest on the mainland; he transmitted it to the exile's family and thence to the imperial authorities, who pardoned the exiled water-messager. As of this footnote, the dissident Wei Jingsheng has not been as fortunate as the priest Yasuyori.

satellite messages to outer space). A dandy find, no doubt, such gadgets, for today's beachwalking counterpart to yours truly in his tens and teens, but no more the Real Thing than those afore-deplored advertising, "educational," or party balloons released by salesfolk, schoolfolk, or celebrators, which — when deflation turns them from aerial- to water-messages, become last suppers for pelagic turtles taught by eons of evolution to misread the message. What one yearns for — your solitary preadolescent beachcomber in dreamy search of signs from the world as well as clues to him-self — is nothing less or more than a bona fide message in a literal bottle, washed into the Choptank from Portugal, Chile, China (though Maine or Florida would suffice), and ostensibly declaring *Here is the key to the treasure* or *Rescue me and I'm yours* but secretly whispering *It is all right. We understand. Things will not always be as they may seem to you now. A quite wonderful life lies ahead for you, comprising not only the best of what you've seen around you thus far but many things of which you can as yet be aware no more than dimly, if at all.*

Heaven knows how many water-messages I myself posted from the rivershore in those days (always on outgoing tides), most declaring no more than *Set adrift in the Choptank River on 27 May 1941* [say], *by* [myself], *301 Aurora St., Cambridge, Mary-land, USA,* but others saying . . . I don't remember what; all of them, anyhow, announcing, *I exist. Here I wait. Give me some sign.* And none — Needless to say? — ever replied to. But we're talking a mere half century; Jay Scribner would have it that Columbus's message floated for 499 years before being received and responded to, in the 500th, by himself. Perhaps mine, too, then, some of them, bob about somewhere yet in the world's waters, barnacled, beweeded, en leisurely route to wherever, whomever, as their youthful sender floats into his elder decades.

Once, mirabile dictu, I found one. On the pebbly beach near the jungle dump, in a clear glass gin or vodka bottle not entirely dry inside (I used to cap my own messages tightly for the long haul) and too slimeless outside to have drifted long, it nevertheless bore, by god and in fact, a small sheet of white paper once rolled to fit through the bottleneck and now unrolled to the point of irretrievability except by smashing the container with the usual handy brickbat. Surely my heart beat fast; I can't imagine otherwise, though I half remember an exhilarated calm — *Yes. Of course. At last* — and I was not after all so gone in fantasy as to expect anything more glamorous than *Set adrift off Baltimore*, say, maybe a few days before, maybe from a freighter bound up to the Chesapeake & Delaware Canal or down to the Capes, but, you know, possibly of Liberian or Panamanian registry. In fact the message read, in its ink-run, splotched, block-capitaled entirety, IT WAS BILL BELL. Not *if you find this, please reply to* . . . Not *For a hot time, call* . . . Not even *I am* . . . *And you?* Only the cryptic expletive and past-tense copula, quasi-accusatory or confessional, its noun-clause subject unsupplied, and then the ding-dong predicate nominative proper name. Even our thin Cambridge phone book listed both a *Bell, Wm* and a *Bell, W*; I had not nerve enough to call. *What* was Bill Bell? Fifty years later, I still wonder; hence, no doubt, this aria.

The theme of water-messages, I note, itself bobs through my fiction, from my first novel (*The Floating Opera*) to this. In a short story explicitly titled "Water-Message" (in the series *Lost in the Funhouse*), the bottled inscription IT WAS BILL BELL becomes the salutation TO WHOM IT MAY CONCERN, followed by the closing YOURS TRULY. "The lines between were blank," reports the narrator, "as was the space beneath the complimentary close" — a blank, it might be said, that my life's labor has aspired to fill. All my books, it goes without singing, are water-messages, posted to whom they may concern, quite as the nameless stranded minstrel in the story "Anonymiad" (also from *Funhouse*) posts into the Aegean his private versions of the Trojan War, written on goatskin with squid-ink and sealed in emptied amphorae:

> There [he declares], my tale's afloat. I like to imagine it drifting age after age, while the generations fight, sing, love, expire. Now, perhaps, it bumps the very wharfpiles of Mycenae, where my fatal voyage began. Now it passes a hairsbreadth from the unknown man or woman to whose heart, of all hearts in the world, it could

speak fluentest, most balmly — but they're too preoccupied to reach out to it, and it can't reach out to them. It drifts away, past Heracles's pillars, across Oceanus, nudged by great and little fishes, under strange constellations bobbing, bobbing. Towns and statues fall, gods come and go, new worlds and tongues swim into light, old perish. Then it too must perish, with all things deciphered and undeciphered: men and women, stars and sky. . . .

whether or not I find it washed up one day in our marsh at Langford Creek.

In earlier chapters of my personal life-story, like that stranded minstrel I more than once drained literal wine jugs in search, let's say, of their fluid message, while filling figurative amphorae with my fiction. In later decades I put by that line of inquiry, chastened by the sad alcoholic pattern of male American writers in this century. In vino may sometimes be veritas, but that particular bottled truth may include as well cirrhosis of the liver and the muse, delirium tremens, corroded minds and noses and talents, and early death: As Salman Rushdie nicely puts it, "Djinn and tonic."

Better places to look: in marshes, as aforesung, the whole catalogue of whose treasures may be read as messages from other shores. In libraries and good bookstores — for what is all literature if not bottled missives awaiting degustation? If serendipity is to operate, however, one must be in the Browsing mode, not the Directed Search. It was in that former mode and venue, bookfiling in the Johns Hopkins library to help defray my undergraduate tuition, that I first found and read such floating marvels as *The Ocean of Story*, *The Thousand and One Nights*, the *Panchatantra*, the *Satyricon* — none of which was in my excellent regular curriculum and all of which "impacted," as they say, my subsequent writing and thus my life.

Let's get cosmic: Our lives are messages, brethren, by our bodies embottled, afloat in the great sea of the world. We wash up on other folks' shorelines, they on ours. Many go unread, some are unreadable, many are misread, some are read to death, and a lucky few meet their ideal readers. Our Earth is an intricate, lovely message, bottled in its fragile biosphere as in fine crystal and adrift in eddies within eddies of the black universal sea.

Let's get homely: My wife and I plant messaged bottles on our own beach at Langford Creek, to be found serendipitously by young beachcombing grandkids summer-visiting from California (*Help! We love you! G'ma & G'pa*, etc.). And like the Christians' bread cast upon the waters, certain messages to myself, never meant to be aquatic, were lately lost and floated back to me as water-messages, in the following wondrous way:

At the turn of the decade, December 1990, my wife and I celebrated our twentieth wedding anniversary and the aforesung close of an eventful year with a Caribbean vacation, in a rented beachfront condominium on Grand Cayman. As I have a leaky memory for details — Have I mentioned this already? — I habitually keep, along with other sorts of notebooks, a circumstantial log of our travels, usually a yearsworth at a time. This being a busy year's end, the log then contained not only the data of our latest Caribbean arrival but full notes on memorable sojourns in Italy and Japan as well as the record of my monthly lecture-sorties here and there in our republic: what and where we ate, whom we met, what we saw and did, what we missed, what we thought of it all — verbal photographs for the household archives and for possible future use in and out of my fiction.

To our disappointment, we had been assigned a ground-floor condo: easy beach access at the expense of privacy, and in the tropics as in Langford Creek summers we enjoy leaving everything as open as possible to the breeze. Ah well, we said to our joint self: Cayman is a well-run British isle with full employment and the highest living standard and lowest crime rate in the Caribbean Basin. We'll be obliged to keep some clothes on in the apartment, but be damned if we'll seal out the tradewinds and air-condition ourselves at night. Latched screen doors will do for security; it's not as if we're in the USA.

A reasonable enough judgment call, we still believe, and all might have gone well had we not left a nightlight on in the unfamiliar living room, which revealed to the beach that the sliding glass doors between our screened porch and that room were wide open, and that a beach bag was perched temptingly on the cocktail table just inside. My wife heard mid-night noises; her sleepy husband dismissed them as the sweet tradewinds blowing through the condo (and welcomely over our skin) and rattling the large vertical slats of the porch blinds. Unconvinced, she walked as was into the living room, noticed nothing amiss, but thought she saw figures out on the beach and so returned to bed before they ogled her. All okay, she guessed.

Morning, however, showed we had been B & E'd, as we say in America all too often: Broken into and Entered, after all. Porch screen punched through, screen door unlatched, apartment penetrated as we more or less slept. Alarming indeed, especially upon reflection that my bedmate could well have been B & E'd herself. But what was missing? Our snorkel gear was as we had left it on the porch; every native Caymanian and tourist is already equipped in that line, no doubt. The beach bag we had emptied of in-flight gear on our arrival and not yet filled with go-to-the-beach stuff; it sat still empty on the cocktail table. Everything else ours of value we had fortunately stashed in our bedroom, where our burglar fortunately had chosen not to venture, and the condo's own appurtenances seemed undisturbed. My wife's bold, even reckless approach had evidently spooked some amateur prowler looking for items quickly grabbable and easily turned into cash; we shudder to think of her walking in like that on your average American housebreaker at work.

But even as she telephoned a calm report to the condo manager and the Cayman cops, my second review showed that we had been robbed after all, of items valueless to the thief but of considerable importance to us: her eyeglasses in their case and . . . my leather-bound, rubber-banded, loose-leaf travel notebook, left out like the eyeglasses on that cocktail table for A.M. repacking in that beach bag and snatched by the burglar faute de mieux, we presumed, in hasty hope that they might turn out to hold jewelry or cash.

Amid our relief at having suffered nothing worse, distress! How was my friend to see Grand Cayman without her specs? And from

me had been stolen, in effect, Tokyo/Kamakura/Kyoto/Hiroshima/
Miyajima, also Firenze/Siena/San Gimignano/Bologna/San Ma-
rino/Macerata/Assisi/Perugia/Orvieto, not to mention Bethlehem
PA, Seattle WA, Buffalo NY, and High Point NC — memorable
visits and revisits all, doomed now to fade betimes from my lax
memory as if logged in disappearing ink. Irreplaceable — and
maddening to know that the thief or thieves would simply toss
that notebook and that eyeglass case with a Grand Caymanian
curse once they saw them for what they were.

In quixotic hope that that curse and toss might have happened
promptly, I hurried out (easy beach access) to comb the beach,
pool area, parking lot, and immediate environs while our neighbors were still abed or breakfasting, and — Mirabile, mirabile
dictu! Not washed in from the sea, quite, but beside the beachside
pool, *at the bottom of the Jacuzzi* — into which they had been
dumped in disgust — there they were: the eyeglass case and my
precious travelog, quite soaked.

More than soaked: marinated, simmered for hours in heavily
chlorinated water at 100°F. Her eyeglasses and their case were simply rinsed even cleaner than usual. His Japan, however, his Italy,
and the rest (including what-to-pack lists refined over twenty
yearsworth of vacations, and a life-list of every United State and
foreign country I've set foot in), were messages watered blank now
as that unfillable space between TO WHOM IT MAY CONCERN and
YOURS TRULY: a pale wash of ballpoint ink on the looseleaf pages,
not a word legible, and the inch-thick book one sodden wad.

Damn. On the scale of human misfortunes, not enough even to
jiggle the needle, and yet . . . damn. That ryokan with the unfor-
gettable sashimi in — Where was it? That storm-turbled Tyrrhe-
nian night in Whatsitsname, upcoast from Fucino. The list of four
remaining United States I've yet to be invited to lecture in — gone
with the water.

Idaho, I muttered to myself. *Montana. New Mexico. South
Dakota.* There's those. But it's bases touched that count, not bases
untouched: the name and year of that particular dry white wine
in that Orvieto trattoria, our collection of cryptic English-

language T-shirt mottoes noted in the Ginza — dissolved. The very covers of the notebook, a simulated leather thickly padded with pasteboard, held water like a sponge; the leaves themselves could scarcely be separated without their disintegrating. Yet separate them I did, peeled them apart as carefully as if they were those other famous water-messages, the Dead Sea Scrolls, to confirm that all was indeed lost, lost.

And as I did — she standing by in full sympathy when we both had hoped to be out snorkeling the reef by now on what was, after all, our China Anniversary morn — I found that I couldn't bring myself to throw away those ruined, ink-run runes. Like some Venetian art restorer after high water in the Piazza San Marco, across the condo kitchen I spread square yards of paper towel, laid out the pages in sequence like limp tesserae, and sandwiched them with a second layer of towel. The cover, too, I pressed as dry as I could, wrapped in absorbent paper, and set out on the sunlit porch to dry. That, perhaps, was salvageable; I could buy new loose-leaf paper down the road in Georgetown and open the new year's travelog with an account of our Caribbean B & E. But in such tropical humidity, after such a more than tropical immersion, my washed-out pages I had no hope of ever seeing dry again, much less restored to legibility. Disappearing ink indeed. It was only a consolatory exercise, this elaborate stanching: a last rite for *temps perdu.*

When all was laid out, we turned at last to what we had come there for. We swam and snorkeled, reading the reef's water-message of environmental stress from "development" since our previous Cayman visit just a few years earlier. We strolled the tourist-booming Seven-Mile Beach, where the shelf life of an attractive seashell, not to mention a note washed up in a bottle, we estimated at thirty seconds tops. We sunbathed in lounge chairs, reading extended beside-the-water messages: Julian Barnes stories of Noah's ark and the wreck of the *Méduse,* Gabriel García Márquez's novel of Bolívar's long last river-journey. At midday I changed the paper-towel bandage on my massively hemorrhaged pagelets, resqueezed and rewrapped their erstwhile binder as one might reswathe a mummy.

No hope. Tropical showers moved in, between which we drove about the island, checked out new restaurants and old, rejected the Chinese place we'd had in mind for our China Anniversary in favor of something rather more elegant, did a bit more submarine reef-reading. As we dressed for dinner, I re-rebandaged my hopeless patient and observed — Could it be? — that while the towels were still coming up wet with Jacuzzi water and pale blue with blotted inksplotch, the pages between them were not only less limp and sodden but rather less undifferentiatedly blue. I could in places distinguish their ruled lines now from the watercolor wash of ink, and a hint of the pen-strokes themselves. I could even almost imagine — no, not imagine: I could actually make out *words* here and there, dehydrating palimpsests emerging from the wet like the first amphibians. There's *Todi*, that handsome little Umbrian walled city between Perugia and Orvieto, whose name we couldn't come up with last time we tried. There's *Happo-En*, Tokyo's shrine of a restaurant with its 350-year-old bonsai garden and perhaps the most magnificent fare we've ever been treated to. Happo-En! Could it be . . . ?

At an Austrian-Caribbean eatery far less memorable than Happo-En but not bad at all, we toasted twenty years of marriage, twenty-one of loverhood, our immeasurable good fortune at having washed ashore each on the beach of the other. We toasted Todi, Happo-En, and whatever other fragments might reswim into our ken back there between the paper towels: flotsam from the wreck. Though, to be sure, never imagining . . .

Time to end this aria. That night, and in our Cayman days and nights thereafter, we duly though relucantly sealed, secured, and air-conditioned the condo, promptly caught colds from that unnatural air, but by the way dehumidified both the apartment and the drowned record of our year's adventures. By New Year's Eve, through some negentropic miracle of reversed capillary action, the washed ink appeared to have resorbed into the lines from which it had leached. Italy, for some reason, remained a low-contrast indigo on lavender, though every word was there again; Japan and our domestic excursions returned against a pale blue-white field

to black distinctness, no less legible than any other of my penmanship — e.g., the manuscript of this aria, drawn with my immortal
Pumblechook Parker in Feb '91 in my battered and doubtless mortal but still intact old three-ring binder. My Skrip dries word for
word as I scrawl this latest water-screed, crisp black on clean
white, whose aim and shape I trust to gather as I watch it go where
it has to go. "Borne by currents as yet uncharted," the "Water-
Message" narrator says of that story's young hero's find, "nosed
by fishes as yet unnamed, it had bobbed for ages beneath strange
stars. Then out of the oceans it had strayed; past cape and cove,
black can, red nun, the word had wandered willy-nilly to his
threshold."

Just so, perhaps, figuratively speaking, *this*, to who knows
whose. And just so, evidently, the cask that launched it.

Story:

"How's it going?" You've been briefly down in the galley, firing
up the LPG oven to warm both the cabin and the French rolls
scheduled to accompany our thawed-out beef stew bourguignonne. The Caesar salad, you remind me from the companionway
ladder, remains to build. Shall you relieve me at the cask-work
while I build it, or put dinner on Hold and rejoin me in the cockpit, although it's turning a touch chilly out there for you and I'm
the one who usually gets antsy for dinner first? No way you're
going to miss the grand opening.

An honest-to-god cask, I reply not quite to your question, is not
a vodka bottle or an empty jeroboam,* nor yet a marine distress-
flare canister.† Cask hath not lid nor screw-top nor opening port
nor inspection window but an equatorially positioned bung, and
that, in this instance, not of cork but of two-inch-diameter pine or
fir, softer than the staves but beyond corkscrewing and slightly

---

*Of the sort into which the character Ambrose Mensch stuffs his life-story in my
novel *LETTERS*.
†Of the sort in which the crew of the sloop *Story* improbably find serial instal-
ments of a seminal playscript in my novel *The Tidewater Tales*.

beveled to boot, it appears, for tapping tight without tapping through. Hence the absence of internal slosh, after who knows how long a float, which has swelled the fine coopering to water-proofhood and seized the bung even faster. It is chisel it out or bash it in, and our vessel's tool locker is chisel free.

"So bash. Enough low-grade suspense."

I bash, the flashlit cask cushioned on a folded scrap towel on the engine hatch in the cockpit sole, bung banged with peen of ballpeen hammer once twice thrice, not lightly, and then (there being in English no single adverbs for times past three) again, with all my strength, which just suffices to drive the plug inside.

"Force majeure," you remark, approvingly. "Quick and dirty."

'Swhat made our country great. I suppress an aria on that theme — e.g., Mark Twain's time-travel mechanism in *A Connecticut Yankee in King Arthur's Court*: crowbar upside the head, and the Yank revives in Camelot — and invert and shake cask over towel while you aim the light.

Nothing: only the tock of the bung inside. I peer in with the flash — not easily done through a two-inch hole with a three-inch lantern, but I would surely see *something* in there if the cask held the lost log of Columbus's first voyage, say, or even a foolscap valedictory from Jay Scribner.

"We'd hear it and feel it, too," you affirm. *You* shake it this time, side to side, up and down, yourself still standing half up the companionway ladder and leaning into the cockpit. Rattle rattle, tock tawk tuck. Nothing.

"The container *is* the thing contained," you offer, "more or less. The bung to the brandy *is* the brandy, et cet."

I carry that ball a bit while making salad. The medium *is* the message: in this instance, casked kenosis. An owl hoots at that from the woods astern, but I feel I've banged some Gordian bung. My suspended passage . . .

"Fill 'er up," you advise at dinner. "Float 'er off." Cabin cozy from our cooking, squat glassed candle burning on the dinette table, gimbaled brass lamp lit on the teak bulkhead, low-volume High Baroque adagios denying on the tape player that the Age of Reason was short on passion.

It's my characters who do the real thing, beloved shipmate, I reply, not their author. But while you're not the only of his readers (only the most important) perhaps surfeited with certain of his themes — No more sailboats! No more Scheherazades! No more water-messages! — what's a writer to do with such a full-fledged empty portent, such a floating metaphor as this contentless cask, if not put it on the payroll? Indeed, it's *on* the payroll, no? It's aboard, whatever we do with it: Fill it and toss it; *don't* fill it, just toss it; fill and don't toss; don't and don't — whatever. Now that our imagination contains this particular container, *we're* the thing contained. I'll wake you when it's over, now that it's waking me.

Meanwhile, Albinoni and company, beef stew bourguignonne, French rolls, and Caesar salad, washed down with a 1975 St. Emilion brought aboard to be enjoyed before one day's bumpy sailing undoes seventeen yearsworth of undisturbed aging in our cellar. After dinner cleanup and crew washup, in flannel pajamas and ski socks you settle in on the starboard settee with Scott Fitzgerald, whose *Gatsby* you've agreed to teach to your high schoolers for the umpteenth time; I on the port, first with *US*'s log (in which I bring our post-anchoring activities right up to Time's rolling ballpoint, as it were: *Update log*), and then, half guiltily, with my dapper blue full-size "Friday essay" binder, which I've made no attempt to conceal but didn't announce I was bringing aboard, either.

"What's that?"

I actually blush. And, not without a semiquaver of defensive challenge, I reply: Friday binder. Okay, so it's Saturday. But that passage I mentioned before . . . the suspended one . . .

"Never mind the binder."

Okay, okay: my good pen. I felt the need, is all. I hold it up, uncapped and in position in my writing hand, for both of us to regard. How perfectly fitted to my fingers, my hand and arm, mind, life! And they to it, through which they flow, not always so effortlessly as does their instrument.

You return with a shrug to Jay Gatsby and the green light on Daisy's dock, and as you've said no more, I say on: hunches born from decades of professional experience; muse as B-movie monster, trying to tell us something; learning by going where we have to go.

"I love that poem."

Kenosis. Suspended passage, dot dot dot.

"We suspect that that particular kenosis is history. You'll wake me when it's over?"

Like P. Charming his S. Beauty, I promise, except that *I*'ll be the one who's been being tranced and may need waking. Auto-mesmerized. Astray in Time's funhouse.

"Time's?"

I did say that, didn't I. Upped and popped out: Time's funhouse.

"See you later. Tuck me in after a while?"

Reprise: "Kenosis"

I will, and presently I do: a habit from our younger married years, when not infrequently I used to sit up sipping, reading, and note-taking, my motor still running past your bedtime, having paused at that hour to come upstairs in Baltimore or down-hall at Langford Creek for a good-night word, embrace, whatever our combined moods called for, before going on with it till near midnight. Nowadays it's rare for us to end our days (*as we end our days*, I almost add, mildly horrified) otherwise than together, half-past-tennish, just when for example a proper Madrileño settles down to dinner. Rare indeed in recent years, absent illness or a previous night's insomnia, for you to need "tucking in" except aboardship in cool-weather cruising, when the early darkness, the silent anchorages, the snug but confining cabin (in summer, we would be out night-swimming now), and reading-fatigue all conduce you to earlier bedtimes. We've come so to relish beginning and ending each day in each other's arms (When did we not? But time has enhanced our relish), our one serious complaint about *US* is that, for people really comfortable only in a king-size bed, its officially double berths amount to singles. To make love we can always make shift, but we sleep alone — she in the quarterberth, he in the forward V — and while almost invariably we sleep well, it is not our way of choice for approaching and returning from oblivion.

Tucking done, by a single shaded and focused cabin light I ply old Pumblechook to my suspended passage as if the hour were ante- instead of post-meridian. Astray in Time's funhouse, I cease to hear the ship's clock's light tick above my head. A touch awkwardly in the Friday binder in my shipboard reading/writing position (back rested against cabin bulkhead, feet on settee cushion, knees drawn up), I draw sentences like these about kenosis: the vessel no longer absent presence but filled with the presence of absence and refilling, word by word, with the presence of presence. A presence . . . new but familiar. This.

Story:

This penned, I quit while I feel myself ahead, my passage still suspended but no longer stalled. You're asleep, both fast and quickly. I'll need a good-night beer to change my head's channels if I'm not to wander in Time's funhouse till morning. I tuck away the Friday binder behind *US's* pinrailed library and, at risk of waking you, decide to take a quiet turn on deck with watch cap and nightcap before bed. Unaccountably (What premonition tells me that that will prove the most consequential adverb in this overture?), I have not clipped my Parker into the binder's rings as usual, perhaps because it's not the usual binder. I've simply laid it, capped, candleside on the dinette table. Unaccountably (not to make noise refetching the binder, I suppose, but still . . .), instead of leaving it there till morning or stowing it on the fiddled "dresser top" area of my berth along with pants-pockets stuff, I clip it into the breast pocket of my PJs before quietly slipping into watch cap, windbreaker, and carpet slippers, quietly fishing up a Beck's Dark from the fridge and our main flashlight from its night-place on the ladder step, quietly quietly easing back the companionway slide and lifting out the top dropboard and, much cumbered, stepping up and over and out into the cockpit, then reclosing all, quietly, behind me.

Hello there, world by night. I know you're out here, but until my eyes accommodate, you exist mainly in my head. I close and reopen my eyes, inverse of the companionway hatch, and can now just make out the boat's stern rails, the lifelines, cockpit cushions, binnacle, and braked wheel. There on its bed of towel is our unbunged water-messenger, its message sent but only beginning to be received. Yonder's Queenstown Creek, I'll bet, the world, the universe — that last obscured almost entirely by unforecast clouds. Our low-magnitude anchor light on the staysail stay is the sky's only. No breeze, and so the night-cooled air is not uncomfy. What ambient light there is, I reckon, must be reflected off that cloudcover onto the placid Eastern Shore from bustling Baltimore, some thirty miles up and across the Bay. I reflect upon this reflection.

Aria: "What are we doing here?"

The question forms itself with the crew of *US* as its subject and Queenstown Creek as the reference of its adverb; in that sense, it may still be responded to, if not quite answered, by our aforesung aria "Why not?" We aren't really chasing *American Century* down the Chesapeake and out from the New World back toward the Old; we're simply enjoying a late-season, open-ended, middle-aged little cruise. Why not? But by the time I've uncapped my nightcap,* the question has expanded like the universe itself: The "here" now *is* the universe, the "we" we all, not just us U.S. *US*ers.

I'm too old, I decide, to address such cosmicality, though not too old to be stillstopped thereby from time to time. In less than half a Beck's, I've scaled the question down to less than half its expanded size: Whither *our* life, hers and mine, now that we've reached together the age and stage wherewhen our personal universe shifts from net expansion to net contraction? Ambitions in the main fulfilled or gently relinquished; capabilities gently but

---

*How? asks the sharp-eyed reader: As of this penning (7 March '91), Brauerei Beck of Bremen neither makes twist-off bottle caps nor offers its Dunkelbier in cans, although its Heller Lager comes in poptop aluminum, and you forgot the opener. I reply, for openers, that by the dark night of this aria, 12 October '92, the good Brauerei may well have sunk to canning its Dunkel as well, for the American trade, or to bottling with twist-offs for the world's convenience. Remind me, reader, when we reach that juncture in Time's funhouse, and I'll either twist, or pop, or lift the cap with some opener that I've neglected to mention but not to pocket before exiting the cabin.

inexorably reducing or at best holding their own; life plentifully blessed, but nothing *remarkably* better any longer reasonably to be expected. On the contrary: just a matter of time now, and not exceedingly much of that, until one or the other of us runs afoul of cancer, stroke, life-changing accident, whatever, or until those inexorable changes in degree of capacity become changes in kind. What I'm singing — in a tenor meant to be reflective, not self-pitying — is the somber hue these commonplace contingencies take on in the reflected light of that age and stage: One feels in a terminal but far from interminable holding pattern, circling comfortably and sipping nightcaps while waiting for collision with another aircraft or exhaustion of fuel, whichever happens earlier.

What are we doing here?

That is the question, we imagine, that drove my counterself Jay Scribner and *his* skeptical friend Beth Duer to sally forth new-lifeward, together or separately, burning bridges behind. To that extent, they *know* what they're doing; what they're doing is what they have irrevocably done, wherever it may lead. But Jay/Jerome is metaphysically antsier than I, ontologically more agnostic, always has been. *His* real and ongoing question isn't What are we doing here? but the logically prior Who are we? To which I am disposed by temperament (and perhaps Beck's Dark) to respond, We're the ones who're here doing whatever it is we're doing.

And what is that, exactly, and why are we doing it?

Faute de mieux, the stolid German in me replies in his tidewater French, and inclines to contentment with that reply. He writes as well as he can within his limitations; he does and bes and lives likewise, and that not poorly, he inclines to think — even quite well, although he can not only imagine better but point to examples. Maison Faute de Mieux, we call our little house in Baltimore; Villa F d M our Langford Creekery. Neither will ever be written up in *Architectural Digest* (or would not have been, had I not written of them there, in this vein). La vie faute de mieux, then, too, let it be, our many-blessinged life: I affirm it; I salute it with the last of my Beck's; I let it be, and get on with it. That's what we're doing here.

Story:

Between that aria's lines I've been hearing a new westerly in the treetops, next to nothing in snug Queenstown Creek, but maybe as much as ten knots out on the Chester. With the flashlight, I confirm that our dinghy is still back there on the end of its thirty-foot painter (fully extended, to keep the sound of wavelets lapping at its bow from disturbing your quarterberth sleep and to reduce the odds of its drifting up, as nighttime dinghies like to do, to bump our hull a few inches from your quarterberth ear), comfortably streamed aft on this new little breeze. The sight inspires me to go forward and let out more anchor rode, fair forecast notwithstanding. Our current five-to-one scope (five feet of line out for each vertical foot between bowsprit and creek-bottom) will almost certainly suffice in so sheltered an anchorage, barring real storm; but there's swinging room to spare hereabouts, and we have been disagreeably surprised before by unpredicted middle-of-the-night blows of anchor-dragging potential. In a rising breeze, I'll sleep better on seven to one. We anchored at low water in five feet (Dear shallow Chesapeake!) — ten, say, from bow roller to bottom muck, plus two more for high-tide allowance — and I duly paid out the 5/8-inch nylon to its sixty-foot mark. Another thirty should hold us through anything short of a hurricane.

Lamp- and candlelight glow through the cabin ports onto our dew-soaked gunwales. After tucking my empty bottle out of harm's way beside the more or less empty cask (and resisting any parallels), I douse the flash and make my way forward by that gentler illumination. I could do it eyes closed, so familiar is the way, my free hand guiding me from lifeline to shroud (we resist the metaphor), back to lifeline and on to bow pulpit. There I prop the relit light against a bulwark, uncleat the rode, and feed out extra line from one of the twin deck-pipes leading down to a locker at the vertex of my V-berth. This too I could do blind; our Chesapeake creeks and coves are so uniformly shallow that we have secured rubber chafing gear at the sixty- and ninety-foot marks of our main anchor line — the former for light weather and anchorages short on swinging radius, the latter for breezy evenings, squalls actual or threatened, and less-sheltered parking places — and rarely do we need to reposition that gear, although the line runs to two hundred feet. But so slight is the new breeze here in the lee of the woods, and so gentle or contrary the tidal current, *US* is in no hurry to settle back on its lengthened tether. The fresh slack loops down between cleat and bow roller for lack of sufficient pull to take it up; several times I go out onto the bowsprit platform and hunker down with the light to pay out that slack by hand.

The little chore done, I take a leeward pee (returning Beck-message to medium), slip quietly back into the cabin, replace flashlight on step, out candle and oil lamp (you stir, but do not waken), off watch cap, windbreaker, and carpet slippers, climb into my berth — and realize that my pajama breast pocket is penless.

Buzz of nerves! as in that moment between when you see that you've just cut yourself, seriously, and the arrival of blood and pain. I did put it there, unquestionably though unaccountably, pen in pocket, and am unquestionably accountable for not having sensibly unput it. It is not there now. Stradivarius of pens! My instrument! Partnership older than my marriage, and in its peculiar way as close! My hand is on my heart, my heart as full as the pocket over it is empty. Chagrin at my double folly! Anger at myself, to distract me from the size of that folly's consequence! It has to have been that in my squatting, bending, and hunkering on the foredeck to adjust (no doubt needlessly) our scope, the Parker unpocketed itself inside my half-open windbreaker, down through or up out of which it then made its way, to drop . . .

I'm sweating. Surely I would have heard a little cluck and scuttle if my pen had fallen to and slid along the deck; a plick (more a *ploick*, actually; I can conjure the fell small sound) if, when I was stretching through the bowsprit pulpit rails to feed out that slack, my pen had slipped directly overside into Queenstown Creek; a muted *pook* or *took* (echoing *buuk*) if — Happy possibility! — it had dropped to the portside settee or the cabin rug when I pulled that windbreaker off. But I heard none of these. Oy, veh is mir: my pen, my pen. Surely now I must at least —

But among my shortcomings I number this, that in situations calling for extraordinary response, I do not always respond extraordinarily. Some deep-grained distaste for (no doubt some fear of) emotional extremity and bravura action intimidates, numbs, restrains me — particularly, but not only, when I'm in the go-to-sleep mode. Oh, I've here and there done the macho thing, gone flashlight in hand (and heart in throat) to check out untoward late-night noise on our various premises, that Grand Cayman instance to the contrary notwithstanding. I have gone abovedecks in crashing midnight weather to refurl storm-loosened sails, and overside in inhospitable water — chilly or sea-nettle infested — to unfoul a fouled propeller or unclog an engine intake line. Not spineless, then, quite. But I haven't my mate's courage at "standing up to" people, say; at "making a scene" where, I agree, a scene needs making. I'm capable of rationalizing inaction where prudence calls for action (those "tradewind noises" in Grand Cayman that turned out to *be* burglars; certain foul-weather nights at anchor when I've crossed my fingers and said from my berth to yours, "We're okay," instead of suiting up at three A.M. and hauling out into the blast to make sure).

To this weakness now is added my disinclination to a well-earned reproof: I not only brought my precious Pumblechook aboard, but (unaccountably!) carried it up on deck, at night, *out onto the bowsprit* . . . ! And you're sleeping so soundly. I've managed once already to exit and re-enter the closed companionway without waking you, light sleeper of a mate; I won't likely twice.

So look, I reason painfully to myself: Either the dear thing is on the bottom of Queenstown Creek, in which sad case that's that, or else it's up in the cockpit or somewhere on deck or somewhere in the cabin after all, in which cases it will be there in the morning. We are in no peril. The dearest such item in the world is still only an item, not a child or a limb or an irrecoverable manuscript or an actual Stradivarius. The water-messager is at worst returned to its medium — as I myself, I remind me, have often wished my body to be returned upon my death, to recycle the seafood that it has so relished in its life.

So instead of rousing all hands to a midnight search or attempting one singlehanded, I spend the next dark half-hour trying to reconstruct from memory Elizabeth Bishop's lovely poem "One Art" (another villanelle, like Roethke's "Waking"), which begins, *The art of losing isn't hard to master,* and goes on to catalogue various of the poet's losses — her mother's ring, her house, the beloved to whom the poem is addressed — with the operative refrain *but that was no disaster.* And although my reconstruction goes little farther than that, I reflect determinedly on the triple arts involved in "One Art": the knack for losing valuable things (not among my afflictions, fortunately), the ability to come to terms with loss, and the gift for turning such setbacks into, for example, memorable verse — no doubt the key to that second art. One day, I suppose (I reflect), I'll write of my lost pen.

With what?

Too old to cry about such things, I sigh and sleep — quite soundly, as nearly always at a quiet anchorage, though toward dawn, when I haul out of my berth to pee, I am restung by recollection of my loss. Maybe the Parker company's customer relations people will be impressed enough by my devotion to their product to search their archives for a duplicate. Would I do a commercial for them? Not for money; otherwise, I've just done one. I hear the wind still busy in the creekside treetops and now occasionally in our standing rigging as well. Weather often sounds inside the cabin as if it's going to be more formidable to deal with than it turns out to be; but even after so many years of sailing, that small apprehension together with the mishap of my pen keeps me now from better than fitful sleep.

From which I take my waking slow. In the early light, you come forward to use the head and then — since we both sense that we're both awake now — join me in my berth once we've turned its V into a solid triangle with a filler-cushion designed for that purpose. Our legs entwined down in the vertex, we embrace and half doze.

"Wind's up."

Some.

"Was it forecast?"

Not really. But wind, we know, is the trickiest thing to predict in these latitudes. Listen: I lost my good pen last evening, probably overboard. I'm trying not to be too upset about it, but I *am* upset.

You've drawn away from me already, wide awake — as you can become in five seconds at a two A.M. phone call, while I'm still trying to recollect who I am and where. I tell you the story.

"I can't believe it."

Me neither.

"You've looked everywhere?"

You won't believe this, either: I haven't looked anywhere.

"I believe it. But we're awake now: How come you're not turning the boat inside out?"

Busy holding you. Anyhow, it's either et or cetera, no? Let's take our waking slow.

"I can't believe it." However, no chiding my carelessness; thanks for that.

When presently we do haul out and fire up the gimbaled gas stove to warm cabin, croissants, and coffee, the morning is crisp and bright, and the wind is in unmenacing perspective: just a fine brisk sailing breeze, though more than was forecast, and the forecast itself is less ideal than before. In Papermate ballpoint I tell the ship's log, *Sunday 13 Oct: Q'tn Creek– ____ : 0730 up to a fine A.M. after OK night. Cabin 60°, breeze W 10 + . Lost dear Parker last night from PJ pocket, evidently overside. Stupid. Am inconsolable.* For I've checked upstairs, recapped and windbreakered over my flannel pajamas, while you've searched the settee cushions and other possible falling-places. Even in summer there would be little use in my going overside with mask and snorkel (swinging on wind and tide, we've traced a ninety-foot-radius semicircle in water that one can't see more than two feet through); as is, that water's a hypothermic sixty Fahrenheit, like the wake-up cabin air, and pulsing with Medusa jellyfish.

Gone.

"Pack it in? Home for lunch?"

I've been thinking such thoughts, too, especially as the Weather Service forecast changes: Tropical Storm Jerry ("Come *on!*" we chorus) is picking up speed and intensity as it moves north off the coast. Although still reassuringly offshore and not expected to turn landward, it may well trigger tides higher than normal, gale winds, and heavy rain in some coastal areas, particularly if and when it reaches hurricane strength. But the Beths and Jays, I reflect aloud, won't be turning tail for home.

"We're not them. We *have* a home. On the floodplain."

Granted. But our project isn't their project, either: just a little middle-aged, open-ended etc. If we go straight home, I'll get depressed about this Pumblechook business, whereas aboardship I'm *used* to not having it (So why did I bring it? you don't ask), and maybe by cruise's end I'll have begun to get used to having lost it. The day, meanwhile, we agree, is certainly Go. So maybe the best thing to do is go, one day at a time as they say, keeping an ear on the weather and *not dwelling on my dumb mistake.* Shall we see where we are this time tomorrow, and how the weather looks from there?

Suits you.

On with the story, then,

Which I'm still resolved will not be one more sail-tale, but rather an opus that happens at most to begin afloat and possibly end there, with some sort of non-nautical middle. Let's get down-Bay:

I lash "CC"'s empty cask under the thwartships dinghy seat, to get it out from underfoot. We weigh anchor and motor out of Queenstown Creek (auf Wiedersehen, dear old pen, faithful old pen, pen meant to outlast this penman), into the wind and down to Kent Island Narrows, under the new high bridge there and through the old low one, after which we pick up the good west-northwesterly square over our starboard rail for a brisk reach down behind Kent Island itself under all plain sail, a spanking close reach out into the Bay, and then a booming broad reach down, down, down under main and genoa, no staysail needed, no spinnaker wanted, in brilliant sunshine, eighteen knots of true wind on our quarter but only ten or so on our backs, as we're surfing along at seven-plus ourselves — hull speed, nearly: the fastest this design can be pushed through water — with our autopilot at the helm and little for us to do but exhilarate, hour after hour. It is so ideal a day of sailing that we can't bring ourselves to end it betimes at the mouth of the Patuxent, while there's still late-afternoon light to enjoy our anchorage by. We stretch it out, keep on and on, wondering Are we crazy? but knowing that a lifetime offers few such perfect sailing days and happy indeed that we didn't run for home this morning.

Down, down, down; lunch under way at speed and now, five hours later, a glass of red wine and clam-dip hors d'oeuvres under way at speed, sky suddenly overcast in the last of the afternoon; down, down the ever-widening Bay past the Patuxent's lower lip, Cedar Point, and along the featureless, all but shelterless twenty-mile stretch of high bank or low cliff to westward between Patuxent and Potomac, the various low-lying Eastern Shore marsh islands nearly invisible across the broad, rather lonely expanse of water. Empty.

"Where are we going?"

Taking your question most literally, I report from downstairs (where I'm doing chartwork at the nav station) that half an hour at our present course and speed should fetch us abeam of Point No Point:* the point of no return between anchorages on the Patuxent, now well behind us, and on the Potomac, still well ahead, except for a single harbor of refuge called — What have we here? — *St. Jerome Creek*, just past pointless Point No Point. Thereafter one must sail on, sail on, past Point Look-In — an antipoint, actually: an *indentation* in the shore — to Point Lookout and several miles up the Potomac to its first decent anchorage.

"So where are we going?"

I'm the one, typically, who's ready to drop the hook early and loaf about a bit in cockpit and cabin before dinner and bed, whereas end-of-day sailing is your favorite kind even when we've been working the ship since breakfast. But the pretty light has disappeared now, and the absence of other boats is a mite spooky in all that gray-and-silver seascape. When I reckon further that to

---

*So called because there's a lighthouse offshore there but in truth no proper point, only a shallow angle in the western shoreline.

turn Point Lookout — a bona fide point, that one, the southern extremity of Maryland's western shore and entrance to the broad Potomac — and then to motor upwind upriver another six miles to anchorage will take more time than we have daylight left to us, we decide faute de mieux on Point Look-In and . . . St. Jerome Creek, a harbor unknown to us.

You recite from the cruising guide: *"Don't try this creek in a hard onshore wind or if you draw three and a half feet or more. The depth in the dredged channel — 5 feet on the chart — cannot be depended on."*

No problem: The wind is "offshore" — westerly — and gentling by the minute; we draw a mere three feet with centerboard tucked up, and our depth sounder is reliable.

"Do we know who Saint Jerome was?"

Well, we know one who wasn't, isn't, though in his way would be. But we lapsed Protestants and secular Jews aren't strong on saints. Jerome, Jerome: Not one of the martyrs, we think we remember. Biblical scholar, wasn't he? Somewhere between second and fifth centuries? A flash flashes from my undergraduate years, when I had *everything* to learn and (as aforesung) learned a fair fraction of it as a bookfiler in the old Johns Hopkins Library, replacing books in the stacks of Greek and Latin classics and of William Foxwell Albright's Oriental Seminary, and interfiling new entries in the massive card catalogue: For *Jerome*, I learned from that latter activity, *see Hieronymus.* Intrigued, I did (and for a while thereafter called Jerry Schreiber by that Greek equivalent, until he self-metamorphosed into "Jay Wordsworth Scribner"), and now it comes back to me: great biblical scholar, fourth or fifth century; retired from Rome to Bethlehem in his old age, I do believe, and first translated Old Testament into Latin directly from Hebrew texts with aid of Jewish scholars. The Vulgate. There.

Your husband's memory being such an undependable combination of sieve and flypaper, you are duly impressed. I forget names of your colleagues of fifteen years' standing; you remember first names of my colleagues' *children*, even if met only once and years ago. I can't find my way confidently to certain outlying Baltimore shopping plazas that we've shopped in dozens of times; you can remember which restaurants we ate at in St. Lawrence Gap, Barbados, in 1985, and in many instances what we ordered and how we rated chef and service. But I can — unreliably — come up with *Jerome: see Heironymus*, etc., forty years after my one and only seeing of his catalogue card. Wasn't St. Lawrence, by the way, the one martyred on a barbecue grill?

"Never mind Lawrence. Let's have a look-in at your pal Hieronymus."

We pass without difficulty between the entry day beacons and find the shallow creek inside pleasingly ramified in true Chesapeake fashion, coves and forks every which way, most occupied by workboats and none particularly handsome or "unspoiled," but who cares about that when there's not much daylight left anyhow and we'll be leaving after breakfast? The guide recommends anchoring in a cove due east of the point between the words *Jerome* and *Creek* on the nautical chart, but we don't like the look of a two-foot sounding exactly in that cove's small mouth and so park instead just under said point, in a nameless five-foot-deep cove just off the *-rome* of *St. Jerome* as lettered on our chart.

"He did spend time there," you confirm later that evening. We keep a pocket encyclopedia in *US*'s reference library, for you are a dedicated looker-up of things. "In Rome. Your friend Jerome-See-Hieronymus, circa Three-Forty-Seven to Four-Twenty, question mark. And he's buried there, in Santa Maria Maggiore. I don't remember that church; do you?"

Only its name. What else?

"Engaged in high-tech theological catfights. Corresponded and argued with Saint Augustine — How about that? And defended Our Lady's perpetual virginity against the guys who claimed she had normal children by Joseph in the normal way after her Jesus episode —"

The Maggiore connection.

"And get this: Was spiritual adviser to a clutch of noble Roman ladies and toured Palestine and Egypt with them. One ladyfriend even built him a monastery in Bethlehem to do the Vulgate in with his rabbi pals. Quite a mensch, this Jerry."

In his fourth-century way. The Rome of Saint Jerome . . .

"How'd we get a creek named for him out here in the boonies?"

Very R.C. boonies, I remind you, this neighborhood: Lord Baltimore's first colonists landed just around the corner on Saint Clement's Island in the Potomac — 1634? — and founded Saint Mary's City on Saint Mary's River in Mary-land. They were refugees from antipapist England, and they sainted everything in sight: Saint Leonard's Creek, Saint Inigoes Creek, Saint Margaret's Island, Saint Catherine's Island. . . .

"Did we touch bottom just then?"

I felt it, too: a moment's hesitation in our idle anchor-swing, as if our shoal-draft keel barely grazed soft mud. Only veteran thin-water sailors would have registered it at all, but we are that. The small sensation brings us at once, as one, from the fourth and seventeenth centuries to the fin-de-twentieth; from the Rome of Jerome-See-Hieronymus to the -*rome* of *St. Jerome Creek*, regarding which the U.S. Coast Guard's weekly *Local Notices to Mariners* has lately listed three several reports of shoaling to less than charted depths. Had we expected to be down this way at all, I would have made note of the affected areas. Anyhow, we came in cautiously without incident on a fairly low tide, and if our depth sounder never showed more than five feet (which is to say, six, corrected for placement of the transducer), neither did it ever show less than three, which is to say four. We are used to such narrow margins. All the same, you switch the instruments on, and I go upstairs to have a look.

3.*1*, the dial reads, which is to say etc.: close, but acceptable, for the tide has turned, is on the rise now. The flashlight shows us to be a comfortable couple of boatlengths from the nearest cove-bank and oysterboat piers. Not impossibly there's a one-foot hump or bottom-wrinkle somewhere within the arc of our swing; maybe a sunken log or a discarded engine block once used as a mooring anchor — though what we felt a while back was sound-less, and such obstructions usually go bump. Our nerve endings in this department will no doubt remain deployed and fine-tuned for the next hour or so, but we ought to be all right.

It is dark indeed, the universe round about the softly glowing capsule of *US*. No lights ashore, as it happens, nor any aloft besides our anchor lamp. Only the mildest of breezes, southeasterly now. Socked in. Somewhere aft is our dinghy, fraught with its fruitless freight. Somewhere forward are Beth and Jay/Jerome/ Heironymus and *American Century*, very possibly out of the Chesapeake already if they've been standing watches, and either motoring down the ICW below Norfolk or close-hauled out in the Atlantic, beating for Bermuda.

Small boat, black ocean, black night: The image chills my soul as does the black space above, vertiginously signifying Nothing. I crave, suddenly, an updated weather forecast. Whatever its tidings, however, we can't act on them before morning, and a worsening forecast on top of our little bottom-nudge would blow our night's sleep for sure. We are okay. We will assess the situation bright and early, or gray and early.

We're okay.

"Okay."

Distracted aria: "Bad J Good J"

Where is my pen, to sing Bad J Good J, the dark without and the dark within, and thus to begin refilling a certain old sailor's emptied cask? Full foot five, or six, on the bottom of Queenstown Creek. Our P.M. duly logged in ballpoint and nightcapped, good nights kissed, all lights out, in my coffin-comfy berth I stare Nothing to another draw. The darkness here is total: not stunningly endless like the space between visible stars, but softly enveloping, claustral. No sound save the ship's clock's tick aforeregistered and the small, high-frequency tinnitus in my skull: An effect of aging on the auditory nerves, ever-present since my fifty-fifth year like the Big Bang's rustle, it would drive a higher-strung sensibility mad, but I seldom notice it except with earplugs in at my writing table and in night-meditative spells like this.

Dead on the bottom, dear deathless Parker, a touch slimed already by one day's marine growth and ever-settling silky sediments, the black creekwater sliding gently over it. I ponder the hydraulics of a half-filled fountain pen two meters under: whether tidewater will literally seep into the barrel and mix with the ink, as it always did figuratively, or, contrariwise, my pen literally empty itself into the Chesapeake, ditto. Either way conjoined, the dark within and the dark without: one darkness.

Talking to each other in recent years, "Jay Wordsworth Scribner" and I have found that despite our growing attenuation we still share opinions on sundry matters. In the public sphere, e.g., neither of us is a flag-waver on the one hand or an America-basher on the other, but we shake our heads in synch regarding aspects of life in the USA, particularly in our century's latter decades. Political agnostics both, we nonetheless deplore our republic's living on borrowed money, borrowed economic time, and, largely, borrowed brains — brains drained (not for no reason) from other countries, our own public school system being so inarguably mediocre and our college undergraduate curricula by and large ever less demanding and coherent. We frown, do Jay and I, upon our government's propensity through the 1980s to deregulation of what for the public weal needs intelligent, scrupulous regulation, and to gigantic investment in the military and in highly fallible "big science" at the expense of social programs, public education and transportation, civilized cities, the country's infrastructure. You get our stock-liberal drift: We tisk at our national addiction to violence, drugs, material consumption and waste, the commercial pop culture in general, network television in particular, and despoliation of the natural environ — heavily overlapping categories of tisk. Shake shake go our heads at declining American technological competitiveness and SAT scores, booming teenage pregnancies and young male homicides in our bleak inner cities, TV evangelism, AIDS, the National Rifle Association, and — Let's see, now — Oh, you know: a sentimentality, a vulgarity, a *silliness* about our national life almost as ubiquitous as its violence. A loose cannon on the deck of history, our USA, we often sigh, with an inane happy-face plastered on its muzzle and a wiseass bumper sticker on its undercarriage.

We then endeavor to look at our coin-of-the-realm's other side, for both of us acknowledge feeling American to the marrow (even our essential alienation is in the native grain), and we do not exempt ourselves from certain of those regrettables at which we tisk and frown, sigh and headshake. Here are our celebrated open candor, our Yankee straightforwardness, energy, resourcefulness, and irreverent indocility (where television has not mesmerized us altogether), our personal liberty verging upon anarchy, our ethnic pluralism a general value despite abundant bigotry, our cultural enrichment by all those immigrants, our prevailing guilelessness and good humor, our cheerful near-nihilism when you get past the superficial pietism, our comparative classlessness, opportunity more approximately equal after all than in most venues, the insouciance of our unhistoricity, the magnificent geography, and one or two other things we're no doubt forgetting. Credit where due!

"The Devil his due," growls Bad Jerome Schreiber, my old East Cambridge nemesis, my counterself.

Cet diable, c'est nous, I French-rhyme him.

"To hell with us, then."

Speak for yourself, Jerry Schreiber/Jay Scribner.

"Amen. I've *had* it, man. You know?"

I know, and know *he* knows that shifting citizenships won't serve. We're at least as ambivalent about other countries as about Yankland (have spent time in several, he more than I), and are incorrigibly, if only residually, American. So?

So here this pair of Js part company, reopening a split that's been there from the start, however sometimes grafted, and that echoes a fault line running separately through each of us. Bad Jay *has* finally had it; can't make peace with either his country's failings or his own; knows better than to imagine grass greener otherside some fence; has therefore burned his bridges, cut his cables, laid his course toward nowhere, really, except away from Chris Columbus's discovery and its consequences. Palos will be for him no more than a fractionally serious port of call, "to hand-deliver CC's water-message to King Juan Carlos"; likewise those projected subsequent waypoints back to "where it all began."

Whereas, on the other hand, Good J —

"Tame J. Timid J."

Okay. But not *just* those, Jay, as you well know.

"I do."

Well, I'm doing what I'm doing, have done what I've done, will do what I'll do: with sigh and shrug, incline to accept my country's shortcomings as I accept my own, without pretending they don't exist or misreading them as virtues or abandoning all effort — not to eliminate them (too ambitious, that; too . . . American), but here and there at least to moderate, ameliorate them. Leopard can't change spots, but can maybe shine 'em up a bit, lick 'em into better shape? Thus *don't* turn my back on CC's northern-hemispherical legacy or my personal story thus far. Acknowledge reduced capacities; plan no radical changes in work habits, residence, worldview, only somewhat more leisure, less pressure, fewer obligations in that story's late chapters. Count self blessed in marriage, health, career; cross fingers; hope for twenty able years more. *Enjoy* kenosis while gravitating at my muse's pleasure toward whatever next large Attractor, and neither expect nor strongly wish myself to be very different from what (in face of that black wind from the future, resonating certain black winds from the past — the dark within, the dark without — and picking up, picking up like the southeast breeze now in St. Jerome Creek) I am.

Story:

"It doesn't sound good."

Indeed it does not, we agree over breakfast, neither of us as refreshed as we wish we were. Wind in the standing rigging has kept the pair of us edgy since 3 A.M., despite all my usual be-quiet measures upstairs. It's blowing yet, and now the National Weather Service advises us that Tropical Storm Jerry, cruising north-northeastward a hundred miles or so off Cape Hatteras —

"Off Hatteras! How'd it get so far up the map in one night?"

— while still expected to remain offshore, will quite possibly cross the seventy-five-mph threshold into hurricanehood later this morning. Although winds on the Bay are forecast only in the neighborhood of twenty knots today, gale warnings have been extended up the Atlantic coast as far as Cape May, New Jersey.

You swallow your carrot cake. "Remind me again what's the order of increasing seriousness: Alert Watch Warning? Watch Warning Alert? Warning Alert Watch? And while you're at it, is the number of possible combinations the square of the number of elements, or the cube, or what?" You sip your freeze-dried coffee. "I hate being innumerate; it's like only knowing one language. Knowing *only* one language."

I answer your first question but can't your second until, sipping coffee too, I've spelled them all out on a yellow notepad, using ABC for Alert/Watch/Warning. To sound my own innumeracy, I search then for the principle, in final vain: Of A and B there are, obviously, only two possible permutations, AB and BA; of ABC, to our joint mild surprise, there are, not nine or twenty-seven permutations, but only six. Add a fourth element, however — Alert/Watch/Warning/Notice, let's say — and the number of possible combinations leaps to twenty-four. So, fellow dodos: If two elements yield two combinations and three yield six and four yield twenty-four, what's the principle? How many combinations are possible with five elements? You are a superb teacher of high-school English, the daughter and sister of engineers, our house logician and logistician; I'm a professor emeritus of fiction, a novelist of some accomplishment, our house accountant, a faithful subscriber to both *The Sciences* and *Scientific American*, and a tailorer of computer spreadsheets to our domestic purposes. Once upon a time, to amuse myself, with the aid of a calculator and a standard medical manual I worked out to my satisfaction the arithmetic of Scheherazade's menstrual/obstetrical calendar as a key to the *1001 Nights*. Yet neither of us, staring at the progression *2 is to 2 as 3 is to 6 as 4 is to 24*, can confidently extrapolate *5 is to x*. We are not, in fact, dodos; following the series of implicit multiples (2×3, 6×4, $24 \times 5 \ldots$), we both would bet that that $x = 120$. But where is the principle (obvious, we're certain, to any mathematically gifted junior high schooler) that would let us calculate the possible combinations of nine elements, say, or thirteen, without tediously extending the chain of ratios all the way from 2 : 2 :: 3 : 6 :: 4 : 24 :: 5 : 120?

You shrug your shoulders: one more girl no good at math and heavy lifting, also short of sleep, and the logistician in you wants to get to the more pressing question of where we're going this fine ominous windy morning. Ought we to stay put in the -rome of St.

Jerome Creek until Jerry blows by? Run for home (we'll never get there in one day, especially beating into the predicted northerly)? Shoot for some anchorage more familiar and secure, a proper hurricane hole — snug Mackall Cove on the Patuxent, say, with its all-but-encircling hundred-foot banks?

Or, I remind you, carry on with the cruise, right down into the Chesapeake Triangle, and take cover when wind or Weather Service tells us to? Dopey like yours from restless sleep, my mind nevertheless won't leave my innumeracy alone; it returns to and probes that adumbration of its limits like a tongue a missing tooth. Any reasonably sentient taxpaying citizen, I maintain, ought to be able to intuit the requisite algebra; *invent* it if necessary. But I myself can no more do it than stand on my hands, wiggle my ears, or pencil-sketch the likeness of your face. So be it: Accept thy limitations, I remind myself. Rejoice, even, that natural gifts and capacities are distributed as unequally as money, though less unjustly, and that we are not among the destitute. So be it. In that case, however, one incarnation is not enough; I would like next time to be a whiz at math and foreign languages, say: also an adventurer and an athlete, while we're at it. Maybe a Jay Wordsworth Scribner, even — not that he's every one of those.

Thus these pages, I daresay: another imagined alternative identity. Thus all the other pages, back when I had my trusty old Pumblechook to pen with.

"Carry on? You're kidding."

Maybe. No, not really. I'm thinking again now of Jay and maybe Beth out there, down there, probably as more or less snug somewhere in the Dismal Swamp Canal as we are in the -rome of St. Jerome, but just possibly bracing for the worst, not in the "Chesapeake Triangle" (a mere house levity) but in the infamous Bermuda one. No story, I reflect, without a plot; no plot without a triangle of one sort or another. . . .

Trianglish aria:

Books both sober and sensational have been penned (My pen! My pen!) about the Atlantic area approximately bounded by

Bermuda, Miami, and Puerto Rico* — the venue of many unexplained disappearances of ships and aircraft. Were they beamed away by UFOs? Destroyed by Soviet submarines stumbled upon in mid-hugger-mugger? Zapped by some unknown natural force so formidable that no one encountering it survives to report its existence, maybe a monstrous anomaly in Earth's magnetic field, a maelstrom flukily spun off now and then from the Gulf Stream, or spasmodically active power-generators from the lost continent of Atlantis? Cooler heads hold that the Stream itself — that great warm river fast-flowing northwestward through the colder ocean — with its notoriously bumpy weather, is sufficient to account for the casualties: wind-shear and microburst effects like those that plague certain airports under certain conditions; "white squalls" like the one that capsized and sank Maryland's own *Pride of Baltimore* just east of the Bahamas in less than a minute on 14 May 1986, with the loss of four of the crew: a replica clippership professionally skippered and worked by seasoned hands. A few skeptics question whether there's any statistical significance at all in the number of vanishments from the area (don't ask us borderline innumerates). But fact or fancy, the lore lives on, and it must be a rare sailor who enters the Bermuda Triangle for the first time without some tingling of nerves.

In our house, the lower Chesapeake — from the Maryland/Virginia line (Potomac River on the west, Pocomoke River on the east) down to the Bay's entrance — is called the Chesapeake Triangle, both because it is, as aforesung, *mare incognitum* to us and because in fact the weather is often rougher down there than up our way. The Potomac's wide mouth is a famous breeder of summer thundersqualls that then roar down into the Triangle or smash across into the Eastern Shore marshes; the Bay itself is at its widest just there, giving wind and waves a long fetch; and the ocean's increasing proximity as one moves south — both the approaching threshold of the Atlantic proper and the ever-narrower peninsula dividing the two bodies of water — makes the Chesapeake Tri-

*Some enlarge it to a rectangle: Virginia Capes/Florida Keys/Virgin Islands/Bermuda.

angle more vulnerable than the upper Bay to the effects of coastal storms. We keep all this in perspective: The whole two-hundred-mile length of our Chesapeake, from Virginia Capes to C & D Canal, is a mere milk run for seasoned traversers of the Intracoastal Waterway and for bluewater sailors en route to or from the ocean. Beth and Jay chuckle; the incidence of charted wrecks down there is no higher than elsewhere on our Bay, and in both venues they are more often the casualties of leaks, fires, accidental groundings, and deliberate abandonments than of storms. But we've never sailed those waters, and so for us the CT has still the little frisson of adventure.

We might consider, I suggest now, simply scaling down our original objective for this ad-lib odyssey, itself a scaled-down version of Beth and Jay's. Instead of southing on until we cross the Bay's Atlantic threshold for the first time in our nautical lives, we could merely lay our course for the morning's first leg southeast into Virginia waters, over toward Smith Island and Tangier Sound, monitoring the weather radio as we always do when things are meteorologically uncertain, and thus at least cross for the first time the threshold of our Chesapeake Triangle. Should TSJ turn out to sea and the forecast improve through the morning, we can carry on southward as originally half-planned. If not, we can sail up Tangier Sound (where we've never been either) to some new anchorage on that part of the Eastern Shore; or take shelter on colorful Smith Island itself, an isolated watermen's community that we've long meant to visit but have never managed to; or — since the marshy geography over there offers no truly snug sailboat anchorage — retreat across the Bay to the Potomac, the Patuxent, or even the -rome of St. Jerome before heading for home and real life.

I know without my voyage-mate's reminding me that this proposal is imprudent under the circumstances. Quite apart from our house half-joke about the Chesapeake Triangle, the waters on its lower Eastern Shore side are shallow and unfamiliar, the anchorages likewise and exposed as well. We enjoy our life together too much to be reckless with our safety, and there's always next summer, isn't there? Granted, there won't *always* be next summer, tick

tick tick; but this particular Quincentenary fall there's almost certainly next summer. Inarguable, all that; goes without saying, but we've said it anyhow: My suggestion is imprudent, imprudent, and we are prudent sailors, prudent souls, characteristically. . . .

But my trianglish aria is not done. The percussionist's shiny little chrome-steel equilateral does more than tinkle; its diminutive size notwithstanding, it can assert its high-frequency *ding* through the entire orchestra. In like fashion, through the chatter of the foregoing I hear the high, clear, insistent ring of other triangles, sounding Prudence's countertheme. Story-plots are triangular, in at least two ways: The "curve" of dramatic action is classically a nonequilateral triangle, a ⟋b⟍c, where *ab* represents the "rising action," or incremental complication of some conflict; *b* the climactic "epiphany" or reversal of fortune; and *bc* the denouement, or resolution of dramatic tension. But the dramatical conflict, sine qua non, itself most often involves a triangle of forces: not just *x* versus *y* (Jack v. Giant, Oedipus v. Fate, Hamlet v. Hamlet), but *x* versus *y* catalyzed and potentiated by some *z* (the magic beans, Tiresias the prophet, Gertrude/Ophelia), as crucial to plot-combustion as is the third log in a fireplace to successful ignition of the other two. In the novel, particularly, given the nature of its writers, its readers, and their society (another triangle of forces), this plot triangle is famously often of the amorous, even the adulterous, variety. The late-medieval Italian *novelle* from which our novel descends together with its name (in English, Spanish, and Portuguese, at least) are typically ribald tales of jealousy and cuckoldry; the canonical novels of the European eighteenth and nineteenth centuries famously focus their themes through the dramatic lens of adultery; the vulgar conflation of Romanticism and sentimental-erotic "romance" is close to the essence of the *roman* (another triad, if not quite a triangle), whether the triangle's third vertex is the "other woman" or man, the ogre/father, or the dragon mores of the tribe.

Commonplaces, all these, not worth singing were it not for my growing realization (the thin, insistent ding of that triangle) that the two of us on *US*, even the two of us plus *US*, won't suffice to

turn this overture into a proper opera. Heaven forfend that our
two-decade marital harmony, with its occasional inevitable disso-
nances but thus far no false notes, be soured by some adulterous
third party for this story's sake: Get *that* triangle out of here! By
going where I've had to go thus far in this overture, however, I've
come to learn — inveterate narrative course-plotter that I am in
this incarnation, triangulating our dramaturgical position from
bearings on these several sorts of triangles — that a (fictional)
domestic internal storm is brewing, *must* brew and burst upon us,
together with Tropical Storm Jerry upon *US*. In a tightly bonded
couple, the spark that dings the triangle (Mix that metaphor!
Ignite that brewing intramural storm!) can be almost anything.
     Prudence, say, versus its opposite. . . .

On with the stormy:
     On with the cruise, say I. In bocca al lupo. Into the Triangle.
     "You're kidding."
     Nope.
     "You've lost it, then."*
     Yes, well. I lost it, all right: overboard, two nights ago, in
Queenstown Creek. I was empty before; now I'm bereft.
     "It was really dumb to bring that pen on board," you remind
me. "It was dumber yet to take it up on deck. And it would be
dumb-dumber-dumbest to sail farther down the Bay in the face of
that forecast." Having said what until now you had considerately
refrained from saying, you retreat a bit. "Not dumb. Imprudent."
     Yes, well: prudence. We are, beyond question, characteristically
prudent people: a strictly reared and dutiful though temperamentally rebellious Nice Jewish Girl and a Good (Tame, Timid)
Goy. Prudent, the pair of us; no Beth and Jay we. On the other
hand, we owe our life together, long may it wave, to certain
uncharacteristic imprudences on both our parts. Middlescent
forty-year-old WASP divorcé novelist/professor with three high-

*American slang, possibly out of date by October '92, for *You're crazy.*

school/college-age children, small-town born and bred of stolid, low-strung German stock, marries twenty-seven-year-old urban high-energy former student of his, no idly decorative "trophy wife" but a workaholic high-school teacher — Was that prudent of us? he asks her. Imprudent of her, the year before that marriage, to have driven through a blinding Boston blizzard to hear her old teach give a public reading at a crosstown college, and then all but crash the reception after it to reintroduce herself to him; imprudent of him (rash, anyhow, and anticharacteristic) to have urged her to dinner after and then to nightcaps back at his motel, to continue a conversation that goes on yet.* Thanksgive for such imprudences!

"That has nothing to do with this," she declares. "You're not listening." Will she go on to say . . . ? She will, this broody morning: "You don't *listen*. You lecture."

In very truth, I was . . . not lecturing, but blandishing her with Blessed Imprudences to get her off the painful subject of my Dumheit in bringing my Parker aboard *US* and then up on deck for no good reason that first night out, almost as if — but I'll wait for her to say that.† Irritation turns me toward stubbornness; no need to tell me that "that has nothing to do with this"; what I'm trying to say without saying it is that I *know* my proposal to be imprudent, but that my situation aforesung, while by no means desperate, is unusual and, under my temperamental placidity, a touch anxious-making, perhaps inclining me toward some therapeutically distracting . . . imprudence.

"Right. Like drowning. But is that an inclination to be pursued or resisted?"

Maybe he's inclined to pursue it only because she's resisting it? Maybe if she had understood and seconded what he proposed, or had even just shrugged her shoulders, his native prudence would have reasserted itself and he'd have resisted his own proposal? It was only a suggestion, for pity's sake!

---

*On these blessed imprudencies, arias to come.
†She wouldn't, would she? Sure she would; either of us, furious enough, and we've known such furies, can be provoked to fire almost any available artillery, and later wholeheartedly to regret having fired it.

"Who's not shrugging her shoulders? Shrug shrug shrug." She shrugs. I am in love with those shoulders, even under a Peter Storm oiled-wool sweater. "You want to sail into the eye of a hurricane, let's sail. I just want it established that we're being damnfoolish."

Damnfoolish we're being, all right: not only in upping anchor, feeling our way out of the -rome of St. Jerome and into the uninviting Bay (cirrus clouds turning into cirrocumulus, something unfriendly in the fifteen-knot breeze) and then reaching briskly southeastward under main and reefed genoa toward a landless gray horizon, but even more so in setting out with this voltage undispelled between us. I ought to have come off it back there and tried to touch or kiss her. I didn't, and am now the more irked at the recognition that if I had, she would likely have rebuffed my overture as phoney-baloney. On the other hand, she might not have — What do I know, having lived with the woman for only twenty-plus years and in the world for some forty before that?

Unprogrammed aria: "Sturm und Drang"

I know that now we're in love and trouble, is about all — the love abiding, the trouble not — and that in this couple's chemistry neither of those precludes the other. Given the closeness of their connection, the differences between them, the amount of time they spend in each other's company, and the very little time they spend apart, these domestic storms used to beset them once or twice per season, interstitched with passionate reconciliation and overarched with indubitable love. In latter years, the love and commitment have, if anything, grown; time, experience, fatigue, and reciprocal understanding have happily decreased the frequency, duration, and damage (if not the occasional intensity) of such in-house blowups. Perhaps for that reason, they have still a way of taking us by surprise: The emotional fuel-air mix builds almost imperceptibly in the house until some spark — typically a thoughtless word of mine, some small thing done or neglected, inconsequential in itself — blows the roof. Our adrenalines surge; each charges the other with initial provocation; we watch and listen appalled as the angry words scarify; we exhaust ourselves into the night (What home-brewed tempest ever didn't rage past bedtime?). . . .

Whereupon these two tempers most markedly diverge. Spent, he'll sleep soundly, realizing with a pang only some moments after waking that we're still at odds as well as in love, much discharged but nothing resolved. Accepting that we're pretty much who and what we are, he's skeptical of "resolutions." Moreover, he's purged, catharsed, and well rested — that's who and what he is — ready to embrace her, apologize for his contribution to our Sturm und Drang, and get on with our good life. But who and what she is is not purged; she will have fretted the night through, the more irked for having tossed sleepless beside his obtuse sleep. The night will have magnified her grievance; her recollection of which of us said what to whom, and in which order, rivals a master bridge player's ability to reconstruct a whole evening's play. If at such a time he reaches out to touch — Nothing doing! Once upon a time it took days for the clouds to lift, more days yet for the air truly to clear and love freely to reassert iself. Once upon a time it took also solemn pledges of never again, vows of future spotlessness that, for *this* leopard (to his fault, no doubt), were ever more hope than expectation, more wish than hope. It can still, on infrequent occasion, take till breakfast.

Thanks be, then, that since this pair's early years together such full-blown storms have come to buffet them ever more rarely. Both of them are abler than once they were at containing and deflecting the inevitable frictions of conjugality. *Weather the storm you cannot avoid*, goes the old sailors' proverb, *and avoid the storm you cannot weather*. Every lasting marriage follows those advisements (I sing here of storms engendered by temperamental difference, not — Heaven forfend! — by infidelity, gross abuse, and suchlike misconduct); a happy one like that here sung avoids much more than merely the unweatherable — and, to be sure, involves much more than merely avoiding storms.

But the same experience that teaches longtime shipmates those useful skills has a debit side: Seeing certain familiar horizon-clouds, clouds no bigger than a man's hand, can lead such shipmates to expect a storm where none need be, and by preparation contribute to the forecast's self-fulfillment. One battens a hatch.

"What's that you're doing?"

Oh, you know: closing this hatch, sort of.

"You're *battening the hatches*!"

Well, yes, I suppose; this one, anyhow. That particular little cloud over yonder . . .

"Why are you battening the hatches? You're *looking* for a storm, right? You *want* a storm!"

Not that I know of. But who knows?

In any case, next thing one knows, one has one.

Storm:

Et cetera, and excuse the unprogrammed aria. But —

"But you sang it anyhow, right? To the whole world."

Nobody out here but us chickens.

"Who oughtn't to be. But it's all grist for the mill, we bet, dear old pen or no dear old pen."

What mill? The millstream's dry just now; otherwise we wouldn't be out here, being damnfoolish.

"Speaking of *that* . . ." And she does: how she's been being patient, patient with this kenosis business, this whole megillah of Suspended Passages and Emptied Vessels and Beths and Jays (They aren't, like, *friends*; they aren't, like, real *people*), this tsimmes about Dear Old Binder Dear Old Pen — because those things *do* matter. But what a mothering *opera* I've been making out of them!

What opera? So I lost my damn pen! So the damn cask is temporarily empty! It always fills up. I'll find another pen. . . .

"So why the opera? Why are we out here? I'll tell you why."

In full-storm mode now, she does, her anger three-sided like the Chesapeake Triangle that we have by this time crossed into without, in our building squall, remarking it. She is one-third angry at him: his *characteristic* occasional recklessness, his absentmindedness (inattention, she's convinced, not innocent forgetfulness), his hyposensitivity, his emotional shoal draft — the whole catalogue of his shortcomings, not excluding nit-picking pedantry (he has just riposted that she's not "one-third angry" at him; she's entirely angry at him, but her anger is not entirely at him). She's another third angry — *angry another third*, damn it, the second third — at herself, for having yet once more deferred to his judgment in this on-with-the-cruise nonsense, putting her own judgment (in this case better, as in many others) in abeyance, as she so *characteristically* does: a self-infuriating reflex of her femalehood and of her having known him first as her teacher, among other factors. And the third third —

But we won't get to the third third for quite some stormy while, and that's a pity, as it happens to be the third that could bung the running cask of anger and let it refill with love. I mean that fraction or aspect of her rage directed at the blind, ineluctable circumstance of our separateness despite our love: that we are two and can never be one however intense our intimacy; that life is short and we must die, he no doubt before her, as he's thirteen years older and of the male persuasion.

How we now go at it, you at the helm of our storm and of *US*, I at their sheets and cleats and winches, appalling ourselves at the force of our fury as we happily haven't in many a season — while all the while our metaphor for that fury, the literal spin-off from TSJ, has been figuratively following suit. Call it what you will (I'm calling it *coaxial esemplasy*, as aforesung), it's as if the two tempests each feed the other's tempestuosity. It is an ugly sky now, an ugly Bay, nobody in our neighborhood but us and *US*. The wind has shifted a remarkable hundred-plus degrees through our morning's quarrel, north-northwest to southwest, steadily increasing, and seems bent on carrying on with both. Too busy being angry to keep close tabs on the forecast or even properly to navigate, we've been roaring southeastward and at each other, sailing ever-closer reaches with less and less sail to keep the same course, until now as the wind draws even more southerly we're no longer reaching across it but beating, banging into it. Slabsided seas with a fifty-mile fetch are stopping *US* dead in our tracks under single-jiffy-reefed mainsail and a genoa roller-reefed now down to half its full foretriangle. In twenty-five knots of apparent wind, gusting now to thirty, I reckon we're making as much leeway as headway. I've fetched up from the crashing cabin our life vests and foul-weather gear and mean to go forward to double-reef the main and maybe set the small forestaysail so that we can furl the big genoa entirely and better balance the rig. A sudden thirty-five knot gust, however — perhaps the most wind we've ever been under way in — lays us almost over on our beam-ends and mercifully makes clear our folly (I'm calling it ours) in holding this course to nowhere. I wanted the Triangle? I've had the Triangle. Let's get the hell out of here. One-eighty to starboard.

More often than not, I am for better or worse the one who gives these "orders." This one — to come about through the eye of the wind and retreat Potomacward — you don't question, but the maneuver proves undoable. With our shortened sail, we can't manage enough headway to punch through those wall-like seas onto the other tack; the boat stalls, hobbyhorses madly in the steep short chop, and falls back off to port. Yet reversing course the other way around would cause a violent, possibly gear-damaging gybe. Start the engine, then, to help us around? As I'm about to climb down into the cabin to set the battery switch for that purpose, another shrieking gust knocks *US* scarily far over. I happen to be clinging to the mainsheet cleat; I cast off the sheet's hitches to ease the sail and get us back on our feet, then suggest, more than order, a quarter-turn to port. Let's turn ninety degrees to port, I suggest: off the wind, but not enough to gybe. Let's run homeward, anyward, but off the wind.

We do, and although straightway a wild rain pelts after us, as if the Triangle is spitting us out or the storm is spitting its fury, the boat is decidedly more manageable on this heading. Now I want the mainsail down entirely; we can run with better control under jib alone. The prospect of turning partway back into that wind and rain to lower and furl sail is intimidating, but if we don't and the storm intensifies, the job will become even more hazardous. We have to get the main down, I declare. Let's start the engine, and I'll harness up and go do it.

No reply needed. In secret truth (as I go below to set the battery switch to ALL and fetch the safety harness that we've carried aboard for nearly twenty years, on three different boats, and have never once used before now) I am as gratified as frightened by the task ahead. For some merciful minutes already, since we tried and failed to come about, the storm and our labors have shut us up. Now the wind and rain and the physical distance between us will extend this welcome pause, while my putting myself at necessary risk affords me an illegitimate but not disagreeable high ground. As you hold the boat at the steadiest close angle to wind and seas that you can manage, I must make my way to the mast, clip my harness onto something, stand on the pitching cabin top, wrestle down the flogging sail, and furl and lash it to its boom. Passing through the cockpit en route forward, I believe I see tears mix with rain on your cheeks, and at once his heart goes out to her, to us. Although the worst of our literal weather may lie ahead, for him our storm is over. For her, I know, it's not that easy to come off it — these dust-ups hurt her more than him — but I have reason to hope that the noisy part has peaked and passed.

And so I do what must be done up there, and it is a properly macho, scary, and not undangerous ten minutes, everything heaving and slamming and flailing until finally secured, while the wind batters and the waves pound and the rain strafes. But in both of these areas we are seasoned hands; the differences we're coping with are only in degree (and that only in the literal storm). My satisfied relief at having done the job — and at our being able now to bear off and run before the wind under a reefed headsail alone, furlable if necessary from the cockpit without altering course — completes the purgation of my spirit by alarm, anger, fright, and sympathy, and leaves it free to love.

Seasoned hands, we let things between us be — not the moment yet for apologies, embraces — while we tear northward, cooling off, speaking only and tersely of ship's matters. How's the helm now? "No problem." I'm raising the centerboard halfway, but let's keep the depth alarm at eight. "I'd better take a Bonine, just in case. And unfortunately I need to pee." I'll fetch the pill (banging into rough weather never makes her seasick, but the rolling motion of seas astern can do it, and a trip through the cabin to the medicine locker guarantees mal de mer. As for the other, she has been known to use a bucket in the cockpit rather than make her way to the head in such conditions. Given this rain and our self-draining cockpit, no bucket needed). "Thanks. So where are we?"

Where indeed? Out of the Triangle, I guess, or all but, and into the redemptive third third of your treble emotion aforeanalyzed.

While you, I imagine, are reconstructing what led us into our blowup and shaking your head that two people who so prize each other can nonetheless be so provoked, I try to reconstruct our course and estimate our position. It is no easy task in the absence of landmarks. The arithmetic is simple enough, even for us innumerates: So many hours of southeasting at such-and-such average speed while tide and leeway set us severally thus-and-so puts us exactly here on the chart. We even have a distance log on our knotmeter to tell us that we've traveled precisely x miles through the water since we turned the instruments on in the -rome of St. Jerome. But all of those numbers are approximate indeed, especially leeway and current set, but including even distance through water (a function of the meter's calibration, and not to be confused with actual mileage over the bottom), and the error enlarges with time and distance. Allowing generously for leeway, we could be anywhere in this roomy ellipse down here on the chart, off the west side of Smith Island — it's a wonder we can't *see* the island now, despite its low profile and the poor visibility — but neither is it at all unthinkable that we're somewhere *outside* that ellipse, and so maybe let's aim a touch west of north, not to plow into the shoals off Smith. . . .

You consider our sail trim, the wind angle. "We'll need the jib on the other side."

We will, but as it has no boom, gybing it over is no problem. Thank Whatever (our prudence will do) that we doused our mainsail, for the hard wind seems perversely to be shifting back west. We're under secure control now, with an easier motion, and fairly flying along. Our leeway, however, if not our headway, must be setting us into the ever-shallower water bounding Smith Island. We strain to see landmarks to starboard, where the island must be: navigation buoys, anything identifiable. But the rain is almost white; our eyeglasses and binoculars are running with it; our depth sounder is holding in the low teens (not bad by Chesapeake standards, but not easy-making either), our knotmeter in the neighborhood of six under reefed genoa alone, our windspeed indicator at twenty-plus apparent, to which on this point of sail must be added our boat speed — and we really don't know where we are or what we have in the way of sea room. This is perhaps not yet the nautical most danger we've ever been in; cautious sailors and seasoned hands, we've not been in much, but there've been close calls: accidental gybes that could have killed but didn't, a heart-in-mouth passage through unfamiliar Caribbean reefs in weather that obscured our steering marks. It is, however, by far our most sustained *potential* seagoing danger: danger not of drowning or even particularly of losing our boat (if we run aground, it will be on mud or sand in waist-deep water; there are no rocks hereabout to hole the hull, and boats can be refloated even if hurricane-driven high and dry), but of injuring ourselves, sorely damaging *US*, perhaps having to radio for rescue or salvage.

And the storm, which has stormed for too many pages already, shows no signs of sharing our fatigue. How to short-cut it, for the reader's sake and ours?

You're pointing eastward. "Is that a line of utility poles sticking up out of the water over there?"

Brava. Just what I needed: the overhead power cable shown on our chart as running from Smith Island four or five miles south along shoals down to Goose Island. What's more, we catch a glimpse of it doglegging eastward just off our starboard quarter, and here's that dogleg on the chart. We know more nearly now where we are: We're skirting this wiggly twelve-foot depth contour here just below the Maryland/Virginia line (farther south than I'd guessed), about a mile off the southwest shore of Smith. And look here: About three miles up the road — half an hour or less — we should see this pair of day beacons marking this skinny entrance channel into the island. We can duck in there and anchor up here in this nine-foot spot and ride the storm out. No great shelter from the wind, but we'll be out of the wave action, and it ought to be safe enough, and I love you completely and wish we never, ever, quarreled the way we just did.

"Me too, [*pet name, not the general reader's business*]. Me too."

Dearest particular reader: What's a mere near-gale, now that *our* weather is so improved? *There's* a shortcut for us! Let me spell you at the wheel while you keep an eye out for this U.S. Navy marker here on the chart or these orange-and-white state line markers up here or this day beacon farther along here that'll tell us we're coming up on our entrance marks. Blow your damnedest, Tee Ess Jay! *Our* weather's clear!

Mini-duet: "It's not that easy"
    "Clearing the weather's not that easy, [*pet name*]."
    Dear [*pet name*]: I know.
    Sigh.

Back to the difficulty:
    As if responding to my dare, the storm blows away our harmonious sigh and cranks up its volume to a perfect fury. Have we ever *seen* so wild a seascape, much less ever sailed through one? The reedy shoreline to starboard that we just now welcomely caught sight of — Hog Neck, if we're where we think we are — disappears in the squall. We won't see those markers I mentioned unless we run into them. You're feeling the windchill, but retreating to the closed-up cabin is out of the question; we absolutely need both pairs of eyes on lookout, and if we pile up, better to be on deck. Can our dinghy possibly still be back there? You sneak a look and advise me not to: The dinghy's there, all right, surfing crazily on the following seas; if it trips and swamps, we'll have to cut it loose — but the world astern, you report, is Apocalypse Now.
    "Don't look back."
    Eurydice advising Orpheus? He perpends the advice and reflects that if Beth and Jay really happen to be out in the Atlantic, their situation is both worse than ours and better: more wind and higher seas, but endless offshore sea room for heaving to or running before the gale, and the waves out there assume their longer, more "natural" deep-water frequency instead of this wicked short chop. Nevertheless, all in all I'd rather be where we are, wherever that is — and there, I suppose, is the difference between my counterself and me.

Another trial shortcut: We never do see the Navy marker, the state-line markers, or the single day beacon just below the pair we're after. We do, however, see in time what we take to be — what *must* be, unless we're off the chart altogether — that pair: the triangular red and square green dayboards on steel pilings marking a narrow, shoal-girt channel leading into the labyrinthine interior of what might better be called the Smith Island Marsh Complex. But the wind by then has pulled south-southwest again, straight across that channel, and the tide is flooding in with it. I furl the last of the genoa, and we approach the marks at half throttle, angling our bow well into the wind and tide and seas. No good; we sweep to leeward. Even at three-quarter speed (your suggestion) we seem unable to keep the entrance marks aligned with the next pair in, half a mile shoreward. The boundary-shoals give us no margin. Rolling and pitching, we pass between the entrance beacons at almost a forty-five-degree angle to our course; another minute or so will commit us to continuing, come what might — and just here the blastiest blast yet, a *rogue* blast from southeast instead of southwest, stops us dead. You gun the engine, but our stern lifts under the next wave, and our propeller chews air. We begin making sternway toward the shoal. Although I'm standing just beside you, holding onto a backstay, you cry out my name. . . .

Hard over. Let's get out of here.

Somebody has to call these shots. Hard over, but not all at once; keep some way on. Get our bow across the wind, and then the weather will bring us around. Mind we don't snag the dinghy on that leeward beacon on the way out. Let's get ourselves some elbow room, and we'll reconsider.

You do all that, dear seasoned hand, while I keep one eye on our dinghy, another on those unherculean pillars that we're threading our way out between, and some third on our options. You are of the opinion (you let me know as soon as you can) that we were being overcautious back there; that at *full* throttle and less of an angle, always favoring the upwind shoal, you could have barreled us through. I concur with your reasoning and don't question your competence, but I was shaken by that rogue blast, the shortage of maneuvering room, the unfamiliarity of that in-

hospitable-looking maze inside. On the other hand, the next feasible sailboat anchorage is . . . who knows where in this shallow
quarter of the Chesapeake, no place for sailors, not far from my
birth-marshes, so to speak: the trackless wetlands of lower Dorchester County.

Moreover, in your voice I hear a familiar harmonic: that (once
again) he wasn't trusting her to size up the situation back there
and take appropriate action on her own. True, her crying his name
was a call of alarm; it was also a protest that the larger angle and
lower throttle that he was urging upon her weren't working.

This is a wire that I hope not to trip. There is justice in her (so
far unvoiced) complaint; otherwise she wouldn't entertain it. But
while I consider myself a far from domineering husband, I have
and accept the habit of final responsibility in certain matters, as
does she in others. What's more — but hey, our weather was clearing, and here I am battening another hatch.

Take us back in, I suggest. I promise to shut up unless I see
trouble.

Brava encore for your not shirking at this point and returning
the ball of responsibility to my court: You open the throttle gamely
and head up to regain the leeway we've made while pondering.
Might it not be that in the aftermath of our recent squall, what
I've privately decided is that I would rather put the ball in *your*
court, at risk of mishap, than hazard reopening our argument?
Not impossibly, but in truth our alternatives are so comparably
unappealing, it's well that one of us has a decided preference.

And not impossibly you could have pulled the thing off. At
hell's very gate, however, in very bocca al lupo, TSJ takes matters
out of our (seasoned) hands. That rogue blast reprises as a steady
state; a wall of wind and white rain blanks out the inshore beacons
and almost the outer ones as well, just a boatslength off. Headway
is impossible; we're blown right abeam and half over under bare
poles, spun right around. Good-bye, last-chance harbor of refuge;
addio, Smith Island (named for Captain John, who in 1608 also
had navigational difficulties hereabouts); auf Wiedersehen, narrative shortcut out of this stormy passage. Will-we nill-we, our only
course now is dead before the wind, straight up the Chesapeake.

How long can this last? We're wet, cold, tired, frightened, discouraged — and, unlike a summer thundersquall, this gale could blow all night and tomorrow. Once again we're tearing off northward; sore-muscled, I've cranked out just a tiny triangle of jib to keep the overtaking seas from broaching us side-to or fetching our dinghy up into our laps. The steering is tricky, but ought to be manageable until fatigue slows our responses. When pee-time comes, we can wet our pants if necessary; sooner or later, however, we're going to need nourishment. And although we're reasonably safe just running up the Bay's long axis (provided we hit nothing), we can't imagine doing this through the night.

So let's come up with something, to keep our floating-opera-in-the-works from turning into *The Flying Dutchman*. Between Smith and the next two islands up — uninhabited South Marsh and Bloodsworth, used for much of this century as naval aerial bombing targets — is Kedges Straits (called "Limbo" by Captain John), leading over to Tangier Sound. I propose we try to motorsail a right-hand turn into that limbo. If we manage it, we'll be in the low lee of Smith Island, out of the worst of wind and waves. We'll hope to avoid this two-foot spot here on the chart and maybe scrooch in here, near Solomons Lump Light. We'll set out both anchors in five or six feet somewhere along here and ride out the gale down in the cabin. It isn't what we'd call shelter, but —

"Better Limbo than Hell."

The trick will be to spot this quick-flashing beacon here on a rock —

"A *rock*?"

The chart says *Rk*, just off Fog Point —

"*Fog* Point?"

Our turning point.

"There it is. Two o'clock."

Right you are. So we'll nudge around it, looking out for these red nuns here and here, and we'll make a wide turn over to Solomons Lump Light — forty-seven feet high, a six-second flasher with a bell.

"I don't see it. I see it." And there is, welcomely, less wave action once we turn Fog Point, the island's northwest corner, although this wind would make waves on a swimming pool. Even with all sail furled, it heels us ten degrees over. The water depth, I notice, is several feet more than the charted figures: the surge from TSJ. That should let us scrooch in closer to shore.

"Some shore." All we can see over there through the rain in our faces is a sea of gray-green marsh grass, its edges indefinite. But let's scrooch in, scrooch in, dead to windward, one eye on the depth sounder. I'll ready the anchor and come back to confer. It looks feasible.

"Unless the wind shifts. Was that thunder?"

Thunder it was, unless the Navy does bombing practice even in storms. And there's lightning! And now that we've given Zeus the idea, sure enough the wind wildly veers *west*, wham bang, at the edge of a thundersquall spawned by the gale spawned by Tropical Storm Jerry. We must expect gusts now from any quarter: downbursts, the works.

"So what do we do now?"

Mini-soliloquy: "What do we do now?"

What do we do now.

I almost answer *Don't ask me*, for yours truly is out of expedients. But while there are numerous situations in which I would be the one asking you — logistical screwups, e.g., and interpersonal matters, wherein your intuitions and resourcefulness exceed mine — here's one (there are others) where it's finally up to me to make the call. Sailors have been known — even Columbus's journals report such instances — to deliquesce in these circumstances like infantrymen under sustained artillery barrage. Amateur skippers unused to the role, and occasional pros unfit for it, can be reduced by compounded stress to dithering helplessness or induced to mad courses like abandoning a still sound ship and swimming for shore. No better way to turn alarm into hysteria than for the person "in charge" to panic, and no better road to panic than to throw up one's hands. Thus the calm last words of so many professional airline pilots, as overheard from control towers or found on their flight recorders after the crash:

"We're going down, Captain." "I know it." (Air Florida Flight

90, shortly after takeoff from Washington National Airport on 13 January 1982, and just before striking the Fourteenth Street Bridge over the Potomac)

"Uh-oh." (Space shuttle *Challenger*, 28 January 1986)

Thus too the skipperly habit —- I have it — of running silent *What if?* scenarios even when things are going well. What if the diesel were to conk out just as we're passing through this drawbridge against the tide with another boat right on our tail? What if, on this spanking fair-weather beat under full sail, one of the windward shrouds let go? What if, as we're running delicately balanced wing and wing with spinnaker flying, our nine-year-old granddaughter, up there on the bow pulpit aiming her camera, should lose her balance and plop overboard?

And what if, so close to real though limited shelter in the lee of Smith Island, a crazy rogue thundersquall should come barreling right out of the west into the limbo of Kedges Straits? What do we do now?

Damned if I know. But

Back to shot-calling:

There's no anchoring here now, for sure; we would drag right into the marsh or onto Solomons Lump. Work us back into Limbo, s.v.p., and then hang a left up into Tangier Sound. We'll see what's what in the lee of Bloodsworth.

These orders — desperate suggestions, shot-callings — have to be shouted; the weather's that loud, our diesel too when you open it up now to get us back into Kedges Straits and down the new wind. I'm obliged to crawl forward to resecure the anchor and its coil of line, lest they pitch overside and foul the propeller. Lightning and thunder bang all around us. In our years of sailing, we've weathered dozens of thunderstorms in more or less protected anchorages around the Bay — some fairly hairy, most just pleasurably exciting — but this is the first we've been "caught out" in. The noise and motion are terrific. We can see nothing except gray-white seas, gray-white rain, and the pitching boat; we could scarcely steer otherwise than downwind even if we wanted to, and downwind is by no means a constant heading. Some of my *What ifs* at this point draw a private near-blank: *What if the furled mainsail blows out of its storm lashings under these conditions?* It would simply have to blow: no more leaving the cockpit. *What if we can't hang that left up behind Bloodsworth Island?* Then we get blown straight across Tangier Sound into one of the rivers over there, is all, unless the wind abates or shifts before we get that far. There's got to be shelter over there somewhere. *What if we're blown aground?* Then we're aground, mates, as aforewhatiffed: The boat might get hurt, but we're not likely to. We would hang on and radio for help when the storm's done with us. *What if we sink?* Come on: Nothing less than a full hurricane or a tornado could capsize *US* with sails down in the Chesapeake, and short of a capsize nothing can sink us but a hole in the hull: a major collision. So we keep a double lookout.

What if —

"Red bell-buoy to starboard! One o'clock!" Exclamations for audibility, not excitement, and I reply likewise: Okay! To port now! Forty-five degrees if possible, and then another forty-five behind Bloodsworth!

The first you accomplish; we can verify as much by compass, even though landmarks are scarce and the wind- and wave-angle shifts a bit with us as we exit the straits into the broader waters of Tangier Sound. A few minutes on this new heading ought to fetch us into easier seas.

"That's what we thought before!"

Don't I know. And as before, it may not be that easy. But our luck can't be *all* bad, can it?

Unsung duet: "Sure it can."

The storm, the storm:

Did we imagine all hell loose two arias back, or three, or four? Well, here's more: It blows our "Sure it can" back down our throats (some songs go without singing). Indescribable, TSJ's newest escalation, but Parkered or Parkerless I must try to register the nightmare slams of wind from here, from there, as the squall-center overruns us.

Nature, wow: The thunderbolts rain down like lightning; the seas, confused as storm-mixed metaphors by conflicting winds, no longer roll, but slop in crazy peaks and pits. We flinch at the terrifying racket; we can *feel* electricity in the air. Not much to be done except hang on — and you remind me, just in time, to hang onto something less conductive than the steel-wire backstay. In electrical storms, sailboat masts simultaneously attract lightning and provide a theoretical "cone of protection" from its bolts; the wire shrouds and stays, however, like the aluminum mast itself, are the current's natural pathways. As if to demonstrate, a stunning bolt now strikes very close by indeed. You cry out involuntarily and let go the wheel (with your hands — steadying it, however, with deck-shod feet). It's stainless steel, unconnected to the rig but metal-to-metal through bronze rack-and-pinion gears to the rudder post down there in the water, and you'll swear you felt it tingle in your palms. We wonder: Aren't all those lightning bolts in Tangier Sound like so many hair dryers dropped into the bathtub? We can *smell* that lightning! Can it actually have struck *US*? You're convinced it did, and another *What if* occurs to me: Knowledgeable opinion on what constitutes proper lightning protection for sailboats ranges from the battleship-impractical to the shrug-shouldered fatalistic, and one supposes that the grounding measures in production boats are a cost-conscious, cross-fingered compromise. Even in the sailboat-thronged, summer-storm-rich Chesapeake, after all, very few vessels are ever actually struck — yet one reads accounts in the literature not only of electronics being fried but of through-hull fixtures being melted or blown right out of the boat. *There's* a way to sink that I hadn't allowed for. What if —

But this is no time to open the cabin and rummage under berths and lockers to verify that all half-dozen or so of our through-hull fittings are intact and their wooden emergency plugs standing by: wash-basin and sink and shower drains, head and engine intakes and discharges, knot meter and depth-sounder sensors. When you retake the wheel, there comes a short, spooky pause in the wind, as if it's drawing its next great breath. For some moments, as the seas slurp up into frothing pyramids and the thunder brackets us, the rain dumps straight down like a waterfall.

"Instruments are out," you let me know. "Compass, too, I think."

I had just noticed, all except the compass: windspeed zero, although the anemometer cups are still spinning up there as the masthead pitches about; knot meter zero point zero despite our headway; depth sounder flickering crazy readings in crazy non-digits, its liquid-crystal display gone haywire. Only the engine gauges, on a separate panel and circuit, seem still to be functioning normally, as is the diesel itself: 1800 rpm, on who knows what course. I lean over you to confirm that the steering compass is swinging dizzily.

We took a hit, I acknowledge. I'll bring up the hand-bearing compass. Damn.

"What'll we do without the depth sounder?" You sound near-desperate.

And without the radio, I don't bother to add, fairly desperate myself, and without who knows what else. But look: We've managed without depth sounder before, in the old days, in our first cruising boat. . . .

"Would you steer? I'm going to be sick."

Hold out for a second, if you can, while I pop down and get the hand-bearing compass. But as I move to lift out the companionway drop-boards, the wind, which had been drawing its breath —

"*!*"

A cry of pure terror, as a virtual tsunami of sudden wind overwhelms us — from astern, luckily, or we would surely be laid flat. A screaming wall of air (anemometer: zero) from what I have to suppose is south; I just manage to clamber aft to help you with the helm before that avalanche of air wipes out those water-pyramids and corrugates Tangier Sound into ranks of following seas, larger by the moment. Off flies our vinyl-cased chart — okay, you've got it; quick reflexes, not that we can navigate. . . .

Indeed, we can do nothing now except hunch down, hold on,

and steer before the nightmare as best we can. The engine is doing little for us; I throttle down to half speed for standby steerageway. We may be thankful that the empty islands in this neighborhood aren't likely to thrust docks, moored vessels, or breakwaters into our path. If a buoy or a day beacon lunges at us from the murk ahead, we can perhaps avoid it. If a marshy shoreline suddenly materializes across our bow, we simply plow into it and hope for the best.

This helplessness is perversely calming. We may get very inconveniently stuck, but we'll not likely get hurt. Property damage and bother, then somehow home and to hell with Jay Wordsworth Scribner, *American Century*, the log of Columbus, the Chesapeake Triangle, this abortive floating opera of a cruise. Meanwhile, ride it out and ready ourselves for the pileup. You've huddled down onto a cockpit cushion for small shelter, your nausea under control but hypothermia not far ahead. The wind and rain and waves are at my back, scary but not wretchedly uncomfortable now. With my foul-weather hood up, I can see only ahead, and that's just as well. I sit on the chart: no further use in trying to locate us on it. At who can say what speed, in what direction, and through how much water, we are going where we have to go. The learning, we presume, will follow.

Here it comes! I warn you when, sure enough, a drowned shoreline emerges to confront us: a line of marsh grass over which the storm waves break as into a flooded paddy. No beach or bank or other ground in sight, but no doubt there's a bottom not far under. You sit up to help me watch it happen.

"Off to starboard: Is that an opening?"

I'll try for it: the space break you've spotted in that surging field of reed-tops. At risk of running even harder aground, I throttle up enough to slew us somewhat astarboard.

We're going to hit the point, we predict — the submerged point that doubtless corners that "channel" through the marsh. We wait for the thud: But although we think we feel our keel brush bottom in a wave-trough, we find ourselves shoved will-we nill-we right through the spartina-tops into what we're calling our channel — a shallow gut, no doubt winding up into the Bloodsworth wetlands or even the lower Dorchester "mainland" if we've blown that far: canoe country, normally, with perhaps one foot mean low water, made unnaturally "navigable" by the storm surge. Already the wave action is damped, though the wind's still fierce.

We'll simply ride it up as far as we can, we decide, until we run aground or can anchor in the lee of something, whichever happens first. Let's shorten up the dinghy line.

A wild, waste place, flooded marsh on all sides now as we negotiate the winding waterway through waterland. The rain lightens. We see green-brown marsh to the limits of visibility all about us: sometimes lakelike stretches dotted with hummocks and islets; sometimes, inversely, dense marsh-meadow dotted with ponds. What we take to be our channel forks and reforks. At first we follow whichever branch is downwindmost, but presently we find we have enough maneuverability (Is the wind dropping somewhat? Anemometer zero) to motor into whichever fork looks likelier — wider, maybe deeper (depth sounder indecipherable), maybe leading into taller reeds. Look: We can actually make this S-turn without being blown into the high grass! And what relief, to be out of those waves! Can it be we've *survived*?

"Don't tempt the gods. But there's a lot less wind in here, and the rain's letting up for sure." You can actually stand and con the scene with binoculars. "Not a tree in sight. But hey, there's a bush!"

A by-god bush, half swamped, around the next drowned bend. So exhausted are we, we're tempted to anchor behind it as if it were a wall of trees. A bush! Terra almost firma! But there's a mean-looking snag just visible across the narrow channel from it (How many more out of sight beneath us?) and no room to swing. That's evidence of trees ahead, though, no? Like Columbus's crew, or was it Noah's, jubilating at sight of a straw on the water. . . . Onward and inward, we decide, although we're bone-weary and apprehensive about getting too far into a maze that we may have trouble getting out of when the surge recedes. Feel how that wind's going down, we urge each other: fifteen/twenty tops, even broadside to it. The rain, too: scarcely miserable now. We can ride on the anchor in these conditions, if we can find swinging room.

"Let's poke around one more bend. How can we not be bumping bottom?" You have the chart out now, inspecting the possibilities of South Marsh and Bloodsworth islands: "One foot. Two feet. *Half* a foot. There's a 'Great Cove' on the east side of Bloodsworth with a three-foot hole in it after you cross a two-foot bar, but I see nothing that winds around like this till you get up to Tedious Creek in lower Dorchester — and it has day beacons and stuff. We're nowhere."

We round the next bend. No trees, no banks, but voilà: a whole stand of scrubby bushes backdropping a half-submerged gooseblind to windward, in a bight of sorts enclosed by flooded marsh, with enough swinging room (so it appears on the surface, at least, in this abnormally high water) for a sixty-foot radius, if not a ninety. Let's get ourselves parked and explore no more.

You're all for it. You retake the helm, I reprepare the plow anchor, we swing out and then up into the fast-falling wind, aim straight through the light rain toward the gooseblind clump, and at a safe distance drop that anchor and back down to set it, expecting at any moment to strike mudbanks or sunken snags astern. Out of habit I call back from the bow: What's the water depth?

"Shnaffel point shmumf," you remind me.

So we'll use our old low-tech depth sounders, as we did on smaller boats in years past. I lean far over the side with a telescoping boathook taped at one-foot intervals, which we sometimes use for taking soundings from the dinghy: Can't touch bottom. I lower our centerboard experimentally to its full seven-foot draft and maybe feel it nudge mud as we swing, but only maybe, before I tuck it back up.

We are parked. We are, for the present at least, safe. We are one hundred percent spent, but we seem actually to have weathered this mothering storm. Our faces and eyeglasses adrip with rain, we embrace. Wherever we are, for the present we are okay.

The wind has dropped to no more than ten knots, the rain to a light bluster, and both bid to go on dwindling. The air has cooled, but remains mild for the season. You withdraw to the cabin, to begin restoring order down there; after a few minutes of monitoring our easy swing on the anchor, I follow. My watch says late afternoon; we've been hard at it since early A.M. No matter what the weather does now, we agree, we're staying put until tomorrow morning — when, conditions permitting, we'll make our way back to open water and homeward. For now, warm dry clothes, nourishment, rest. Presently I'll check for further lightning damage and find that the cabin lights and running lights are operative, the bilge pump and freshwater pump likewise, and our little portable FM radio and cassette player but not the main VHF radio. We're on our own. The small secondary compass mounted in the nav station reasonably agrees with our hand-bearing compass; it would appear that only the main steering compass was magnetized out of kilter by the bolt that cooked our electronics. Slouched now on settees port and starboard, we shake our heads at what we have come through; we sip a Maryland beaujolais nouveau, not bad, and nibble mushroom brie on rye crackers and apologize freely to each other for the afternoon's fuss. Presently we'll catch a storm report on the portable (no hurry about that; whether we hear that TSJ has passed or that the present lull is the proverbial one before the *real* storm strikes, we're staying put, faute de mieux). Presently we'll wash up and build dinner; I'll log our day in ballpoint on the log's last page as the most weather we've ever weathered, and we'll read and maybe even make love on His settee (Hers is confined by the dinette table) and, weather permitting, most certainly sleep. For the moment it is unspeakably balmy simply to sit still, spent, calmed inside and out.

Reprise: "Calmed, becalmed"

All the aforeforeseen has come to pass: We are logged, fed, laid, read, early-nightcapped — Beck's Dark for him, a small brandy-and-Kahlua for her — calmed, becalmed. The merest rustle of rain strokes our cabin top; the breeze sighs a recollection of its former force. My quarterberthed shipmate sleeps her deep first sleep; her shipmate, propped in the mini-triangle of his forward V under an adjustable cabin light, with calm concentration scribbles these words in his "Friday essay" binder — not, alas, with his old pen. He wonders, calmly, where we are; what he has gotten us into; what lies ahead.

And I — at Langford Creek and in Baltimore a full year and a half before the events here overtured — I share his wonder as I pen *these* words in my battered old "fiction" binder with my faithful Pumblechook Parker, dearer than ever to me now that I've rehearsed its loss. It is a sweet May '91 morning in this beflowered city, after a violent quick storm last evening that downed trees and outed power round about and may or may not have damaged our Eastern Shore retreat (we'll find out tomorrow, when we drive over there for our first sailing weekend of the season). I've two weeks more of being sixty before another birthday plunges me unequivocally into my seventh decade; I'll spend the working mornings of that fortnight winding up this unorthodox extended prologue and reviewing it, as the crew of *US* must review their position tomorrow morning, to try to determine where they might be and how to proceed. To what will this overture prove an overture, other than to the reader and the muse? Quo vadimus?

Between our first "Becalmed" duet, sung last October, and this Maytime reprise, much has happened on the earth and not a little in our house: Iraq has all but destroyed Kuwait; the U.S.-led coalition has all but destroyed Iraq; a typhoon in the Bay of Bengal, dwarfing our "Tropical Storm Jerry," has quite destroyed much of Bangladesh and killed maybe 200,000 people. Infinitely luckier, my comrade and I have lecture-toured through Italy, book-toured through the United States, and vacationed in the Caribbean and Hawaii, as well as teaching our respective classes, tending our property, visiting our far-sprung offspring, and (one of us, who will presently seek the other's readerly reaction) making this overture. That novel that most lately and satisfyingly emptied me, *The Last Voyage* etc., has been duly published and promoted, praised and blamed, and has joined its predecessors in my bibliography. Its American first-edition hardcover life already all but run, it awaits the commencement of what I hope and expect will be its longer half-life in reprint editions and foreign translations, while into its post-partum kenosis, like a man singing into an emptied room and listening for the echoes of his voice, I've pitched these "arias." Teasing the future. Provoking time.

Preludial coda: "I know these waters . . . and yet . . ."

I know these waters wherein we lie — calmed, becalmed, eighteen months from now — and yet they seem to me defamiliarized, estranged, somehow dismaying. I suspect our venue to be uninhabited Bloodsworth Island, just below my natal bog: an island that I have never visited, but to which I have dispatched sundry of my fictional creatures over the decades, no doubt because its portentous name (accompanied on the nautical charts with warnings: DANGER AREA; PROHIBITED AREA) appealed to my apprentice imagination: a place in which to lose and find and test oneself, assay one's blood. However, as the crew of *US* has speculated, they may well be in the vast Dorchester wetlands themselves, or the vestibule to some Beyond, or nowhere. They'll learn, by going where I'll have them go — and I with them, coaxially esemplastic.

What if? We'll see.

Although we're becalmed, I feel (with a familiar shiver) our story under way. Its overture is finished: gone, with Time's tide. Curtain's all but ready for some Act One.

INTERLUDE
"We take our waking slow"

W E TAKE our waking slow; let the morning warm a bit; give Time time after our profound and well-earned sleep. In early light I murmur aft from my berth through the chilled, still cabin: Are you awake?

"Not yet. Crazy dreams."

Likewise, and I'm soon back in them. But "dream sequences" in fiction make me fidget: dreams within dreams, hyped phantasmagoria. So never mind.

Presently we're up, more or less.

"Look at it out there. We must be near Fog Point, all right."

My mate stands sweatsuited on the companionway ladder, her feet snugged in quilted slippers, her hair piled up the way I most admire it. She's peering out over the hatch dropboards at what was, once upon a time, the world. Who could resist nuzzling her nape and shoulders, regarding with her the socked-in scene? The storm surge has receded. Our stern has drifted around toward the gooseblind, relatively high and dry now on its bushy hummock, and although we are not aground, the roomy-enough "bight" that we anchored in has ebbed to half its last-evening's size, a mere meander in a marshy gut. Beyond the encircling wall of scrub and high spartina, all is fog.

"Getting out of here will be interesting."

Indeed. But we are unhurt, undamaged except for our zapped

instruments, and well rested; the unusual fog, we suppose, together with the dead calm, made for as quiet a night as we've known afloat. There appears to be a sun up there somewhere, which ought to burn off this fuzz by midmorning if we're in our usual and regular solar system. We'll just take our waking slow, check the forecast on our little portable, and then set about threading our way back to open water while the tide's rising.

Through breakfast you're subdued. "Weird dreams. I don't want to talk about them."

I'm used to that: She dreams apocalyptically, often whimpers in her sleep (it hurts my heart to hear, but my standing orders are not to wake her), and seldom cares to rehearse her anxious mind's night's work. My own latest would alarm the bejesus out of her; I report that I've forgotten it (she hadn't asked; dreams bother her, despite our agreeing that they're all but meaningless), as indeed in large measure I have, and content myself with appending to our log's last page the principal cue-phrase from that dream: *an easy death by sea* — Tiresias the prophet's promise to Odysseus in the underworld.

That's that for Nineteen Ninety through now, I declare. Time to start a new book. First day of the rest of et cetera.

"Let's get to it, then."

Why not. The fog has thinned enough for us to see a few hundred feet ahead (marsh, marsh all around, the reeds much taller, the watercourse much lower and skinnier than when we came in), there's no wind to complicate our maneuvering, the forecast reports that Tropical Storm Jerry has fizzled out at sea, and the tide should rise for several hours yet. You'll drive; I'll unanchor us while you shorten up the dinghy line in case we need to reverse —

"In case?" You survey our shrunken anchorage.

Yes, well. We'll feel our way out dead slow and call the turns as they come. If the water gets really thin or we bump in midchannel, I'll take soundings from the dinghy.

"Let's not forget to notice that this place is beautiful, in its way."

Noticed. Spooky, but beautiful indeed: the haunt of Tory picaroons in our Revolution and of other dissenters and outlaws in other times, down to the moonshiners of my youth and wildfowl poachers to the present day.

"No birds."

Nor bugs. Spooky. TSJ must have blown them all to Pennsylvania.

"It's as if we're the only living creatures in the scene."

To life, then, and here we go, out of this beautiful though spooky wetland labyrinth, we hope; at least not farther into it. To begin with, we agree, we'll head *this* way from the blind, not the other way. After that, no doubt, there'll be twists and turns and doublings back; if the gut forks and both options look feasible, we'll prefer the southmost — Southmore? — using our hand-bearing compass for general direction. Okay?

"Anchor aweigh."

And aweigh we go — for about three bendsworth, it turns out, before we first bump bottom. We back off easily, make another dead-slow pass closer to the outside of the bend, where normally the water's deeper, and bump again. On third try, really hugging the outside bank, we squeeze through. Nothing we pass looks particularly familiar: generic marshland, mudbanks, green-brown water, reeds. The nursery of the Chesapeake, ecologists say, but this morning all the cribs are empty; not even a periwinkle snail to be seen on the stalks of spartina.

The first fork in our road presents a dilemma several times repeated thereafter: The more navigable-looking tine goes off in the less likely-looking direction, and even without fog we can't see far enough ahead to help us make the call. Our rule of thumb becomes to take the "wrong" fork when the "right" one looks really tight or otherwise unpromising, but there are a number of coin-tossers. We consider logging our turns, then decide hopefully that there won't be all that much retracement. One promising branch peters out after two bends; we run aground twice while backing and filling to turn *US* around and retreat to the alternate fork. Where the watercourse threatens to narrow beyond our turn-around capacity, I take the dinghy ahead to see whether the path rewidens farther on or cul-de-sacs — push-rowing so that I can see forward.

Slow progress, if it's progress at all. In yesterday's wind and rain, floodwater and fatigue, we made no usable estimate of how far we penetrated this marsh. Couldn't have been *this* far, we begin to think by late morning, but who knows? Always better than I at maneuvering clumsy *US* in tight quarters, my helmsmate performs virtuoso backings-off, three-point turns, squeakings-through — but for all we know, we may be elaborately side-tracking or even working ourselves farther into wherever we are.

"Look."

To southwestward, you've espied a small stand of loblolly pines that we certainly didn't notice yesterday. Our fork of current choice seems to wend their way; we'll use them as a reference mark.

"To where?"

I share your concern: Before long the tide must turn, and our repeated soft groundings will become less extricable. Nothing for it but to stay busy. The watercourse just here seems reasonably promising, although it appears to narrow as it turns the next bend. We consider anchoring and exploring ahead together, with the little outboard engine on the dinghy. You're spooked a bit, you confess, whenever I disappear around a bend in the dinghy and leave you idling *US* in place, unlikely as it is that we'll lose each other in the maze. On the other hand, anchoring and unanchoring use up valuable high-water time.

We compromise: No anchoring, but I'll hang the little outboard on the dinghy transom and poke ahead solo one stretch at a time, sounding bottom with an oar. At each bend, I'll pause and either wave you forward or signal you to stand by until I come back and confer — unless you feel that we've strayed completely and ought to backtrack. . . .

"We'll never get back to where we started," you opine: "We have to hope this will lead us out by a different door."

Our new way of going works, for a while. The pines shift position bend by bend, but draw ever nearer; the waterway widens

and narrows, deepens and shoals, but remains just navigable.
Quite near the higher ground of the pine stand, it forks southeast
and southwest into near-identical branches, another coin-tosser.
The two might even rejoin behind the trees to make a loblolly
island. Into neutral you go, while I try the right fork first. I'm
going to pursue it a little distance this time, if I can, before returning to try the left; time ticketh. Don't be concerned if I'm gone for
a little while.

"I'll be concerned. But go."

It proves a manageable passage, seldom less than oar-grip deep
in the middle and never less than an *US*-length wide, but a real
spaghetti-bender. At its first turn, I glance back. Your hand flutters
a good-bye — rather wistfully, it seems to me, as you stand gamely
at the idling helm. I lift my chin in reply and motor on, through
reeds so tall and thick that I have to stop and stand upright in the
dinghy to see our mast, sometimes even to see the stand of pines.
The bends are innumerable, and before long my fork forks and
reforks into further coin-tossers. I begin keeping count — right,
left, then left again, to see whether I circle the pines — and like a
wilderness hiker, I look astern after each choice to get a sense of
the backtrail. At the fourth fork, finding that I can no longer see
either our mast or the pine grove even when I stand on the dinghy
seat, I decide to lead *US* this far in before I go farther, lest I miss
my way. Right left left — which is to say (played backward now)
right right left. The fog, thank heaven, is all but gone; there's a
clear blue sky coming through up there, a lot less spooky, and the
air is comfortable, even warm: shirtsleeves weather. Right right
left.

I do get things wrong, I remind myself; perhaps more often than
I used to. A couple years back, I accidentally killed our prize cut-
leaf maple, centerpiece of our streetside yard, by spraying it with
the wrong stuff for scale insects — so confident it was the right
stuff that I didn't bother to reread all the fine print on the label.
And only last spring — but let's skip the tiresome catalogue. I forget things. Frequently, as my shipmate charges, I don't pay enough
attention, or the right kind of attention. After a quarter-century of
sailing, I've been known to say port when I mean starboard. Once

in a while I drive up to the wrong side of the gasoline pump, even after reminding myself which of our cars I'm in and which side its filler cap is on. Absentminded. But right left left (and it *was* right left left), retraced, means right right left, no two ways about it, and this is my right hand and this is my left. Even so, I pause at each turn and stand to orient myself with the pine grove, which, now that I'm headed *this* way, has to be over *there*.

Well, it isn't. But the spartina is particularly tall here, and chances are it wasn't exactly at this spot that I took a fix on the pines coming in. Right right left is what matters, and I've made two rights, and here I come, patient helmsmate.

She's not there. Rather, *I'm* not there, back where I left her. No pine grove, no *US*, just another fork in the gut where they ought to be. This one makes a near-even triad of 120-degree angles, identical spartina right around. Unthinkable that I could have passed it without noticing before I took my first right fork and started counting. I'm a-tingle — sweating, even, with dismay. The damned marsh grass! I'd need a ten-foot ladder here to see over it. I curse myself as well, briefly: no gain there. The hand-bearing compass, which I've brought along, machts nicht; who cares which way's north, after so many turns? The only thing to do is poke a short distance into each of those forks, maybe somehow marking the one I just emerged from so that I can't mistake it when I return. No sticks or stones or shells lying about with which to blaze its muddy point, just beginning to uncover on the ebb tide. My options for marking it are an oar (nope), the spare outboard fuel can lashed under the dinghy seat (nope), or —

The empty cask beside it, still wedged neatly in place despite yesterday's wild ride. *That* job, at least, I managed competently. Better this objet trouvé be lost than my motive power; it's nothing but an old empty cask; couldn't possibly be . . . authentic, let's say. And who says I'm going to lose it? I am not by nature a loser of things, except in memory, as I may have said already. When I find you, we'll be passing back this way to proceed right left left, and I'll retrieve the thing.

Now I'm really sweating. The air is becoming almost summer warm, in fact, but that's only half of it. I guess I've been gone from

US twenty minutes or more already — I neglected to note the time
and set the bezel of my watch when I started out — and it's going
to take that long again to probe these forks, unless I'm lucky on
the first try. You'll be anxious already. For all I know, you might
have heard the dinghy outboard winding about you from time to
time; might even be hearing it now, unless *US*'s idling diesel
drowns it out. Perhaps you've been calling to me, and I didn't hear
you over my own engine racket. Could that racket cover even the
blast of our compressed-air horn, I wonder? *There* would be a
possibly useful locator signal, if you thought to sound it. What if,
trying to hold position for so long in such confined space, you've
drifted aground on the falling tide and are stuck fast, in no present
danger but mildly alarmed and beginning to be mildly frightened?
In my mind's eye I see that wistful good-bye wave. I sweat.

Fork One (the leftmore) quickly iterates, anyhow seems to do
so. From that vertiginous prospect, I retreat to my cask-marked
point — *that*, at least, is still where it should be — and try Fork
Two, which wends and winds but presents no choices other than
forward or back. I am uneasy about the time all this is taking; I
know I've spent longer now "returning" than I spent on my original right left left. You must be climbing the walls — the *rigging*,
I correct myself, chagrined that I never pursued my frivolous but
longstanding wish for ratlines on our shrouds, such as tropical
sailors use for easy lookout from the mast spreaders; from that
height, in this flat landscape, we could perhaps have overviewed
the maze and seen our way out. All the same, I go on a bit farther,
faute de mieux, round yet another bend, and find myself for the
first time all day in more open marsh. I can see some distance
ahead now, and to both sides; the reeds and grass are shorter here,
and the winding corridor of water reticulates among ever more
widely spaced hummocks. No sign, alas, of *US* or of truly open
water, although the trend seems promising; I much wish we could
pursue it at once, together, from this spot.

Maybe a quarter-mile ahead over the hummocks is another
stand of loblolly pines, the palms of the Eastern Shore, their
straight scaly trunks rising thirty, forty, fifty feet before branching.
It is not the same stand as before: considerably larger and thicker,

suggesting a sizable area of high ground. And do I see, just to starboard of and a bit beyond it, a utility pole and what might be a ramshackle pier? The first sign of civilization since . . . Solomons Lump Light, I guess, unless I'm forgetting something,* and it makes for a difficult call indeed. I have back-checked my exit from the taller marsh, a dozen yards astern: It's a twenty-foot break in the cattails and spartina back there, not remarkably different from other such openings along that terrain's irregular edge. Either I retreat promptly before I lose track of it, make my way back to the cask-marked Place Where Three Roads Meet, and resume my thus-far-fruitless search for *US* (How? I ask myself, a touch desperately: by pursuing Fork One through its iterated dilemmas? By backtracking up the marked stem and hoping for better luck this time?), or else I invest the red plastic spare fuel can to mark *this* portal — after topping up the outboard's self-contained little tank — and check out that pier over there, that pole, that pine woods, in hope of finding, if not open water, perhaps more local knowledge of where it is, where *I* am, and where my mate might be with *US*. In the best worst case, I might be able to telephone the Coast Guard for a helicopter search, or importune some fellow Marylander to report our plight, and then either wait for help or begin backtracking in the dinghy.

No: That last would only compound and complicate the search. If I'm lucky enough to find anybody "home" over there (I'm already refueling the OB and looking for the most conspicuous place to put my gas-can marker), I'll do whatever is necessary to get the Coast Guard notified and then follow their advice. I have no money or even identification with me — one of the minor pleasures of sailboat cruising is not to carry the omnipresent male wallet in left hip pocket unless we're going ashore for dinner or supplies — but who could refuse belief and assistance to such plain (and embarrassed) distress?

Murmuring a pained auf Wiedersehen to you — Be steadfast, Love; be brave — I set forth. My course through the hummocks is necessarily indirect. The fuel-can marker, although I lashed it

---

*I am: that tumbledown gooseblind at last night's anchorage.

head-high to an improvised fasces of cattails just reachable from the dinghy, is soon lost to view, but I've taken a stern-bearing on it with my handheld compass — almost due east — and the pine woods, I'm gratified to see, hold still on the average reciprocal of that bearing. If nobody's over there and I find no road or telephone or other avenue to assistance, I should have an odds-on chance of refinding Fork Two.

And what then? And what if . . . ?

As I near the pines, the water broadens but grows shallower: a tussocked swamp, an everglade. Over the last stretch of it, I have to tip up the outboard and row. When the dinghy itself mucks to a stop, there's still a wide marsh meadow between me and the pines. I shuck off deck moccasins and socks, roll up my jeans, and step into the ankle-deep ooze — surprisingly warm, as is the water over it — to haul the dinghy securely up into the cordgrass before striking off across that meadow toward the corner of the woods where I reckon that pier to be (I understand now that it must have been more in the nature of a walkway out over the marsh grass).

But — as is often the case in marsh country — the lay of the land changes as I pass through it. My meadow turns out to be coursed by tidal rivulets, a couple of them large enough to float a canoe, if not a dinghy. What had looked from a distance like a straight wall of pines I see now to be an irregular, less well defined boundary between woods and marsh, some odd corner of which must somehow be obscuring from this perspective the "pier" that I saw rather plainly from back in the dinghy. That stout little vessel itself is now out of view behind me; although I have a rough visual bearing on where it should be, it might have been prudent for me to stick one oar upright in the mud beside it.

To my surprise, one of those meadow rivulets — near what I had thought to be the "corner" of the woods but see now to be just another projection of their ragged perimeter — widens and divides into a pair of little coves or cattail-bordered creeklets with a fine sandy point between them (that pier, then, might turn out to be a pier after all): a not especially remarkable prospect, but one so strikingly familiar in its particulars that I'm stopped as if by déjà vu. This sandspit, these reeds, those twin creeks or coves, that grove of pines (some juniper and white cedar in there, too, I see now: trees that, for as long as I can remember, I have felt to be inspirited) — I *know* this place.

From where?

Well, from my fiction, to be sure: In at least three of the later novels, very possibly in earlier ones as well, a setting like this — I'll even say *this setting* — is the mise-en-scène for critical disorientations of the main characters. Typically they *wake* to find themselves here stranded ("knowing better *where* they are than who and when and why . . ."), whereas I've long since finished my slow waking and am not the least drowsy; I'm alert and anxious. Typically too my strandees are naked at this juncture, nothing on or round about them in the way of time cues, whereas my rolled-up jeans and university sweatshirt (into which I'm duly sweating), my canvas sailing hat and waterproof quartz wristwatch and plastic-rimmed bifocals fix me as late-twentieth-century American. All the same, looking back from the sandspit itself (to which I've waded for that purpose) I'm scarcely surprised to see that from its viewpoint my approach route is scarcely recognizable. The most I can venture is that my dinghy is back yonder somewhere, as are my wife and US.

Vertigo! And why, exactly, do this setting and this scene recur in my writing? No doubt I've stood on many such reed-girt points in my tidewater lifetime (though never to my knowledge on this one, *the* one, wherever it is); they are beyond counting in Chesapeake country. I am not in the habit of dozing off on sandspits or of wandering about buck-naked except at Langford Creek in summer, but on our sailing cruises we do a fair amount of skinny-dipping when conditions permit, for the sensory delight of utter unencumbrance, and plenty of times we've swum naked from our anchored vessel to explore a nearby empty beach or shaded bower of honey locust. To stand or sit in such a place in such circumstances, especially in the relative absence of time cues, feels agreeably primal, a touch uncanny. Even clothed and anxious, I sense the voltage of . . .

A threshold.

Uh-oh, I say aloud, my nerve-ends buzzing: I may not know

where we are on the map, but I recognize where I am in the program. It is imperative, I understand, not to stand mesmerized on this spooky point. I must either head back promptly in my companion's direction (Which way is that?) or forge on into those woods in search of pier, walkway, cabin, road, whatever. Another yearning look "back" — away from the woods, anyhow — suffices to convince me that retracement is out of the question now, if it was ever in it. Dinghy, fuel can, cask, *US* — the only possible route to them at this point is the long way around: forward, through the woods.

My eyes fill. By temper a skeptical rationalist, secular to the bone, I am an entire stranger to mystical experience, though not to my profession's daily mysteries of language and imagination. What's more, I'm too old for this: sixty-two, Social Security age, a junior Senior Citizen. All I want — and I've never wanted it more — is to live out my remaining years with my beloved friend, dreaming up the best stories I can and finding the best words to tell them with, maintaining our modest properties, enjoying our boats and bikes and books and bodies and other blessings for as long as we're able until the Destroyer of Delights has his way with us. But into the woods it must be; I know that for certain, and to the woods I turn: barefoot, unwalleted, almost shivering with apprehension, but resolved to look back no more.

Aria: "This is a story I've told before"

This is a story I've told before:

In the second half of my twenties, having published two relatively short, relatively realistic novels, I wrote a long, elaborately complicated "historical" comedy, *The Sot-Weed Factor* (colonial American English for "tobacco trader"). It retails the misadventures of a factual early Maryland colonist, Ebenezer Cooke, the self-styled poet laureate of Lord Baltimore's fledgling province. My Ebenezer comes programmatically innocent from the Old World to the New (the opposite, it now occurs to me, of Jay Wordsworth Scribner's condition and trajectory); he loses his estate, regains it at cost of his innocence, and in the process "finds himself" as a poet: author of the satirical mock-epic "The Sot-Weed Factor, or, A Voiage to Maryland."

I did not have in mind the "Ur-myth," that archetypal pattern of wandering-hero myths the world over. Indeed, I was scarcely aware that such a pattern existed, although I had of course read particular literary examples of it in my college years: Homer's *Odyssey*, Virgil's *Aeneid*, Sophocles's Oedipus tragedies. My models were Henry Fielding's *Tom Jones* and the actual Ebenezer Cooke's actual poem. Cooks Point, the ancestral property, is at the juncture of the Choptank River and Chesapeake Bay, five portside points downriver from my native town, but although I knew Cooks Point, I was unaware of Cooke's poem — often billed as "the first American satire" — until graduate-student days. The coincidence inspired the novel. My objectives were several, not all of them articulable in the late 1950s. Looking back, I am inclined to declare grandly that I needed to discover, or to be discovered by, Postmodernism. At the time, I contented myself with vowing to devise a plot at least as complicated as Fielding's, in a novel at least as long: a novel fat enough to wear its title right-side up across its spine. I was *not* thinking of, e.g., Lord Raglan's *The Hero* or Joseph Campbell's *The Hero with a Thousand Faces* or Otto Rank's *The Myth of the Birth of the Ritual Hero* or other works of comparative mythology. Hadn't read them.

At least a few of my reviewers had, however (likewise Jay Scribner, as shall be seen), and when the novel appeared in 1960 they remarked my debt to such works as those abovementioned. The adventures of my virgin poet Ebenezer Cooke, they observed (especially in tandem with those of his tutor and counterself, the "cosmophilist" Henry Burlingame), exemplify and satirize the wandering-hero myth. Intrigued, I read my alleged influencers and was delighted to find that while the imputation of influence was technically untrue, it was altogether valid; in my own innocence, I had absorbed the mythic pattern unawares. I felt marvelously validated as a storyteller, the muses' conduit. Unlike Homer, Sophocles, and Virgil, I had not orchestrated an established myth; except for Cooke's poem (which itself has only a few of the Ur-myth's features), my material was largely invented — yet I had unconsciously conformed it almost point for point to the pattern.

Thus my initial reaction. My second, as I read more deeply into the subject, came to be the contrary: So far from its being a remarkable coincidence or evidence of my calling as the Muses' Very Vessel, that correspondence between the sot-weed factor's trials and those of mythic wandering heroes came to seem to me inevitable. How could one write what is, after all, a maturation novel *without* echoing the literal or metaphorical rituals of passage? Don't all children regard their fathers as god/kings, more or less, their mothers as royal virgins, and certain other adults in the extended family as nemeses? Aren't all our childhoods more or less misty, ontologically obscure, "in another country," rich in riddling intimations, even after destiny and hormones have summoned us to our vocation? Don't we all then have thresholds to cross, monsters and ogres to battle, pitfalls to avoid, princesses to rescue (if we happen to be male heterosexuals; otherwise, mutatis mutandis), and various helpers (those princesses included) to abet our triumph? Mustn't we all lose our way and ourselves, go down into darkness, return transfigured to the daylit world if we're resourceful and steadfast and lucky enough, bring with us the wherewithal to rout pretenders, proclaim and establish our administration, beget and minister for a time — and then inevitably fall from favor, put our house behind us, and confront the terminal mystery? It is this ubiquitous correspondence to our ordinary lives (among other correspondences) that validates the myth, I came to understand, even as the myth validates our ordinary lives.

Et cetera. Thus to "explain" the great model, however, or at least to account for it, was not to explain it away. My third reaction, if that term applies, was no longer imaginative possession of the myth but my imagination's possession by it. Everything I considered in the way of material for a next novel was transformed and directed by what I had learned of the Ur-myth — and therefore, it seemed to me, contaminated by self-consciousness in a way that *The Sot-Weed Factor* had not been. Homer and Sophocles had presumably been innocent of the mythic template, although no doubt they were richly aware of the relevance of Odysseus's and Oedipus's adventures to more ordinary life-passages. The case of Virgil, on the other hand, came to interest me sharply, for while innocent of the Ur-myth, he was exquisitely aware of Homer's *Iliad* and *Odyssey*. Virgil's literary project in the *Aeneid* is a model of uninnocence: to vindicate the Roman empire and Latin culture in a verse-epic systematically patterned after their Greek heritage. Not only the project is self-conscious; so, famously, is its hero, who, like his author, knows he has a script to follow, so to speak. Although Aeneas is less wily than Odysseus, his mission is more problematical. Both make mistakes and midcourse corrections, but the Ithacan wants simply to get home to Ithaca, whereas the Trojan's destination and destiny are revealed to him only incrementally. Aeneas learns by going where he has to go, as perhaps did Virgil in composing the *Aeneid*, and the poet's sophisticated literary self-consciousness (as compared to shadowy Homer's) leads to effects almost "postmodern" in their self-reflexivity: the celebrated set piece of Queen Dido's unfinished Carthaginian frescoes, for example, in Book Two, wherein storm-battered Aeneas, still struggling to learn where he's supposed to go with his band of Trojan refugees and what exactly he's supposed to do when he gets there, sees his Story Thus Far already transformed into art. He recognizes in the frescoes the likenesses of fallen comrades, and (himself still disguised by Mother Venus from the Carthaginians as well as, metaphorically, from himself) espies — Hair-raising moment! — *his own face* in Dido's painted narrative-in-progress, the narrative to whose continuation he will presently be summoned — like the reader, like the poet — from Dido's bed.

Newly interesting to me too, in this particular, were the gospel narratives of Jesus, whose history in general famously follows the model of mythic herohood. Like Virgil vis-à-vis Homer, the authors of the gospels (St. Matthew especially) seem aware that their hero has a script to follow — the messianic prophecies of the Old Testament — and this awareness leads them to such arresting formulations as this, from Matthew's report of Jesus's confidential healing (12:15–21): ". . . many followed him, and he healed them all, and ordered them not to make him known. This was to fulfill what was spoken by the prophet Isaiah: . . . '[The Messiah] will not wrangle or cry aloud, nor will any one hear his voice in the streets. . . .'" The ontological situation is particularly intriguing — indeed, vertiginous — if one regards Jesus not as a false or self-deluded prophet but as a devout Jew who knows by heart the Old Testament prophecies *and who happens also to be the true Messiah*. He thus does *a*, *b*, and *c* not simply because the script directs him to, but because the script *predicts* that the Messiah will do *a*, *b*, and *c* and he happens to be not an actor playing the role of Messiah but the Messiah. In short, it is a case not only of the prophecies' validating him, but coaxially of His validating the prophecies. As Jesus himself poignantly observes at the Last Supper (Matthew 26:24), "The son of man goes as it is written of him. . . ."

At thirty, myself approaching with this enhanced awareness the critical age of Jungian "differentiation" (departure, descent into abyss, crucifixion, loss of way in Dark Wood, other "thresholds"), I came to regard what I called the Jesus Paradox as that of more ordinary self-consciousness writ large, just as the Ur-myth in general may be regarded as our ordinary lives writ large — in particular the lives of people with a deeply felt vocation and some "tragic" sense of life. I did not regard myself as any sort of hero, not to mention savior. I did, however, feel an utter and unequivocal authorial calling — all the more so after my belated encounter with the Ur-myth and its retroactive application to *Sot-Weed*. Hence that work's successor, *Giles Goat-Boy*, which with its right hand parodies the model and the Jesus Paradox (the goat-boy believes himself to be the "Grand Tutor" but has himself been tutored assiduously in the Grand-Tutorial model) while its left sympathetically explores that paradox and the general problematics of self-consciousness, self-knowledge, and self-transcendence.

That large project completed, its author found himself not thereby freed from its preoccupations — read "obsessions" — but still wandering, professionally and personally, in a labyrinth that had lost its appeal himfor though not its power himover (I was given to such coinages in those days: fretting, fretting with the great instrument of English, as I was fretting at numerous other things). The story-series *Lost in the Funhouse* ensued: "Fictions

for Print, Tape, Live Voice." Its title speaks for itself; so did several
of the stories, whose heroes are the stories themselves, speaking
themselves, or the hero metamorphosed into his own story — an
occupational hazard, it may be, of self-conscious storytellers, perhaps even a general aspect of the postmod condition. In one of
those stories, in particular — "Night-Sea Journey," narrated in the
first person by a spermatozoon afflicted with both self-awareness
and skepticism — I sought to purge my imagination, extricate
myself from the maze, by a reduction to absurdity of the model
(though indeed the "life history" of a spermatozoon hauntingly
replicates the Ur-myth). I succeeded only in reimpregnating myself
with it: self-insemination where I had intended abortion.

I'm ahead of myself. *Giles* was begun in State College, Pennsylvania, extended in Spain, and completed in Buffalo, New York,
as its author moved through the first half of his thirties and America moved out of the Fifties into the High Sixties. As aforenoted,
I was not blind to the workings-out of the Ur-myth template in my
own, undramatic life-story: an example of "coaxial esemplasy,"
inasmuch as my understanding of the model was being shaped by
my experience of life as well as vice versa. Having wed quite young
and green and quickly bred a family, I attained Threshold Age
(thirty-three and a third, by my satirical computation) with fourteen years of prevailingly happy marriage under my belt, three
children sired and already parented to the threshold of their adolescence, three novels published and critically well received though
not commercially successful, a fourth in progress that would turn
out to be my first and only best-seller, and, thanks to them, an
academic career moving agreeably toward full professorship by
age thirty-five.

Of even such modest triumphs, the gods take corrective notice.
And indeed, those callow, money-poor, hard-striving, energetically
exploratory years, however productive and deeply satisfying, had
exacted a toll on my innocence, as in turn my innocence (and a
certain innate obtuseness) had exacted a toll on my marriage: a
toll increased by maturation, "differentiation," and our quota of
scarifying experiences as parents, spouses, lovers, friends. Enough
here to acknowledge that by their thirty-third year this couple had

known separate dark nights of the soul; that their connection had gone through thick and thin; that their exfoliation into their thirties was not, alas, bringing them closer together; and that round about their thirty-third birthdays (both in May '63, but she Taurus, he Gemini), returning on the S.S. *Rotterdam* from their first sojourn in Europe, they found themselves embarked upon a literal westward night-sea journey as well as a figurative one, with Raglan/Jung/Campbell looking over their shoulders (over his, at least) and Giles the goat-boy — that creature of the American Sixties — capering about in his author's imagination.

Through the rest of that decade, while for our children's sake and our own we tried in vain to preserve the marriage in rambunctious Buffalo, the myth of the wandering hero preserved its hold on my fancy despite my growing weariness with it and my several attempts to purge it away. It informs, is indeed the armature of, the novella-triad *Chimera*, which followed *Lost in the Funhouse*. Only a new marriage, a new life, new professorships in Boston and Baltimore, and the investment of my forties in the enormous, intricate, stock-taking novel *LETTERS* flushed the Urmyth from my system — whereto it soon after returned, but on *my* terms, at my invitation, with an unmistakably middle-aged mellowness, in the novels that followed.

Attender of this aria: I had not been unaware, through the writing of *Giles* and those other myth-driven comic *opera*, of the danger of trivializing what is, after all, as profound and ubiquitous a "paradigm" as any in the human repertory, the template of the story of our lives. Against this risk I paid my dues to the paradigm: by way of tribute, not only a dozen years' hard, lifesaving work (those *opera* weren't *simply* comic) but a decade's fruitful tribulation, a tempestuous night-sea journey that scuttled my domestic vessel, sundered and seared its skippers, and doubtless scarred the innocent young passengers as well. If my muse is, finally, the one with the grin instead of the grimace, she's so only finally. That smile of hers is not fatuous; her laughter is net, not gross, as she watches me still watching my life fit itself to the cycle's final quadrant: the wandering protagonist's "reign" and death.

Three times that cycle's protagonists are summoned: first, from obscure childhood across the threshold of adventure to the initiatory trials and ordeals of their quest — divestments and disorientations and dismemberments, night-sea journeys, swordbridges, labyrinths, lethal riddles, father/brother/dragon battles, princess-rescues, elixir-thefts, and category-transcensions; second, from the ecstasy of unitary transcendence, the arms of the awakened princess, the paradise in Davy Jones's locker, back across the threshold of the daylit world to eff the ineffable, translate enabling revelation into worldly work (never without some loss in translation, for these wanderers have left the hemisphere of Mystery for that of Tragedy); and third, from that edifice of their own construction out to the closing of the circle: Oedipus to Colonus, Odysseus out upon his last voyage — a mysterious Tod und Verklärung with implications of return, apocalypse reverberant with genesis, a finale that reprises the overture.

Happens to all of us, no? Or nearly all. Anyhow to many, in our smaller lives' prosaic terms, no doubt particularly if we're half looking for it to happen ("You're closing the hatches? How come you're closing the hatches?"). Although we're far from resting on our laurels, there is slippage in our muse's credit rating. New prophets woo our parishioners; younger minstrels distract an audience attrited already by other sorts of spectacles. Our life is comfortable; we're lucky in love (and we don't play cards); our metropolis of words remains commodious, stable, not unhandsome — a formidable construction, really, even imposing from some perspectives, although *imposition* is not exactly what we had in mind. And yet . . .

We grow fidgety. This particular fall of late-afternoon October light, this particular stirring in the air, we half recognize. A certain grove awaits — off the charts, but we'll know it when we see it; we've been there before. One early morning soon — still nighttime, really — in our last, restless sleep will come the call. We'll hear and not hear it; half hear it, through the low-level tinnitus in our aging ears; hear it most clearly in retrospect, after we've responded. . . .

On with the interlude:

In a needle-carpeted vestibule of old junipers and white cedars in the shaded margin of the full-growth pines, at a rotting picnic table camouflaged with lichens chartreuse and loden green, a woman and a man chat easily, both of them smoking cigarettes and sipping from aluminum cans in orange foam-rubber sleeves. The man's back is toward me; a lanky, dark-curled fellow in belt-less jeans, light blue workshirt that looks soaked through, and deck moccasins sans socks, he sits on the pine-spritzed tabletop's near end, his right foot on the bench below, his left leg crossing his right knee. He rests his drink-can on his left foot between sips and makes conversational points with his cigaretted left hand. The woman — thin, light-brown-haired, bespectacled, not tall — sits sidesaddle on that bench's farther end, in quarter profile. She, too, gestures with her cigarette-arm as she talks (cigarettes were good for that; I had forgotten) — the right arm, in her case, its elbow resting on the table. Her left hand balances the can on her left thigh-top, trousered in doubleknit apple green.

My nerves thrill. Of all people: my twin sister, Jill to my Jack.

She has, evidently, seen me approaching; without lifting her elbow, she waggles the free fingers of her cigarette-hand in casual hello. My impulse is to hurry herward with my urgency — *How in the world*, and *You're not going to believe this, but* — but something checks that impulse: perhaps the recognition that that lean fellow with her isn't our brother (How could it be? He lives cross-country. But then, this isn't Jill's neighborhood, either; she lives in the next county over and up from our native Dorchester), perhaps something else. I finger-waggle back and stroll her way, shaking my head. The air has turned midsummerlike, even August-like, still and sweatsy. My sister sips what I now see to be her beer, taps her ash into one of two empties on the table (the other is accordioned flat).

Her companion, also bespectacled, turns his head — and I'm stopped in my tracks, momentarily, by disbelief.

"Hey," Jill says when I'm near enough for her unraised voice. "We wondered how many beers it would take to get you here."

Jay Wordsworth Scribner, as is his custom, doesn't greet me directly. He replies to my sister in her own down-county-bantering tone, "Di'n't take us but two. We hardly got caught up."

Nor does he hold out his hand to shake. My counterself doesn't shake hands, as a rule. His explanation has always been that to a left-hander, thrusting forth his right feels backward ("Try shaking left-handed; you'll see," Jerry Schreiber told me back in grade school, first southpaw I'd known). But there's more to it: a disinclination to many social rituals when the society is his own; an impatience with others' assumptions that sometimes leads him to offer his left hand to your right. Instead — Familiar gesture! — he tips back his head and beer can for a long pull while keeping his bright dark eyes upon me, a salute of sorts that I remember from high-school and college fraternity days. Then he sets the sleeved can down on the old planked table, permanently damp and black with dry rot where it isn't greened with moss; he wipes his turned-back wet shirtsleeve across his lips, slightly scarred from decades of trumpet-playing (there's more to that story, too), knuckles up his wire-rimmed eyeglasses, and stands.

Your fly's open, Jay, I point out as if in countersalute or self-defense. How the hell'd you get here? Where's Beth?

"You might say *that*'s how he got here," Jill says in her wry drawl, cigaretting toward Jay's jeans. "He'll explain; don't get the wrong idea. Do I get a kiss hello?"

I miss her point but buss her near cheek; it has been too long since brother and sister have seen each other, given that we live in the same state. I hear myself reply in mock complaint, Don't I get a beer? — the familiar raillery of our house, common among tidewater folk, which I took for granted until age thirty or so and have found ear-grating since. What do I want with beer and banter, even with the how and why of Jill's and Jay Scribner's being here and their unsurprise at my joining them, when so more urgent business presses? Never mind the beer (which I don't seem to be being offered anyhow): Look, guys . . . I've got problems.

"Don't we know it," responds my counterself. Meaningly, but not unamiably, my twin adds "And don't we all have." As children, she and I felt ourselves to be as close as two souls can be, an effect in part of our unfortunate nursery-rhyme naming; at adolescence, regrettably, our lives diverged, and have not since reconverged more closely than a real but distanced affection. My life has arguably been the more wide and various, hers the more deeply rooted. I've undergone divorce and enjoyed remarriage; she has endured untimely widowhood and the protracted management of our parents' last age. I had almost forgotten you two knew each other, I hear myself saying, as if my real priorities won't stay in place in the presence of such ambient unlikelihood.

"Oh, Jer and I go way back," Jill replies, and her use of that nickname reminds me that of course they do — Hadn't they even "dated" once or twice in my early college days, when I worked in Jay Scribner's dance band both in the city and all over the Eastern Shore? In the decades since, Jay has seldom mentioned their brief connection; it's an effort for me to imagine that they were once rather close. Jill drops her cigarette butt into the empty can: L.A. Light, which I can't imagine Jay drinking except to be neighborly. He's a Beck's Dark man like myself, when he drinks beer at all; in his role as my counterself, however, he has gone through extended periods of teetotalling on the one hand (as through vegetarianism and macrobiotic diets) and of serious wine connoisseurship on the other, when my house jug wines were to him what Jill's low-alcohol beer is to me.

"And we have a long way to go," Jay adds — in his "real" voice now, no-nonsense, without a trace in it of our shared tidewater origins. In my head, my own voice sounds close to that, but when I hear a taped interview played back, for example, I'm struck by the amount of down-home brogue still in it: somewhere between Jay's and Jill's, as I myself am now positioned between my counterself and my erstwhile other self, even the erstwhile *rest of* my self. "Time to get started."

He has made no move to rezip his fly. That, too, is rather *like* Jay Wordsworth Scribner — not to go about unzipped, but unapologetically to decline rezipping when the oversight is brought to his attention — though I can't recall its ever happening before. His shirt, I re-remark, is soaked through in places, not as if with sweat;

his jeans and deck shoes, too, as if he had waded ashore. Again my nerves tingle.

"Let's use the facilities." He cocks his head toward a nearby screen of younger junipers. His manner signals conversation more than urination. My sister confirms: "He'll brief you, honey." That endearment, while characteristically Chesapeake, is unironic, as is the advisory. I follow Jay into the grove, asking again Where's your wife? Where's your boat? Where the hell are *we*? This time he replies, though without quite answering — and without peeing, either, for all it's he, not I, who has been drinking beer. As I relieve myself onto the pine-needled ground, he calmly recommends that I set aside for the time being my concern for both his shipmate and my own (my concern for *her* concern included), as for both our vessels. They're all okay — "On Hold, you might say. This isn't their story any longer, man, for a while at least." I'm not looking at him directly, but I hear his voice grin as he echoes the old television series: "*This is your life*, more or less."

His too? That isn't at all the question on my mind, but it's the one I ask, to which Jay answers Yes and no. Yes, to the extent that he's a character in my opera, let's say. But do I think that his fly is open and his clothes are soaked, for example, because his aim is bad?

Ah, Jay! But his tone waves off my concern, as it has ever done in the area of his distresses ("Somebody opened a door on me while I was practicing," Jerry Schreiber informed me curtly when I first saw his smashed mouth in fifth grade. A decade later I learned that his hungover alcoholic father, furious at Jay's waking him with reveille, had slammed his open palm against the bell of his mischievous son's bugle, driving the mouthpiece into the boy's lips. Characteristically, Jay claimed when the injury healed that the scar improved his embouchure). "*Don't piss overside in foul weather*," he reminds me now. "First rule of offshore sailing.* That's how old Odysseus got it, by the way."

---

*In fact, an informal Coast Guard survey of offshore sailboat drownings revealed that a surprising number of the (male) victims were found with trouser fly open.

Stricken but unsurprised, I find myself saying to myself *An easy one, then, at least.* Jay smiles ruefully (at our most close, we've often thought in synch): "Not as easy as the old guy promised, but that's water over the threshold now. All set, man?"

That "man" is from our bebop musician days: pegged pants, lapel-less jackets. Somehow it empowers me to ask — the dreamer questioning his dream's ontology from within it — *All set for what?*

"Goes without saying, doesn't it?" I've shaken, tucked, re-zipped. Jay's rhetorical question is a coded challenge, to which I give the coded reply: It's *his* job to answer rhetorical questions. At the close of our graduate-school years, when he and I both were determined to become "significant" writers (we never used the adjectives "great" or "famous"), and had decided after much discussion of alternatives to support ourselves by teaching as we pursued our larger goal, and had agreed that one ought not to shortchange the work that pays the bills, we addressed ourselves to the question of what we might honorably do with the academic side of our lives. Only half joking, I vowed to devote mine to saying and resaying to my students "all the things that go without saying" about their subject; to staring down its presuppositions and first principles until, defamiliarized, they take on a renewed, high-order interest. What is literature? What is fiction? What is a *story*, and why is it what it is, rather than some other thing? Jay topped me — par for our course in those days — by vowing for his part to answer, in rigorous detail, all rhetorical questions. Should a student ask, offhandedly, "Who's to say, finally, what's reality and what's illusion?" Jay would tap his own chest, lead that student through the history of metaphysics, and conclude with the charge, "Now *you're* to say which is which. Okay?"

He and my sister, he tells me now (who in her current role, he assures me, is no more impatiently awaiting our post-urinary return than my wife is fretting over my whereabouts — "We're *out* of that movie, man"), will explain this and that from time to time, more or less, as we go along — although "with any imagination" I should be able to answer my own questions. It is, after all, my story ("Sorry, there: your *opera*"), not his or hers; they have their

own stories, "needless to say," in which *I* play a more or less sup-
porting role — no criticism intended, necessarily. But inasmuch as
we are where we find ourselves — in this bepisséd grove, Jay
means, where he'll linger now for a bit while my twin sees me
through the "first reel of my replay" or first "island" of my "voyage" and thereafter remeet me in time to steer me through my
second (of three, I might want to make note) — he'll take a
moment to remark a few more things that go without saying. E.g.,
that that empty cask was where it was not so much because he put
it there (he can't say he didn't, although *his* version of the thing is
on his boat, in *his* floating opera) as because that's where and how
it needed to be in mine. That it was my idea, not his or my wife's
or any soul else's, to set the action of this narrative not in "real"
time but in an imagined near future that the present will presently
overtake, and further — for all my talk of "coaxial esemplasy"
and "learning by going where I have to go" — to conceive as its
plot vehicle a voyage out of the time of its imagining and writing
into the time imagined and written. Thus I needn't bother him or
Jill (it should go without saying) with such irrelevancies — unin-
telligibilities, in fact — as whether he "really" fell overboard and
drowned while taking a leeward leak in mid-TSJ from the gunwale
of *American Century* at the threshold of the Atlantic, or whether
my twin is "really" going about her daily business in Hurlock,
Maryland, while my projection of her is running me through the
guided tour of my first two decades. As well ask whether the "I"
who just now peed on pine needles is the same fellow who's writing this sentence in Baltimore on 10 June 1991, with the very pen
that he lost overboard in Queenstown Creek a few nights ago —
12 October 1992. Do I get the idea? And shall we get on with the
show?

Jay himself makes no move to leave but extends his arm like an
usher toward the juniper screen as toward a stage curtain. The old
picnic table is there, I'm half relieved to see, but no Jill, and she
must have taken the empties and the orange foam sleeves with her.
Hang a left in the neighborhood of that table, Jay instructs me,
and I should see a wooden footbridge over another part of that
same little creek that I forded earlier in this interlude. My twin

waits for me across that bridge. As he understands the scenario, he himself will see me again farther along, when the time comes. "Ciao now, Oatmeal."

Both the wry expression of farewell and the nickname are so familiar and so long unused between us — the former from early-undergraduate days, when we thought it as "cool" to flavor our speech with foreignisms as we later thought it gauche; the latter a childhood tease to be later explained (I sometimes called him "Wordy," to tease his reticence) — that I'm suddenly on the threshold of tears. So many times he and I have parted company, sans handshake, much less abrazo.

I hope you're . . . *okay*, Wordy, I manage to say.

He regards me. "That makes two of us."

You're . . . every important male friend I ever had.

"Plus a few you didn't have, right? Plus imaginary ones you wish you'd had, plus maybe a touch of Marley's ghost. The usual mix."

Okay: altered egos, like all close friends. Counterselves.

"*And with a friend like me*, et cetera? Hey —" He fishes into a side pocket of his damp jeans. "We almost forgot your passport."

He presents it held delicately upright with three fingertips of his left hand. The talisman swims through my tears as if I had, after all, snorkeled it up from the bottom of Queenstown Creek.

Ah, Jay!

"Ah-ah," he chides, withdrawing my lost Parker just out of reach. "Not till we've briefed you. It *looks* like your precious pen, right? It may even *write* like your precious pen. But what we have here, says the script, is a super-high-tech, made-in-Japan *replica* of your precious pen. Or maybe it's your precious pen itself, sea-changed into a solid-state, hypertech, multifunction *ree*mote, okay? And not to be deployed before checking out the user's manual."

He proceeds — Who can tell how straightforwardly? — with that checkout. Filling this souped-up pen I should now consider as "loading the program," so to speak, with an "ink" ("to be supplied") home-brewed, my friend solemnly declares, of sweat and tears and tidewater, the sexual fluids of both sexes, and, well, home brew: in short, "the usual mix," not to be loaded until I'm on that footbridge. The clouded gray glass stone set into the pen's cap-top I am invited to regard as a super-duper laser holograph, and its arrow-shaped clip as the notorious Arrow of Time. "Once the fun starts," I am to place the cap in normal writing position on the barrel butt for Forward, remove it for Freeze Frame (*"so to speak,* so to speak"), and recap for . . . Recap? Anyhow, not to worry: The program is alleged to be user-friendly, even user-seductive; Jay doesn't doubt I'll quickly get the hang of it, late as I was in coming to word processors, VCRs, telephone-answering machines, and the like, and stubbornly as I've stuck by This Old Pen. We are, after all, talking metaphors.

I reach again — gratefully, unquestioningly — and again he tantalizes. "You think it's free, man?"

Come on, Jay. It's paid for.

"You wish. Your watch, please. Not *my* idea."

I understand, of course, having invented this device myself for my time-tripping *Last Voyage* novel. Reluctant but willing, I hand over my trusty sailor's wristwatch: rotatable bezel, twenty-four-hour dial, case waterproof to a hundred meters. I even kiss it hasta la vista — Why didn't I you, dearest shipmate? — trusting now its return to me at this adventure's farther end.

"What a sentimentalist." Jay pockets my watch and this time genuinely proffers the pen. "Time for writing, okay? Ciao now, old buddy. Auf Wiedersehen."

In his gruff tone I hear the familiar mix of goodwill and irony, even sarcasm: affection with a chip on its shoulder, which my friend himself, when I once taxed him with it, dubbed his "friend-chip." I take dear Pumblechook with my own left hand and deliberately offer him my right. Jay parries with a smile, twitches his freckled nose (a boyhood tic that I had forgotten), and thrusts both of his hands into the hip pockets of his jeans.

"Time to turn yourself around, comrade," he advises me. "Turning time around seems to be the name of this game." Serious but wry as ever, his voice is behind me now. "You've taken the first step already, no? Forward to Square One. Don't look back."

ACT 1

Look at us:

"Look at us."

Her voice a head-shaking sigh, with her free left hand Jill indicates the baby twins before us, life-size in faded black and white — Two years old? — rather stiffly embracing for some camera on a three-dimensional but featureless light-gray beach or rivershore. The darker-gray water beyond is riffled to crested wavelets by what my sailor's eye now recognizes as a ten- to twelve-knot breeze, although nothing's moving. In the "picture," chubby-faced and birthmarked Jack stands wincing cameraward, an unyielding little post hugged by more demonstrative (or more directable) Jill in . . . 1932? Spring or fall of the year, my sister now infers from our matching lightweight sweaters and knit caps. Regarding our near but so-distant selves from "offstage," she hugs me lightly with her right arm — and gets from her normally affectionate twin no more reciprocation just now, sixty years later, than she got on that lost afternoon Back Then. I'm too preoccupied with *us* — and *US* — to pay attention yet to "us."

Because just look at us: In the single page-turn since "Interlude," per Jay Scribner's delphic instructions I've crossed that momentous footbridge (aria to come). What was to happen there — and more! — has happened, and has vastly though by no means totally eased my spirit with respect to what's at hand. On the bridge's farther side, as foreappraised by Jay's . . . ghost? . . . I found duly waiting for me my twin — or some viable projection thereof, indistinguishable by yours truly from the original — ready to tour-guide me through Act One of this floating opera, or the "first island" of My Story.

I wondered aloud to her then: First Island?

"Don't ask *me*." Good-humored impatience, impatient good humor, whichever; I know the tone. She flicked her cigarette-end into the street. We are, somehow, no longer in the lower-Dorchester marshes, if we ever were; we're on the sidewalk before 301 Aurora Street, East Cambridge, Maryland, USA, Earth, Solar System, Galaxy, Universe, the concrete slabs dappled gray and white *like old saltines*, I used to think: the saltines that "Dee-Mom," our dour Germanic paternal grandma, gave her twin grandkids to teethe on as we sat side by side in our double stroller, dressed for picture-taking in our matching light-gray sweaters and knit caps. . . .

Vertigo!

Grown-up Jill — growing-*old* Jill, my sexagenarian coeval — gave me a quick hello-hug, this one reciprocated by her brother.*

"Something to do with your fountain pen, is all *I* know," she offers. "Are you getting the hang of it?"

Yes and no. I will, of course; I know that now. But you have to understand. . . . What am I saying? You *do* understand —

"Don't bet on it."

I mean understand how I'm feeling, Jill. You've *lost* your partner; I've only lost track of mine — temporarily, I'm assuming, or I'd be a lot less coherent than I'm being. But who knows? Do *you* know, by the way?

"Nope. I just work here." There was in her tone just a

---

*Chronologically prior but narratively posterior to the hug of some paragraphs past, was this one a reaction to distracted that? Vertigo. But the time sequence in Act One's opening is likely to remain a touch vertiginous until I get the hang of things. I have crossed that footbridge; I'm with my twin, reviewing with her a scene from our childhood while I review with you my rejoining her on the bridge's far side — and I've yet to rehearse my singular meeting with a different Her on that singular bridge itself. Vertigo! But vertiginous Time is the very medium that floats this opera.

touch . . . not of indifference, certainly, but of the moral high ground of having suffered worse, and earlier.

Yes and no, I was saying, about getting the hang of what's going on here. *No*, in the first and final senses: Fine-tuning the metaphorical mechanics of this Parker *ree*mote, as Jay called it, will take some practice. Don't be surprised if things go a touch chaotically for a while. . . .

"I s'pose we'll just learn as we go along."

I looked for evidence that my twin, not by habit a reader of poetry, was consciously echoing the Roethke line. Saw none. And *no*, too (I went on), in the bottom-line sense of my understanding what's happening here *really*, and where it's going, and what it means. But between that top line and that bottom, yes, I have some sense of what's afoot: the passage out of time, tourist-visa to the Axis Mundi, etc. Remind me to sing you a few bars of my Urmyth aria, I told her, when I've acclimatized a bit.

"Over *my* head."

Come on, Sis: You've been saying that ever since the hormones hit us at age thirteen. As if we didn't have the same stuff upstairs: the same gray matter.

"Maybe. But who went to Johns Hopkins and who went to secretarial school?"

I let that pass, busy musing that just as I had said "the same gray matter," I'd registered that the mottled sidewalk under our feet — its squares heaved so familiarly out of level by the maple roots beneath that we had given names to the major bumps as we tricycled over them: Ralphs' Bump, Leaps' Bump, Moores' Bump, after the neighbors' houses they happened to front — along with our whole 3-D Aurora Street surround, flicked erratically from "color" to "black and white": full color when maple leaves and Depression-era cars and figures were in motion, B&W when (presumably by some pen-fiddling on my part) the "frame" "froze" — always the scene of some old photo from the family archive. One more aspect that I was getting the hang of, I supposed, of this *This Is Your Life: The Walk-Through Laser-Hologram Video* that I appear to have gotten myself involved in. Yet another such aspect is that I hear myself now — heard myself then, back at the chro-

nological opening of Act One — no longer addressing "you"-my-
mate, my (temporarily!) lost Reality Principle, my sine qua non,
my love, but rather "you" the reader, whoever you are,* just as in
any other of my fictions.

That realization stopped me cold. It stops me again now, and
the scene goes gray from some distracted pen-push: the freeze-
framed water, the beach or rivershore, baby Jill hugging unrespon-
sive baby Jack. Small wonder that the little chap has gone rigid
and winces usward out of the scene: Something in his two-year
old gray matter has whispered Don't look now, kid, but you're
stranded.

"Look at us."

I will. Directly. After this recitative retrospect:

Retrospect: "If — when, pen in hand"

If — when, pen in hand, at Interlude's end I exited that grove
of spooky junipers and white cedars, looked leftward from that
moss-grown picnic table as directed, and saw in plain view close
by not only a footbridge that I had somehow failed to note before
but, more remarkably, that it was an old-fashioned *covered*
bridge — if then I had turned to protest to Jay Wordsworth Scribner that there are in fact no covered bridges in Dorchester County,
Maryland, in 1992, would the grove have been still there? Perhaps.
Would whom or what I'm calling Jay Scribner have been still in
it? Less likely, perhaps. But had I done so and had they been, I can
imagine Jay raising one left-hand finger at a time, his right teasing
my wristwatch in his pocket as he set me straight:

"*A,* my friend: There are no animated ghosts of drowned imaginary pals to be found in these parts, either, outside of fiction. *B*
and *C:* Who says you're in these parts these days (I mean Dorchester County, Em Dee) and/or that these days are still Nineteen
Ninety plus Two? Me, I could swear I just heard the Great Crash
of Twenty-Nine off yonder, unless it was your parents' bed-slats
letting go — young Georgia and Whitey bonking upstairs at Three

---

*You're me just now, as I read this footnote freshly penned in Baltimore on 3
October '91. Vertigo.

Oh One Aurora, while the Twenties roar their last! And *D* (for *Dumkopf*): You've blown it, boy, by looking back this way instead of going on to meet your better half on that bridge. Tant pis for you."

Therefore I didn't — didn't look back, didn't protest, didn't imagine Jay's wiseass reply.* I was instead simply stopped in my tracks, not by the surprising sight of a weathered but sturdy old covered footbridge bridging this new bend in whatever creek, but by a smiting concern for *you* (we know which You) in the predicament that I feel responsible for having gotten us into by . . . by being who I am; by imagining all this; by penning such fell sentences as these with this old pen.

"Covered shmovered!" I hear my imagination cry: "Fussbrücke schmussbrücke! Where am I? And *where are you?*"

My eyes watered the Parker out of focus; I felt at once like kissing it hello (as I had lately kissed my watch good-bye) and like flinging it back into the creek, any creek. Of what earthly use was it to me, sans She?

No sign of sister over there; I doubt I could have made her out through that obscure tunnel in any case, and in any case it wasn't *that* She that I was looking for. Dizzy, stricken, I was obliged to sit on that everdamp picnic bench to steady myself, my back against the green-black table edge. I stared stunned at the capped old instrument I held in the fingertips of both hands, cap-top left, barrel-butt right. My eyes squeezed shut. I rocked, I *davened* like a praying Hasid in my crisis of concern.

Then, out of an impulse — call it a *com*pulse — deeper even than grief, almost angrily I opened my eyes, yanked off the pencap, and winced at the pair of parts, parallel now, ready for reconnection in whichever mode. (I repeat the action here at my Baltimore Invention table, Monday 7 October '91, to feel how it would feel.) Unimaginable, to carry on! On the very cusp of my recapping

---

*To which I now hear him add this *E*: "A covered *foot*bridge? Weren't bridges covered to keep horses from bolting as they crossed?" But a covered footbridge is what's before me, up there in the text.

it, however, as if from the dark interior of that unlikely bridge, I heard (I hear) *you* calling me.

I hear you call, essential partner, as I've heard you call to me a thousand times through the rooms of our lodgings owned and rented, here and there, over the years of our partnership. None of your numberless, ever-evolving pet names for your mate this time; you call from in there the straightforward interrogative given name that signals measured concern, means business. At sound of it, a sound comes from me, involuntarily — your name, to be sure, but fraught with much else — and my call so mixes with the repeat of yours that this time I can't tell but what yours *is* mine, reverberant. Or, it occurs to me, perhaps this one's my sister's after all, or perhaps some older summoner's: my mother, say, calling her kids in from Aurora Street; who knows who.

Anyhow, it's *me* calling now, calling *you* as I spring from that bench, pen in right hand, cap in left, and, calling you, call myself forward into the cover of that bridge, where . . .

Where, half framed, half silhouetted by the square of afternoon light at its farther end, I see what I recognize to be not the second-person pronoun I'm calling you by, but its antecedent and true referent, whom in unspeakable relief I hurry to embrace.

"So what exactly happened in there?"

The voice is Jill's, but the question is mine, I realize, on behalf of all reasonable readers. I put it to my imagination, which replies . . .

Listen: I'm not being coy. I am, however, constrained to speak in images and to choose my words carefully. My summoner was whom I recognized her to be: my missing shipmate, Reality Principle, muse personified . . . in her aspect as my muse. We embraced, to put it mildly. She reassured me — vastly, vastly, although it was not in her considerable power to remove my apprehensions as to either what lay behind or what lies ahead. She encouraged me to go forward with . . . with this going back, I could say, in Jay Scribner's half-teasing terms, or (in my own) with this most considerable *What if* of my what-iffing career: What if, some October down the line, she and I were to set out in a certain humor on an impulsive late-season cruise to nowhere special, and (heaven forfend) . . . ?

"In short, let's say she filled your pen."

She tendered me my ink, let's say — to which her own contributions are major. But I filled old Pumblechook myself, as I have ever done, like a seasoned lab-techie drawing a blood sample, while she held the cap. Then I wiped the point (my pen-wipe, faute de mieux, my own left-hand fingers), took back that cap, fitted it in its working place, and let my faithful implement lightly assume as of itself its Ready position against the callosities of our joint making. I held my friend then by her shoulders (see how she fades now in the telling, from second-person back to third) and kissed her (*You*! Come back!) a much more easeful though far from easy au revoir, knowing better now how things stand. Following then "Time's arrow" on that pen-cap-clip, per program (it points to the pen's own moving point: to *this* point, this, this), my imagination turned as difficult a turn as it has ever turned and strode figuratively forward, friction free, away from Her, back toward where my time began.

On with the past:
    "*Our* time."

Right you are, Sis; sorry there. That first-person plural, however, was still half singular back then, like chestnuts two to a hull, each flattened to a hemisphere.

"Say what?"

Let it go. In fact, my skull *isn't* quite symmetrical; pressed out of round, I like to suppose, either by overpacking in Georgia's womb — we both were eight-pound-plus newborns: Seventeen pounds of baby in there, and nobody suspected twins! — or by insufficiently frequent crib-turning in our infancy, when 301 Aurora suddenly had its hands full. When my hats feel straight, they aren't. Are yours?

"Never noticed. And with those knit caps, who can tell?"

Speaking of which, look at us: "strandees on that vast desert island called the world." Don't say "Say what?"; I'm quoting from

my recentest, which I wonder whether you've read. Anyhow, I'm
not necessarily *saying* all these words; I'm running on to myself,
still nervous about what's going on here and upset by that covered-
footbridge scene, consoling as it was in several respects. I take
what comfort I can in what I know about the nature of these off-
the-chart excursions; I understand better now, for example, what
it meant that I "wasn't quite myself" at Langford Creek on Columbus Day morning 1992, et cetera. And "she" herself — my real
other half for the past two decades — she herself reminded me,
back on that bridge, that the time I'm moving in here may not be
her time, and that while she and I truly are "one person" in our
voyage through life, pardon the cliché, there are side trips that
each of us must make solo. I believe and accept that; no doubt
we've made minor such excursions already in our shared past,
although I can't recall them, to address matters that the most loving helpmeet in the world can't help us meet. This present business
may take longer — or it may be done with "in no time." All the
same, meanwhile —
    "Whoops."

Prospective arietta: "Whoops indeed: This new old pen"
    Whoops indeed: This new old pen, the hang of which I thought
I was getting, has inadvertently fast-forwarded us a couple of
years, into Franklin Roosevelt's first term and the depths of the
Great Depression. By the time I manage to freeze-frame us (i.e., to
cap Time's flow by diddling this pen-cap thus and so), the twins
are maybe four years old. Improbable instrument! And yet . . .
    To us diehard word-by-worders, the trouble with such high-
tech illusions as those multisensory hyperworlds envisioned
(enheard, ensmelled, entasted, enfelt) by computer simulation is
that their wraparound virtual reality is *real* virtuality, really appre-
hended by our physical senses thus elaborately deceived. Whereas
poor good old fiction, such as good old Pumblechook used to pen
one friction-free word at a time, hath not sight nor sound nor
smell nor taste nor feel, only the names therefor. Its virtuality is
virtual, not real, and by virtue of that second-order virtuality it
transcendeth mere physical sensation to tell us what things look/

sound/smell/taste/feel *like*; it accesseth the worlds inside our head and under our skin — worlds at least as real and considerable as those reported by our gullible senses — and it so doeth by no trompe l'oeil (l'oreille/le nez/la langue/la touche) but by straightforward address to the imagination: "Once upon a time," etc.

"We are, after all, talking metaphors," J. W. Scribner cautioned or assured me when he re-presented my sea-changed instrument with a quick and possibly tongue-in-cheek mode d'emploi. As I pen this arietta with my old real Parker (well before the fact of its fictive loss and restoration), I begin to grasp in prospect not this new one's barrel but its point — to be sung further shortly,* when I have its hang.

Meanwhile, a quick rewind, and

"Whoops"

Whoops indeed. By the time I manage to freeze-frame, the twins are maybe four years old — it's a series of frame-by-frames, actually, and quite endearing, actually, in the side yards of 301 Aurora and our grandparents' house next door, "up on the corner" of Aurora Street and Maryland Avenue. We wear the same clothes in all four shots: light sweaters again, though not the same ones as back on that beach; socks and sandals; short pants for him (nobody called them "shorts" in those days), short dress and large hair bow for her. We're a touch dressed up for the photo session, in similar but, thanks be, not matching outfits to match our lamentable nursery-rhyme names. *My* sweater has a dark vertical offset stripe with a motif of . . . Can those be sailboats? Sailboats they are, fuzzed as is the focus and grainy the "print": a row of sloops or cutters stands under all plain sail toward my pendant left arm while with my right I sort-of-hold Jill's hand in this first one (our expressions engagingly serious) and collar her in this second, the pair of us amused at our own antics. In this third, some headless elder woman stands on the background wooden steps before the latticed rear porch of 301 — It will be Mother's

*Fast-forward, s.v.p., to aria "What I've noticed, reader," a few pages farther on. Or just take it word by word.

mother, "Mommy" Simmons, who lived her widowed last years
with us and, family tradition has it, unfairly favored Jack over
Jill and both of us over our three-year-older brother. Appropriate
therefore, I suppose, that I'm foregrounded alone in this one,
astride . . . my beloved hobbyhorse! Sturdy, nameless sire of all
I've ridden since, it had a gallop that springs even now to my muscles' memory. But was the thing dark green? Dark blue? Dark red?
Can't remember, and can't bring back the animated color of some
pages past. Mounted, I wince into the sun and barely smile,
whereas in this fourth and last of the series —

What are we doing this for, Jill?

"Don't you remember? It's Dee-Mom and Dee-Pop's yard, up
against their white picket fence, and my guess is that Aunt Roon
and Uncle Doc or some of the other New Jersey people have come
down on vacation and that's why we're dressed up for picture-
taking, 'cause Mother and Dad never took pictures. But something
rubbed me the wrong way in this one, and I wouldn't turn around
and face the camera with you and Bill; that's why you're grinning.
They coaxed and coaxed, and then gave up and took the picture
as a joke."

Not what I meant, but let it go. I remember all that very well,
and plenty more, though not what it was that's making you contrary. I remember that Mickey Mouse sweatshirt Bill's wearing. . . . Were they called sweatshirts in 1934? That would be the
year they finished building the Choptank River bridge, that Dee-
Pop used to walk us down to watch being built, and he complained that you ran too far ahead while I stayed with him,
well-behaved Deutscheskind that I was — and once he hand-
carved me a dandy wooden train wheel to replace a busted one on
my toy locomotive; I can see it plain as day, no bigger than a half-
dollar but complete with a perfect flange and low-relief spokes,
and that's about all I *do* remember about Herr Dee-Pop except
that when he died they laid him out in the Good Parlor up on the
corner, and either we were allowed to go in and look or else we
sneaked in; anyhow, the first deadie we'd ever seen, and the parlor
was chilly, and I remember he had this brown stuff stuffed in his
nostrils, as if they'd sealed his big nose with wax. President Roo-

sevelt sailed over on his yacht to dedicate the New Bridge when
its lights were finally installed, and even though they tore down
the old freight house at Long Wharf for fear some anti–New
Dealer might hide in there and take a potshot at him, he never
came ashore, and nobody got to see him. The *Potomac* anchored
out by the channel, and they broadcast FDR's dedication through
loudspeakers on Long Wharf, and then he or somebody pushed a
button to light the bridge lights and everybody said *Aaah* and back
he sailed across the Bay to Washington. Poor Bill: He must be
seven already there, second grade, but this is the earliest shot I
remember of the three of us, and I see Trouble written all over it.
Look how cutesie you and I are dressed, and how rough-and-
tumble his clothes are: a normal kid called in for one shot from
playing with the other kids on the block, while *we* go from pose
to pose. Look how *regular* his face is — an ordinary second
grader, out in the neighborhood — and how . . . spoiled? . . . no,
not spoiled, but vulnerable, delicate, sort-of-sissy-looking, anyhow *sheltered* our faces are. Mine, I guess I mean; yours is okay.

"You're reading too much into the picture. Bill's seven; we're
four."

But when we're seven and he's ten, the difference will be even
sharper. Let's see if I can fast-forward a few years. . . .

"Not yet! I like seeing these old scenes in this new way, though
my memory's getting to be as bad as Mother's was. Let's go back
before we go forward."

Back to my question, then, if I can keep it in focus —

"What's the earliest scene? Where does this show start?"

Neither of those is my question.

"Okay: They're mine."

And quite in order. What's your earliest memory, Jill?

"I don't remember. Standing on that beach, I guess — with
Aunt Fanny and Uncle Edgar? But it's probably the photographs
I'm remembering."

I "rewind" to the shoreside sequence. Look how spiffy Mother's
brother is in this one, squatting behind us in his and the century's
early thirties: suit and tie and Panama hat and cigarette holder, on

the beach. The Depression doesn't seem to have hit Edgar Simmons yet, but his melanoma will have been at work already under that coatsleeve. What did he do for a living, by the way?

"Something with railroads? Insurance? All I know is that he and Aunt Fanny favored me 'cause Mommy Simmons favored you, and that the New Jersey relatives favored Bill 'cause the family's first grandchild went from all the limelight to nearly none when Jack and Jill upstaged him."

He had his innocent revenge in advance, however, hanging those names on us.* So there's the diagram of forces. But we're skipping over Family Mysteries: What exactly did Uncle Edgar do for a living over there in West End? Whatever happened to Pop Simmons, whom we don't even have a shot of? Why did Mother always refuse to talk about her down-county childhood? What happened to Aunt Roon's first marriage, and Aunt Rose's marriage, and Cousin Eleanor's first marriage, in a town where and a time when divorce was all but unheard of?

"Abandonment wasn't unheard of, but I guess neither one was spoken of. Hey, you're getting the hang of that *ree*mote now, and I can't even set the clock on my VCR. Does our story start on this beach? And I'm supposed to remind you not to forget your earliest memory."

Or my basic question. My earliest memory is visual, but not photographic; I'm sure of that, because there's motion and color. I'm on the front porch of 301 Aurora, summertime, either on the glider or in a baby carriage, anyhow lying on my back in the corner of the porch where the glider always was. I'm looking up and out through the porch screen at the leaves of the big silver maples of Aurora Street moving in a breeze, their dark green tops and light undersides. It's an agreeable memory, Jill, from god knows how early: tranquil, crystal clear, and empty of significance. The flickering leaves have caught my eye. I'm not thinking anything about them; I'm just comfortably *registering* them there on the glider,

---

*"Now we have a Jack and Jill," Brother Bill is alleged to have declared, gamely, when told of his siblings' birth.

mesmerized, as my mind's eye's doing right here right now. And it's the opening deposit in my memory bank. Did I ever tell you that I have flying-dreams maybe once a year?

"Nope."

They're the classic flap-your-arms-and-levitate kind that Freud says are exhibitionist, but I happen to know mine aren't. Nobody's watching, and I'm not showing off; it's just easy and delightful to flap arms and levitate, as if the air were water. Anyhow, in these dreams it's always summertime on Aurora Street, and I'm never flying high — just up among the maple leaves in front of 301, hovering in the treetops, enjoying the elevated view of our street and our house.

"Where am I?"

Change the emphasis, and you've got my basic question: Where *are* we? I don't mean in this scene or that; I mean where are we here, *among* these scenes?

"Say what?"

What I've noticed, Jill . . . What I'm trying to say —

"Was it Mother or Mommy Simmons that used to say 'If you can't say it, sing it'?"

Aria: "What I've noticed, reader"

What I've noticed, reader, is that there seems to be no scene-between-the-scenes; no theater, so to speak, where this show is taking place. My sister and I stroll amid these tableaux vivants and freeze-frames of our East Cambridge childhood as though through some high-tech lifesize 3-D projection of a sort not yet invented as I draft this aria (Columbus Day eve, 1991). We are at once *in* the scenes and apart from them: an ongoing "out-of-body experience" in which the bodies are ours (and the family's) of the 1930s, speeding from scene to scene through their black-and-white lives more swiftly than figures in an old silent movie. So far as I've discovered, my sea-changed Parker has no normal Play mode: In its Ready position, Time's arrow streaks forward through the past; when I uncap, the scene freezes, and it rapid-rewinds when I recap. I mean to experiment with this ground conceit after I've acclimatized a bit, for my strong sense is that this can't be all there is to it, and/ or that I haven't yet got it quite right. Earlier on, e.g., I observed that the scenes were in color during the fast-forwards and went black and white when I stopped the action, but now it's B&W all the way; when I attempted, some pages past, to put my hobby-horse in motion in order to recall its color, the dear thing galloped dark gray both forth and back.* Only we twin sexagenarian inter-lopers maintain our natural color and solidity as we stroll through the arrested scenes or stand dizzied during the "rewinds" and "fast-forwards" like spectators in a runaway cyclorama.

It is my hunch that despite my knowing the conceit's me-chanics to be metaphorical, I'm still handling them too literally; too . . . mechanically. All this Jay-Scribnerish rigmarole of pen-cap positions and the like is really no more than a manner of speaking, meant to suggest a manner of going and of telling; *that*'s what I must get the hang of. I believe that I understand another aspect now of that covered-footbridge scene: What drives this opera is *vocation*; the ineffable, indispensable upper-case Calling. Life-experience — shaped by memory and shaping memory, molding imagination and by imagination molded in coaxial esemplasy — is *called forth* into language by the fortuitous confluence of innate gift, assiduous practice and training (especially self-training), and temperamental vocation: the Calling, in itself nothing, but without which nothing.

That said, however, among the several things that still puzzle me is the nature of our ontological space, so to speak. I mean the grown-up, here-and-now Jill's and Jack's: what continuitous ground we stand on as the scene around us vertiginously shifts. Without asking or experimenting, I understand that the people and objects in these scenes are, from our point of view at least, mere images, projections insubstantial as light — although some-

---

*At the same time, I discovered that my approaching the horse's rider did not extend the scene's field to complete the headless woman on the back-porch steps. Nor did I, turning, see the photographer and the reciprocal perspective of our yard — merely the space of lawn that I had crossed and blackness beyond it, on the near edge of which Jill waited.

thing tells me it's *words* they're made of.* No use trying to address them — and yet surely what we're involved in must be more than a tour through the family album from which the scenes thus far derive. My guide or companion, on the other hand, is touchable and be-touched-byable, Q.E.D., as is her twin astray in Time's funhouse — although neither of us can imaginably be her/his "real" self: the Jill who minds her business over on the Eastern Shore, the Jack who pens this aria in the city across the Bay.

A better way to put my question, then, maybe (and I break off this aria here to do it), is

Back to the question:
Who *are* you, Jill?

My twin or her likeness looks me straight in the face and dryly drawls, "I thought you'd never ask. Could you put us on Hold, please, before I get seasick?"

Sorry.

Alas for coherent inquiry, I seem to have capped my Parker in order to deliver myself of "What I've noticed, reader." Throughout that aria, the action all about us — our silent past — zipped backward from the shoreside sequence at an ever-accelerating, soon unfollowable clip. But even as I make now to uncap, the motion stops of itself at a scene I recognize at once from my favorite photograph of our parents, and instead of replying to my question, Jill says tenderly, "Look at them."

With pleasure. Young John Jacob "Whitey" B. — hardworking proprietor of Whitey's Candyland, Est. 1922 — and Georgia Vivian Simmons, either in mid-courtship or not long wed, pose nattily for their joint portrait some years after the sweetshop/soda fountain's establishing. On what must be a backless bench at the base of a large tree (its sunlit scaly bark is a giveaway: the silver maples of Aurora Street), the pair sit close but not quite touching,

---

*I say "without experimenting": Walking up to Uncle Edgar, however, as he squatted behind baby us in that primeval beach scene, I impulsively "touched" his left shoulder (so it occurs to me now, or occurs to me to declare) as I asked Jill what the man used to do for a living. My hand passed right through.

he on stage left, she right, at a small angle to us, both figures truncated at mid-calf and slightly cropped at the outboard shoulder.
Georgia's hands nestle in her lap (Is she wearing a ring? Can't tell,
no matter how we shift our position). Whitey holds a cigarette in
the lean long fingers of his right hand, resting lightly on the top
knee of his crossed legs. His left hand is out of sight — on the
bench, it appears, between him and his girlfriend/fiancée/wife/
whichever, and hidden from our ring-seeking view both by Georgia's shadow on his sleeve and by the nature of these projections.
He wears a three-piece pinstripe suit, appearently light gray — the
vest's top button open, a watchchain threaded through the next
buttonhole down, a handkerchief-corner peeping from the coat's
breast pocket — a dress shirt with French cuffs, a short thick bow
tie of indeterminable pattern, and a light felt hat with dark band
(my guess is that under that hat he's bald already, as was I by age
thirty). Except for that hat, that watch chain, and possibly that
style of bow tie, his outfit would not look odd if worn these nearly
seventy years later, so comparatively little has this category of
western male dress changed. Georgia's, on the other hand, is pure
period late-1920s/early-1930s, no further fine-tunable because of
my ignorance of couture, of whatever fashion-lag there was in
those days between small-town and city women of the middle
classes, and of the degree of my mother's attention back then to
dressing in fashion. On reflection, I imagine that last to have been
at least average within her limited means and sophistication, for
at the time my parents met she had moved from down-county up
to Cambridge and worked as a milliner, the highlight of whose job
was to take the excursion steamer to Baltimore from time to time
in order to note the new season's hat styles and copy them for the
homefolk. Although we children don't remember her ever men-
tioning details of these excursions — where in the city she ate,
whether and where she slept over, what she did for amusement on
the daylong boat trips and downtown — our mother recalled the
fact of them with wistful pleasure for the rest of her memory's
life, which ended a considerable while before her body's. My impression is that they were her brightest recollection of young-
womanhood.

To a more knowledgeable viewer, therefore, it might be historically revealing that Georgia's hat here, doubtless fabricated by its
wearer along with the rest of her demure ensemble, is a dark straw
affair, round-crowned and considerably brimmed, its circular rim
turned up on the side facing us and perhaps down on the far side,
perhaps not (the chiaroscuro lighting makes it difficult to say), and
that she wears it cocked down on the right and forward almost to
her eyebrows to expose a short wave of hair behind; that the sharp
shadow of that hat on the maple bark suggests a perky flare of stiff
netting behind the crown, invisible from in front. . . . What are
those called?

"You're asking me?"

Why not? Don't you wish you knew the name of everything in
the world?

"I wouldn't remember them."

Anyhow, the hemline of her dark, conservative outfit is not
flapper-short but well below the bottom of the tight-shot scene.
Most pertinently, perhaps, her ensemble is set off by one of those
fox-fur scarves complete with heads, so popular in Whenever.
What at first I took for blemishes along the right edge of this projection I see now to be the little ears, muzzles, paws, and beady
glass eyes of the two or three red foxes whom I well remember
staring back at me from Mother's bedroom closet later in the
decade, when we used to sneak peeks to see what was what.

"You've decided it's the Thirties, then. I guess it looks that way
to me, too."

Almost. Georgia's getup certainly isn't Roaring Twentyish, but
who knows whether young married East Cambridge women wore
cloche hats and short beaded skirts like John Held Junior's cartoon
flappers? It's our folks' faces, their general air, that tell me they're
past the courtship stage and have a few things under their marital
belts. Their handsomeness is composed, mature; there's gravity in
their half-smile. The honeymoon is over. They're established in the
new house at 301 Aurora, next door to Dee-Mom and Dee-Pop,
and their first pregnancy has miscarried: *Infant of J.J. & Georgia
Barth*, her little gravestone reads, carved by her grandfather. Their

second hasn't; Herman William the Third's been born and is doing just fine, and so there go 1927 and '28. Mussolini and Stalin are in place; International Modernism is riding high; Lindbergh and Heisenberg have done their very different things. This is Labor Day weekend, Jill, 1929.

"Say what?"

Did you ever count back 266 days from our birthday? You never did? Count back 266 days from 27 May 1930 and you get Labor Day weekend, 1929 (3 September, actually; a Tuesday that year, actually — but 266 is just the statistical average pregnancy). For seven years, John J. has been working his butt off to keep his nickel-and-dime business afloat: eight in the morning till nine in the evening, six days a week and no vacations, selling Whitman's chocolates and Dolly Madison ice cream and sandwiches and Cokes. His chronic sinusitis has triggered the massive infection that left him three-quarters deaf; by all accounts a real sport in his twenties, with his boutonnieres and his red Ford roadster, now he'll never have a normal conversation for the rest of his life. Georgia's been working every bit as hard, keeping house and raising baby Bill and making kettles of soup every night for the store and hooking rugs and sewing window curtains and all her own clothes to save money. But they're still early-thirtyish, vitality to spare, and they're doing okay by local standards and their own. So here's a welcome break in the grind that hasn't ground them down yet — the Sunday, I'll bet it is, with the Monday holiday still ahead: a chance to get dolled up for church and then take a spin in the open red roadster even though it's unusually cool for the first weekend in September (that explains the wool suit and the fur neckpiece). Maybe they'll pose for a snapshot before or after, and then this evening enjoy a glass of beer or some of Dee-Pop's wine, that he makes from his own grapes in the long backyard of the corner house. Tomorrow morning they can sleep in again for a change, if young Herman William lets them. Nothing indolent, not to mention sybaritic; just a welcome half-hour or so of extra sack time like this morning's, when the daylight waked them as usual, but instead of hauling out and up and at 'em, they had leisure enough to stretch and sigh and snooze and then reach out to each other, and never mind the condoms way over there in the top drawer of the big armoire. . . .

"Come on."

They don't know it yet, but that handsome fellow with his legs crossed and that attractive woman with hers pressed together and her hands clutched lightly in her lap are pregnant again: pregnant with *twins* this time, one month before the stock market crashes and the curtain comes down for keeps on the century's twenties and their own. Our clock has started, yours and mine. Time's begun.

"Uh-huh. How'd you find out that September Third was a Tuesday in Nineteen Twenty-Nine?"

Tricks of the trade.

"Did you allow for leap years, smarty, when you counted back through February?"

That's more like it. Did I need to?

"Four into Nineteen Thirty won't go; you're clear."

Here's a more prickly one: Does time begin at the moment of conception?

"I don't remember. But no matter how cool that weekend was, they wouldn't have their furs and woollies out of mothballs yet on Labor Day. This can't be early September."

Now your head's working, Jill. I just like to imagine all that. For all we know, this could be Columbus Day . . . or maybe October 27th, the Sunday before Black Tuesday. Georgia has missed two periods already, so they're pretty sure, and they want another kid. The Candyland's doing all right; President Hoover has assured them on the radio that the country's economy is fundamentally sound, and they don't play the market anyhow. The tough Tuesday for them will be one hour and twenty minutes after you're delivered next May 27th, when to old Doctor Wolff's surprise he finds that neither Georgia's labor nor his is done for the day. What a cluck.

"Everybody loved Doctor Wolff! And you're forgetting that you and I were delivered by different doctors. Old Doctor Steele delivered me while Doctor Wolff was en route to the hospital; he got there just in time for you."

Yes, well, anyhow. Georgia must've been a blimp by May Day; any small-town doctor worth his salt would've suspected twins and checked with his stethoscope. And then when double-delivery time came, instead of doing an episiotomy they let 'er rip, old Steele and/or old Wolff, and she was never sutured up until she had her hysterectomy, years later! Cluck cluck cluck.

"Good enough for us homefolks, I guess. *Does* time begin at conception?"

Thanks for asking. Our family's time begins indistinctly in 1881, when fifteen-year-old Herman B. leaves the village of Schmölln, in the Herzogtum of Sachsen-Altenburg, and crosses unescorted on North German Lloyd's from Bremerhaven to Baltimore — steerage fare twenty dollars, bring your own food except for a barrel of pickles at one end of the deck and a barrel of salt herring at the other — since there are no family records or transmitted memories earlier than that. Young Herm the First is more or less adopted by German-Americans on Aliceanna Street in Fells Point in Baltimore and apprenticed to the stonecutting trade. He marries Anna Derr of that neighborhood, makes his away across the Chesapeake to help build the Episcopal Church on High Street in Cambridge, and stays on to set up what must have been a fairly prosperous stonecutting business of his own — tombstones, cornerstones, mantelpieces, lintels and doorsills — since he and Dee-Mom built that not-so-bad frame house in brand-new East Cambridge and raised six children in it, most of them born before the century turned.

"You say prosperous, but Dad remembered eating lard sandwiches and snitching turnips from Old Man Wright's field down by the rivershore."

Boys will be Lausbüben. But he also remembered homemade wursts and sauerbraten and five kinds of grapevines in the backyard and German farm families gathering there on Sunday afternoons. Look at the pair of them here in their lawn chairs in their old age, surrounded by us grandchildren. Dour German faces and comfortable paunches — it isn't affluence, but it's solid bürgerlich comfort.

"No running water or central heating. Outside privy. Chickens in the backyard."

No car or telephone, either, but a summer kitchen on the back porch and two other porches for sitting, plus the living room and the good parlor and three or four bedrooms and a row of out-buildings and a white picket fence. They were nineteenth-century Dorfbewohnern who never moved out of the 1890s.

"Say — ?"

Villagers, reasonably prosperous within the parameters.

"And yet Dad quit school at age sixteen to work in Charlie Corkran's soda fountain, down by the creek bridge. . . ."

While his older brother went off to the Maryland Institute of Art to become a sculptor, and his older sister went off to nursing school to become an R.N. My reading of it is that Whitey was Number Two Son. Like Herman Junior, he was put to work help-ing out in the stone shop after school when he was still a little boy, polishing flat marble surfaces with a heavy piece of railroad iron and a grinding compound. But on his very first day he mashed his finger with the iron, and Dee-Pop sent him home crying, and that was that for John J. and stonecutting, not to mention sculpture.

I've always been touched by that anecdote, Jill. As I see it, Uncle Herman and Aunt Roon are the favorites; they get to go away to school, and they never come back to stay. Herman fills the corner house with apprentice Beaux Arts statuary and then jobs around in the city until World War One, while Dad stays home and quits high school and works in Charlie Corkran's store, four blocks down the street. Both sons enlist to fight the Hun, and Dee-Pop turns the Kaiser's picture to the wall for the duration. Fair-haired Herman dies in France in the flu pandemic, and we don't get to find out whether he would've discovered Modernism and become a real sculptor or just have followed his father in the tombstone trade. Dropout Whitey comes home from military service next door in Virginia, opens his own soda fountain uptown, marries a local hatmaker, buys a house next door to the corner house, and dutifully sees his parents through their old age.

"*My* guess is that they loved him and he them."

No doubt you're right — though what comes to mind when I look at those stern faces is *duty* more than love. I don't remember any *warmth* from that pair when we were kids. Our visits up there were never more than dutiful except when Aunt Roon and Uncle Doc and the rest of the New Jersey relatives were on hand; we used to scram out of there as soon as Dee-Mom paid us our lemon-drop reward for coming to see her. Compare that to real grandparents and grandchildren! I don't remember any back-and-forthing between the two households. Did Dee-Mom and Dee-Pop ever come down to 301 for dinner? Did we ever do dinner with them or stay overnight in the corner house?

"Okay. But the whole New Jersey crowd *did* come down for holidays, and there was plenty of back-and-forthing then. We're probably forgetting stuff; we were still little kids when the old folks died. But I think you're right that there was nothing much between Mother and her parents-in-law."

I'd go further than that, Jill. The family genes are prevailingly undemonstrative, to the point of stolidity. There wasn't much between Whitey and his parents beyond genuine affectionate loyalty. There wasn't much between Whitey and *us* beyond genuine affectionate loyalty.

"I disagree. Anyhow, there's something to be said for affectionate loyalty."

There is indeed. So I speak for myself. But I'll sing for the two of us:

Interrupted aria: "Affectionate loyalty; benign passivity. The best complexion"

Affectionate loyalty; benign passivity. The best complexion that I can put on our parenting at 301 Aurora is that our father the sport — the gay blade who tooled through the Twenties in his red Ford roadster and took night swims with the New Jersey relatives down off the rivershore and enjoyed steamed-clam-and-hardcrab fests with the fellows from his store — was all but KO'd by the one-two punch of his sudden deafness and the Great Depression. He and Georgia lost their savings (we kids even lost our little ten-

and twenty-dollar accounts) in the 1933 Bank Holiday; they
would have lost the Candyland to mortgage foreclosure if the local
bankers hadn't understood that their only hope of eventually
recouping such loans was to let hardworking debtors like John J.
stay in business. So the guy worked and worked and worked,
and despite his deafness became a fixture in the community: a
successful merchant who chatted with his fellow townsfolk (in
raised voices) all day long; a volunteer fireman who responded
to fire calls at all hours of the day and night for decades (*"Fire
whistle, Dad!"* we learned to call out to him) and helped the down-
county communities organize their own volunteer companies; an
Orphans Court judge for Dorchester County who out of civic-
spiritedness and the need for a little extra cash first ran for that
elective office the year we twins were born and held it thereafter
for forty-eight years (forty-four as Chief Judge), a still-unbroken
record in the state of Maryland; impresario for years of Cambridge's annual Armistice Day parade, which under his organizing
became an event of regional renown. All this over and above those
sixty-hour weeks in the store: never a vacation-trip after his honeymoon, no hobbies or leisure pursuits beyond his civic activities,
no time for family recreation except our ritual Sunday drives —
always within the county, our mother at the wheel. Uptown to the
store after early breakfast and the morning newspaper; home for
supper and the evening newspaper; back to the store to close up;
home for a beer and a bit of reading, the eleven o'clock radio
news, and bed — from which, several times a week, he would be
roused by the fire sirens (*"Fire, Whitey!"* I can still hear Mother
call from beside him in bed, and he would stumble into his clothes,
blow his nose, and go off in our big LaSalle, his pride and joy).
On Sundays, Men's Bible Class at the neighborhood Methodist
church — out of propriety more than piety, I believe: Our parents
never "went to church"; God and religion played no part in our
home life; the spirit of the house was secular. Then Sunday dinner,
the family drive, three Sunday newspapers, a bit of work on the
property. All the while plagued by the sinusitis that at its most
severe had damaged his eardrums and at its least caused his nose

to run almost constantly until his death at eighty-five. Yet never (in our presence, anyhow) complaining of his lot — indeed, prevailingly cheerful; never cross with us children so far as any of us can recall (we were well-behaved kids, except for the continual squabbling between Bill and the twins), and, without prodding, uncritically supportive of our several interests and ambitions. To imagine John Jacob drunk, say, or abusive, or unfaithful, or in any way out of line is . . . unimaginable. Between our parents, although surely they must have had serious disagreements from time to time, never a quarrel that any of us can remember; no bickering or cold silences; not even brief displays of exasperation, that we can remember. Only consistent goodwill and good humor; affectionate loyalty; benign passivity — and, I daresay, very considerable fatigue as the years ground on.

The raising of us, auditor of this aria, fell altogether to Georgia, whose benignity was, in the early years at least, less passive. Frugal, hardworking, sweet-tempered, somewhat simpleminded perhaps and short-memoried, but long on patience and cheerfulness (her husband was alert, quick-witted, well informed, and sharp of memory up to his death), she saw to it that there was a piano in the house, for example, and money for lessons for us kids, and she played sheet music herself for pleasure and obliged us docile twins to practice regularly for years, often against our inclination (no dealing with stronger-willed Bill, on this and other fronts). She saw to it that we three were supplied with expensive encyclopedias and sent to Miss Ridah Collins's private kindergarten over in West End — no public kindergartens back there back then, and Miss Ridah's would prove to be my best education until Johns Hopkins — even though, in the lean Depression, she was obliged to relinquish her extension telephone to help pay the modest tuition. Between making and shlepping those kettles of soup for the store, doing the marketing, cooking, and other housework (aided, be it said, by her mother and a faithful maid we called Colored Mattie, to distinguish her from one of Whitey's sisters of the same given name), supervising our homework and adjudicating our frequent quarrels (never between us twins), and in later years working in

the store herself, she found time that our father couldn't or
wouldn't find actually to *do* occasional things with us, or at least
to put us in the way of their doing. She it is I remember lifting me
over the breakers at Ocean City before I grew large enough to
handle them unaided. Several times per summer week, when we
were too young for unsupervised swimming in the nearby Choptank, she drove us crosstown to the better rivershore beach in West
End and worked crossword puzzles in the pine-shaded car while
we twins romped in the warm tidewater (Where was Bill? Off
playing with his neighborhood friends, I suppose; anywhere but
with us). Most important, she was available for us to laugh and
argue with, complain to, interrogate and be interrogated by, try
out our attitudes and opinions on, and, as we grew older (it pains
me to recall), join in our father's good-humored but relentless
"razzing" of — a sometimes witty but most often heavyhanded
and reflexive raillery, the prevailing mode of our dinner-table talk,
whereof Mother was the standard, mock-exasperated but always
accepting butt: "I swear!" she would reply, or "That's a big not-
so!," or "I don't see how I've stayed married to him all these
years!" . . .

That ragging, broad sarcasm; that ponderous, pointless, typically raised-voiced teasing, as I have sung earlier, I associate not
with our household only but with us tidewaterfolk in general. I
am no expert on its sociology, but I hear redneckery in it: the caus-
tic banter of watermen's bars and blue-collar eateries, where the
barmaids and waitresses give as good as they get — though even
folk of characteristically finer, more soft-spoken sensibility will
often affect it in such company, not to seem "superior." I sometimes hear it in the houses of my siblings, good people both. My
hackles rise; I'm back at the dinner table in 301 Aurora; I programmatically will not join in.

Ah, well, so, there's the best complexion: an affectionate loyalty
that subsidized my first drum set when I took up jazz in my teens,
and put up with my noisy practicing in the extended living room
and with group rehearsals there when things reached that stage;
that helped support me through college (though scholarships,
musicianship, and other employment paid most of the freight);

that never discouraged my quixotic ambitions, first to be an orchestrator and then to be . . . a writer; that put up patiently with the airs and pretensions I brought home from the city, and managed to appear, perhaps even to be, more proud of than distressed by the distance I was putting between myself and them. It stings me to recall what sanctimonious-liberal grief I gave them during the local civil-rights ruckus of the 1960s, when Whitey's Candyland (on Race Street!) and the all-white clubbiness of his beloved Rescue Fire Company were obvious targets; my failures of historical and personal sympathy for a man of my father's generation and position, confronting sit-ins and incendiarism face-to-face while I tisked righteously from the bucolic white enclave of the Pennsylvania State University. Forgive me, Father (and Mother), for I sure did sin; my position was correct, but not my attitude.

There's my *up*-side view of our parenting. As for the down side —

Interruption:
"Do we have to hear the down side?"

Insistent aria: "Of course we do"
Of course we do, yea though I sing here for mine own ears alone. The bane of these nursery-rhyme twins' childhood was their older brother; yet it's evident in retrospect that that fellow was by no means a "bad boy," just an only child virtually orphaned by his siblings' birth. I must sing that I believe that our parents — out of ignorance, insensitivity, indifference, whatever — managed wretchedly their firstborn's radical status change. Granted that children (I've had three) have minds and wills and dispositions of their own, Brother Bill maybe more than most; granted that Doctor Spock wasn't around to help, and that *sibling rivalry* had yet to enter the East Cambridge vocabulary: Folk wisdom has nonetheless always recognized the phenomenon, and more capable folks would have taken steps to defuse it. Strained as the domestic system was by my unexpected appearance in it, our older brother should have been given more attention thereafter than he got — and been given it in our presence, at 301 Aurora, not up at the

corner house and off in New Jersey. The twins' act ought to have been broken up more, for the good of the order, to make us less of a world unto ourselves (our names, to start with, were an egregious misstep, and ought to have been changed to protect us innocents): less Jack and Jill, that brace of binary solipsists; more Jack and Bill, Bill and Jill, Jack *or* Jill with other kids our age. Okay, so there *weren't* any others our age near to hand, as it happened, except certain unacceptable roughnecks from Byrn and Henry streets and worse — the likes of bad Jerry Schreiber, soon to begin the action of this act — whereas proper Bill's-age boys and girls happened to be on hand. Okay, so the house had its hands full, and ours was an unsophisticated time and place, and worse things than sibling rivalry can happen to the best of parents. My sense remains, however, that little effort and no imagination was brought to the matter: It was let to get out of hand, to polarize and aggravate, each sib-side baiting and blaming the other; it marred our childhood and distorted both parties' personalities until Bill finished high school and left home. Indeed, although we've been cordial and reciprocally respectful in our adult life (and we are in substantial, head-shaking agreement concerning our case history), the fact is that between us yet there's a low-level voltage that impedes our being ever really close, not to mention temperamental differences that themselves are in part the consequence of our sore upbringing. Forgive me, Herman William III, those bluff and bullying elder brothers here and there in my fiction. The problem wasn't your fault, lad — at least by no means all your fault.

I sing next Dad's deafness, the third great debit entry in this accounting, after the mutually reinforcing ones of too-close twinship and elder-sibling rivalry. Who can fault a no-fault infection, back when even Old Doctor Wolff, cluck cluck, would no doubt have knocked it out in a week with antibiotics, had antibiotics been invented? Who can doubt the severity of the blow to a temperamentally gregarious and lively fellow (and his wife), or not admire the fortitude wherewith he bore up under it, when deafness was added to economic hard times and more new heirs than he'd reckoned on? In his scarce and weary leisure, do I expect him to have got down and played horsie with us, and Hide and Seek and backyard ball and all? Do I expect him to have tried one cumbersome and costly hearing aid after another (a far cry from today's high-tech, lightweight unobtrusives) in unremitting effort to improve communication — no matter how the contraptions stigmatized a chap only in his forties — when raised voices could accomplish almost as much? Do I expect that multiply burdened fellow to have been not only the passive model of rectitude, patience, and good-natured authority that he was but our active senior pal as well, our encouraging instructor in sports and crafts and skills, the facts of life and the principles of character?

Yes, actually, to all of the above, whether or not I myself would've done better in his position — for John Jacob's children still pay the price of his incapacities. With our father we never had real conversation; our raised-voice verbal transactions were necessarily minimal: reports, requests, notifications ("*Fire whistle, Dad!*"). Our worries, problems, opinions, inclinations, and speculations all had to go to Mother — unfailingly sympathetic, but not particularly imaginative or knowledgeable — whose own exchanges with her husband cannot have been much more extensive than ours. His verbal distance from us was not merely oral; a number of times in my young-adult life I attempted in letters what we couldn't do tête-à-tête, for he was an articulate fellow and a ready raconteur, who I thought might enjoy communicating by mail. No go. Nor was his distance from us merely verbal; that affectionate loyalty was physically undemonstrative, with wife and children alike. After I had children of my own, I insisted on embracing and kissing my father at hello- and good-bye-time when my family visited Cambridge (he never visited his grown children); before that, our physical contact had been limited to manly handshakes.

What went on in the parental bedroom, I do not know. There was that armoire drawer rich in condoms that I came upon in later years, when I was dispatched upstairs by Mother to look for something or other in there (they would have antedated her early hysterectomy). I recall her remarking with a chuckle, many years after the fact, that upon the belated suturing of her non-episiotomy, Whitey had teased her about being virginal again. And — once only — in the wee hours, through the partition between their bedroom and what was by then a guest bedroom I heard Georgia protest mildly, loud enough for him and therefore me to hear, "Oh, Whitey, not now!" — in the tone, however, of one yielding.*

All that bespeaks at least an average degree of physical intimacy between them, which I prefer to imagine was less perfunctory, more tender and loving, than the one-way razzing and the benevolent, passive unphysicality of their daytime relation. But I can't help feeling that the hard coin of my father's deafness had another side for him. Men of his time and place and class, just as busy and no wealthier, managed to do more with their families than share dinner and take Sunday drives. Dad's deafness *excused* — was permitted to excuse — a distance, a mild indifference, even a selfishness, to which I suspect he inclined in any case, or in any case inclined once afforded that cover. I do not doubt that he was gratified by, even proud of his children and their accomplishments — academic scholarships, advanced or professional degrees, successful careers, the production of grandchildren — but he took little active interest in those children and virtually none in those grandchildren. His interests were the town and the county, his cronies at the firehouse and the courthouse, the fire-company ham-and-oyster suppers that were his and Mother's only social occasions, and where the glad-handing, loud-teasing "Judge" was respectfully regarded as "a real character."

Astonishingly, to me, this Chief Judge of the Dorchester County Orphans Court, who every Tuesday afternoon for four dozen years directed the legal paper traffic of the county's dead, himself died with irregularities in his will and without any sort of life insurance. No serious dereliction in that former, a mere matter of renaming executors: "It all goes to your mother," he had let Jill

---

*What was I doing there? Visiting with my own small children, I suppose, and they asleep in the rear bedrooms. My parents, then, would have been late-fiftyish.

know, who presided over our parents' last age. But "it all" comprised no more than the Aurora Street house in which the couple had spent their entire married life (a high-upkeep, uninsulated, termite-troubled frame structure in need of serious renovation top to bottom, inside and out), a savings balance inadequate to the house's and his widow's maintenance, and three well-enough-off grown children — who willingly took up the financial slack, but with whom he had not troubled to discuss their probable need to do so. In short, no realistic provision for his spouse and no real review of that circumstance with his "heirs." It is difficult to believe that he was much concerned.

Deeply mixed, then, my feelings, toward Whitey especially — for Georgia was a sweet and selfless spirit, in many ways oblivious, but in her passive manner entirely loving, and up to the moment of her death (early in the morning of her ninety-third birthday) as constitutionally good-humored as her husband.

I sang above, and now sing further, the price my parents' children paid and pay yet for their parents' shortcomings, Whitey's especially — as no doubt they in turn paid for *their* parents' shortcomings and they theirs, back to Adam and Eve, and as our children pay for ours. Needless to sing, I do not mean the literal dollars we contributed to make good the shortfall between Georgia's "estate" and her expenses. No burden, that: Our own children were by then self-supporting, and my sister's accountancy managed Mother's slender resources well. Nor do I mean the cost in time and worry of keeping the old couple in their homeplace — their preference — for as long as possible, with round-the-clock attendants, and then Mother in an invalid apartment nearby when (some years after Dad's death) the house really had to be sold or totally renovated, and finally in a local nursing home for her terminal few months — the personnel problems, the house-maintenance headaches, the massive medical-benefits paperwork. Jill and her accountant husband, to their enduring credit, took care of all that, for the elders of both families (the price of living as responsible adults where one lived as children), and did it scrupulously well, while from our different distances Bill and I had little more to do than send our monthly support checks. To this day,* I remain innocent of how social workers and live-in nursing attendants are located, hired, and payrolled, how Medicare and Medicaid and other such benefits are managed, and how funerals are arranged — matters in which my twin has become grimly expert.

Do I sound, in that innocence and distance, unadmirably like my father? I am his son, and Georgia's. To be sure, we three siblings are not alike. My brother inherited, as we twins did not, Whitey's bluff gregariousness and his penchant for back-to-back anecdotes (the deaf man's one-way conversation); Bill's impressive vitality, range of interests, and general appetite for life are unconstrained by Dad's deafness and fatigability; he is made of sturdier stuff — some of Georgia's hardscrabble stolidity, perhaps, or our stonecutting grandfather's, though Bill's quick-wittedness and formidable memory are our father's. Like Dee-Pop, like Whitey (and like me), he is for better or worse a self-made man; none of us followed in our sire's footsteps or owes very much, careerwise, either to mentors or to friends in high places. Bill's childhood battle for ego-maintenance, one against two in that mismanaged siblingship, toughened him more than it did his twin adversaries, who had each other for reinforcement: Him it drove out of the house, into the neighborhood, the world; us it drove all the more into each other's company, self-sufficient (together) *against* the world, and self-insulated from it, to our cost. His blunt extraversion is perhaps at least in part an early reaction to our somewhat sissified JackandJillery: those twin strollers, twin beds, complementary baby outfits and stuffed animals (Jill's Gingham Dog, Jack's Calico Cat), piano-duet recitals, and the rest. The poles, once polarized, each potentiated the other. Given that poisonous potentiation, it is to all hands' credit (including our easygoing parents') that our adult relations are as cordial and reciprocally respectful as they are. So affectionately loyal is my brother to the

---

* 29 October '91, our Langford Creek flotilla decommissioned for the winter. *Next* fall, we hope, we'll do more end-of-season sailing than this year's calendar permitted; perhaps an extended Columbus Day Quincentenary cruise. . . .

non-sibling aspects of his childhood that, alone of the three of us, when the time came he wanted from the homeplace souvenir furnishings for his own house — three thousand miles away, at the opposite end of America from East Cambridge, Maryland.

The price: When puberty and high school mercifully broke up the nursery-rhyme duo, Jill accepted her tracking into the "Commercial" curriculum and thence to secretarial school in Delaware, although her high-school academic record had been consistently better than mine. While I studied Latin and Spanish and literature and trigonometry in the "Academic" curriculum and aspired to some undefined future distinction, she studied typing and shorthand and bookkeeping and aspired to secretaryship — an honorable occupation, to be sure. Neither of us had enough imagination (or, on my part, unselfish concern) to protest this arrangement, common practice at the time: Jack would have a family to support; Jill would have a husband to support her; ergo etc. I believe I did encourage her, from the distance of Baltimore, to work in some city when her secretarial training was done, rather than return to the hometown that I presumptuously felt myself to have outgrown. She tried that, briefly — a short spell in Wilmington, another in Washington — but soon retreated to live happily at home and work in a local bank until she met her accountant husband from an even smaller town nearby and settled with him there to live out a modest, agreeable, responsible life.

A life, that is to say, much on the contented model of her parents, who seldom ventured far from Dorchester County or enjoyed unfamiliar foods, people, experiences, ideas. If its radius is short, however, its roots go deep into her community, as mine have never done. She has friends both old and close, as I do not, and a genuine community life — the salvation of her untimely widowhood — of which her twin's involvement with his university is his only and much-attenuated simulacrum. We erstwhile wombmates, formerly so indivisible that we believe we once literally dreamed the same dream, have come to have so little in common that although her house is no more than two hours from Baltimore and less than that from Langford Creek, we see each other at most twice or thrice a year. Affectionate loyalty; benign passivity. . . .

The price: If I am blessed with my parents' robust constitution (except for Dad's sinusitis, neither was prone to illness, anxiety, or depression, and both lived long, though Mother's last two decades were a slow slide into cheerful senility and invalidity) and my father's lucky metabolism, which with minimal exercise and no dietary constraints keeps me a fit and paunchless middleweight (the clothes I wore at age twenty-one would still fit me these forty years later, as would his have him), and if by imagination, ambition, hard work, and happy accident I've lived a wider, more varied, more materially prosperous, perhaps more rewarding life than theirs, I have also an ample measure of their shortcomings, the more painfully apparent to me precisely because education, experience, and imagination have afforded me the wherewithal for such self-assessment, to which my parents did not incline. Granted that not all of one's traits come from one's parents, I nonetheless thank you, dear folks both, for vigorous health; for a peaceable temperament and a prevailingly good-humored disposition; for a model of unresentful patience, uncomplaining hard work, honorable behavior, domestic tranquility, harmlessness, stoicism in the face of hardship, and a fundamental self-acceptance inclined to shrug off disappointments and get on with it. Thank you, Whitey in particular, for what wits I have and for my inclination to apply them to telling stories. Thank you, Georgia in particular, for whatever gentleness is mine and whatever capacity for giving love as well as accepting it.

But some of those capacities, folks, are neither so large nor so active and imaginative as I wish they were. I'm short on thoughtfulness, empathetic sensitivity, tact, subtlety, interest in others — How do we suppose I came by those deficiencies? I'm terrible at gift-giving, at remembering details of even my children's and grandchildren's news; they and we see one another far less often than we all agree we should. Whence my merely (though genuinely) affectionate loyalty and benign passivity? Cordial acquaintances I have aplenty, but each decade fewer close friends — in recent years none, if such a friend is one with whom one enjoys "doing things," exchanging confidences, sharing one's life. My wife is my only such friend, I hers; our life together approaches that solipsism à deux of which her fictive image spoke in this opera's overture, discomfitingly reminiscent of my early twinship, and while we shake our heads at this state of affairs — People shouldn't live in such isolation! — I find that it troubles me more in principle than in fact. Except for visiting family, we seldom entertain at home, and I "go out" only to university social functions, which I enjoy. Were it not for our separate academic connections and my literary lecture-travels (which I also enjoy), we would be recluses indeed. Whence (on my part) that tendency, if not from chip-off-the-old-blockhood?

In a word, if I am not selfish, I am decidely self-centered; inclined, if not to narcissism, most certainly to that sort of solipsism aforesung. My father's son and the Jack of Jack and Jill, although I do not think myself immodest (Who does?), I am gratified by audience attention and applause and by my moderate literary success, mildly envious but unresentful of those with more. As I draft this insistent aria in my old binder with my old pen in our Baltimore house on a sunny end-of-October forenoon, I wear the wax earplugs with which I imitate Dad's deafness, and with affectionate loyalty I sing . . . myself.

Rest in peace, dear Whitey; yours was no easy road. Rest with him, dear Georgia, down there in the family plot in the county cemetery that your son (in this, too) doesn't often get around to visiting. You guys did your best, I'm sure, within your parameters; may I have done no worse within mine. Bad luck for you, you spawned a singer inclined to arias on such themes as (all together now) affectionate loyalty. Benign passivity. Cordial etc.

For the record. A new twist. Aha:
   "Well: For the record, I *enjoyed* our childhood."
   Likewise, Image-of-my-sister. But.
   "Did you do a better job of parenting?"
   In some ways, for sure: more *relating* to my kids, more widening of their world, a little help from Dr. Spock. But changing social classes took its toll, from small-town-storekeeper to urban-

professorial. My children's home base wasn't as stable as 301 Aurora, either geographically or emotionally; there was more active love in it, certainly, for their first ten years, but they were still high schoolers when the scene broke up. They paid a price for that, and for their parents' other failings. I'm not about to catalogue all of mine, and I discreetly pass over my then partner's.

"So?"

So rest in peace, dear G & W, as I said. Let's get me back to my *present* partner.

"I sympathize."

And I with you. What I can't tell you — but why not? What I can't quite *believe*, let's say, is that the Jill I'm lost with, here in Wherever, is my literal sister from Hurlock and Hunting Creek. I think of her as going about her business there while I pen these words here with her image. . . .

"The Jill is as real as the Jack, seems to me. Speaking of your pen, can you give it a twist? We've lost our picture."

Indeed, we stand now in a blackness illuminated only by our projected selves, as in some avant-garde stage set or outer space. At that insistent last aria's end, brooding still upon the scene that prompted it, I capped my Parker with some sort of sigh. A few older views rapidly thereupon ensued, for moments each: the "corner house" done up in tricolor bunting (its red, white, and blue three shades of gray in this projection) for some pre–World War One Independence Day parade; the interior of Dee-Pop's stoneworks, a turn-of-the-century-looking shed uptown behind the Post Office, replete with slabs and dollies and serious-faced workmen in coveralls; an artist's-studio view of our uncle Herman's full-scale bust of Laocoön (copied after the Vatican group that inspired Lessing's famous treatise on poetry and the plastic arts) — a bust that family tradition, until I corrected it from college, held to be the head of Christ crucified, and that when it came into my possession inspired my early novel *The End of the Road*; finally, a sepia-toned series from early Kodak days, of folk anonymous to us; then nothing but our own present images.

I could, I suppose, return my pen-cap as before to Ready, then "fast-forward" to where we left off and proceed to whichever next view comes up: J & J playing among the buried cat turds in their jim-dandy sandbox, maybe, whose bright-striped awning our mother accidentally set afire one fine afternoon by flipping her cigarette through an open bedroom window lest *her* mother, who must have just moved in with us, discover that her fortyish daughter was, after all, a smoker of cigarettes. Or whatever, while the Chinese communists march their Long March and Hitler rejects the Versailles Treaty and Mussolini invades Ethiopia. But I'm suddenly depressed: the aftereffect, perhaps, of delivering myself of that judgmental aria on my parents, or perhaps the prospect of reviewing sequentially sixty-plus yearsworth of such archival views in hope of finding my way back to US — still stymied, our passage through the maze suspended. "Give it a twist," Jill has suggested — and for all she's my old twin, I sense her to be in this projection something more, her as-if-casual utterances worth monitoring with some third ear, the way I monitor my tentative notebook notes from my muse. Some new twist, it occurs to me, may be quite what's *called for*; some different way of going, before the goer loses heart and interest in where he has to go.

As if cued by my unvoiced recollection of that sandbox-awning fire, my sister's image (I'll call it Jill) lights another cigarette from her pack, and for some reason I'm reminded of our favorite childhood storybook, *365 Bedtime Stories*, a joint Christmas gift from which for a full year thereafter Mother faithfully read to us when we tucked into our twin beds — and which, aha, in early highschool years, when we had outgrown it, we carefully hollowed out as a cache for verboten cigarettes, its innocent narratives supplanted by uninnocence, like those seventeenth-century Italian breviaries hollowed and fitted with deadly little pistols. For a season we kept that deflowered volume up in the rafters of our garage clubhouse, where we and . . .

Aha.

With a sudden fumbling confidence, I twist off Mr. Pumblechook's cap. It isn't threaded, as is the Montblanc Meisterstück's that I keep at Langford Creek for drafting Friday pieces; it pulls straight off over its simple spring-and-ridge detente, but habitually I uncap with a slight right-hand-clockwise twist of which I've scarcely been aware before now. I ready it on the barrel-butt with a different twist — a new, experimental one — checking the scene around us as I adjust it. I couldn't say what I'm up to, exactly, but as to what I'm after I feel a certainty tantamount to inspiration. Not this, not this, not this . . . wait, now . . . not quite . . .

Aha.

"Where's *that* from? Who in the world . . . ?"

Still in black and white, a bawling, brawling, scrapscruffy brat of a bullyboy, kindergarten age but urchined out of such privilege, is being lifted right off the sidewalk of 301 Aurora by his tough-looking teenage sister. With her formidable right arm she suspends him by his left, half a foot above our saltine pavement, while in her no less formidable left she holds a shiny red tricycle, the missing of a matching pair. . . .

"Good lord! Is that Jerry Schreiber?"

With the same stumbling sureness, I twiddle my cap; the scene jerks forward and backward in a frame-by-frame sort of way. I'm then inspired to . . . How to put it, especially as I'm making this up as I go along? . . . to do something-or-other with that gray glass stone in the captop ("We're talking metaphors," Jay Scribner reminded me back in that pine grove, himself a talking metaphor) . . . et voilà, with sudden color, sound, and vigorous 3-D action:

Not an aria: "Gawdam cunt!"

The black-curled, brown-freckled brawlbrat — our then age and size, but a different piece of work from little JackandJill, who witness this scene with awe from our safe screened porch — has been dragged and hoisted half around the block from bluecollar Byrn Street, down by the hospital, where the clapboard houses are a touch less tidy and a touch more crowded than our stretch of Aurora's, and the households are headed not by clerks and shopkeepers and schoolteachers but by carpenters, watermen, mechanics, jacks-of-all-trades. Barefoot and shirtless, soiled and sunbrown, he has hollered and flailed in big Patsy Schreiber's inexorable grasp past Whissy Moore's house down on that corner, where the ruddy-cheek bachelorman dwells with his infirm parents and whistles wonderfully on his natty walk to and from his uptown clerking; past Old Misternmiz Leap's, where the elders live with their church-organist spinster daughter, just across Aurora from the Other Leaps' house, their married son's; over Leaps' Bump and past Miss Emma Ralph's house, where abides our sturdy-waisted, impressively mustached neighbor lady, the much-dreaded Sixth Grade Math Teacher, with her broad soft elder sister Miz Helen Fell (not *Miss* like Miss Emma Ralph, we don't know why, after whom the house is invariably called, we don't know why) . . . to our house, from before which one of our brand-new birthday trikes was stolen only this morning.

The big girl drops that gleaming object with a rubber-tired clatter onto our walk, beside its companion, and squawls at her captive brother "Yew tellm yer sorry, doanchewl getchew a switchin!"

"Gawdam cunt!" bad Jerry Schreiber bellows back — a startling volume of enraged male voice from so wiry a brat. We contemporary witnesses, porched and appalled, comprehend only his furious tone, but the grown-up narrator sees that the lad must know whereof he bellows, for as he bellows it he slugs her right there with his free fist, and when Patsy grabs that wrist too, he crotches her yet another with one bare foot.

"Lil shitass!" She wrestles her kid brother safely hind-to — "Seef I don't wale yerass blacknblue, calln me names!" — and pitches him bodily into our overgrown spirea.

Scratched but unfazed, the boy bounds from that bush, free of her now, and finds time and presence of mind enough, even as she lights out after him, to feint porch-stepward (we two retreat as one toward the open living-room door). He makes a jeering face at us with thumbs in ears and fingers waggling, dodges quick Patsy in the nick of time, and hollers a mocking "*Jack eats Jill!*" before thumbing his nose at his pursuer (both hands again, in line now, as if keying a wind instrument) and bolting through the shrubs toward our alley.

"Damn lil cawksker," Patsy grumbles, to herself and to us, as she retucks her shirttails into her skirt. "Caint do a thing withm." To my grown-up ear, her tone sounds half admiring.

"Thanks, Patsy!" Jill and Jack chorus from the porch, for we've learned her to be the inconstant warden of her brawlbrat brother, our Byrn Street nemesis. Of those several naughtinesses, *shitass* was the only one we understood, to our shocked amusement. I, for one, however, sensing the category, carefully filed the others in my memory. It will be this same tricycle thief, the Byrn Street bad-boy until he moves to even rougher Henry Street, who in another context presently explains their meaning to me.

"Whoa, now,"

Jill objects as this scene dissolves: "Something's wrong here. It wasn't our tricycles that got stolen; it was our Goodyear junior bikes, so we have to've been seven or eight, not five or six. And it wasn't Jerry Schreiber that took them. There wasn't any Jerry Schreiber yet, back then."

There may not have been then, Image-of-my-twin, but there will be now, or we'll never get out of here. I'm not interested in the blow-by-blow of all four hundred blows. What I want is to get through this movie — no offense intended — and back to my ship and shipmate.

"What four hundred blows?"

The thousand natural shocks, let's say, that flesh is heir to. Truffaut. Shakespeare.

"Mommy Simmons used to say we have to eat a peck of dirt before we die."

Close enough. We're going to skip the grain-by-grain.

"So you're making stuff up now with that pen?"

That's what I've mainly always done: imaginary gardens with real toads, as a rule; this time vice versa. Never mind the allusion.

"For the record, though, it was Travers Bradley that took our bikes — *both* bikes — and Patsy Bradley brought them back and apologized, but I don't remember either of them behaving like that. Travers would've been about the age you showed, but you and I were second or third grade by then. Why not show the real thing?"

The "facts," you mean. Because there's no end to them, Jill. Because their nature and status are arguable, not to mention their meaning. Because they're not my stock-in-trade, except by the way. Because they're fine-grained to the point of quicksand. I don't know what "Travers Bradley" is *for* — was for — in our lives. He played no part in them, that I can remember, after the bicycle episode. But I'm getting a sense of what Jerome Schreiber is for.

"In our lives?"

In our story: the mother of all fiction.

"Come again?"

Aria: "The mother of all fiction"

Elsewhere with this old pen in this old binder, I have remarked (let the where of it go, along with Truffaut and Shakespeare and Marianne Moore) that the story of our life is not our life; it is our story. The mother of all fiction, reader, is surely our common sense that our lives are stories — more exactly, that each of our lives is a story-in-progress, whereof each of us is perforce the central, if not necessarily the dominant, character. We may be Ishmael to some Captain Ahab or Moby-Dick, Nick Carraway to some Great Gatsby; nevertheless it's we who are the "receptive lucidity" about whom our life-story finally *is*, with its more or less misty beginning; its ongoing, sometimes confused or episodic middle, perhaps as replete with missteps, setbacks, and digressions as a picaresque novel; its ending as certain in its approach as it is uncertain, for most of us, in its where/when/how; with, above all, its *why*: its meaning, perhaps obscure to us mere protagonists — who are, after all, inside it — but unwaveringly clear to its Author (if we are a certain sort of believer) and at times at least fitfully to ourselves, if we happen to be visionary, existentialist, or possessed of strong vocation.

Now, then: I myself do not accept the proposition, at least not a priori, that our lives are stories. Our lives are *not* stories, although we may make stories of them. In this singer's opinion, our lives are not inherently dramatical, not intrinsically meaningful. In most instances, our little victories and vicissitudes — even our mighty triumphs and disasters — are, from the dramaturgical point of view, meaningless, their only coherence the circumstance that they all happened to us, the central character, with or without our agency.* "It was the culmination of all my labors," this one declares; or that one, "It was the shattering of all my hopes." Well, it was not: only of all your hopes and labors in that category, however principal, of your multifarious life, however "single-minded." And your death will not likely have significant bearing upon the life it ends.

To those of you given to reading and reflection — and who else will attend this aria? — I owe an apology for so belaboring what no doubt goes without singing. The fact is, however, that while I truly believe our lives to be in themselves without meaning, I honor our persistent human urge to find meaning in them or give meaning to them (even to impose meaning on them), and our common inclination — an effect of evolution, I am persuaded — to make or find that meaning in the form of *stories*. Some cognitive scientists now maintain that consciousness itself is the brain's biologically evolved narrativity: the necessary process of making sense out of the senses' instreaming data-flood by what we call (misleadingly, as it implies a yet "higher" consciousness) selecting, editing, recollecting, associating, projecting, cause-and-effecting — in short, making sense by making scenarios. After forty years of making up stories professionally and sixty of hearing, reading, watching, and telling them extraprofessionally, I still don't know which is chicken and which egg: whether our "dramatistic" sense of life comes from a lifetime of absorbing stories — bedtime stories, anecdotes, comic books, novels, movies, TV dramas — or whether, on the contrary, our sense of what constitutes a *story* comes from our innately narrative, even dramatistic sense of life: the mother of all fictions.

"We mustn't believe that life makes sense," Jay Wordsworth Scribner once exhorted me (we would have been upperclass col-

---

*In this respect, the most "lifelike" of novelists is Defoe, of whose Moll Flanders and Robinson Crusoe so many irrelevancies are extensively reported by the author precisely for their verisimilitudinous irrelevancy: e.g., Crusoe's meaningless and anticlimactic adventures in *France*, of all unexotic places, after rescue from his desert island.

lege undergraduates then, just discovering our vocations in postwar, Harry Truman America, pleased with ourselves for having
climbed out of the marsh, so to speak, attained the high ground
of a good university, and begun the altitude adjustments of scaling
Parnassus), "or history, either. On the other hand, we mustn't stop
trying to make sense of them. But let's never imagine that by
explaining things we explain them *away*."

My ex-brawlbrat, trike-thief friend was given to such oracular-
ity in that period. Less so was I, if only because less ready than he
with the spoken word; but on this occasion I found it in me to
reply, "Of of what one can't make sense, one may make art." Jay
liked that: the alliterative and assonant, quasi-stammering monosyllables, the not unclever mimetic syntax. Already, though we
hadn't yet acknowledged it, we were beginning to think of him as
the Intellectual and me as the Artist. The scene was a dark, all but
empty student bar on St. Paul Street, near the Johns Hopkins campus, in mid-brilliant-April afternoon. We were discovering Proust
and Joyce and, just then, Hemingway's *The Sun Also Rises*, which
we admired despite its portentous borrowed title. Jay stood me a
bock beer, in token of the season.

"Why are you singing me all this?" asks Jill.

I could reply: In hopes of making art of of what I can't make
sense — i.e., what we're doing here; what this opera is all about.
Instead, I give my trusty Parker *ree*mote this time no new twist,
but the oldest one in my book, to wit:

A story: The Brawlbrat

Pick a card, Jill. Any card. I'll pick one, too. We're ready to get
on with it.

"With what?"

I spoke before of our "diagram of forces": East Cambridge, 301
Aurora, the Choptank rivershore, Dee-Mom and Dee-Pop's corner
house; Dad's deafness, the Depression, the store; our Jackand-
Jillery, Bill's Billery. Jay Scribner preferred the image of a hand of
cards (we're back in college again, drinking National Bohemian

beer on a scaling rowhouse porch in the student warrens of North
Calvert and St. Paul between Twenty-ninth and Thirty-fourth
streets): that life deals every writer — every person, for that matter, but we were talking writers — a limited hand of cards to com-
bine and recombine, play and be played by. As in certain poker
games, one may discard a few, pick up a few new ones, and re-
figure accordingly. Essentially, however, one's hand of cards is
one's hand of cards: Proust's asthma and his madeleine; Joyce's
Irishness and apostasy; Kafka's overwhelming father, his neuroses
and tuberculosis. JackandJill's hand has now been dealt, with one
wild card in it: the brawlbrat Jerry Schreiber from around Moore's
corner, on Byrn Street.

"It wasn't Jerry Schreiber —"

Jerry Schreiber it has become, and our tricycles he stole at age
five, not our junior bikes at age eight or nine, and the reason for
that is this: We're in a *story* now, and it happens that bikes come
in His and Hers, whereas a tricycle is a tricycle is a tricycle — or
used to be, anyhow. Either of ours could be either of ours —

"I don't remember this story that way. I don't remember our
tricycles at all."

— just as either of us, et cet., for all your bow-ribbons and my
short pants and our pet names for our privates when we were sent
to the bathroom together every morning for the sake of family
efficiency, there being only one bathroom in 301 Aurora until we
"added on" in '36 or '37.

"You're not going to put *those* in this story."

Discreetness is for more important matters. Tommy and Susie.

"You did it. Then I'll complain out loud that you always got to
sit on the toilet while I used the potty, on the floor over by the
washbasin. Except I guess I didn't mind."

The entering wedge of gender-discrimination, I suppose. My
point, anyhow, is that notwithstanding Tommy and Susie, in those
days we were still more JackandJill than Jack and Jill —

"But never Jill and Jack."

— and that's when I want the brawlbrat to impinge. Hence
trikes, not bikes; hence Jerry Schreiber, our age but not our class,

so far as such things went in the scrappy Fifth Ward of Cambridge, Maryland, USA.

"I guess I don't understand fiction. It was Travers Bradley."

Now it becomes Jerome Schreiber the brawlbrat, while we stand wide-eyed on the porch, one person, and he makes his nyah-nyah face and hollers *Jack eats Jill!* We didn't know it at the time, but the serpent had just entered our garden. Show me your card, and I'll show you mine.

"I'm lost."

Nope: *I* am. Look: You've picked the 365 *Bedtime Stories* card, and I'm astray in what may be the last of them.

"I don't remember a single story from that book. But we loved it, and we loved Mother's reading to us from it."

I remember a stiff cardboard four-color binding with 1930s graphics of something sentimental — Bedtime candles? Kiddie-nighties? — and the coarse paper of the pages with their twelve-point type and echt-Thirtyish line drawings and the stories numbered like Scheherazade's, except by calendar date. And, of course, my later gutting of that book to stash Lucky Strikes in. So your card is on the narrative table: our First Book, in effect, and let's get on with the first story in it: the brawlbrat, gawdam cunt and lil shitass cawksker and Jack eats Jill, and suddenly we're out of the Eden of Miss Ridah Collins's kindergarten —

"I was Bo-Peep in the graduation pageant, up in the Arcade Theater. Mother sewed my costume, and I had a big shepherd's crook wrapped in silver foil. Who were you? And where's this card you're supposed to show me?"

I wasn't anybody yet. I was the secondo of our JackandJill duet, just beginning to divide from you at our conjunction, with a little help from the brawlbrat. My card's a book-card, too: *The Book of Knowledge*, published by the Grolier Society, whose sales reps knew how to work on well-intentioned Depression-era moms like ours. Twenty blue-and-silver-bound folio volumes in their own brown bookcase, just inside the front door of 301. I read every article in every volume of that kiddie Britannica, and it became my bridge to the brawlbrat. Remember *The Book of Knowledge*?

"Of course I do. But can you talk so us homefolks can understand?"

How's this:

> *Jack and Jill*
> *Went up the hill;*
> *They each had a dollar and a quarter.*

> *Jill came down*
> *With two and a half:*
> *D'you think they went up for water?*

We're in East Cambridge now, not being chauffeured to and from Miss Collins's, where the nice boys and girls were, and no rough stuff at all that I can remember. Now we're walking the three long blocks of Aurora Street from 301 down to Ground Zero: East Cambridge Elementary, where for the next five years our street begins and ends. If the brawlbrat doesn't ambush us from the alley between our house and the corner house (tall privet hedge on our side, high board fence and hollyhocks on Dee-Mom and Dee-Pop's side), we're clear as far as Maryland Avenue. After that, on the left-hand side comes Crazy Alice's yard, where she lopes about in her flowered print dresses and white socks and big shoes and raggly hair, talking to herself and shouting at schoolgoers who run a stick along her picket fence to get her going. Then we cross Henry Street, where the serious trouble lives — including young Jerome Schreiber after his father goes to the dogs and the family has to move several notches down. . . .

"You're making this up!"

Not Henry Street. Mostly decent bluecollar families there, I'm sure, then as now, but a handful of truly bad apples, too — not to mention the even harder cases from "down by the creek," whose route to school leads through Henry to Aurora. Once we've passed the No Man's Land between Henry Street and the schoolyard, our troubles are pretty much over except on the playground at recess, until time comes to walk the gauntlet home again. Not to overstate: All this was tame compared to postwar urban ghettos; we didn't live in daily fear or otherwise hate our schooldays. We were sometimes teased and taunted, but seldom physically bullied, and we came to have our sort-of-friends. But there were some scary characters back there: the Aaron brothers from down by the creek, louse-ridden, torpid as sloths and pale as albinos, who spooked through East Cambridge alleyways at night, raiding garbage cans; some other boys in and out of Reform School for car theft, general incorrigibility, whatever — in fifth grade! Granted, these were the days when children were actually "held back" if they did poor schoolwork, and some of those Henry Street fifth graders were hulking fellows in their early teens.

"*The Book of Knowledge* didn't have naughty nursery rhymes."

Certainly not — but the book of *our* knowledge did, from first grade on, years before we understood them. No discussing those things with Mother, not to mention Dad. It was Jerry Schreiber who mainly kept at us with stuff like that — at me, especially, at recess-time and to and from school. . . .

"My first 'boyfriend,' sort of, in fourth grade. Have I got the idea?"

You have. And *my* first out-of-the-house friend, sort of, by that time, although there was always a voltage between us, a volatility. I admired Jerome Schreiber and was half afraid of him; *he* wasn't afraid of anybody. I had to learn how to manage him, like a courtier managing a capricious prince.

"Jer was no prince in those days, if I've got it right. That was the problem: He wasn't our kind. I think Mother worried about his influence on us, although she never said anything about it."

Who *was* our kind, Jill, among the kids our age in that neighborhood? The truth was — Jay Scribner told me this later, in college, but I think I sensed it at the time — the truth was that the brawlbrat couldn't leave us alone, because he was as fascinated with us in his way as I, at least, was with him in mine. Schreib was the world outside our house: naughty, rough, unpredictable, mysterious and a little scary, but interesting indeed.

"What were *we*?"

Strange as it seems, from the perspective of Henry Street we must have been the children of privilege. Fresh clothes and a clean house — spacious and stable by brawlbrat standards. A piano —

remember how Schreib used to hang around it as much as he could, picking out melodies and chords, when I had come to hate the thing? And *books.* . . .

"He poked fun at our books. That's why you cut up our *365 Bedtime Stories.*"

He had to poke fun at them, to maintain face. But he *read* them, as transfixed by *The Book of Knowledge* as I was by the Two-by-Fours he stole from his older sisters' boyfriends.

"Dear god, I'd forgotten Two-by-Fours!"*

The *real* Blondie and Dagwood, Popeye and Olive Oyl, Dick Tracy and Tess Trueheart — just as Jerome Schreiber the brawl-brat, with his foul mouth and his horny mind, was in some respects the real Huckleberry Finn. I was astounded.

"I was disgusted. And I'm thinking there may be things down the line that you really have no business putting into this story."

So there may be. By and large, though, Jill, I'm impressed in retrospect by a kind of intuitive discretion on our part, which — together with a certain accident of brawlbrat temperament — kept us out of real trouble on that score. When you and I played Doctor, for example —

"Objection."

Overruled, please; it's important to get things like this on record, exactly to establish our relative innocence. You and I had a busy fantasy life in those early years, no doubt an effect of our twinhood, the diagram of forces at 301, and the absence of real outside friends. While Bill was doing rough-and-tumble real-world stuff out in the neighborhood, you and I spent a lot of time making up situations, acting out roles. For instance —

"All kids do that."

Not Jerry Schreiber. The brawlbrat was as fantasy-proof as Huck Finn; that's the lucky-for-us accident of his character. He might play along for a while with us Tom Sawyers and Becky Thatchers, but not for a moment did he ever lose sight of his real self and his agenda.

---

*So, perhaps, has the reader: pornographic parodies of popular comic strips, thus named for their dimension in inches.

"Don't remind me."

What I want to establish is that we never played Doctor with *him*, or Desert Island, or any other such etceteras, and for that reason they remained quite innocent explorations, within their category. It was Doctor Me, not Doctor Schreiber, who took my patient's rectal temperature with a forest-green Crayola in second grade, and the patient wasn't you. You were the nurse, and the patient was your girlfriend Whatsername from around the corner on Maryland Avenue.

"Who shall be nameless."

And when I first practiced boy-and-girl kissing, at about age ten, up in the attic, as part of some soap-opera story we were acting out, all hands kept their hands in hand, and the girl wasn't you; it was your other girlfriend Whozits from around the block on Franklin Street.

"Who shall be nameless."

Innocent innocent innocent is my point. Whereas if Jerry Schreiber had been in on our make-pretend —

"I shudder to think."

But his problem was that he couldn't fake it; we could see right through his seeing right through our games, and something told us where to draw a line that he even tried to bribe me to help him cross. Fifty cents, on one occasion, that he had earned standing watch for his sister Ramona while her boyfriend shagged her in their Henry Street woodshed. I said no.

"Thanks. Jerry knew too much too early."

In *that* line, for sure — whereas *The Book of Knowledge* was all news to him. It's to our credit that we knew how to turn him away from the make-pretend stuff when things looked to get sticky, and to hook him into "Why Is the Sky Blue?" in Volume Seven, or the reduction gearbox for a traveling crane in my Gilbert Erector Set manual, or a six-handed rendition of "Chopsticks" on our piano.

"He was terrific at 'Chopsticks'!"

Ten years later I did a full swing-band arrangement of it for Jay Scribner's Bluejays. But back there in brawlbrat days it's to Jerry Schreiber's credit that he let himself be sidetracked. The bedraggled brawlbrat, we know now, was in fact a highly intelligent, deeply principled kid in a Huck Finn situation, unsanitized by Mark Twain's Victorianism. Old Man Schreiber was an abusive drunk who beat up on the whole family, tried to hump every one of his four daughters as they reached puberty, and probably succeeded with at least one of them. His mother was a battered fishwife who held the household together mainly with her mouth, between KOs. His sisters were streetwise survivors who took their pleasures where they could and got out of that house as early as possible. You'd think that Jerry might have been spared, as the youngest kid and the only boy, but in fact he was targeted — until he reached puberty and could really fight back. His sisters stood up for him as much as they cared or dared to, just as he stood watch for them; but he was a battle-scarred hellion in a houseful of battle-scarred hellions, and an aggressive survival expert. He must have felt at 301 Aurora the way we'd have felt in Windsor Castle, except that where we'd have been intimidated, he preserved his self-respect by burping and farting and sneaking cigarettes and flashing stolen condoms and baiting us with naughty nursery rhymes and poking fun at *The Book of Knowledge* — every time he returned a volume that he had borrowed and read from cover to cover.

"He spoiled one, didn't he?"

And lost another, and was too proud to tell me until years later that the damaged one had been thrown across a room at him by his mother, who swore he'd stolen it, and the lost one had burned up in their chicken-coop fire, started by a sister's cigarette during a midnight tryst. Jer had hidden it out there for safety after the earlier ruckus, and I had to make up a cockamamie story about its being taken from my book bag during recess. Volume Sixteen.

"You're making up a cockamamie story now, I think. I don't remember any of this."

Maybe here's the genesis of my vocation.

"I do remember that toward the end of fourth grade or beginning of fifth, he learned better manners and spent more time in our house instead of out in the garage."

Better manners with you and Mother. It was an *exercise* for him, to see whether he could behave like somebody that Henry Street was telling him he wasn't, but that he had an image of from our weekly trips to the library: those well-mannered chaps in the Hardy Boys and Tom Swift series. You were his official sort-of-girlfriend that year, in a time and place not much given to boy- and girlfriends at age ten. He was Huck Finn trying to meet Aunt Sally standards, tongue half in cheek. With me he let it out a bit, but even then his horniness took a different slant. When we hung out in our garage clubhouse, he quit asking me "What'd you *get* for your dollar and a quarter, up on that hill?" Instead, he would pose me such heavy general questions as whether, when I was grown up and married, I intended to fuck my wife.

"Maybe we could fast-forward over this part?"

I wish. No, I don't wish, because we're dealing with a *real* Huck Finn here, warts and farts and all, and because his question reminds me that as of age ten, despite Schreib's naughty rhymes and horny jokes and Two-by-Fours and fabliaux of his busy sisters —

"Say what?"

— Despite all that, I managed still not quite to know what the F-word really meant. Not *fabliaux*. Don't I remember you and me agreeing in third grade or thereabouts that it probably meant that the husband puts his Tommy up against his wife's Susie, or she holds it there between her legs somehow, and they both pee?

"I'm not saying a word."

We agreed it sounded icky, and we had no interest in trying it — certainly not with each other, far less with some outsider. We were innocent! Nowadays, I suppose, my nine-year-old granddaughter knows all about Safe Sex; I'm not inclined to ask. Oh my . . .

"What's the matter?"

Everything! When I mentioned my granddaughter. . . . *What am I doing here, Jill?* Who cares about brawlbrats, and East Cambridge, and what you and I knew or didn't know at age ten in 1940? I don't think I can go on with this.

"Maybe do your pen?"

Hell with my pen! But you're right, you're right. I told him . . . Come on, Pumblechook . . . I told Jer I guessed we would, yes, probably, my wife and I, when we were married . . . *fuck*. Would he? He cut me a sly look — bright-eyed and black-curled, freckled and jut-jawed, a look from his brawlbrat period, which he was fast outgrowing; a look that dared me to acknowledge that he might be thinking of my sister — but by the time he answered, that look was gone. "Man!" he said, and the point of this anecdote is that his tone and expression were more reverent than horny: "When I'm married, I'm going to fuck all day!" It strongly occurs to me to imagine that despite the household he grew up in and his inventory of obscene words and ribald jokes and innuendo, Brawlbrat Schreiber might not in fact have known a whole lot more than you and I did in this line, at this age. Standing watch is not the same as watching, and even those Two-by-Fours had their informational limits. In any event, we-all hadn't reached puberty yet; I didn't know what *masturbation* was, for example, and Schreiber never spoke of it, much less proposing a circle-jerk out in the clubhouse. All that came a few years later.

Silence on my sister's-image's part. Our brawlbrat dialogue, I sense, must for one reason or another become a monologue, or end here. Were I to join her silence just now, however, it's not the brawlbrat who would come crashing down on me, but rather . . .
    I push my pen.

Monologue faute de mieux: The brawlbrat brawl
    Back there in East Cambridge, the 1930s have run out: dreary decade of a catastrophic century, and its survivors are in for worse. The Depression is ending because world war has re-begun, though East Cambridge isn't in it yet. Much as I've penned here about JackandJill's first years, I've left most out. History is a Mandelbrot Set, infinitely subdivisible. Narrating it is like measuring a coastline: Its length depends upon the scale of measurement, which has a lower limit but no upper. In Zeno's paradox, swift Achilles can never catch the tortoise — yet catch it he does, with ease, in the world we know. In Time's infinitely forking funhouse, the Thirties

can never reach the Forties, or JackandJill reach puberty and
become Jill and Jack, or *Once Upon a Time* attain Act Two — yet
all of those came to pass, or surely shall come if pen push on. Like
real-world coastline measurements, stories accomplish their end
by selective omission; Achilles accomplishes his by ignoring the
terms of Zeno's paradox. But Time, mirabile dictu, omits nothing,
ignores nothing, yet reaches 1940, even 1941, in only ten or eleven
years! My frictionless Parker races to keep up; its pusher still wonders why.

Too late now to sing the death of all three or four of our grandparents, virtual ciphers in our life. Through the Forties, the corner
house will be intermittently occupied and maintained by widowed
or maiden aunts (our father's younger sisters) and by the New Jersey relatives. One of those — Aunt Roon's husband, Uncle Doc,
the alpha male of that part of the family, a knowledgeable ex–New
Yorker and prosperous dentist who loved tidewater East Cambridge the way his East Cambridge wife (our father's older sister)
loved New York City — explained to me what the word *Schreiber*
means auf Deutsch, and my own surname as well — the latter in
Plattdeutsch, he supposed, as the spelling wasn't given in Dee-
Pop's old gothic-print dictionary. In our garage clubhouse, I passed
along that revelation to my brawlbrat sort-of-friend. We were
trying just then, with small success, to smoke bitter "Chinese
cigar" seedpods from the catalpa trees in JackandJill's side yard —
and although Schreib scoffed "So what?" I sensed his perpending
of that datum. Maybe he would grow up to be some kind of a
writer, I suggested — the first time, surely, that that vocation had
ever been mentioned or even imagined in East Cambridge.

"And *you*'ll grow up to be some kind of a beard. Ha ha."

The original Cambridge Schreibers, my Aunt Roon or Aunt
Mim or Aunt Rose or Aunt Floss thereafter declared, had been
one of numerous more or less desperate families "brought over"
from the old country early in the century by Dee-Pop, in his moonlighting capacity as ticket agent for North German Lloyd's. Having trekked west from Baltimore to try their luck at homesteading,
some found the bitter prairie winters beyond enduring and trekked
back east, all but ruined. A few of the most enterprising picked up

for a song some acres of the cheapest land available thereabouts: Dorchester County fresh marsh, regarded in those days as good for nothing. They laboriously drained the wetlands and, to the ecosystem's loss but their personal gain, became the reasonably prosperous farmers who used to gather at the corner house on market day. Others worked in the building trades around about Cambridge; Jerome Schreiber's grandfather had been a respected carpenter, who had helped build 301 Aurora and its clapboard neighbors. His father had followed that trade as well, once upon a time, and (like mine) had married a down-county Scotch-Irish dirt farmer's daughter, but drink had been the fellow's ruin. These tidings, too, excepting the last item, I conveyed to my friend, who affected both to have known them already and to be indifferent to the knowledge, but who in fact, it pleased me to believe, was hearing his family history for the first time.

Too late now to sing our fishing off the hospital seawall with Uncle Doc–rigged bamboo poles, cork bobbers, and two-hook spreaders, using peeler crabs to bait white perch and spot and sunfish and occasional croakers — all which "Schreib" took home for his sisters to clean and cook; of our prowling the rivershore Jungle between the Nurses' Home and the New Bridge, and its adjacent rat-rich dump, elsewhere aria'd. I pass over JackandJill's piano recitals with the rest of Miss Agnes Hubbard's clientele (Rest in peace, dear Georgia; you did your best). Likewise the July Fourth parades that outstripped our famous Armistice Day extravaganzas as war drew nearer: Every peninsular volunteer fire company and high-school marching band passed down Race Street between patriotic floats, platoons of gussied-up baton Twirlettes, American Legionnaires (Whitey among them), uniformed Boy and Girl Scout troops, and the festively crepe-papered wares of local automobile dealers; by far the liveliest music and most spirited strutting was provided penultimately by the "colored" Second Ward high schoolers and ultimately by their elders in the New Orleans–style Merry Band, who together always brought up the rear. And, that night — no time to sing them — the annually more resplendent fireworks displays subsidized by some minor Dupont who maintained an estate downriver from Cambridge; displays shot off from barges moored out in the river-channel and witnessed by uptown Cantabrigians from the Long Wharf municipal park, by us wrong-side-of-the-creekers from our hospital seawall, and by Second Ward coloreds from the marshes out past West End.

"They beat their drums differently," I happened to observe to Jerome Schreiber on the afternoon of 4 July 1940, as the Merry Band high-jinked past Whitey's Candyland. We were eating Dixie Cups of ice cream, half chocolate, half vanilla, the underside of whose collectible lids now featured Stuka dive-bombers and Ryan trainers instead of Tom Mix and Hopalong Cassidy. Schreib gave me his What-am-I-going-to-do-with-you look, by now a commonplace of our relation.

"That's jazz, man. The afterbeat."

Come again?

"Taintnyer Bookanollidge, Oatmealarino," he let me know. As I had come to call him by a contraction of his last name, he teased me with variations on his ancient nickname for me. It had become increasingly Schreib's pleasure, and therefore ours, to play with words, particularly coinages based on how the people around us actually spoke: uptada Cannylann, danny shore, inna Bookanollidge. "Whaja git?"

U.S.S. *Arizona*. Whajoo?

"Gene Autry. Yroleman must be selling stale Dixie Cups."

What's an afterbeat?

He knucklefisted my bicep, an ouchy form of fifth-grade harassment in that period, designed to raise lumps on upper arms. "The backbeat, man." This *man* was something new; not so the blackface accent in which my comrade now explained, "White folks go *one* two *three* four, *one* two *three*. . . ." He clapped his Dixie Cup with its wooden paddlespoon and falsettoed: "'*Jee*-sus *loves* me, this I *know*.' Cullud folks go 'Jee-*sus* love *me*, this *ah* know, *yeah!*' Afterbeat, man."

Hey, neat! I probably said, for I found the simple illustration as remarkable as my friend's unsuspected knowledgeability in this area; the more so when now he discarded his paper cup and snapped his fingers jazzily for emphasis:

"One *two* three *fo*, aint-gon-*hit*-one-three-no-*mo*! Den we drums a liddle syn-co-*pation* into you big bone head —" I knew the word, but not its meaning until he then did exactly that, with his fingerflats — "Bididdlydiddly *bump*bump, bididdly bump*bump* —" whereupon I grasped, instantly and forever, the principle of syncopated rhythm.

"Cmonnalonga mahouse now, man, and we *ree*hearse it."

His possession was contagious: All the way from steaming Race Street, over the creek bridge to East Cambridge, down Maryland Avenue and over to Henry Street, we pranced and snapped our fingers on the afterbeat, singing (as best I could, who scarcely knew the words) "Alexander's Ragtime Band" and drumming syncopated paradiddles with sticks from the gutter upon lampposts, bridge railing, car fenders, each other.

> Come *on* along [*bump* bump],
> Come *on* along [*bump*ity bump],
> It's *Alexander's* Rag*time* Band [di *bump*ity bump]. . . .

I was razzed for my having taken music lessons for years already and learning little or nothing about the subject — and indeed, my friend had opened some odd door in me, for I had a sudden intuitive feel for what we were doing such as I had never experienced in Miss Hubbard's studio, laboriously counting out the values of dotted eighth notes and sixteenth-bar rests in six-eight or three-quarter time. Before we had passed the rank crab-houses along Cambridge Creek, I was as dexterous a maple-twig percussionist as Jerome Schreiber — whose sisters, he informed me en route, were practicing the new jitterbug dance all over their house at every opportunity to the accompaniment of recordings by the King of Swing and other notables, all unknown to me. Ramona, the second oldest, was moreover dating a trumpet player from a dance band over in Easton, who, to ingratiate himself with their occasional watchman, had given Schreib a beat-up old bugle and was teaching him the standard calls.

> *They* can play a *bu*gle call *like* you never *heard* before [*bump*]:
> So *natural that* you want to *go* to war [*bump*]. . . .

Under our antics lay an awareness, surely mutual, that often as
Jerry Schreiber had been on the premises of 301 Aurora and even
inside our house, he had never until now invited me to his; nor,
given his stories of what went on there, had I yearned to visit. I
was flattered, curious, a touch apprehensive. My friend was every
bit as intelligent as my sister and me; our teachers all acknowledged that JackandJill and Jerry were the bright lights of the class,
while scolding Jerry for a disruptiveness and laziness that I was
certain they misunderstood, although I could not have articulated
how — except that those traits were of a piece with his scoffing at
our Bookanollidge while devouring it volume by volume. Even
better than with my sister, I could do "word stuff" with Schreib,
one of several ways I had learned to deflect his fits of bullying. We
thought it hilarious that summer, for example, to make mock-Irish
names out of locutions with Os in them — Buck O'Knowledge,
Tim O'Clock, Tubb O'Shit — just as, a decade later, in our work-
ing-musician days, we would amuse ourselves with imagining such
Italian characters as good-hearted old Ma Nontroppo ("Take it
easy on old Ma"), her sexy daughter Ann DiAmo ("I'm ready if
you are"), and Ann's chaperone, Aunt Dante ("Take a walk, Aunt
Dante"). Easy to see in retrospect that as JackandJill began to dis-
join, Jerome Schreiber was my mercurial surrogate for and relief
from that long conjunction, as I was his equivocal relief from
Henry Street. By his lights I was a bit of a sissy, but he needed me
even in that aspect; by mine he was a bit of a lowlife, but I needed
him in that aspect as well. It was a friendship faute de mieux, each
of us the mieux for the other's faute.

As we turned off Franklin Street onto Henry, my heart misgave
me. Only three blocks from home, it was a stretch of East Cambridge that I had never traversed in my ten years. The houses there
were not shacks (as were whole blocks of the Second Ward), but
several were in notable disrepair, and even the tidiest were bleak.
There was little in the way of trees and shrubbery; front yards were
brown and weedy from summer drought and inattention, and the
landscaping ran to such ornaments as whitewashed tractor tires
and halved furnace boilers planted with red, white, and blue petu-

nias. From some backyards (as still on Byrn Street but no longer on Aurora) roosters crowed.

"Wait here till I signal."

The yard we had stopped before was poorly picket-fenced, the lawn dead and unornamented but for a faded blue crystal ball on a concrete pedestal, the crabfat-yellow clapboard house neither the most dilapidated nor the least among its neighbors. Old washing machine with hand-cranked wringer on the screenless porch, which however also had a peeling swing and weathered wicker chairs. At the windows of both stark storeys, roller blinds but no curtains, the blinds drawn to varying degrees and some askew. In the crushed-oystershell driveway, an old Chevrolet coupe, its hood halves folded up like black bird's wings. Schreib identified it as "Mona's" boyfriend's, then vaulted the low sagging fence and took cover behind the car for a moment before zigzagging to the house corner like a movie cowboy dodging Indian rifle fire. I had no idea how much of this caution was meant seriously or what he was reconnoitering for. His covert approach was spoiled by three mixed-breed dogs, who now bounded from behind the house to leap and yelp at him enthusiastically; nevertheless, he skulked from window to window down the driveway, cuffing the dogs and peering over each sill into the house before moving to the next. I crossed my fingers that he would pen those dogs, for I had not yet entirely outgrown a childish fear of any except the most quietly affectionate canines. But soon after he disappeared behind his house and presumably slipped inside, the mongrels frisked back into the side yard, caught sight of me, and sprang full cry at the fence corner, from which I retreated across the sidewalk.

A full minute later, Schreib stepped onto the front porch and waved for me to come. Two of the dogs ran to him; the third — half spaniel, half English setter, by the red-eyed look of him — stayed at the fence to bark warning of certain dismemberment if I trespassed. Call off your dogs! I pled with a laugh, hoping he might if I showed I wasn't really afraid.

"Paym no nevermind. They don't hardly never bite."

He was clearly teasing, and as clearly testing. I knew him well enough to understand that I was not to assume myself safe just because he jokingly suggested that I wasn't — and as I moved to the fence-gate, the two mutts who'd left came charging back to assist the third.

"Don't showm yer scared!" Schreib called, in high glee, as I felt my fear broadcast like radio waves from the RKO tower in their movie trademark. I was more terrified at the prospect before me than I could remember having been at any in my life till then. I would have seized any honorable excuse not to open that gate. On the other hand, my regular post-piano-lesson Saturday matinees at Schine's Arcade and my busy reading through the shelves of boys' novels from the county library, together with the racks of comic books from Whitey's Candyland, gave me to recognize my situation: the ordeal that the Main Character must surmount if he is to remain the hero of his own story. It was only that summer that I had begun to think about such things, though I could not have said what kind of things they were: the range of actions permitted to the Lone Ranger but not to Tonto; the reasons why although Flash Gordon's enemies on page three of the comic book seemed this time to have sprung a really fatal trap, one needed not doubt for a single panel of the story that he would escape it; why, on the other hand, we could be fairly certain that this particular secondary member of the polar expedition or of the desert island castaways was foredoomed from Reel One, or Chapter Two — and the extent to which such considerations did and did not apply to real-life predicaments. I had found that even my sister, not to mention our mother, took no more interest in these questions than in the Word Stuff, whereas Schreib could be counted on to engage them as spiritedly as I, unless one of his ornery spells was upon him. As I write these lines with old Pumblechook in my old binder on the fiftieth anniversary of the Pearl Harbor Day then just a year-and-a-bit ahead for America and the world, I can still summon to tactile memory the feel of my left palm upon the coarse end grain of the pointed gatepost as *he steeled himself* (I found myself narrating to myself), lifted off the makeshift rope-loop latch, and stepped forward *to confront the raging beasts, come what may*.

"See?" From his grinning porch-rail perch, Schreib didn't budge until I had crossed the dreadful distance from gate to front steps, the three mongrels yipping, leaping, nipping almost hysterically at my pants legs and bare raised forearms, snuffling at my crotch and backside, forepawing my khaki slacks, terrifying me beyond measure every step of the way, but in fact biting neither me nor my clothes. Once I had passed my unacknowledged test, he demonstrated to me how he could wrestle with the biggest of them, thrust his bare forearm into its jaws, even bite its nape until the animal shrieked, all with impunity, before dismissing the pack with a mighty *Git!* and leading the way indoors.

I myself was much impressed with what I had done; I had been genuinely *brave*, as surely my friend was aware. But if he registered my courage at all, it was only by not teasing me for having been so frightened in the first place. The test was dismissed as the dogs had been. "Cmup," he bade me, and I was not too shaken by my dooryard ordeal to register, en route to the stairs, the differences between his family's living room and mine. On the floor, linoleum, much worn in the traffic areas, instead of carpets on high-gloss hardwood. No coffee tables, bookcases, houseplants, or knick-nacks, not to mention a piano; no chairs, even: only three couches (two slipcovered, one threadbare), a couple of scruffy floor lamps, an old console radio with much of its veneer peeled off, and one end table crowded with movie magazines and a battered electric fan. On the walls, no pictures such as our reproduction of Millet's *The Gleaners* and Mother's framed needlepoint floral designs, only a blemished mirror over one of the couches and a small colored print of Jesus like those in our Sunday-school leaflets. The ceiling plaster was stained and sagging in places from water leaks. I had never before been in a Poor Family's house, not to mention one stripped to hard-use essentials like (I would learn a few years later) a college fraternity's make-out room. I followed Schreib closely up the worn wooden stairs, trying not to let on how struck I was by the contrast with 301 Aurora.

From the kitchen, where I had heard someone bustling about and clanking cookware, a young woman's voice called "Hoozat wichu?" and the sister I guessed was Ramona appeared in the doorway, toweling a large agate saucepan. Ram O'Na, as Schreib

Irished her name, was attractive in a slatternly way, with her kid brother's wiry black curls, dark eyes, and freckles, a skinny bare-foot figure in T-shirt and pink pedal pushers, high pointy breasts, and a mouthful of gum.

"Nunnayerbeeswax," Schreib let her know — having, however, dutifully paused on the stairs at her call.

"I'll show you whose beeswax, smartass."

I politely supplied my name and added "from over on Aurora Street."

"Well I guess you are," Ramona granted, unimpressed but mol-lified, and snapped her gum and returned to the kitchen. Schreib thumbed his nose after her with both hands, as he had done at JackandJill in our first encounter, and carried on up the stairs with his impudent trick of farting audibly at each step.

"Never saw this dump so empty," he remarked, as if grudgingly pleased. I had the feeling he didn't want to speak about the place or have me in it longer than necessary. By unusual chance, his mother, his several other sisters, and most importantly his father were nowhere about just then. We went down a linoleumed hall-way past small bedrooms crammed with double bunks, chests of drawers not neatly shut, discarded girls' clothing on the beds and floors, movie-star photos pinned to the walls. His own room, at the hallway's end — not much more than twice the size of its single bed — was the smallest yet the most commodious because unshared. No head- or footboard, no dresser or desk, not even a chair, only the unmade bed on its low iron frame, a wicker hamper with a gooseneck lamp atop Volume Fourteen of our *Book of Knowlege*, a small doorless closet with a clothes rod and two stacked orange crates by way of shelf storage. The roller blind was rain stained, torn, and taped, the one windowscreen punched through in places, the humid heat oppressive even by local standards.

Neat room, I actually said, only dimly registering the inappro-priateness of our standard adjective of approval. The fact is that while I was appalled at the cramped and squalid space, I rather envied my friend his privacy. To the growing embarrassment of my sister and myself, JackandJill still shared the same twin bedroom, such was the friction between me and my older brother. When I changed bedrooms, as was scheduled to happen before school resumed, I would be obliged to share Bill's room, against both our wishes.

"Jeezy peezy, Oats." Schreib shook his head at my fatuity, set aside the gooseneck lamp, returned Volume Fourteen to me without thanks or comment, and from the wicker hamper fished out a dented but carefully polished brass bugle and a tin kazoo. "Let's clear out before the twats come home."

The word was new to me: I sensed its general reference and was embarrassed to ask for clarification. Schreib provided it, indirectly, by snatching back for a moment the borrowed volume, retrieving from it his bookmark, a soiled ten of diamonds, and flashing me a glimpse of the card's backside: no naughty Two-by-Four cartoon drawing, but an actual black-and-white close-up photograph of a naked woman's wide-open legs and the hairy precinct between, which she herself appeared to be spreading with two fingers.

"Look familiar?"

His tone was teasing, even taunting — but I failed to recognize the taunt and was so startled by the photograph that I said only Wow-*ee* before he popped it into his polo-shirt pocket along with the kazoo. We then withdrew via what Schreib called the Fire Exit: through his window onto the rear-porch roof just beneath it, across that roof to the overhanging lateral of a half-dead walnut tree, along that limb to a knotted hemp rope, and down that rope (no easy matter with book and bugle) to the hardpan ground of his backyard, where the still moderately alarming dogs already barked and leaped. Between a wire-fenced chicken run and an unstacked pile of cordwood, we made our way to the row of outbuildings still standard behind East Cambridge houses. Chicken coop, wood- or coalshed, toolshed, and privy would have been the original foursome when these turn-of-the-century neighborhoods were built. By 1940, most of the privies and many of the coops and woodsheds had been converted to miscellaneous storage, and more owners than not had either added a garage to the row, as we had done at 301 Aurora, or dismantled the whole array. But the Schreibers were a carless family when my friend's father was "off on his rambles," and they evidently still used a woodstove for either heating or cooking, although I hadn't seen one in their living room; only the privy had been cleared out and departitioned from its neighbor to make a large utility shed. Thither we now repaired, and in the remaining hour of that long and sweatsy July Fourth afternoon, my lowlife friend accomplished what Miss Agnes Hubbard had not in several years of Saturday piano lessons: I became a musician.

More jammed than our alleyway garage, which had become JackandJill's clubless "clubhouse" when Dad took to parking our big LaSalle more conveniently on the street, the Schreiber shed I nonetheless found "neat," like his bedroom-cubicle, because it was exclusively his territory. Sacks of chickenfeed and portland cement were couch and chair and hassock; a drum of coal oil served as table, with a candlebutt fixed atop it by its own drippings. In myriad secret places my friend had stashed a store of stuff: shoplifted candies in an empty paint can stacked among old half-full ones; Lucky Strike cigarettes and paper matchbooks in one of numerous cigar boxes of nails, screws, bolts, and miscellaneous small hardware; behind a sufficiency of feed sacks, a foot-high stand of old numbers of *Spicy Detective* magazine, their covers stripped off like the clothes of the line-drawn women held in durance vile in the full-page illustrations, awaiting rescue by fully clothed male heroes from their salacious but likewise fully clothed male captors; in that same library area, Volume Fifteen of our *Book of Knowledge*, osmosing groundwater from a dry-rotted floorboard. And (worth a separate sentence because the thing was new to me) behind a rusty tin of soldering flux on an upper stringer between the shed's studs, a package of Ramona Schreiber's trumpeter boyfriend's Trojan *rubbers*. From other of Schreib's talk, I had gathered that these were for use in *fucking*, to which end he loaned his toolshed retreat to that couple from time to time, standing lookout as well, in return for the bugle and other rewards. But as with that odd noun that my friend had introduced to my vocabulary up in his bedroom, I was ashamed to reveal the extent of my ignorance in this matter by asking for clarification — and so by pretending to know more than I did, I learned less than I might have, even when Schreib unrolled one Trojan for my inspection. Now I understood that the thing fitted over the man's *dick*, though not quite why; Schreib's Two-by-Four comics, together with that playing-card "beaver" bookmark, gave me strongly to suspect that dick and — well, susie — were not simply pressed against each other. I could appreciate that the woman wouldn't want the man taking a leak . . . *inside* her, any more than he would want her to pee all over his dick; I supposed the rubber had something to do with preventing that, inadequate as it seemed for the purpose. What impressed me most, however — and would mildly concern me for some time to come — was how *long* the Trojan was, unrolled. I had assumed that Popeye's and Dick Tracy's pee-toms, in those Two-by-Fours, were exaggerated for effect, like other features.

In any case, this review of Schreib's den's treasures was perfunctory. I imagined — mistakenly, it would turn out — that I would be visiting it many another time, now that he had so taken me into his confidence; what we had come there for this afternoon was music. From yet another tweensack cache he produced a perfectly acceptable pair of drumsticks: one actual one, cracked but unbroken, discarded by Ramona's boyfriend's band's drummer after a *hot solo* and retrieved by the trumpeter to pass along to his lookout with promise of another by and by — and a slender hardwood dowel salvaged from a wooden chairback and cut to matching length. My friend demonstrated (left-handedly) how each was held, the dowel in his secondary hand and the cracked Slingerland drumstick in his primary, and rattled out a military tattoo on the coal-oil drum-top:

> *Brrrump bump bump, brrrump bump bump,*
> *Brrrump bump bumpabumpa bump bump bump.*

Neat!

"You do it," he then bade me, and — once I got the sticks reverse-handed and correctly positioned — I did, promptly and easily, as if I had been practicing for some time. Embellishments that I didn't know I knew came naturally:

Bumpadiddly bumpadiddly diddlybump bump,
Diddlydiddlydiddlydiddly bump-bump-bump-bump.

"Not bad," Schreib allowed — the most gratifying praise of my life to then. In no time at all, I could smartly accompany his bugled mess call:

Soupy soupy soupy, without a single bean . . .

Likewise taps, simple for him and difficult for me, as it required a single sustained drumroll:

Day is done; gone the sun
From the lake, from the fields, from the sky . . .

Also reveille, assembly, attack, retreat — all easy for me, but trickier for him because of their tempo and wide intervals:

I can't get 'em up, I can't get 'em up,
I can't get 'em up this mor-ning. . . .

There's a soldier in the grass with a bullet up his ass;
Pull it out, pull it out, pull it out, pull it out.

My polite duets with Jill were nothing by comparison. Schreib and I were making heartfelt music; we were a band. In two sentences he explained why all bugle calls necessarily sounded much alike, and why one couldn't play, for example, "Alexander's Ragtime Band" on that instrument. One minute sufficed to show me the difference between the two-four time of all those bugle calls and the four-four (with accented afterbeat) of jazz — to which we now turned, Schreib exchanging bugle for kazoo. Illumination followed illumination like strung firecrackers: The side of my right shoe against the oil-drum bottom made a satisfying bass effect, which I found I could manage independently of what my hands were doing; the click of the sticks against the upper rim and the varying resonance of different areas of the top gave some of the variety of cymbals, tom-toms, and traps; I discovered accidentally what I would later learn were called rim-shots — the pistol-like effect of striking simultaneously the drumhead with the tip and the rim with the shaft of the stick.

"Hey, Oatmeal, you're hot!"

I was indeed — possessed, transported. A few minutes of piano practice was enough to bore me; I never went to that instrument voluntarily. But I would have played that coal-oil drum behind Schreib's kazoo for hours and hours; wanted never to stop. We played "Darktown Strutters' Ball," "Tiger Rag," "Charleston," "Jeepers Creepers," every up-tempo "jazz" tune that we ten-year-olds could think of. Schreib provided most of the suggestions; I was as surprised at how many of them were familiar to me (who had never before paid real attention to music) as at how almost intuitively I understood licks, fills, breaks, stop-time, roll-offs. We played "Camptown Races":

> Gwine to run all night,
> Gwine to run all day.

"Hot stuff, ain't you," Ramona herself acknowledged from the toolshed doorway, and although her tone was sarcastic, she did a frisky little step — a *sexy* little step, I half understood — *to my beat* before telling her brother to get off his lazy tail and feed dogs and chickens and wash himself up before his mother and sisters got home, or there'd be no hospital fireworks for *him* that night. He replied with a splendrous bugle-fart, reached out his hand to me for the drumsticks, then changed his mind:

"Find yerself a drum to go withm, Oats, and we're in business."

We were not to be, for five years thence — whereafter we would be, off and on, for nearly twenty. But I afterbeat and syncopated all the way from Henry Street to 301 Aurora, feeling materially older than I had been when I'd left home after lunch to walk uptown for the parade. I had at once to show off my new-found talent to Jill (on a garbage can lid, far less impressive than Schreib's coal-oil drum) and to tell her of my afternoon's adventures. I was irrepressible at the dinner table with knife and fork on drinking glass and dinner plate. And all through that evening's fireworks — the most splendiferous, everybody agreed, that Mister Dupont had ever benefacted the city of Cambridge with, and the more stirring in view of the wars going on in Europe and Asia, where Hitler and Hirohito had gotten too big for their britches — while I sat among my family and neighbors on the grassy hospital embankment down by the seawall to marvel at the skyrockets, ground pieces, flares, squibs, and chasers, and while the other youngsters (no sign of Schreib) set off their own firecrackers, cherry bombs, sparklers, and Roman candles, I drummed away at my knees and thightops with my precious sticks, already as natural-feeling in my hands as would be, decades later, this old pen. How readily left and right passed accents back and forth and filled in for each other between, while my foot — *both* feet — maintained beat and afterbeat and did a bit of accent-trading between themselves, even between heel and toe, as well as between feet and hands. I must have been absorbing these rhythms for a long time, unawares; their kinesthetics came so naturally that when, years later, I first sat behind a real jazz drum set, my feet and hands already knew basically what to do. Learning to play the instrument would prove to be mainly a matter of adjusting its fixtures to my taste and enlarging my repertoire by careful listening to jazz recordings and radio broadcasts.

"What's come over you?" my sister asked that night across the space between our twin beds — for I was still drumming, drumming with my fingerflats on my chest in the dark, bediddlybiddly-diddlybiddly diddlybump *bump*.

I don't know, I told her truly. Miffed, she said "Well, *I'm* going to *sleep*," and turned her back to me. "I'll be glad when I have some *privacy*."

I was too preoccupied to think about that; too preoccupied to sleep. Long into the muggy night I soloed, recalling from forgotten movies images of frenetic jazz drummers perspiring over their equipment; of restless natives in the Johnny Weissmuller Tarzan series, tom-toming from the heart of Africa aboriginal messages to sheltered white boys on the verge of adolescence in an America on the verge of war: boomily boomily boomily boomily, blip-blip bdlyblop. (*Yeah!*)

The brawlbrat brawl that this monologue extends toward came to pass on the following Columbus Day. In the three-month interim, I did not move heaven and earth, as a more single-minded boy might have done, to secure a proper drum set for the implementation of my new passion. Having sneaked our soiled Volume Fifteen back into place in the special *Book of Knowledge* bookcase, I recovered from our attic the "bass drum" of a long-discarded kiddie outfit that had once belonged to brother Bill and wheedled his indifferent permission to convert it into a snareless snare-drum or shallow-draft tom-tom on which to practice with my makeshift sticks — and practice I did, with some frequency for a while, in our garage, both alone and with Jerry Schreiber. He never saw fit to invite me back to his toolshed retreat, nor I to press him for reinvitation; indeed, I believe that I was never again on his Henry Street premises. Ramona broke off her romance with the Easton trumpeter before a second drumstick came our way. Another, younger Schreiber sister had a friend in the Twirlettes who at Schreib's urging filched me a pair of marching sticks from the American Legion Post 91 Drum and Bugle Corps, with whom the Twirlettes sometimes rehearsed. Alas, I found them too fat, heavy, clumsy for our kind of music and went back to my chair dowel and cracked Slingerland 3A. Twice or thrice we took over the piano end of the Aurora Street living room and attempted a threesome with Jill; Whitey sold piano sheet music in the Candyland along with comic books and grown-up magazines, and my sister obligingly tried her hand at several Tin Pan Alley tunes: "Rosalie," "The Sunny Side of the Street," "I Got Rhythm." But she was not yet musician enough to play only the chords and leave the lead to Schreib's kazoo, and so he had either to double her melody or to improvise little obbligatos where he could. In the absence of cymbals and wire brushes, my "snare drum" accompaniments sounded inappropriately military and always too loud, particularly at slower tempos; and although Jill was more adept at the keyboard than I, she lacked a feel for jazz and for ensemble playing. Her rhythm was mechanical; she inclined to set the beat herself rather than following the drummer, and yet never quite grasped its primacy; her hesitations over a chord or a fingering would throw us maddeningly off after every few bars. Moreover, something about my friend "got her goat" that season, as our mother would have put it: something that I, too, could sense, but not identify, in his teasing manner with her, of a different nature from his ragging "friendchip" way with me. Copies of *Spicy Detective* found their way from his toolshed to our garage, hidden up in the rafters with *365 Bedtime Stories*. He wondered to me, no telling how seriously, whether we could persuade Jill to play Spicy Detective with us, either there or down in the rivershore Jungle.

Exciting as it was at first to have a band of three instruments instead of two, we soon grew unhappy with our efforts, moved our original duo back into the garage, and found ourselves no longer satisfied with the sound that had at first so pleased us. "Dumb toys," Schreib declared of our instruments. He was saving up for a real trumpet; Ramona's ex-boyfriend had been thinking of buying a brand-new Selmer over in Baltimore and might sell Schreib his old Conn for forty smackeroos. I agreed to start saving for a real drum outfit — Slingerlands or Ludwigs, Schreib had let me know, were the only kind to have. But even a basic set without floor tom-tom or genuine Zildjian cymbals cost a couple hundred dollars easy, and my allowance just then was fifty cents a week, of which half usually went for Saturday matinees. And so while I continued to tap out jazz rhythms with my hands and feet "like a reg'lar darky," my father remarked, my energies shifted to activities more usual for a ten-year-old boy. Sports, alas, were never among my interests, either as player or as spectator; but I was passionate about airplanes — reading about them, identifying the few that passed overhead, attempting to build flying models from kits — and I ran through library books at a great rate, and played elaborate fantasy games down at the rivershore, where also I posted messages in bottles as aforesung and kept an eye out for reply.

In August, JackandJill spent two weeks as usual with the New Jersey relatives (I marvel now at the logistics of their generosity: how they shuttled their East Cambridge niece and nephews up to Jersey and back for extended visits without automotive assistance from Whitey and Georgia, and managed seldom or never to have JackandJill in residence at the same time as Bill). Up there, there were neighbor kids to play with — of or above our class, I realize now but did not then — and I put my bugle-and-kazoo friend out of mind entirely while we reveled in the expansive, more affluent life and property of Aunt Roon and Uncle Doc. As Schreib hid out in his Henry Street toolshed, we fixed up for fun an aging Old Town canoe discovered in the well-finished loft of the detached three-car garage that Aunt Roon called "the barn." With our new playmates we staged amateur variety shows up there for the grown-ups. We made sight-seeing expeditions to the New York World's Fair and excursions to Jersey shore resorts — at one of which, Asbury Park or Ocean Grove, I managed to get briefly lost in a funhouse. The New Jersey place was commodious, but there seemed always to be other relatives living there temporarily, and so although all hands agreed that JackandJill were getting too big to share the same bedroom, we did so faute de mieux. Dressing and undressing, however, not to mention bathing and toilet-using, we managed privately, as we had come to do at home — and it was announced to us that back at 301 Aurora my bed was being shifted into Bill's room, and Jill's into the little sewing room adjacent. Our lifelong old bedroom — where we had sent coded messages from bed to bed via string-cable shuttles, and listened to winter mice scuttling in the walls, and endured measles and chicken pox together, and told and heard not 365 but thousands upon thousands of bedtime stories, registering in whispers in the dark our joint and several experience of life until one or the other of us fell asleep — would become Mother's new, more ample workroom. Jill was pleased; I, too, would have welcomed a room of my own, preferably adjoining hers so that we could talk at night as usual. But the disagreeable prospect of doubling up with my brother was still a week and more off, and by some logistical magic Bill was to be fetched up to Jersey for the final fortnight of

summer as JackandJill were being returned to Maryland, and so
the twins would have that time to settle into their new quarters
before the crunch came (for me) on Labor Day.

"So now you cain't just slip across the room and fuck all night,
like you been doing."

Schreib and I were peeing in adjacent urinals in the boys' lavatory of East Cambridge Elementary at the end of afternoon recess
on the school's "Columbus Day": a Friday, October 11, as the day
itself fell on a Saturday that year and the holiday on Monday.
Adolf Hitler, victorious everywhere in Europe, was bombing Britain nightly (I could identify by silhouette every combat aircraft
used by both sides). Unremarked by East Cambridge, the Soviet
Union had annexed the Baltic republics. Although we had not yet
entered the war, President Roosevelt was continuing the state of
unlimited emergency that he had declared on JackandJill's ninth
birthday, and German U-boats were even said to be patrolling the
mouth of Chesapeake Bay. Where once the occasional Piper Cub
or Stinson Reliant had buzzed overhead, we were now permitted
to rush to our classroom windows to see military transports and
even Navy blimps cruise by. But although the highlights of the war
were reported in our *Weekly Reader* and its geography was
pointed out to us on classroom maps, Miz Stoker's fifth grade had
spent the week as usual at that season concentrating on 1492:
King Ferdinand and Queen Isabella, the *Niña*, *Pinta*, and *Santa
Maria*, and the lamentable injustice that the discoverer of "America" had nothing American named in his honor except for one
poor country in South America, a province of Canada, a few
towns here and there in the USA, a river out west somewhere, and
the federal district comprising our nation's capital. Our class had
tabulated those paltry items on the blackboard early in the week.
By the Wednesday, I had added to it Columbia University, in New
York City. On the Thursday, Schreib had contributed both Columbia Pictures, in Hollywood, California, and the Knights of Columbus, which none of the rest of us had heard of but Miz Stoker
verified to be a Roman Catholic social organization. How had
Jerome happened to hear of it? she wondered.

Schreib explained, grinning despite the smashed lips that he had

showed up with at school last Monday: "My sister Maryann had-
erself a Cathlic boyfriend this pass summer that blonged to the
Columbian Squires, which is run by the Knightsaclumbus and is
like their Boy Scouts. Then Maw got wind of it and giver a good
switchin."

We thought that report hilarious. Miz Stoker, however, told
Schreib that he knew very well that the correct past tense is *gave*,
not *give* (indeed, all fall his speech had been belligerently unedu-
cated, as if he were reverting defiantly to brawlbrat days gone by;
we assumed his mouth to have been injured in some weekend
ruckus, although he variously claimed he'd fallen from a tree or
walked into a door). She reminded the class that while there were
no Catholics in East Cambridge Elementary — they had their own
primary school, over by their church in West End — Lord Baltimore's original Maryland colonists had been Catholics fleeing persecution in England. To them our state owed not only its name
(though we Protestants preferred to regard it as honoring the
queen of England, not of Heaven) but its historical tradition of
religious freedom. We Protestants might disagree with the Catholics' beliefs — just as Methodists, Presbyterians, Baptists, Quak-
ers, and whatnot disagreed with one another, and even Methodist
Episcopalians with Methodist Protestants — but they had as much
right to hold those beliefs as we to hold ours. That was the American way, Miz Stoker declared, and we might remember that the
discoverer of our country (which ought by rights to have been
called Columbia, as in the Gem-of-the-Ocean song) had been a
Catholic.

"Maryann sassed back," Schreib volunteered, "that ifn she
couldn't have her cat-licker boyfriend, she'd up and find herself a
Christ-killing Jewboy or a shoeshine nigger, see how Maw liked
that."

At this remove I still shake my head at the precociousness, for
our neighborhood, of my friend's expressed bigotry and the terms
of its impudent expression, for which Miz Stoker — a mild and
pleasant lady who manifested her displeasure constructively as disappointment — firmly but unangrily smacked his open palm three

times with her ruler, stood him to face the cloakroom corner "like a second grader," and wearily repeated her threat of suspension from school if he didn't rein in his late incorrigibility, for she knew him to be quite as bright as . . . Jack and Jill.

That pair were as much baffled as scandalized (and scandalously amused) by his epithets. Here in East Cambridge in 1940 was not only the "anti-Semitism without Jews" that one would hear of decades later in postwar Poland, but Catholic-baiting without Catholics and Negro-baiting virtually without Negroes. Although at least one in five of the town's thirteen thousand citizens was black, except for Colored Mattie and the occasional yard man we knew none of them, so complete was racial segregation in that time and place. Our prejudices in that quarter, while ubiquitous, casual, and complete, were mild and without virulence, if only for lack of contact with their object. Catholics we had heard of but, in our ward, knew none. There being no parochial secondary schools in the county, when the children of the several white wards came together from sixth grade on, we would come to know and befriend our several Catholic classmates; I remember no baiting, teasing, or even remarking their religion. As for Jews, to us East Cambridge Elementarians they were something vaguely biblical; none of us, I suspect, could have defined the term, which I believe had never come up in conversation at 301 Aurora. There were in fact at least six Jewish families in our town — the Cartons and the Frankels, who owned clothing stores on either side of Whitey's Candyland; the less prosperous Garners and the Marmers, who owned the Army & Navy Store farther up Race Street; and the Nathans and the Feldmans, who owned the town's two furniture stores. All were well-respected business people with houses in West End; several had children in the public school system, all of them well-liked by their classmates (a daughter of Mr. Frankel's would become the television sitcom star Beatrice Arthur, of *Maude* and *The Golden Girls*). With respect to Jews even more than to Catholics, we were too innocent of differences to be intolerant. The notion that one might disparage a Catholic as a licker of cats — whatever *that* might be — or, more sinisterly, a Jew as a killer of Christ, had never occurred to JackandJill. Nearly a decade's attendance at St. Paul's Methodist Protestant Sunday School had not equipped us to understand that slander, much less to entertain an opinion on it.

So where'd you pick up such stuff? I would ask Jay Wordsworth Scribner in graduate school, during one of our fierce nostalgia sessions.

He kept his eyes fixed brightly upon me while he tipped back his National Bohemian, pressing the bottle-mouth to his scarred embouchure like a trumpet mouthpiece. "Cat-lickers from Paw, Christ-killers from Maryann's cat-licker boyfriend. Paw had other names for the Jews. Drunk and sober, he was a man rich in negative epithets; said he learned 'em in the Twenty-Ninth Infantry Division in Weltkrieg Ein."

He went on then to tell me for the first time, twelve years after the fact, the truth about his crushed lips on Columbus Day week, 1940: the Henry Street reveille-call prank, done on a bet with sister Maryann that Gabriel himself couldn't rouse their passed-out father from his stupor; the old sot's astonishingly instant and accurate retaliation with the back of one hand against the bugle's bell, followed by his smashing the instrument to junk against a bedpost — all without raising himself from the mattress.

How come you didn't tell us that at the time?

"Us fifth graders or us twins?" He cut me a sidelong smile and thumbed up his new eyeglasses: heavy black plastic frames with straight sidepieces, such as most of us jazzmen wore. "Come on, Oats: You're forgetting a few things about ten eleven forty."

He then reminded me that on our return from New Jersey that summer — as in the previous summer, when Jill and I had been the only kids in our class to be taken to the World's Fair — I had been in no hurry to reconnect with him. Granted that I had been then and was still (and am yet) of a passive disposition, and that the initiative in our relation had prevailingly been his, my apparent indifference had nonetheless annoyed — *disappointed*, Miz Stoker would have said — the lad who had spent part of our New Jersey fortnight sleeping surreptitiously in the garage of 301 Aurora to avoid his returned father's alcoholic rages. I might or might not

recollect that twice that September, Schreib had attached himself
to JackandJill's Saturday-afternoon post-piano-lesson movie matinees at Schine's Arcade, and had proposed playing with us down
in the Jungle afterward, and had been told that we were too busy;
surely, however, it must have been evident to all hands that he had
by that time a shy crush on my sister that he scarcely knew what
to do with. The psychology of his response was obvious — had
been, it seemed to him, even at the time, although he couldn't have
articulated it.

It had not been so to me, I told him.

Jay shrugged his black eyebrows. "You've always been a fairly
unconscious guy. Maybe a side effect of all that JackandJillery: like
you're only half there." To soften this criticism (for we were close
friends then), he added, "Maybe that'll be the making of you as a
writer, somehow or other."

I doubt it.

"Meanwhile, there you come into the little boys' room to take
a leak, with that oatmeal birthmark that you had back then all
over your face, that I told you came from eating pussy, and you
pretended to know what I was talking about and made a not-bad
joke out of it, saying at least it didn't come from licking cats. . . ."

I marveled: How could he remember all this long-ago stuff, and
in such detail?

"Maybe that'll be the making of *me* as a writer. Anyhow, you
tried to change the subject back then, as you're doing now —"

I'm not.

Scrib shrugged and blew a note across the mouth of his near-
empty bottle, a whole tone lower than his latest previous sounding. "You griped about having to share a bedroom with your
brother, at a time when *I* had to scout ahead for Paw before I
dared go near our Henry Street rathole — which we were about
to move out of anyhow, 'cause we couldn't afford even that. So I
said what I said to you 'bout humping your sister."

He said to me what he'd said, and my face had scalded. We
were not the only boys in that lavatory. *You take that back,
Schreib*, I had managed to reply.

"I don't take stuff back," he let me know, his tone amused and gratified. We flushed, zipped or buttoned, and stepped back from our respective urinals. The one or two other fellows — I can't remember who they were* — watched us.

You take it back *or else.*

"Or else what?"

The bell rang for end of recess. My voice was on the edge of failing me: You just better take it back, is all.

"You heard him," Schreib said to the others, and then, much satisfied, to me: "See you after school, Oatmeal."

Half conscious or not, even through the painful balance of that schoolday I sensed what marriage would later confirm: that quarrels between friends and intimates are, as aforesung, seldom about what they're "about." Criticality self-organizes; differences accumulate like vapors from a basement gas leak, perhaps even where you'd thought the ventilation adequate, until any spark blows the roof. The explosion, when it comes, is not about the spark. Between Jerome Schreiber and me that long-ago Friday, the issue was no unreciprocated feeling of his for my sister (we were only ten), much less his gratuitous ugly taunt. It was the impatience of the relatively deprived with the relatively privileged; of the seasoned with the callow, the tough with the tender. Schreib was fed up to the point of fisticuffs with my being me and his being himself. Grievously assaulted by his father, he needed to punch our difference in the face and be punched by it, wrestle it to the ground until either it or he said Uncle.

Sensing this truth (which I was a long way indeed from articulating) was no help to me as Christopher Columbus duly attained the West Indies in our afternoon history lesson, and further thousands were killed in War-Torn Europe and Asia, and the dismissal bell sounded in East Cambridge Elementary. Between recess and schoolday's end, some version of my lavatory challenge grapevined quickly through Miz Stoker's classroom (bypassing Jill, it seems, who learned of it only after the dust literally settled on this brawl-brat brawl). A couple of the boys sneaked smirks my way; Kay Nevermindwho from over on Franklin Street cut me an apprecia-

---

*"Bobby Hurley and Tommy Snelling." If you say so, Scrib.

tive glance, which I savored although it did little to assuage my
fright. I was no fighter, had never really fought, was in general no
rough-and-tumbler, not even an athlete. I avoided confrontations,
I placated bullies, yet somehow managed not to regard myself as
cowardly. Fifteen to twenty years later, when my own three children were small, I would often play-wrestle with them and referee
their roughhousing among themselves, to help provide them the
ancient feel and healthy animal release of physical tussling, sport-
ive combat, as well as to coach them in fair play, the adversarial
form of cooperation. Alas, Whitey had done nothing of that sort
with us. In the Schreiber household, on the contrary, alley-fighting
was taken for granted. Schreib's sisters ranged from scrappers to
hellions, the terrors of their respective school-grades; they and
their brother were inured to blows from their parents for every
variety of infraction, including losing a fight. Mother and father
themselves not infrequently went at it — he the mean but scrawny
aggressor, she the hefty self-defender, battered but unbowed, who
in well-justified retaliation gave almost as good as she got. Schreib
himself liked to boast that his father had threatened him with a
hiding if he ever got caught fighting *fair* in a back-alley dustup. So
far as I knew, my friend had never lost a schoolyard scuffle.

I was, however, accustomed to a posture of militant defense in
my relation with my brother, and to the more or less dominant-
male role in our JackandJillery; a bit of a mama's boy, perhaps,
but Georgia's easygoing passivity was nowise emasculative, and
my "identification" was unreservedly with my father, whose name
I shared and whose benign authority I unquestioningly respected.
If my character was less strong than in retrospect I could wish, my
ego was sturdy enough. I was prevailingly self-confident, used to
success in and praise for my childhood enterprises, had little or no
experience of failure and blame. Moreover, either diet or genes or
pituitary rates gave me some advantage over Jerry Schreiber that
year in height, weight, and reach, though not likely in strength.
Finally and perhaps most importantly, my experience of movies
and of boys' novels had taught me not only to identify with their
heroes, but at least half consciously to regard myself as one, anyhow as one in the making. Ever since that episode with the Schrei-

ber dogs, an invisible narrator had taken up residence in my head
to recount Voice Over the ongoing story of my life, third-person
anonymous: *To discipline himself for the rigors ahead*, this voice
would intone, *he had taken secretly to wearing a leather belt
strapped tightly around his chest, under his clothing, and he never
removed it day or night except briefly at bathtime* (I had in fact
done this for a week or so in September, having read somewhere
of initiatory ordeals undergone by boys in certain Indian tribes).
Or, *Whatever the danger to himself, and much as he esteemed his
old friend and comrade, he could not let this insult to his sister's
honor go unavenged.* . . .

I offer these considerations to explain to myself why my fear
did not lead me either to withdraw my challenge at whatever
humiliating cost or, once the scuffle was honorably joined, to
capitulate early — as one sees beta males do in the breeding chal-
lenges of other animal species on "nature" television, before serious injury occurs. My reality-sense must have been weak enough,
those other factors strong enough, to carry me in a tingling daze
out to the schoolyard in a press of classmates, book satchel in hand
and heart in mouth. I remember a clear October afternoon, chilly
for that time of year in Chesapeake country; most of us were into
corduroys already, of one sort or another. Kneesocks and knick-
erbockers with matching short jacket had been the schoolboy style
until the turn of the decade, done in a tough dark-brown corduroy
flecked with umber to disguise wear and soil. The knicker-knees
whispered to each other when a boy walked; his stockings, usually
argyll, were turned down at the tops over elastic garters, the tops
themselves covered by the knickers' elasticized cuffs. Mothers
bought these outfits large for their grade-school sons, for so rugged was the material that one jacket and two pairs of knickers
would last a boy from October into April, by when he might have
grown two inches. I am not sure what the rationale of this awkward trouser-style was — a leftover, I suspect, from the muddy
generations before paved streets and sidewalks, when a boy's
soiled stockings would have been a lighter night's laundry than
thick trousers. In any case, by 1940 most of us were wearing
straight-legged long pants of that same tough material and stout

leather oxfords (blue jeans and sneakers lay yet a decade ahead, though in warm weather we wore high-top "tennis shoes" of black canvas and white rubber, the *Keds* brand name in molded relief on the ankle patches); but Schreib's family being down on their luck, he was obliged to wear last winter's knickers, too small for him now and patched at both knees — the image of that turn-of-the-century American character, Peck's Bad Boy.

The ritual of these non-spontaneous combats was familiar to everyone at East Cambridge Elementary. Escorted by that press of boys and a few tomboy girls, the adversaries went to the northwest corner of the schoolyard, where an area of level hardpan ideal for mumblety-peg and marble-shooting extended onto an adjacent vacant lot. There, folklore maintained, our teachers had no authority — though in fact those good women would break up any schoolboy fight they happened to espy this side of Cambridge Creek, and the bystanders' functions, along with encouraging and refereeing by rough consensus, included screening the fight from teacherly view and alerting the combatants to the approach of Mizzes Brinsfield, Nield, Haggett, or Stoker. Depending on the season and the pugilists' personalities, there might be a handing of jackets, satchels, and eyeglasses to seconds, perhaps admonitions from certain older boys against fighting dirty (this being no back alley, but *school*, almost), perhaps an exchange of taunts between the principals to get things started. Then would come no more than a couple minutesworth of cautious bare-knuckled sparring — in these pre-television days, the only real *boxing* any of us had seen was in occasional newsreels; we young East Cantabrigians didn't go in for it, nor had we heard yet of jiujitsu, karate, kung fu, tai kwando, and the rest. Presently one party would land a proper punch, whereupon fists would fly, usually for a mercifully short interval, until the antagonists came to grips and the fistfight turned into what we called a "rassle": an apt compaction of *wrestle, hassle,* and *tussle.* At this stage of the fight, while the combatants rolled and scuffled in the dirt, punches might still be thrown, but not far. Choking, biting, kicking, clawing, hair-pulling, eye-gouging, and the use of any sort of weapons, from sticks and stones and bookbags to pocketknives — all were verboten among even the roughest boys (the girls fought less frequently, but with fewer prohibitions). Typically the fight ended when one or the other got his opponent in a physical checkmate — a headlock or arm-twist sufficiently painful and secure to oblige the loser to say "I give up," or "I take it back," or "Okay, you win," whereupon the rassle ended at once. Never did the winner inflict gratuitous further punishment on the checkmated loser; nor did the defeated, once released, seize the opportunity for a surprise reattack. Noses and knuckles got bloodied, lips split, cheekbones bruised, clothing soiled and torn, but as a rule the fights were short and fair, the injuries not severe. In this regulation, too, the bystanders had an active if inexactly defined role, passed down through untold generations of grade-schoolers and surprisingly unaffected by the violent, protracted, and unsportsmanlike movie fights of our cowboy heroes. There was more arguing over rule infractions in games of marbles and kick the can than in schoolyard pugilistics.

One last time, my narrator hopefully declared, *he offered his friend a chance to take back those insulting words before the two of them came to blows.* So dizzy was I with fright at standing actually inside the combatants' circle — ringed by Bobby Hurley, Tommy Snelling, a number of Aarons, Kay Whatsername, Irma Jones — instead of with them on its circumference, I doubt I could have voiced that last-ditch offer. In any case, I had no chance to: His already-scabbed lips grinning, his bright dark eyes asquint with whatever emotion, the instant we confronted each other in the still-forming circle Schreib said "Here you go, Oatmeal," and struck me a gaspingly painful, tear-springing blow alongside my nose.

Interruptive, tear-blinded aria: "Oatmeal: 'He jests at scars'"

Oatmeal: "He jests at scars who never felt a wound," and at birthmarks who never bore one, in the plainest possible view, through an East Cambridge childhood. Goody-goody we might have been, sort of, JackandJill, until puberty broke up our act and made us ordinary adolescents; but unblemished we were not. To the diagram of forces that early shaped us must be added, in my case, a striking, unfortunate birthmark.

Jill was born blemished, too, but outside 301 Aurora no one whom she didn't choose to show or tell knew of the mole-brown thumbprint just above her left hip. Jack, less lucky, emerged from the womb eighty minutes after with a freckly brown blotch smack in the middle of his face. Scarcely visible in those earliest beach and stroller and sideyard shots (though *I* can see it even there), it is conspicuous in our better lighted but unretouched official first-grade photos. Commencing with a ruler-straight edge down the centerline of my nose (a genetic side effect of the bilateral asymmetry of faces), it spreads under the left eye and well over the cheekbone, lightening and dispersing en route into an archipelago of freckles. In early childhood I quite accepted it, as I accepted being half of a pair, as children accept pretty much whatever they're born with or into until they learn comparison. Given the twins' sore rivalry with their brother, it is to Bill's credit (or my memory's debit) that he never taunted me with my mark; nor did Miss Ridah Collins's nice private kindergarteners, although surely they remarked it, as did I — perhaps aloud, as youngsters will, in frank but unmalicious curiosity: "What's that stuff all over your face?"

East Cambridge Elementary was another story. Although even there I was not *persistently* taunted with it (any more than I was persistently bullied or otherwise tormented through what was, after all, a prevailingly sunny childhood), neither was I let long to forget it. My nose was from time to time rubbed in my face, so to speak — no more so than other kids' differentia were rubbed in theirs ("Carrot Top," "Shorty," "Stringbean," "Tubby"), and rather less often than we were teased with our JackandJillery, but often enough to turn the screws of shy self-consciousness.

In the myths of wandering heroes, the child sustains an early, life-imperiling wound that leaves a scar (or limp, or both) by which he will be recognized in full herohood when he emerges transfigured from his harrowing adventures in the otherworld. With us birthmarked, the scar precedes the wound, as the self precedes self-consciousness. Among the several causes of my becoming not only "a writer" but the author of my particular writings, I give some weight to my birthmark, once the world called it to my attention: the Flaw made manifest.

What flaw, for pity's sake? What did my birthmark mark? Some original sin, surely; otherwise I'd not have felt half guilty for its blazon. But *what* original sin? It was in the insinuating air all around us: as elementary as East Cambridge School, but never quite named before Schreib's Columbus Day lavatory insult, and not *quite* named even on that consequential occasion. It had to do with our being twins, more particularly opposite-sex twins. It had to do with our being JackandJill.

Exegetical aria-within-an-aria: "Jack and Jill"

> *Jack and Jill*
> *Went up the hill*
> *To fetch a pail of water.*
>
> *Jack fell down*
> *And broke his crown,*
> *And Jill came tumbling after.*

As is the case with most nursery rhymes, the meter of this classic specimen is simple and rigorous, even monotonous, and exactly replicated between the two stanzas.* There are no variations whatever in the elementary alternation of stressed and unstressed syllables, with a slight delay after each stress: a lilting, skipping rhythm suggestive of carefree childhood — although the action described is not play but a homely household chore from the days before indoor plumbing. A simple rhyme-scheme (*aab ccb*) and stanzaic structure (short dimeter couplet followed by a single trimeter), its single, small irregularity would appear to be the off rhyme of the *b* trimeters, *water/after*.

Close scansion, however, reveals the apparent simplicity of the poem's prosody to be deceptive. Is the foot iambic (da-*da*) or tro-

---

*There are other stanzas (*note to follow*), but what child remembers them?

chaic (*da*-da)? Each stanza opens with an apparent trochee (*Jack and . . ./Jack* fell . . .) and closes likewise (*wa*-ter/*af*-ter), but a glance at lines two and three of each stanza persuades us at once that the foot is meant to be the homely English iamb: Went *up*| the *hill*/ To *fetch*| a *pail*, etc. Once we note that the syllabification of the lines is less simple than their rhyme-scheme and alternating accent — not 4-4-7, 4-4-7, but 3-4-7, 3-4-7 — we can reasonably describe the prosody of the recited poem thus: Two three-line stanzas, *aab ccb*, each consist of an iambic dimeter couplet, its initial unstressed beat not given, followed by an iambic trimeter third line with a supernumerary final soft syllable to compensate for the missing opener.

These preliminary observations made, we turn to the particulars of the poem's signification, beginning with its Dantesque wedding of form and content in both macro- and microstructural features. Just as the three books of the *Divina Commedia* and their *terza rima* building blocks reflect Christianity's tripartite eschatology and the unity of the Trinity, so this blithe nursery rhyme about the fall of an at least originally innocent couple proceeds by duples: *Two* metrically identical stanzas (*twin* stanzas, one is tempted to say) each commence with a *couplet* in a *dimeter* that, whether scanned iambically or trochaically, employs a *two*-beat foot — more levels of two than Dante has threes. And just as the Florentine's *terza rima* interlinks his stanzas — *aba bcb cdc*, etc. — so the twin stanzas of *J & J* are coupled (slantwise, inexactly) by their *b* off rhyme, *water/after*.

Would it not have been more in keeping with the theme of dupleness, or doubling (not to say *duplicity*), to render the poem entirely in couplets — four of them, perhaps, in two stanzas, to get away from threes altogether? Arguably so, but consider the trade-offs: the hobblingly unrelieved dimeters, the loss of interstanzaic linkage (it's either *aa bb/cc dd* or *aa bb/aa bb*, more a cloning than a coupling; or *aa bb/bb aa*, suggesting an ascent/descent in course of which *nothing consequential happens*; or *aa bb/ab ab* — the metaphorical possibilities whereof, this exegete declines to consider).

In fact, as shall be seen, that "odd" third line of each stanza serves a number of useful purposes, not least among them release from the constrictive dimeter couplets: a playing of twos against threes reflected in and reflective of the line's tripedality. "Who is the third," Eliot's "Waste Land" asks, "who walks always beside you?" Let's zoom in:

I.

Jack and Jill. On an empty stage, two characters in three monosyllables. In the minimalist way of nursery rhymes, all "background" exposition is dispensed with: no "Once upon a time, in a land far away, there lived . . ."; none of "that David Copperfield kind of crap," as J. D. Salinger's Holden Caulfield calls such introductory résumés. We are afforded scarcely a clue to the pair's age, relationship, or situation. Illustrators of Mother Goose books regularly presume J & J to be young children, no doubt on the grounds that if both *go* to fetch a single pail of water, both must be *needed* to carry the pail; all illustrations show the pair of them lugging even the *empty* pail uphill together in stanza one* — small children indeed, or else they hold the vessel jointly out of simple reciprocal affection, as unself-conscious youngsters might hold hands while walking or skipping along. A reasonable presumption, but only a presumption. All that we can say with confidence is that the characters are two, not one or several; that on the evidence of their given names they are male and female; that those given names are what they are (English, for one thing, like the poem itself, implying an Anglophone venue for the action to follow); and that in the order of their introduction, at least, Jack precedes Jill.

*E.g.,

A cultural reflex of male primacy? Very likely. Reflective of a customary male initiative in such enterprises as hill-ascending, water-fetching, etc.? Likewise likely — though Jill's relegation to the end of the line may be owing to nothing more invidious than the resources of English rhyme. *Jill and Jack/Went up the track? Out the back? Down the crack?* Unpromising openers. It may well be *the hill* that constrains Jill to her secondary position and Jack, a fortiori, to his primary; one might argue that he comes first because she must come second, instead of the other way around — though most likely the supply of apt English rhymes merely happens in this instance to reinforce the cultural case: the steep and slippery hill of male initiative and female response, male thrust and female parry or riposte. Jack leads, Jill follows, and the rhyme — and thus the topography and its consequences — follows Jill's following.*

Went up the hill. The three monosyllables of character are followed by four of action and scene. The attentive reader notes that whatever the age of these presumable children, they are not obliged to *climb* the hill, although "climbed up" would as easily fit the meter. They simply "go up" it. The implication is that their Wasserhügel is a gentle grade, not a steep incline† — a circumstance that deepens the mystery of their approaching mishap. Alternatively, they may be not such toddlers as would find a moderately steep slope something of a climb, even empty-bucketed. Perhaps they're vigorous teenagers? Young adults? In any case, up the hill they go, without apparent trepidation or difficulty. As remarked above, the cheery rhythm of both the recited and the sung versions suggests that they fairly *skip* uphill.

---

*In autobiographical fact, the singer of this aria would have it remembered, Jill preceded Jack into the world, invariably played primo to his secondo in our piano duets, and took the lead in academic performance, as reflected on school report cards, even after the twins' curricula diverged with their lives in high school. But there is no debating that in most other matters, through the ballad or tale or opera-act of our East Cambridge childhood, it was Jack and Jill, not vice versa. †Scarcely even a grade in some illustrations: viz. the woodcut terrain aforeillustrated (reproduced, with others to come, from *The Oxford Nursery Rhyme Book* [Oxford, Oxford University Press, 1955]) — as flat as Delmarva.

Up what hill? Not *a* hill; not "Lake Hill" or "Water-Well Hill" — simply *the* hill: a proto-Modernist "presumptive exposition" not uncommon in nursery rhymes ("*The* mouse ran up *the* clock"), but scarcely to be found in prose fiction before the twentieth century.* Compare the pre-Modernist, folktaling indefinite articles of that lugubrious Protestant hymn "The Old Rugged Cross," which Jill and Jack used dutifully to intone in meetings of the St. Paul Methodist Protestant Junior Christian Endeavor: *On a hill far away,/ Stands an old rugged cross:/ The emblem of suff'ring and shame. . . .* A hill, despite every junior Christian's knowing it to be Calvary, a.k.a. Golgotha: Skull Hill, outside ancient Jerusalem.

A water-well atop or at least aflank a hill? A clear mountain spring, perhaps, in the days before one worried about Giardia lamblia and suchlike contaminants. Some pleasant, Cotswoldish "Spring Hill," one imagines, of less ominous connotation than the American locus of Richard Brautigan's poem "The Pill Versus the Spring Hill Mine Disaster." To the wellspring is where our eager couple skip; à la source.

And why? *To fetch a pail of water.* What art is in this seven-syllable line, this three-line stanza, this two-stanza narrative! Syllabically equal to but metrically distinct from the preceding couplet, the trimetric third line's stresses are distributed over its seven syllables in a way that effectively prevents its being mistaken for a second three-four couplet. As to the stanza: First it gives us the actors, then the action and scene (rather than the more conventional vice versa — as though the pair's first priority is *to go* and only secondarily to go some particular where), and now, finally, as if in afterthought, the stated motive. One almost imagines a parent calling, "Jack? Jill? Where are you two going?"

---

*E.g., the opening lines of Ernest Hemingway's early story "Indian Camp": "At the lake shore there was another rowboat drawn up. The two Indians stood waiting." What lake shore? What *first* rowboat? What two Indians? In the interest of immediacy, the Modernist pretends that such things go without saying. Literary *Post*modernists, on the other hand, have been known to revert to "that David Copperfield kind of crap."

"Oh, just up the hill."

"Up the hill? Whatever for?"

"Oh . . . [*etc.*]."

"Mm hm. Well, watch your step."

". . ."

To fetch *a pail* of water. Every illustration to the contrary notwithstanding, the line itself does not explicitly provide the water-fetchers an empty bucket, any more than "Let's go for coffee" sets us out cup in hand. A pail*ful*, a pail's *worth* is as much as the text gives us undeniably. But we need not imagine Mom querying suspiciously, "So where's your bucket, young man and young lady?" The illustrators are on firm ground, both because hillside springs are not equipped with pail dispensers like those paper-cup holders beside office watercoolers and because our story *needs* that pail from the expedition's outset. As sung already, it is the link between Jack and Jill: their conjunction, the couple's coupling, and a sign to all who might catch sight of them that their errand is innocent, even commendable.

Their ascent may be sans trepidation or difficulty; is it without hesitation as well? The stanza's architecture subtly hints otherwise. Contrast such monotonously deliberate alternatives as the labored but steady *Jack and Jill/ Climbed the hill./ Up they went,/ Water-bent*; or the unanimously resolute *Vowed Jack and Jill,/ "We'll climb this hill./ We will not fail/ To fill our pail."* Aside from its pleasing syllabic variety, the 3-4-7 of the stanza as given suggests some initial hesitation (on Jill's part, one imagines, Jack having proposed either the project itself or Jill's accompanying him on his errand), followed by further urging on his part and some yielding on hers (I fancy him leading her by the pail handle, uphillward from the dooryard, she fretting, "D'you think it's *okay?*" and he jollying, "Sure it's okay! Come on!") before she puts by her hesitation altogether and skips merrily with him up the springward path.

This masterful stanza's final coup de maître is its final word — more particularly that final word's final syllable. Universal solvent, without-which-not of life, *water* is also the poem's first polysyllable. As such, it ominously foreshadows its correlative, the *double* disyllables of Jill's downfall in line three of stanza two. Moreover, whether or not its unaccented final syllable is regarded as supplying the "missing" first syllable of line one, the word *water* breaks the poem's rhythm in two significant ways: It trips the iambs with a trochee,* and the pacing of its unaccented syllable in fact rules out its being regarded as a complement to the truncated opening foot. Scored rigorously in the accents of speech, the word would appear not as two quarter notes —

— but as a sixteenth and dotted eighth —

— or an even more abrupt pair of sixteenths —

— followed in either case by the ominous silence of that quarter rest on the measure's closing beat.

Wet flagstones beside the well? Mossy rocks in the freshet near the spring? Some moist boundary-mark overstepped? Whatever the efficient cause, in the word *water* we hear the skip become a trip, the step a misstep, the misstep a stumble, the stumble a tee-tering silence before . . .

---

*Compare *Jeannine and Joel Went through the snowl To fetch a pail of* H_2O, or even *Jack and Janel Went down the lanel To fetch a pail of milk.*

2.

Their fall, of course. Better, their *falls*, for whereas stanza one conjoins the couple in an at least ultimately side-by-side ascent — "mutual assent," one might pun, after some small initial misgivings on the part of the party of the second part — stanza two explicitly separates and serializes their come-downance. As the former apportioned its three lines to 1) character, 2) action and scene, and 3) motive, stanza two apportions its to 1) Jack's mishap, 2) Jack's mishap's consequences (for Jack), and 3) Jill's mishap — which last might be read as Jack's mishap's consequences for Jill. Before examining the stanza — more rapidly than we examined stanza one, as to fall takes less time than to rise* — we must ask what happened between the two. *What caused Jack's fall*, and subsequently/consequently Jill's?

On this literally central question, the text is as silent as that aforescored quarter rest. Did the lad slip? Perhaps distracted or unbalanced by his pail-mate, did he misestimate some audacious step? We can only surmise — though the order of events, echoing the order of the characters' introduction, certainly suggests Jack's ongoing primary responsibility. He led, she followed, however willingly; he took her to the heights and then brought the both of them low. Be it on his crown, then, their downfall — though not entirely so.

But we're getting ahead of ourselves, a good way to tumble. *Jack fell down* is all we know for sure, though far from all we need or want to know. The poem contents itself with effects, leaving causes to the reader/listener's imagination, and those effects now concatenate line by line. Whatever the cause, *Jack fell down* — Another instance of hubris (that which goeth before a fall) brought low? — *And broke his crown*. The climax of the poem's action is not merely a skull fracture with possible subdural hematoma on the not-so-gentle slopes of this Anglican Calvary,† but the end of male regnancy, at least of Jack's.

---

*In classical Greek tragedy, a single circuit of the sun suffices for peripety; in Mother Goose, three monosyllables.

†From Latin *calvāria*, skull (translation of Greek *kranion*, translation of Aramaic *gulgūtha*, whence Golgotha).

And [read *whereupon*] *Jill came tumbling after*, in an aptly tumbling line of denouement, with its artful double disyllables for closure. One line for Jill to Jack's two, but a strict equality of syllables. Not, however, an equality of consequences; reversing the order of narration in lines five and six (Jack falls, Jill tumbles after, Jack breaks crown . . .) throws the disparity into high relief. Both fetchers fall, but the other shoe to Jack's crown-breaking never drops. The dramaturgical silence concerning non-consequences-to-Jill is as loud as that quarter rest of unspecified action between the stanzas.*

Justice served, we might feel: Jack led her up there by the pail; let Jack's be the crown that breaks. Punishment enough for the party of the second part that she takes her tumble: soiled frock, mussed hair, perhaps skinned knees and elbows; no water to show for their little adventure and all the explaining to do, as poor Jack's out of it. Assuming she can set things right with the homefolks, will Jill now wear Jack's erstwhile crown, we may wonder, or choose instead to devote herself to "caregiving" for her injured initiator? If indeed she assumes the crown of instigation and primary responsibility, will she presently lead Jack or some other back up that fateful hill (more circumspectly, one bets), or fetch water from some less risky source, or leave water-fetching to those whose fingers, shall we say, have not been burnt in that pursuit?

---

*As aforenoted, some Mother Goose compendia add further stanzas in which Jack trots home as fast as he can caper to one Old Dame Dob, who patches his nob with vinegar and brown paper, at sight of which plaster, when Jill comes in, she does grin, whereupon her mother, vexed, does whip her next, at the spectacle whereof Jack does laugh while Jill does cry, but her tears do soon abate, whereafter Jill does say that they should play at seesaw across the gate. No child remembers these addenda, which however make pretty clear that the pair are siblings — and children, not yet ready for adult responsibilities and adventures, as these alarming woodcuts affirm:

Such conjectures are beyond our given text, however much it invites them. More appropriate to close readership is the question *What happened to the pail?* Outfielders may dive for a fly ball, roll over several times, and come up holding their catch securely, but nobody ever took a skull-breaking downhill fall or heptasyllabic epitumble without spilling his/her water and very likely smashing the presumably wooden pail as well. All illustrators of the rhyme agree (with the spill, at least*); and although the singer of this exegetical aria-within-an-aria remembers, from his undergraduate fraternity-house-bartending days, drunken Kappa Alphas pitching down the row-house-club-basement stairs with their open Schlitz bottles held safely aloft, out of harm's way, he agrees that J & J's fetching-expedition must have been a dead loss, waterwise. Inasmuch as stanza two is altogether silent on the matter of the pail but explicit on the severity of Jack's fall and the posteriority of Jill's, the implication may be not only that the water was spilled and (as some illustrations have it) the bucket de-coopered into its constituent staves, but — contrary to those illustrations — that *no water was ever fetched*; that the obscure mishap mishappened before the pail was ever filled. In any case, by stanza two the couple has been decoupled, their symbolic link unlinked. Together they went up; they come down separately.

Well. Tear-blinded as may be the aria that frames this aria, there's no use crying over spilt water. In that quarter rest between the paired stanzas, what happened happened, what didn't didn't. But Jack's crown was broke, Jill took a tumble, and it's time to stop playing seesaw across the gate. *Jack and Jill* is a reorchestration of the Fall: Adam and Eve rescored by Mother Goose. The unac-

*E.g.,  , which reinforces the causal mystery by showing "the hill" once again to be level, and Jack's right toe beyond the frame, like Jill's left hand.

knowledged party of the third part is not "Dame Dob" but the Serpent; on that hilltop is the Garden,* and in that garden the Forbidden Fruit. As my twin sister and I were taught by our East Cambridge schoolmates before we knew the facts of life, the "subtext" of *Jack and Jill* is sibling incest: in our innocent case, a taboo not only unconsummated but unapproached, even unimagined, for all our general pail-toting intimacy, our early Tommy-and-Susie talk, and those later illustrations from *Spicy Detective*. As was the case with my oatmeal birthmark — to the interrupted aria whereupon I now return — we were altogether unself-conscious about, even unconscious *of*, this out-of-hand-predamning aspect of our JackandJillery, until the figleaved world pointed its dirty fingers and reddened our innocent ears with naughty variations on the canonical text.†

Likewise at

Oatmeal aria resumed and concluded: "My mark"

My mark. In other times and places, twins have been regarded as divine, or one of them immortal and the other not, the superfetation attributed to their mother's insemination by a god instead of (or as well as) by her mortal mate. In yet others, twins have been put to death at birth, one or both of them, the superfetation attributed to mere adultery. And in a few, opposite-sex twins have been killed at birth on the charge of their having committed incest in the womb. *That* is the aboriginal sin, the man would come to know, whereof the boy stood charged (together with his sister; but unlike Eve in the Garden, Jill is clearly the accessory in the nursery rhyme, Jack the party of the first part), and whereof — even the boy now understood — his birthmark was somehow being taken to be the inexpungeable, unconcealable sign. The sting of Jerome Schreiber's lavatory taunt was coupled with and transferred to his follow-up jibe at my presenting stain. Hence my tear-blinded fury

---

*Many Hebrew, Christian, and Islamic divine geographies locate the earthly Paradise on a hill or mountain: e.g. the top of Dante's Mount Purgatory and the Muslims' Adam's Peak in Sri Lanka.
†E.g. Jerome Schreiber's aforetaunting *They each had a dollar and a quarter*, etc. ad nauseam.

when he now not only smote me upside the nose (the first real blow I had ever been struck in my ten-going-on-eleven years) but repeated his doubly charged epithet:

"Here you go, *Oatmeal*."

Brawlbrat brawl resumed and concluded:

Adrenaline. Another year or two would pass before the hormones of adolescence kicked in to send Jill and Jack up separate hills with closely bonded same-sex friends and in time with opposite-sex partners — also, in Jack's case, to erase en passant his facial birthmark, invisible in photographs taken in my teens and after. But my prepubescent adrenals did their fifth-grade-schoolyard job; tear-blinded, I flew at my insulter/attacker friend and, evidently, *overwhelmed* him with a mindless hurricane of fist-flails, a tsunami of outraged/enraged grapple-pushes. Down we tumbled, me on top, leg-locking and pinioning and pummeling and head-butting Jerry Schreiber insensately, sans macroplan or microtactic, until to my own hotblooded astonishment I found I had him face-down on the hardpan, one of his arms up behind his back and the other pinned over his head, my full weight full length on him, corduroy to corduroy, my forehead pressed against his kink-curled hair (I can summon the stale smell of it still), into which I demanded Take it back.

Schreib chuckled into the dirt. "Okay, Oatmeal."

I could scarcely credit my ears and luck, but, winded and heart a-pound, I pressed: *Take it back!*

"Fight's over," some older boy declared, and warned us that Hester Nield was looking our way from over by her car. I let go, climbed off, stood up. Schreib rolled lazily onto his back and grinned up at me with his scabbed lips. Trained by novels, I extended my hand to him; he tucked both of his behind his head and grinned on, as if taking his ease. Therefore I turned my back to him and the others and stepped determinedly off toward Aurora Street, half expecting him to tackle me before I got out of range, or even run up and spring on me from behind to settle the score. He did not, however, and as my narrator intoned *He steeled himself not to look back*, I steeled myself not to look back.

I don't recall telling Mother about my first (and, as of this writing, only) fistfight, its occasion and improbable outcome, nor on the other hand *not* telling her. Neither do I remember speaking of it to Jill, although I can't imagine my not doing so, out of both vanity and habitual experience-sharing. My reading had taught me that Schreib and I thereafter would be closest friends; in fact he remained aloof, though not uncivil, from Columbus Day through Thanksgiving to Christmas vacation, after which he did not reappear at East Cambridge Elementary. The Schreibers, Miz Stoker announced, had moved across Cambridge Creek to Coraxion Hill, over by the municipal cemetery; Jerome would be finishing fifth grade at Peachblossom Elementary, which served that ward. But we would all be together again next year, in junior high.

"Queer Action Hill," Dad told us at dinner, was what kids had called that area when he was a boy: as scrappy a watermen's neighborhood as its counterpart on the East Cambridge side of the creek. I took no initiative to seek my friend out over there, nor he me at 301 Aurora. I set aside my kiddie drum set and turned to building model airplanes from kits. When all the town's white sixth graders came together out on Glasgow Street at the new Upper Elementary (so called because, given our poor county's eleven-year school system and four-grade high school, the sixth-and-seventh-grade interval did not quite correspond to "junior high"), I passively supposed that our friendship would recommence. But Schreib had new Peachblossom pals by then, and I quickly fell in with my bright social peers and betters from West End, most of whom I had met in Miss Ridah Collins's kindergarten. 7 December 1941 ended the American 1930s, which had begun on 29 October '29 — a touch out of synch with the calendar decade on both ends, but so it often goes with cultural history, as with floating-opera acts. Not until wartime Scout camp and early high-school days would Schreib's and my connection be tentatively reestablished, and not until our college years become, for the first time, real friendship.

As with the twin Christian mysteries of Original Sin and Vicarious Redemption, so with my oatmeal birthstain: I did nothing to deserve it, nor anything to be shriven of it. Mercifully, the exterior blemish faded before I reached "dating" age, but together with its misassociations it left an inner mark on the adolescent and the man. We would be shy (though not unsuccessful) with women, tending ever in that quarter toward a kind of solipsism à deux with obvious harmonics of JackandJillery. Indeed, we would be shy and private generally, though not unsuccessful, and in latter decades even a bit reclusive, *as if* there were something to conceal when in fact there was not. By way of compensation, we would become something of a performer, inclined to wear virtuosity on our sleeve rather than up it. For better or worse, my unexpectable victory in the brawlbrat brawl confirmed in me the hedged, unreasonable conviction that I was a winner — more exactly, the protagonist of some unfolding story — with the consequence, among others, that when in 1956, against all reasonable odds and after numerous rejections, my unorthodox first novel finally found a New York publisher and went on to become a finalist for that year's National Book Award, my reaction was the same as upon finding that early water-message on the Choptank rivershore: quiet validation. *Yes. Of course.**

The man would remain fascinated with marks and scars, without before now[†] understanding quite why: the mythic hero's I.D. scar, Cain's mark, Jesus's side-wound, the stigmata of certain Christian mystics, Hindu caste marks, initiation brands, Hawthorne's allegorical tale "The Birthmark," Mikhail Gorbachev's scalp-stain, dear such blemishes on lovers, mates, children, grandchildren. Scars make your body more *interesting*, gentle reader.

His, too, perhaps. *And although that italicizing, third-personating narrator in his head mercifully faded along with his birthmark, our passive protagonist would never, ever, learn to enjoy* oatmeal.

---

*But *The Floating Opera* did not win the prize. Nor did the story-series *Lost in the Funhouse* (1968), also a nominee. The novella-series *Chimera*, however (1972), did, sort of; a divided jury divided that year's award. Quiet semi-validation.
†January 1992, winding up the first draft of Act One of *Once Upon a Time*.

ENTR'ACTE
In the Dark

❧ ❧

"IT WASN'T Jerry Schreiber," I imagine Jill insisting. "Anyhow, *my* memory is that we moved into separate bedrooms before fifth grade. Fourth, wasn't it? After Mommy Simmons died? And I don't remember any such fistfight. For that matter, there wasn't any Jerry Schreiber."

There was a fight, all right. I won it.

She shrugs. "You win. Look, I've got to run along now: Here comes puberty and World War Two. I do wish we got together more often."

Likewise, sister mine: so near and yet et cet — and she's gone, my erstwhile inseparable; had left already, I understand now, during the brawlbrat brawl. In course of my pushing this persistent Parker through its welcomely familiar paces, reconstructing or inventing scenes in my memory and imagination and translating them into scribbled Skrip, I seem to have left off projecting them for the two of us with that instrument's newer-fangled gimmickry. Now I find myself altogether in the dark, no discernible where, neither standing nor sitting nor lying down — yet more than mere floating consciousness, I gather, for I can sense my body (the still-sound sixty-plus version, not its ten- or eleven-year-old early draft). As in thousands of mid-night wakings, I listen for reassuring sign of *you* beside me: your respiration, some stirring in your seldom-heavy sleep. Joy unspeakable, to discover ourselves re-king-bedded at Langford Creek, Columbus Day '92 not yet upon us: no ill-conceived end-of-season sailing cruise embarked upon, no wake-up good-bye conch-calls from "Jay Scribner," all this Once-Upon-a-Timery no more than a sustained and uncommonly vivid dream in progress, or retrogress.

Breathe. Stir. I reach out leftward, *your*-sideward. . . .

No you — nor bed, creek-house, creek; only the omnipresent low-level, high-frequency singing inside my head, the very pitch-pipe of absence's presence. Even if (even though) I'm dreaming up this floating opera, I'm lost in it now, at sea, adrift and freshly stricken. *What if . . . ?*

My movement, I'll suppose, has jiggled this infernal "*ree*mote." As if some stagehand is goosing rheostats, the lights come up: diffused, bright, but illuminating nothing — perhaps because (it occurs to me) my eyes are closed, reluctant to see anything if not my misplaced shipmate.

"Upnatm, Oat-boy!" I know that voice, all right — fake-breezy, friendchippish — "We got work to do." Scrib brandishes my wrist-watch, reads its face, winces his own. "Puberty to paternity in nine action-packed years! We gotta *move*, man." He still wears his drowning duds, hasn't even bothered to rezip the fly of his jeans since last we met at that decaying picnic table — Position Approximate, as they say on the nautical charts.

Take it back, Jer.

"Say what?" he says, to irk me, and twitches his nose.

You never took back what you said in that lavatory in fifth grade. When we rassled, you said "Okay, Oatmeal," but you never took back what you said.

"You wanna rassle again, or what?" Although his expression remains merry, I know that eye-glint, the push-up of his wire-rims. "You wanna take your toys and go home?"

Right. I reach for my watch; Jay holds it beyond my grasp.

Take back what you said about Jill and me on Columbus Day Nineteen Forty, Scrib, or this opera ends right here.

"My big chance." He rotates the watch's bezel. "*You win, Oat-meal. I'll take you back.*"

Reorganizational colloquy: Where the fuck are we?

Where the fuck are we now, besides in the dark again? To Jay — invisible but still present, some sense tells me — I say, What I had in mind, I think, when I began to get the hang and cubiture of this floating opera, was something like maybe three acts, no more: twenty narrative yearsworth each, say, to fetch yours truly tidily up to the present point of his pen. I.e., I hope and presume, back to old *US* and home — chastened, perhaps, but refreshed, enabled, my suspended passage unsuspended.

"But?"

But look: It has taken me one full real-time year and two hundred Parkered pages to get the show overtured, another year-and-a-half and a hundred-and-a-half to trek from birth through our fifth-grade brawlbrat brawl. At this rate, Columbus Day '92 will come and go before I graduate from Cambridge High and lose my virginity —

"In that order, as I remember."

Never mind. We've run afoul of the coastline-measurement problem, if you follow me: so ever more fine-grained a resolution that we'll end up aging faster than we're narrating. We've got to reorganize, old comrade, or the coast will never clear. Achilles will never catch the tortoise. Odysseus will never reach home.

"Among us drowned," my new guide remarks (dryly?), "time presses less. Try this thought-experiment, Oats: If you're lost in the fractal funhouse — every fork reforking, every mirror mirror-ing mirrors — then in effect you've never left the marsh you ran aground in. What you're after may be just around the next bend. In front of your eyes. Right in your hands."

Get thee behind me, Scribner! As well tell Odysseus that if he'll only wake up, he'll find himself home in the sack with Penelope instead of lost in the Mediterranean. It's not that easy.

"Reveille time, Odysseus-babe! Upnatm!"

It's never that easy. Turn the lights back on, Jay; we've got to reorganize. Where the fuck are we, anyhow?

"*There*'s a question we can address." The voice of my acerbic counterself comes to me as easily and clearly from nowhere as from on this page. "Leave whys to the wise; let's us lesser spirits have at the whos whens whats and wheres."

So where the fuck are we?

"Try this, lad: You, at least, are the fuck in Jimmy Whatsisname's parents' car's backseat, double-dating on Senior Prom Night, June Forty-Seven, parked post-promly down by the Choptank rivershore Jungle. You could lose your cherry right now if you had more nerve and/or savoire faire. As you do not, you're only getting your fingers wet."

No names, Scrib, where it matters. And maybe leave the lights off, after all.

"Make time while you can, man; clock's running." What he means, among other things, he goes on to remind me, is that he'll be appropriating that girlfriend from me in the summer ahead, when I go up from (eleven-year) Cambridge High to the Juilliard School of Music to learn that I won't after all be becoming the career musician that I'd had it in mind to become, and *he* comes home to Cambridge from his junior year at the (twelve-year) McDonogh School in Baltimore, already a polished semi-professional trumpeter and lacking neither nerve nor savoire faire, by local standards. "See how we can move when we set your pen to it? June Forty-Seven already! Europe wrecked, Russia ravaged, Japan nuked, the USA transformed for better and worse forever! Zillions holocausted, purged, gulag'd, atomized, and we zoom in on Cambridge High School's Class of Nineteen Forty-Seven's Prom Night."

Why?

"Ah-ah: Ask me X, man; ask me Z. But don't ask me (a-*one* . . . a-*two*) . . ."

Obscured trivial aria: "Y"

Three pen-strokes at nature's favorite angle, 120 degrees, give us this alphabet's penultimate letter, this language's primary-and-ultimate question, this singer's recurrent theme: Y/Wye/Why. How come?

Regard it: The confluence of two into one? The forking of one into two? Oedipus's fateful Place Where Three Roads Meet? Analysis, synthesis, or some third thing? The answer depends on where you're coming from, where headed, where are. The handsome Welsh-English river Wye conflows with its tributaries down to the Severn, e pluribus unum, unidirectional — in its upper reaches, anyhow — like the confluence of Ohio and Mississippi at Cairo, Illinois, or of brown Rhine and green Moselle at the Deutsches Eck in Koblenz (a Germanification of Latin *confluens*). Just so, fallopian tubes come together at the uterus, lovers lose themselves in each other, father-sperm and mother-egg conjoin to make an entity that's both and neither — and Jack and Jill are prenatally twinned into JackandJill.

Reverse the flow — as does our handsome tidal Wye on Maryland's Eastern Shore every six hours, twenty-seven minutes — and the confluence becomes a fork: Front and Back Wyes, East and West Forks of Langford Creek, Jill and Jack at puberty, lovers at upnatm-time, marital unions come to Splitsville: alienation, separation, divorce. Undifferentiated being differentiates into categories: Hey, now we can talk, now we can touch, now maybe even come together — if not in So-and-So's backseat in June '47, then elsewhere and elsewhen; if not with No-Names-Please, then with Elsewho. Your place or mine?

But before we do . . .

At the slack water between ebb and flood, flood and ebb — at, say, Cacaway or "Potamock" Island, in the very crotch of Langford Creek or the marshy conjunction of Tigris and Euphrates at the Shatt al Arab, where some say the Garden of Eden was — behold a third option: *staying put* at the three-spoked hub of things. Y/Wye/Why? The question, put insistently by a child in this ariast's first novel, bemuses the protagonist-narrator into a nihilism that would as leave blow up the whole showboat, *Adam's Original & Unparalleled Floating Opera*. Thirty-five years and ten books later, the upper-case letter initiates the name of Sindbad's daughter, Yasmin, and is glossed by Somebody the Sailor, more or less lost at sea, as the anatomically stylized conjunction of her thighs.* Therebetween, as it were, the alphabetical letter, the river and its name, and the ultimate question together map the coupled plots of two other of this singer's operas: *Sabbatical: A Romance* and *The Tidewater Tales: A Novel*, their principals well married but not merged, embraced and embracing but not conflated; he he, she she, but mutatis mutandis a we, ah oui, US — our passage . . . lovingly . . . suspended. . . .

In ancient Rome, weighty issues were discussed in the Forum, lighter matters in the Trivium marketplace, where three roads (*tri via*) came together, or forked apart, and folks paused to chat. Whence our word *trivia*: street gossip, idle info.

What else is new?

Back to the backseat:

"Shall we get on with it?" Jay suggests. "A-*three*, a-*four*: High school happened, and a priori junior high, in deepest Doubleyou-Doubleyou-Twotime. Brownouts and blackouts, air-raid drills and incendiary-bomb squads, Victory gardens, ration stamps, scrap-metal and wastepaper drives that had nothing to do with ecology, oil globs from torpedoed tankers on the Maryland beaches, Gold Star mothers, no thises or thats for the duration, and Boy Scout troops more paramilitary than woodsy-craftsy. I'm in Troop One Twenty-Eight, you're in One Fifty-Nine, and so here as elsewhere we're on the separate tracks that we'll remain on for six full years: a good time to make narrative time."

Well, Jay: But I hear those bugle-calls up at Camp Rodney, where all the Scout troops on the peninsula summer-camped and swatted mosquitoes and jacked off in our bunks and watched anti-aircraft flak from the Aberdeen Proving Ground, just across the Bay. First we'd see the rows of black puffs, like suspension points in the sky; then we'd hear the guns fire on the ground, and only after that the sound of the shellbursts that made the puffs. . . .

"While I blew assembly on my brand-new Victory bugle made of olive-drab *plastic*, that new invention."

*Y is also ∇ imploded: the deltaic triangle.

My favorite was retreat, at flag-down time. It made my blood buzz.

"That figures: Going forward by backing up is the name of this game."

Enabling regression, Scrib. You know?

"Whistle a few bars, and I'll fake it."

You've whistled your bars, Jay Doubleyou Scribner; *I'll* fake it. I know the changes.

"Back to that backseat, then, Oatmeal: Two. One."

Marking time by making time, while the hormones surge and I fumble in the dark backseat of adolescence, wetting my whistle and groping for Identity under the aspect of Vocation. It's *my* whistle, Jay, my pen, my opera: I'm going to Freeze Frame here with my hand in place while I backtrack from that backseat in order to fast-forward to Senior Prom Night, Cambridge High School, Class of '47. That is our trombonist's parents' car we're making out in: trombonist of a "combo," as we called them back then, named Swingtette, whereof I am the self-taught drummer, my plucky sister the improved piano player, one Jimmy Let's-Call-Him-Calhoun the trombonist, driving spirit, and literal driver (his pleasant Irish surname wrenched into *Cal*houn in Tidewatersville, like *trom*bone and *ree*mote), and a certain Ben from West End the (alto) saxophonist.

"Odd instrumentation."

It's what happened to be available. No bassist to be had, nor even a trumpeter, your father having finally disappeared for good two years before this freeze-frame and his son gone off on scholarship to do his eleventh and twelfth grades as aforenoted at the McDonogh boarding school in Baltimore.

"A semi-military boys' institution back then, for better and worse, with special scholarships for us semi-orphans and a much better faculty than you Swingtetters had. Carry on."

Given our odd and not overtalented lineup, we Swingtetters did rather well: a mark either of the time and place's unsophistication or of the raw dearth of even semi-trained talent thereabouts in those wartime years — when even high-school bands, remember, had been discontinued for want of instruments and coaches. The

Senior Prom was not our gig — the class had splurged on the same "big band" from Easton that your sister Ramona's boyfriend had once played trumpet in — but we had in fact worked the Junior Prom in the fall semester and — remarkable to remember — since *age fifteen* we'd played more or less regular monthly dances at the Cambridge Country Club and the Salisbury Town Club. So we were, I suppose, semi-professionals, though working well below union scale and weller yet below any real level of professional musicianship. The Swingtette was featured in a Teen-Age Revue on the stage of Schine's Arcade; we even cut a one-off recording on somebody-or-other's amateur equipment, and actually heard the thing scabbed from time to time on the local AM station.

"Innocence."

Enabling innocence, in the short run anyhow. Reality testing in this line was as scarce just then in Dorchester County as string bassists in Cambridge High, or genuine jazz groups for us to watch and learn from. It's a wonder to me that we weren't hooted off the bandstand. Fact is, however, that in the absence of real competition we *imagined* ourselves into enough authenticity to keep us in business. By good private-school standards, our academic education was mediocre: not much in the way of science or history or art or music appreciation, but we managed two years of Latin and two of Spanish, a smattering of English Lit, mathematics up through trigonometry, and a fine manual-training course whose tool-use lessons I still apply. *You* were an athlete and a bit of a delinquent until you left us; your pals and fellow troublemakers were the jocks, mostly not from the Academic curriculum. I was a *cheerleader*, I blush to report, and a feature writer for the school newspaper; my crowd were the team managers and class officers and yearbook staff — nice boys and girls, the major frogs in this benign backwater. If I thought at all about Jerry Schreiber, I probably felt sorry for his being "sent off" to boarding school, like the three or four children of local doctors and well-off non-natives. It never occurred to me that they were getting a superior academic and social education to prepare them for college and the wider world (Who thought about college? What wider world?) while we eleventh-grade-senior froggies boogied along.

"You've boogied away from that Swingtette, man. Take it from the edge."

Enabling digression. What I'm leading up to is the minor paradox that *Cal*houn and Ben, for example — not to mention Jerry Schreiber over at McDonogh — knew their instruments well enough to cut the stock arrangements we picked up from time to time on expeditions to Baltimore, and to improvise solos once they'd learned the chord changes; yet neither they nor you aspired to career musicianship, much less to the Big Time. Whereas I, who knew less about music than you guys did, tucked away my Swingtette earnings to pay for a summer session up at Juilliard after Senior Prom Night. I could not have explained why a piano part scored in the key of C requires a trombone part in B flat and an alto sax part in E flat, and yet I was going to be a big-time professional orchestrator. What did I imagine I was doing, Jay?

"A good jazzman has to know how to fake. Let me put in a mitigating word while you carry on in *Cal*houn's backseat. You knew enough not to imagine yourself to be the next Gene Krupa or Buddy Rich, nor even to want to be; *there's* some reality peeping through. You knew enough to know you'd better learn a little music before hanging out your shingle as a big-time arranger. And you seem to've known enough to give Juilliard a summer-session try before committing yourself to an academic year —"

No money for that in any case. Did I imagine I might win a Juilliard *scholarship*, over all those city-trained hotshots? Like an animated-cartoon character, I was running off a cliff onto thin air.

"They manage to keep going, as I remember, until they look down and see there's no ground under them. Hey, man, I shake *my* head, too. *I* couldn't've won a Juilliard scholarship, and I was twice the musician you were."

Three times. Five.

"Twice does it. So what *did* you imagine you were doing? Maybe what you were better at than your buddies was *imagining*. This one goes realistically off from Senior Prom Night to run a local service station; that one goes to work in a local department store. And your down-to-earth twin, with a little coaching from the System, has already made plans for secretarial school. But you've got Something Else in your head, like Mister Frankel's actress daughter, only less well focused. That cornball cheerleading wasn't exhibitionism; it was showmanship looking for a vehicle. The drumming was virtuosity misplaced — and not all that bad, though less than professional. What you were 'arranging' up there at Juilliard wasn't music; it was a calling scored for your horn, which you hadn't discovered yet, and a larger stage to blow it on than Schine's Arcade. *Identity under the aspect of vocation* is what you were groping for in *Cal*houn's car. How're you doing back there?"

Nunnayerbeeswax, Schreib. She'll be yours soon enough, when I take off up the flyway. Before I look down from New York New York and see nothing under me, read ahead in your part as I've scored it: The trumpet's about to come back in and take the lead, with my prom date and elsewise.

"Speaking of scoring . . ."

Our crowd didn't, as a rule, in those innocent days. There were a few "fast" girls, lusted after but not respected, and a few make-out artists among the boys. By and large, however, what little bonking actually transpired was among well-established Steadies, who married and got pregnant or vice versa soon after graduation. For most of us, the backseat action was more or less heavy petting, the privileges carefully metered and the limits constantly pressed — under the blouse, but not under the bra; under the skirt, but not under the undies — and the rare, half-terrifying carte blanche, or all-but-blanche. What a job, being an American teenage girl before the standards collapsed! No picnic for us nice boys, either.

"Sort of a picnic, I should think. Being Peck's Bad Boy, I had different privileges and different problems."

Pretty much of a picnic, actually, if we could've relaxed and made a meal out of appetizers. And as I said, if I had known what was what there in *Cal*houn's backseat — but then, if I had known what was what, I would never have gone off to Juilliard.

"Where your entrance exams, as I *ree*call, placed you bizarrely in Elementary Theory and Advanced Orchestration — a bit like qualifying for bonehead English and a graduate fiction workshop — and you aced both, but learned nothing much beyond the useful lesson that what you had innocently supposed was pre-professional talent was in fact an amateur's flair. There's an inno-cence well lost, I would say, if not especially enabling. NNP told me all about it that summer. If you hadn't been cunt-shy, you might've scored that young lady on Prom Night, and she'd have been waiting for you when you came back from NYC."

She told you that?

"Just riffing, Oatmeal. Would you care to fill in this portrait of the artist as cunt-shy failed musician? Early literary efforts, momentous reading discoveries, role models, jack-offs, corner-turnings?"

Did she tell you that, Jay? What you just said?

"Ease off, man. I was only making out with the girl, not inter-viewing her. She soon enough married somebody else."

Because I *was* cunt-shy, for one reason or another, and didn't get laid till a full fifteen months after Senior Prom Night — and not by No-Names-Please. But such milestones are not what this opera is about, nor even this scene, so all hands rest easy or switch to the Playboy channel, chacun à son goût.

"Now that you mention it, what *is* this opera about?"

This opera, now that *you* mention it, is about getting yours truly back aboard *US* and going on with our story: not yours and mine or mine and NNP's or You-Know-Whom's or Never-Mind's. *Ours. US's*, suspended in mid-passage. Thanks for asking.

"And this stretched-out Backseat scene?"

Now that you mention *it*, it's about a certain sound, believe it or not. A sort of wake-up call, from a certain trumpet in Lew Startt's orchestra on CHS Senior Prom Night, 1947.

"I'm touched, man. Hey, I am."

I was touched, Jay: moved, stirred, in a way I couldn't have explained before now. Here's an analogy: I was already a busy reader-for-pleasure back then, but as aimless in that line as in oth-ers. Nothing in our English classes touched me: not *Macbeth*, not Milton, not *Ivanhoe* and the other stuff we struggled through. Pocket paperbacks had recently been invented, and I was allowed to bring home as many as I wanted from Whitey's Candyland to

read, so long as I didn't spoil them for sale; I went through tons
of Ellery Queen and Agatha Christie and Raymond Chandler and
such — and became a great fan of supernaturalists like Abe Mer-
ritt and John Collier and H. P. Lovecraft in the old Avon Fantasy
Reader series, whom-all I recognized as something different. I
brought home stacks of anything but westerns and "romances,"
and in one of those all-but-random piles I stumbled upon John
Dos Passos's *Manhattan Transfer*, and in another, Faulkner's *The
Wild Palms* and *Sanctuary* — and I managed to notice that these
were not only something other than my usual whodunits and
spook operas, but something *real*. Real literature, I understood
later, but what struck me at the time was a real *sound*, cutting
through and riding over the genre stuff.

Another analogy: Christianity, theism in general, had evapo-
rated off me, I scarcely know why: metabolical secularity, I suppose, since none of us at 301 Aurora was pious, but the others
were at least notionally dutiful. My "belief environment" was
nothing more than a benignant blur; I had no idea what was
important to me, who I was. *Writing* certainly meant nothing yet;
the supposedly humorous gossip column that I wrote pseudony-
mously for the school paper was on a par with my cheerleading:
expressivity in the abstract, rummaging vainly for a vehicle. I
thought about nothing, that I can remember; was ignorant of art,
classical music, history, philosophy, politics — the works. And
what I wasn't quite ignorant of — the tidewater scene, for example — I took for granted, shrug-shoulderedly, although Whitey's
great pleasure in it no doubt rubbed off on me. The marshes and
tides, the crabs and oysters and wild ducks and geese, the bugeyes
and skipjacks and tong-boats and seafood-packing houses along
Cambridge Creek, the Choptank rivershore where we all swam
through the sticky summers despite sea nettles and mosquitoes —
all that stuff simply *was*. It was what was there, like desert to the
Bedouin or snow to the Eskimos.

"Inuit, I believe."

Inuit, Inuit.

"*And then one day* . . ."

And then one *night* — two nights, actually, back to back. The night before Prom Night, some of us seniors had a mudflat beach party at somebody's house down-county, in the course of which a few of the boys went nighttime skinnydipping for the first time and got ourselves duly zapped by sea nettles. Between zaps, however, I managed to have the quite magical experience of floating naked in the bathwarm Chesapeake under a full moon among the noctilucae, which phosphoresced at every splash and made our bodies sparkle like the gods'. And I realized —

"Got it."

Same thing happened next night with *music*, is what I'm getting to. On my last couple of summer visits to the New Jersey relatives, I had gone over to Manhattan to hear bands like Tommy Dorsey's and Benny Goodman's onstage at the Paramount and the Roxy. But astonishingly different as their live sound was, compared to what we were used to at 78 rpm on our low-fi hardware, the difference got lost in my general overwhelmment by the city. And back home I was playing regular gigs myself, but that was *us* — like the sound of my voice in my own head. Neither of those "real thing" experiences was quite real. Then, on Senior Prom Night, my date and I reached the school a few minutes after the first set started. . . . I shake my head, Jay, at how slightly No-Names-Please and I *knew* each other, compared to real boys and girls in the real world! We weren't really friends; we weren't high-school sweethearts by any plausible standard. We were just two odd, amorphous sensibilities groping in the dark —

"Grope on."

Evening gowns. Corsages. *Cal*houn's car Simonized to a high shine, and maybe a few beers stashed in the trunk. The school gym duded up by the Dance Committee to some Hollywood-tropical theme that wowed us all, complete with the de rigueur mirror-ball revolving up in the rafters, at the peak of the crepe-paper streamers. And onstage, among potted palms and banks of real and fake flowers, Lew Startt's big band from over in Easton: five brass, five saxes, three rhythm.

"A-one. A-two."

Even while we were dealing with tickets at the door, my adren-

aline kicked in at the classy sound of those big *sections*, all in
perfect tune and cutting their ensemble passages with polish.

"Well . . ."

We Swingtetters were kids, just winging it. These were grown-
up *musicians* in summer tuxes, on the home turf. Some Glenn
Miller thing was under way, mid-tempo, cool: "String of Pearls,"
maybe; maybe "In the Mood." I'd heard the recordings a hundred
times; we played our Swingtette versions every Saturday night, the
best we could. But I was electrified by the full-orchestra sound of
it — so big, so real. No-Names-Please must've felt neglected; I
couldn't take my eyes and ears off the band. I didn't know any of
Lew Startt's sidemen — *grown-ups*, some of them middle-aged,
playing so well with so little fuss — but I almost thought I recognized the young dude on second trumpet, except for his eyeglasses.

"I'd just picked 'em up, man: big black frames with straight
side-pieces, like the cats were wearing then? I'd worn my eyes out
studying, over at McDee."

It really did look like Jerry Schreiber up there, kinky hair and
all, but I wasn't certain until No-Names and I worked through the
crowd to the footlights just as the brass section came to a rest, and
I saw the trademark scarred lips. Old Schreib, AWOL from
McDonogh!

"Yeah, well. I'd been practicing over there, and Ma was working a new life in Easton. If Lew was one trumpet short, he'd give
me a call, and I'd get a weekend pass home."

So much power under such smooth control up on that stand,
compared to us amateurs. Glenn Miller was jealous of soloists,
and so there's not much showcasing in those arrangements, especially in "Pearls," right? But "Mood" winds up with that famous
four-bar escalation by the whole trumpet section, at the end of
which young Jerry Schreiber rose up and lifted the roof — *my*
roof, anyhow — with that solo climb in the closing bars. Thrilling.

"You never told me this before. I'm touched, man."

The next number was a ballad — "Embraceable You," I'm
going to say — to which NNP and I tried to dance. Neither of us
was at ease in that line, but as best I could I turned my back on

Lew Startt's Orchestra and tried to do what we had come there for, all the while feeling every note from every instrument as if they were playing on my nerve ends. The real thing! In the stock arrangement that you guys were using, the sax and brass sections take turns leading through the first chorus, and then the second swaps solos among the piano, tenor sax, and trombone — all building to the third, which opens with a low-register trumpet solo. It's young Schreiber again, down front at the microphone this time, his face screwed up and his eyes closed, *speaking* through that golden horn to the Class of '47. Big fat warm low growly notes, quiet at first, but full of grown-up feeling: rich, juicy —

"Spit-valve time."

A perfectly straightforward first eight bars, nothing but the melody notes played over sax-section chords and obbligatos, but each note alive, perfectly inflected, and building in volume through the second four bars. Except for a few tone-deaf clucks here and there, we all stopped dancing and gathered in front of the bandstand, passing the word around that that was our old buddy Schreib up there, long time no see.

The eight-bar bridge (I'm making this up, but I can hear it plainly) was sax section first and brass after, building in color and volume as it lilts along, while the boy wonder stands easy at the mike, eyes open now, exercising his lips and trumpet valves as he waits to come back in, tapping his foot and nodding his head a bit with the easy beat, and at the same time surveying the house. He raises his eyebrows in salute to this and that old acquaintance, and as the bridge winds up he catches sight of me grinning and finger-waving down front and gives me a cool wink as he raises his horn to go on with his solo.

After the bridge, the score modulates to a higher key — C, let's say — and the trumpet shifts to upper register for the final sixteen bars, an octave-plus above the opening statement. The soloist's eyes are squeezed shut again behind those big black frames, his face is winced up, his neck and cheeks swell out under the pressure like Dizzy Gillespie's, and the high clear melody sings over us pure and silvery; as full of feeling as before, but at the same time *above* its own feeling. Transcendent.

"Good arrangement, Oats."

In the first four of the last eight of the second sixteen of the thirty-two, if you follow me —

"I'm with you: *Don't be a naugh-ty ba-by;/ Come to Poppa come to Poppa doo-oo-oo-oo-oo. . . .*"

— the whole band blows fortissimo and then crescendos to a mighty cut on the fifth beat of that *doo*. In the suspended silence after, the trumpet finishes the melody not only solo but rubato, taking its own sweet rhythmless time in the upper atmosphere with that revolving mirror-ball, and blowing not louder but ever more softly as it climbs —

My sweet em - brace-. . .

— then not going *down* with the melody, but on up for the next two notes —

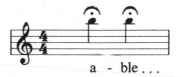

a - ble . . .

— and finally, quietly, perfectly, blowing us all away by closing, not on the corresponding high melody note (in our concert score, the C above that B on -*a-ble*, which happens to be the horn's official ceiling), but on the third above *that*, a sweat-wet but hundred-percent-pure high E:

you.

"Hell, man, Dizzy was doing that all the time by Forty-Seven. Second trumpet wasn't shit by Forty-Seven without a high E."

But who of us had ever heard one live, in the Cambridge High gym? I wouldn't realize it for another year, but the truth is that my musical ambitions were deflated by a silver arrow then and there: not your range on the horn, but the unmistakeable sound of the Real Thing. What I felt at the time was the opposite: inspiration, cool excitement. When set-break came, I sought you out for handshakes and compliments — Hey, Schreib, great *sound*, man! Terrific solo work! — and at intermission I introduced you to No-Names-Please, and we chatted a bit about my plans for Juilliard and who knew what after that, while you had another year yet to go at McDonogh — before college, you guessed, if you could score a scholarship somewhere. Because playing music was cool for now, you allowed, but it was no kind of a life even in the big time, and who fooled themselves that they were big time? *Arranging*, you granted, might be something different; you yourself were sort of interested in *journalism* these days, of all unexpected things. Anyhow, hello to my sister, if she's here, and regards to Georgia and Whitey. Be seeing me around, man, after New York, maybe, and nice to meet you, NNP. Time to climb back on the stand now.

How you'd grown since Henry Street and Coraxion Hill! Polished, cool, polite, perfectly at ease with those older cats in the band. I was proud to know you and to chat with you like one musician with another; I had the feeling that my date was impressed, too, although music was no big deal with her. We two went back to our senior-promming, then off to do some serious necking in *Cal*houn's backseat down by the rivershore, then over to a classmate's house where half the graduating class was having an all-night party and early breakfast. All of my friends were there — good friends, close friends, *factual* friends, not fictional, who haven't even been mentioned yet and probably won't be — and in my heart I was saying good-bye to them already; good-bye to dear Cambridge and East Cambridge and Cambridge Creek and 301 Aurora and the Choptank rivershore; good-bye to No-Names-Please — with whom, however (because those silver notes

hadn't done their work yet), I still somehow fancied myself to be
in love, sort of, although I understood that something was missing.

"Reality, for one."

Yup. Reality was what I'd heard back on Lew Startt's triple-
tiered bandstand and would re-meet head-on up at Juilliard while
you were re-meeting No-Names back in Cambridge. . . .

"Sorry there, Oatmeal. I had a lot of free time that summer and
a regular gig at the Cambridge Yacht Club, where the girl hung
out. So she said hello, and we talked about our Juilliard pal, and
one thing led to another. Nothing serious, though briefly intense
and, you know, real, whether *I* am or not. Reality, I *ree*peat, in
synecdochic form is what you had your hand on in *Cal*houn's
backseat but presently elected to take your hand off of, whereupon
et cetera. The aforesung intersection of the Y, where you neither
stood pat nor pushed on."

Because I wasn't ready, in several respects. I had touched it,
though, the real thing, and at that prom it had touched me. To this
day I can feel it at my fingertips and hear it in my head, but I
needed another year-and-a-bit before reality and I laid hold of each
other, relatively speaking. I needed to learn in uptown Manhattan
what your trumpet had told me in the CHS gym, for one thing:
that music was to be my serious hobby, not my calling. I needed
to go to college faute de mieux, on scholarship, and flounder for
a year as a journalism major, of all things (Where did *that* idea
come from?), and begin to take a sidewise interest in, of all things,
writing fiction (Where will *that* idea come from?) — a notion that
had never occurred to me thitherto — while at the same time discovering civilization in general and literature in particular, with a
little help from certain friends and professors. I needed to pay my
Baltimore rent that year by drumming and arranging in a not-bad
dance band organized by some fellow freshmen who happened to
have prep-schooled together at McDonogh and who therefore
recruited on trumpet their hotshot schoolmate J. Schreiber —
against whom I held no grudge for sort-of-poaching my hometown girl, because that connection hadn't been really real — and
so *our* connection began to become so, for the first time. Enough
so, indeed, that the following summer would prove the most agree-

able of my life till then and a pivotal one in this opera, for the reasons that by that time you and I had become each other's closest comrade; that I had abandoned journalism and was about to hear my true upnatm call; that you had put together your own band for the summer of '48, with Comrade Oatmeal on drums, and scored us a full-time, live-in gig in a casino/dance hall on the pier at Betterton Beach, up at the head of the Chesapeake, where we would be the lords of that downscale little steamboat-era resort. Two hours of dance music in the casino every afternoon, when the Baltimore excursion boat came in; an hour of dinner music at the main hotel, in return for all our meals; and a four-hour dance every evening back on the pier. There, in the midst of one of those seven-hour musical days, you called to my attention a clutch of nifty-looking college-girl waitresses in shorts and swimsuits who had just strolled over from work at the hotel to catch our last couple of after-lunch sets. Of one of them in particular — as we were setting up numbers 54, 146, 17, and 39 — you asked me, rhetorically, "Howja like to slip your hand into *those* pants, man?"

Mm *hm*, I replied — who on that front was still freeze-framed in *Cal*houn's backseat on Senior Prom Night. Although this opera declines to be about what ensued and developed at Betterton Beach, *this* NNP I trust you shall not pre-empt, post-empt, co-opt, or otherwise lay your talented hands upon, Jay-babe — my first real girlfriend and lover-to-be; my first *spouse*-to-be, thereafter and for twenty years thereafter; mother-to-be of the children-to-be of the composer-and-arranger-to-be of *Once Upon a Time* and other floating operas.

"Yes, well . . ."

No names, please.

On with reorganizational colloquy: "Well, then, what?"

"Well, then, what?" Jay Wordsworth Scribner wants to know. "We've got a problem here, man."

We do, as aforeacknowledged but yet to be addressed. The "lights" have come back on in wherever it is we are, and Jay appears to have reappeared: my otherself, lost at sea and then washed up in the marsh of my stranding like an interrogative water-message. We now sit (I realize with a flood of feeling) on the grimy balustrade of the bare front porch of a bare rowhouse on a midsummer pressure-cooker of a Baltimore backstreet, bare of trees but nevertheless called Birkwood Place: It is the last and roomiest of my innumerable student residences, rented cheap from a merry wizard of a Johns Hopkins metallurgist by whom I am also benignly employed this particular summer — the summer of 1953 — to research Benvenuto Cellini's "lost wax" method of casting gold jewelry, with an eye to applying it to the making of large single crystals of that metal for use in materials-fatigue experiments at the university.

Summer '53: At age three-and-twenty, I'm into my sixth and final year of higher academics, my fifth of apprentice writerhood, my fourth of marriage. I have some considerable though gappy and eclectic education to show for the first of those; two small children already to show for the last (plus a third, unbeknown to his parents, in early uterine parentheses); and next to nothing yet to show for my call from the fictive muse. Since *Cal*houn's backseat and Betterton Beach, so much water under the bridge! The Bridge itself included, bridging the Chesapeake as of 1952 and ending forever, for better and worse, the historic insularity of my native bog. The route I had used to spend most of a weekend day hitchhiking and ferry-hopping along — from the Johns Hopkins University to an Eastern Shore teachers college in order to pay court to NNP II — she and I zip over now in no time, with our babies, in the family car (we've just bought our first — There it gleams, at the curb! — a glorious bucktooth-bumpered, windshield-brimmed, two-tone-green Buick Special, secondhand, that still looks yachtlike, even from here). Dwight Eisenhower has defeated Adlai Stevenson with his promise to "go to Korea," and that first of our postwar wars has been stalemated. "The Forties" have gone the way of French Existentialism and my peninsulated adolescence; "the Fifties" have begun, although we scarcely know it, with — choose your milestone — the first H-bomb detonation (Eisenhower hasn't told us yet) by the USA, with the USSR's to

follow later this summer; the death of Josef Stalin and his succession by Nikita Khrushchev; the black blossomings of
McCarthyism and of rock and roll —

"Which you and I wouldn't be caught dead blowing," Jay inter-
rupts this catalogue to declare. "But *our* Nineteen Forties will end
this afternoon, as I remember, with the friendly argument that
we're about to have here on this porch before you drive up to Penn
State in that Buick Special to start full-time teaching, while I wind
up my doctoral dissertation here. And *our* Nineteen Fifties will
begin next year sometime, with a *humongous* falling out between
State College PA and Baltimore that will goose your muse into full-
throated song and spear mine through the gizzard. Felix culpa, I
suppose."

My heart constricts: Let's do it differently! Let's don't do it!

"The congenital novelist's *what if*." Jay fingers his scarred lips;
smiles at me sidewise. "It's our last summer afternoon in Baltimore, Oats O'Rino. How 'bout a bock, for auld lang syne, before
we start our argument?"

Of course — and at once the brown brew is in hand (Gunther's,
I believe, or Hamm's: one of the old Baltimore-German breweries
now gone, that brewed the buck-goat springtime brew over which
we once shared Hemingway/Faulkner/Proust/Joyce/Eliot/Pound,
and more recently have *not* shared Boccaccio/Rabelais/Schehera-
zade [me] and Hume/Hegel/Husserl [Jay], as our trajectories
diverged), although no one fetched it from the Birkwood fridge.
What wouldn't I give to stroll (parenthesized, invisible) through
this roach-rich rowhouse of happy memory and re-see the hand-
me-down Goodwill furniture, the Russell Wright grad-student
earthenware and cheap museum prints and do-it-myself projects!
Not to mention my two-year-old-beautiful daughter and nine-
month-old first son!

"Not to mention Not-To-Mention," Jay reminds me dryly, his
eyes sharp. "That was the problem you mentioned, I believe."

One of the problems — and I here rediddle my Parker before it
mentions too much. The Fifties, you were saying.

"As the literary critic and apprentice intellectual on this porch,"
Jay declares, "I declare *your* Nineteen Fifties to have begun in

utero last year, when your ersatz-Faulkner M.A.-thesis novel failed, and in midst of reading Boccaccio you serendipitously happened across the earliest specimen of North American satire: Ebenezer Cooke's *Sot-Weed Factor* poem, set in Colonial Maryland, of all places. That combination inspired the project that you're working on right now right here in Fifty-Three: one hundred tales covering three hundred years of tidewater history, a kind of Dorchester County Decameron. It, too, mercifully, will fail, but it'll prove to've been the last step but one toward finding your voice — the last being that grand scarification aforementioned and upcoming, which will launch your floating opera and more or less scuttle mine."

Hey: Let's don't do it.

Jay shakes his head. "Don't do it we can't do, man. We *did* it; ergo, we'll do it."

Let's do it differently, then. Less woundingly.

Jay ups his eyeglasses, shakes his head. "No pain, no gain."

I take it all back, Jay.

"You can't, and I wouldn't if I could. *Jay shakes his head*, see? Jay doesn't take things back."

You've taken *me* back, old altered ego, and aback as well. I ponder my pen: rock versus hard place; Scylla meets Charybdis. At least let's *tell* it differently.

Jay tips his bock, regarding me over his cheekbones, after his fashion, as he drinks, then under his black brows as he twitches his nose and blots his lips on his work-shirt sleeve.

"You win, Oatmeal — this round, anyhow. It's your opera; score it to your taste."

ACT 2

※ ⊠

Drum solo: "Cunt-shy"

Safely *out of there* — off that porch of schadenfreudish memory and done with Baltimore student days; safely up in Happy
Valley PA and into the '50s and the end of my twenties; end-
running like a Penn State halfback around that corner-turning set-
to with my fictive friend — from some end-of-the-century end
zone I hazard an instant replay of my broken-field run from Prom
Night '47 more or less to Launch Day '56: the acceptance for publication of my maiden novel, by when #2 was finished and #3 in
the oven, and all three of my literal children were born and thriving. Whatever the quality of the songs, their singer had found his
voice; however green and how evergreen my husbandry, it was
productive.

Cunt-shy, "Jay Scribner" called the boy back there in *Cal*houn's
backseat, and may have re-called the precocious husband/parent
on that Birkwood Place front porch; let's say that that, or something therelike, cocked the trigger for our second brawlbrat brawl,
this one nonphysical but far more consequential than our first,
which he had likewise triggered with a scurrilous taunt. Yes, well:
I could take that bull by the horns here now, that taunt by the
balls, and make this retrospective drum solo a git-down frank
acknowledgment of a minor physical problem that mildly vexed
my boyhood and, less mildly, my late adolescence, until simple
surgery corrected it in '48 — too late for Prom Night, but in good

time for courtship, marriage, fatherhood, and a long and rewarding if less than epical heterosexual career.

Pricked up your ears, did it, that paradiddle? All right: A *con-
genitally constricted foreskin*, O attenders to this drum solo —
neither rare nor common among uncircumcised boys — prevented
normal retraction, once upon a time, of that anatomical item. Had
I been born Jewish, for example, this circumstance would never
have come to light. As I lacked that advantage — and as circumcision of the goyim would not become the pediatric norm in America until the Spockish 1950s, when my own sons were born — it
was my boyhood fate to be visited intermittently by the imp *Phimosis*, a more or less severe inflammation of the prepuce. By kindergarten or first grade, the condition had been diagnosed, but
instead of rectifying it straightforwardly with a scalpel, our then
family doctor — a trim-mustachioed chap piquantly named Wylie
Faw, before whom I quite remember exposing my red-tipped, pus-
oozing weenie — saw fit to prescribe a regimen of manual foreskin-retraction at bathtime (every second evening, as I recall, at
301 Aurora back then, where six of us made do with a single tub)
and thorough washing of the glans to cleanse it of accumulated
smegma. For the first few baths thereafter, Mother herself made
certain, by her tubside presence, that I "did my duty," as she
elected to call it — all most embarrassing for a five- or six-year-
old, perhaps a bit so for her as well. In any case, she and I soon
agreed that the responsibility was mine; after every bath, however,
for quite some while thereafter (I'm going to say for a year or so),
she never failed to ask, "Did you do your duty?" and I with mor-
tified irritation to reply, "*Yes, Mother.*"

But with increasing frequency I did not, or didn't quite, do my
duty. The physical constriction made it an ouchy duty under any
circumstances; phimosis made it downright painful, all but impossible. The yellow-white, oozy-flaky discharge was disgusting (during sleep, it would air-dry and glue my prepuce painfully to my
PJs; the slight Oedipal limp that I sometimes affected in fifth grade
was not all affectation). I was both too old and not old enough to
take bath-time pleasure in fiddling with my pee-tom, as the instrument was denominated in our house. For all these reasons, once a

phimotic episode subsided I would leave off doing my duty and lie that I had done it, until the inflammation recurred.

The consequence, enthralled reader, was that as I and my intromittent organ grew, full prepuce-retraction became impossible. I spoke of this to no one, not even to Jill. By adolescence, I believe, I had forgotten that that was what was supposed to happen, of itself, as necessary — for it wasn't yet evidently necessary. Masturbation could be managed as was; my male comrades and I jacked off, but not as a rule in one another's presence, and in the exceptional case (I seem to recall one cabin-wide circle-jerk in the Waziyata subsection of Camp Rodney), I contrived to stay on the fly-buttoned, cheerleading sidelines. In that time and place there was no sex education whatever of the official sort in either school or church; any routine physical checkups we children had must have passed over the matter of foreskin-retraction, for my dereliction of duty went unexposed, so to speak. Neither Georgia nor Whitey undertook a single sentence in the birds-and-bees way or provided us with informational literature. Our education in the sexual facts of life was left to schoolkids' folklore, Hollywood movies at Schine's Arcade, mildly risqué magazines like *Judge* and *Esquire* and *Spicy Detective*, such notorious Two-by-Fours as came from Jerry Schreiber's toolshed, and page something-or-other of the Boy Scout handbook, which — under the heading Conservation and with more periphrasis than logic — suggested that "self-abuse" was at once a natural urge and an unclean habit, and concluded with the exhortation "Don't do it." Nowhere was foreskin-retraction mentioned, or phimosis.

Yet I must have sensed that something was amiss, pee-tomwise, for I hung back, e.g. at that Waziyata whackoff-fest, and was a touch uncomfortable in locker-room showers with my Phys. Ed. classmates (whereas one of my pals, unfortunately afflicted with penile infantilism, exposed himself unabashedly and took his ribbing with good humor), and could, I suppose, be said to have been . . .

Cunt-shy? Yes, well, sure, maybe: a touch shy generally, for whatever reasons, not excluding the JackandJillery aforesung and the subliminal innuendo theresurrounding — often far from sub-liminal in East Cambridge Elementary. Contrary to what one might expect after so close a sister-siblingship, I was easier with my high-school male than female friends and by no means bold or rich in self-confidence with my high-school dates and my first sort-of-steady girlfriend. In that last connection, on the couple of occa-sions when the petting heated up by our then standards, it was I, if memory serves, not No-Names-Please, who sang so to speak *I'd Better Go Now* — but Mnemosyne is a fallible servitor in such matters.

So, yeah, okay, sure: *cunt-shy*, sort of, even by the measure of a sweetly cunt-shy era, in comparison with the promiscuous decades to come. And some portion of that shyness, more than likely, can be attributed to pee-tomic uncertainty. Freudians ahoy! Have you here the explanation of that slight streak of exhibition-ism that leads to cheerleading and drum solos, a hankering more for performative virtuosity than for self-effacing virtue? Is our man's ongoing fondness for public readings and lectures not a sort of self-exposure, compensatory for that boyhood foreskin-constriction? Does he not let it hang out here on the page because he kept it buttoned up in Scout camp? Are the erotics of his novels not a career-long redress for the adolescent cunt-shyness uncon-sciously attendant upon phimosis? Alternatively, might it not be argued that just as his attraction, at Juilliard, to such Modernist ingenuities as the Joseph Schillinger system of musical composi-tion by mathematical and other algorithms* was a compensation for his shaky grounding in basic musical theory, and his subse-quent similar attraction to the devices of literary high Modernism was perhaps a compensation for his less than massive and system-atic acquaintance with the corpus of literature, so that latter, together with his inclination to fictive "fabulism" over straightfor-ward realism, issues from a basic innocence concerning the ins and

---

*E.g.: Transfer the Manhattan skyline to graph paper and convert it to melody by plotting time on the x axis and pitch on the y. George Gershwin, among others, was fascinated by the gimcrackeries of the Schillinger System.

outs of human experience — and *that* from his having been, early, sort of . . . How to put it? . . . cunt-shy? Or that his so-early marriage (to that attractive coed pointed out to him by Jerry Schreiber from the Betterton Casino bandstand, with whose ardent collaboration he contrived to put virginity behind him in September 1948, in circumstances that he warmly recalls but declines to report, which however made plain to the pair of them that a certain functional difficulty of his was both real and readily correctable) after such limited experience with women, and his subsequent prompt serial paternities, was a kind of joyful catching up on the long-neglected doing of his duty? Ought you not to remark in passing, Freudischers, that among his first undergraduate, post-circumcisory literary efforts was — surprisingly, from so parochial a sophomore — an ode to Rosh Hashanah, and that his first published fiction* was of a Jewish character as well, as if his elective surgical foreskin-excision had both eased some constriction with the muse and prompted an "elective affinity" (in Goethe's term) with the Chosen People, from among whose number he'll eventually choose and be chosen by the wife and present shipmate that he's currently seeking his way toward: the other half of *US*? Have you not explained, in a word (the word *cunt-shy*, or, alternatively, *phimosis*), not only our man's certain diffidence back there in *Calhoun's* backseat on Prom Night '47, but his essential personality and the entire course of his life and work, from his cheerleading and drum-soloing to his literary aesthetics and fictive preoccupations, his early marriage and paternity, his fairly formidable production of more or less erotically charged narratives from a conservative domestic life lived in tenured Academe — even unto his characteristic shyness at social gatherings, which however he rather enjoys if adequately fortified with unfortified wine? Have you not?

You have, you reductive smegma flakes — the way the blind men in the parable explain the elephant by grasping, one its tail, another its ear, a third its trunk, et cet. You have me by the fore-skin, excised in the hospital at the foot of Aurora Street some eigh-

---

*"Lilith and the Lion," in *The Hopkins Review* IV:1, Fall 1950.

teen years after Jill and I were born in that same building. Wear it on your collective head for a dunce cap, with my blessing.

"Me," the trumpeter-bandleader Al Hirt used to announce as he left the bandstand during his drummer's showcase stints, "I've never liked drum solos." Me neither, Al, although I regularly did my duty as best I could when my turn came. Same goes for solo sex, literal or figurative. Love duets are another story: one in which exhibitionism is a disvalue, and virtuosity, while not to be sniffed at, counts for less than reciprocal deep feeling, ardor, tenderness, and the rest.

Cunt-shy, gentle reader, can be cunt-happy. Praise be to Eros Incorporate for that.

Back to the metaphor: Broken-field end-run rerun, with footnotes
My message to the less simplistical is that although a dinosaur may be inferrable from any one of a number of its bones,* one mustn't mistake one's bone of choice for an "explanation" of the beast or imagine even that *all* of them, explaining it, thereby explain it away.

Jay Scribner taught me that, and a thousand and one other useful things, in our undergraduate years together, including but not limited to how to drive an automobile, how to tie a full-Windsor necktie knot, how to shoplift (but only from large, anonymous emporia, never from small shopkeepers, and only the "necessi-

---

*I could sing this opera as a bibliobiography, for example, its corner-turnings a procession of other people's books: *365 Bedtime Stories* and *The Book of Knowledge* and *The Land That Time Forgot* and Richard Halliburton's travel-adventures and Schreib's Two-by-Fours, through all those pocket mysteries and fantasy-readers from Whitey's Candyland to *Manhattan Transfer* and *Sanctuary*, through my extended immersions in Proust/Joyce/Mann/Kafka and my off-the-cart discoveries of Scheherazade and Boccaccio and Petronius and Somadeva in my Johns Hopkins Library bookfiling days, through my stumbling upon Ebenezer Cooke's *The Sot-Weed Factor* and my "breakthrough" discovery at Penn State (on a tip from Jay Wordsworth Scribner) of proto-postmodernism in Joaquim Machado de Assis's 1881 Brazilian novel *Epitaph of a Small Winner*, which gave form to *The Floating Opera*, etc., etc. I could sing it as a series of corner-turning connections with women; of academic/geographical job changes; of social-historical "decades," to any of which series the production of my books is more or less incidental. Conversely, its episodes might be sung as the serial gestations of those books, to which the rest of their author's life is a mere extended footnote.

ties"), how to drink, how to think, how to use the bass drum for accents only instead of for beat-keeping, how to be literarily and morally self-critical (we quickly argued ourselves out of our experimental shoplifting). . . . What in the world, I wonder, did I ever teach him, in return for so much and various tuition? Herewith the recitative of Jay's Second Ascendancy — musicianship being his First — and its unintended end: the (edited and reimagined) replay of my broken-field end run from Prom Night '47 to Launch Day '56.

Sending seventeen-year-old yokels from Dorchester County's eleven-grade public schools to any serious university was a bit like sending green infantry troops over the top into a field of machine-gun fire. My brother, at least as intelligent as I and made of tougher stuff, had gone off to Johns Hopkins on a state-senatorial scholarship at age *sixteen* (he'd skipped fifth grade) to study engineering, and had dropped out after one semester. I knew of no Dorchestrians who had survived that school: America's first research university, founded on German rather than on Scottish and Oxbridge models — a sort of academic Marine boot camp, whose undergraduate college (all but devoid of social life) was regarded as a vestibule to the university's real precincts, graduate research and professional schools, especially the medical institutions. While Jerome Schreiber was getting himself a proper twelfth-grade preparatory year at McDonogh, I boarded a Trailways bus in September '47 at the defunct Cambridge railway station down by the creek bridge and went up the highway and across the Bay to Baltimore (where I had gone a few times before with *Cal*houn to buy drum equipment and stock arrangements for the Swingtette) and The Johns Hopkins University — to which I, too, had won a state scholarship, but which I had never seen. When I observe the patient care with which most parents nowadays (and some parents thenadays, too, I'm sure) shepherd their high schoolers from campus to campus at college-selection time, and at matriculation time shepherd them and their abundant equipage to the institution of their choice, to help them settle in . . .

No matter: I was pleased enough to be going it alone, girl-friend-free, with a few dollars in my pocket, my parents' blessing on my pompadoured head, suitcase in one hand and laundry-mailing case in the other* (and Juilliard, after all, under my belt and out of my system) to major in *journalism* at JHU, sight unseen. Cunt-shy I may have been, sort of, but in other respects I was a not-uncocky kid.

What was journalism? I enjoy believing that I believed that it had to do with keeping journals, an activity that I was not then nor have ever since been much inclined to (travelogs and ship's logs are another matter). No doubt I knew better; I had been "Ash Can Pete," the anonymous "school prowler" columnist for the CHS *Hottentot.* But I had elected my major by default, absent any interest in the other humanistic or the scientific disciplines, and prompted perhaps by Schreib's casual mention of that field at intermission-time on Prom Night.

The bus's first stop was Easton, home of Lew Startt's Orchestra and, by then, of Schreib's mother and assorted sisters. Among the boarding passengers was a fellow I recognized from Easton High's cheerleading squad; he, too, was Hopkins bound, it turned out, to study engineering, and before the bus reached the Chesapeake ferry-slip we had agreed to room together after Freshman Orien-tation Week. Strolling the car-ferry decks as we crossed the Bay from Matapeake to Sandy Point, we met a third incoming Eastern Shore freshman, this one from Chestertown and also an aspiring engineer. The three of us taxied up from the Baltimore Trailways terminal to the Homewood campus fast friends: boondocks mus-keteers (Muskrateers? But Chestertown's father was a civil engi-neer, whose son had graduated from Staunton Academy; nor was gentrified Easton as close to muskratland as was Cambridge), of whom only I, the greenest of the trio, was fated to survive the ensuing Slaughter of the Innocents.

---

*In 1947, Laundromats were not yet common in American cities, and were unknown in East Cambridge, Maryland. A boy mailed his dirties home to Mom for washing.

We oriented: a week in the Hopkins dormitory (back then there was only one; it is not an on-campus-housing sort of place) before the other students returned. In point of fact, Johns Hopkins is one of the smallest bona fide universities in the nation: no more than four thousand students on its Homewood campus, the distinguished tail of the very large dog of the Medical Institutions across town. But half of those students are advanced-degree candidates in plenteous labs and library stacks, busily adding to the sum of human knowledge, and so the physical plant gives the impression of a more populous enterprise, at least to an alumnus of Cambridge High. Of that week I remember little more than buying the looseleaf binder in which I write this sentence, being impressed by the presence among us of so many war veterans — older, less callow, some of them married, entering college on the GI Bill — and the absence of girls, which seemed to bespeak academic seriousness, all right. There were "mixers" with all-female Goucher College, whereat shy I didn't mix, but drank more National Bohemian with my new comrades than is good for a chap. I met a couple of ex–McDonogh boys who knew my old buddy Schreib and steered me to some fellow musicians among their number. Even at so academically rigorous a place, there was social stratification: old-line preppies en route to law or diplomacy, medicine or business; second- and third-generation academics en route to professorships in every field; All-American lacrosse players; streetcar-commuting locals with slide rules at their belts — and us rubes, blithely ignorant of and/or indifferent to all this, as to the social fraternities that "rushed" the other strata but not ours. At Orientation's end, unaware of the long true orientation-work to come, I moved with my Trailway comrades into a furnished row-house room that we had found near the campus, and I settled in to becoming not a journalist but a Journalism major.

That major was offered by a new department of the university called Writing, Speech, and Drama — only the second such degree-granting "creative writing" program (after Iowa's) in the land* — and turned out to be something of a fraud, although no

*At my recentest count, the number was above 400.

less a future journalist than Russell Baker of the *New York Times* was among my course-mates. There were no offerings at all in speech, next to none in drama, and nothing like a pre-professional program in newspaper and magazine work: only a single course, as I recall, presided over by a civilized and literary senior editor from the Baltimore *Sun*, who spoke more to the Large Issues of the profession than to nuts-and-bolts reportage. To learn that latter, he sensibly encouraged us to "go out for" the campus newspaper, which had had such notable student editors as Alger Hiss. I never did — being, among other things, too . . . shy, let's say . . . for the hurly-burly of even a weekly campus paper. Pursuing news stories, *interviewing* people, getting facts straight and deadlines met — not my cup of tea.

What the fledgling department did in fact have, and required of all its majors, were professionally directed graduate and undergraduate workshops in the writing of verse, to which I had no inclination, presided over by Karl Shapiro and Elliott Coleman, the former a Pulitzer laureate for *V-Letter and Other Poems*; and less professional but not incompetent workshops in the writing of fiction, presided over by moonlighting doctoral candidates in literature who were not themselves publishing fictionists but who would prove to be able enough coaches for us utter greenhorns. The program also offered well-taught courses in twentieth-century literature, which the traditional departments stopped short of, and access to the splendid core curriculum required of all liberal-arts undergraduates in those days: two-year surveys of the physical, biological, and social sciences, of classics in the history of (western) literature, and of landmarks in the history of (western) thought. The first two of those courses were interdepartmental, taught serially by professors of the sundry sciences and experts in each of the literary works — a classicist for Homer and Sophocles and company, an eminent *Dantista* for the *Commedia*, etc., up to Flaubert and Thomas Mann. The third was a virtuoso solo of unflagging reasonableness, civilization, and wit by the natty aesthetician and historian of ideas George Boas, who conducted our two-year trip through western philosophy from the pre-Socratics up to Bertrand Russell and Ludwig Wittgenstein, and along the way role-modeled us into rational skeptics disposed, as one of his innumerable advices put it, to "credit one's adversary with at least as much common sense as oneself."* Thus I had the remarkable privilege of an extended though eclectic grand tour not only of occidental literary masterpieces but likewise of the gray eminences of the professoriat — scholars of international renown — and a relatively systematic (as well as systematically relativist) run-through of western philosophical history by a suave and masterful historian of ideas, in classes seldom larger than a few dozen students. Nothing comparable to those splendid surveys is to be found in the university's curriculum today; they would be, I suppose, "politically incorrect" as well as administratively unmanageable. I was able to study simultaneously Homer's *Odyssey* and Joyce's *Ulysses* with a specialist in each, while in the middle distance wrestling *Don Quijote* out of Spanish with the refugee poet Pedro Salinas, and sneaking time with Scheherazade on my book-filing cart back in the stacks of William Foxwell Albright's Oriental Seminary, and pondering with David Hume, via George Boas, the Problem of the Retreating Subject — a made-to-order education, one would think, for a potential Postmodernist.

Alas, I was anything but an able student. I learned much — but how could I not, as I had *everything* to learn, not only about the subject matter of my courses but about the cultural-historical context that they comprised and were comprised by, about habits and disciplines of study, about self-discipline in general, and self-responsibility, social presentability, general non-jerkhood. On the several accounts of inadequate high-school preparation, inadequate daily lesson-preparation, inadequate vocational orientation, and inadequate general maturity and character, I barely survived, academically, those first two undergraduate years, in particular my freshmanhood. I failed two required courses, political economy and *physical education*, the former through incomprehension of its principles (though I managed to squeak through the exams the second time around), the latter by neglecting to show up at the

---

*"Common sense," however, ran another of Boas's graceful obiter dicta, "is the faculty that assures us that the Earth is flat."

gymnasium. In its grown-up way, the university exacted no penalty for class-cutting except the self-enforcing one of ignorance and its consequences; by reason of laziness, discouragement, hangover, and general numbskullery, I cut many of those marvelous lectures. My Easton buddy dropped or flunked out; my Chestertown buddy likewise, and numerous other of my new friends and classmates, especially in the unforgiving disciplines of science and engineering. I lost my state scholarship, but got by on my danceband earnings, a modest monthly allowance from 301 Aurora, and tuition reduction by library bookfiling — the best work-study program imaginable, given that my stacks included the Greek and Roman classics as well as the Oriental Seminary. I was still a virgin — not so unusual then among college freshmen, the war veterans excepted — and a bit of an odd duck. I had exactly one "date" in the first semester (with my sister's business-school roommate in Wilmington, whereto and back I hitchhiked for some chaste social occasion), another in the second (with an old high-school classmate down at Hollins College, in Virginia, whereto and back I hitchhiked with my Chestertown friend for a decorous formal dance), and no other connection whatever with girls, as there were none in my classes. I was, in a word, a nerd, without the nerd's redeeming specialized competency. I farted around too much on weekdays and drank too much on weekends: a floundering, identity-blurred, low-caliber dork.

The forgivingness of my liberal-arts curriculum, and perhaps the greenness of my department, spared me from quite flunking out; inertia and lack of better alternatives kept me from quitting of my own accord; my musicianship alone, such as it was, afforded me a saving measure of self-respect. My new jazz-friends, Jerry Schreiber among them, were more accomplished than my former Swingtette comrades, myself included. The dance band that I mainly worked in (and scored a few arrangements for) was of a gratifying competency and size — four saxes, three or four brass, three rhythm, and a female vocalist. While I was not a star performer, even Schreib agreed that I "held the section down" and urged me to stay on as a regular when he assumed the band's leadership in June for the Betterton Beach gig. Since I worked in such able company more weekends than not, my drumming in fact improved, as did my general musicianship. I could earn more income than most of my working classmates could, in fewer hours of much pleasanter labor, and the band provided me a range of friends and experiences — indeed, an interim, provisional identity — that offset my poor academic performance and kept me in the city and the university, enjoying myself much more than not despite my vocational indirection.

Sophomore year was another story. Although I still had no idea what I wanted to "be," by the end of that delightsome Betterton Beach summer with Jay Scribner's Bluejay Orchestra* I had my first serious steady girlfriend, whom I hitchhiked to visit on every free weekend or rendezvoused with elsewhere if the band had an Eastern Shore date, as we frequently did. I had in "Jay Scribner" my first really close college friend and my first serious intellectual friend ever; and to tide me over until something better came along,

---

*An extended footnote is in order here. The original Jay Scribner was a GI Bill pre-law Hopkins senior and piano player in whose well-established Baltimore orchestra Jerome Schreiber played regularly and I with increasing frequency through my freshman year. When the original graduated and went off to Columbia Law School, the coincidence of surnames and first initials led Schreib at first, upon assuming bandleadership, to bill us as "Jerry Schreiber and the Jay Scribner Orchestra." But that billing was less mellifluous than "Tex Beneke and the Glenn Miller Orchestra," for example, and Schreib had anyhow grown unhappy with his German surname, which reminded him of his alcoholic father and his wretched boyhood, whereas "Jay Scribner" pleasurably invoked for him Scott Fitzgerald's self-invented Gatsby and Ernest Hemingway's American publisher. With our former pianist's shrug-shouldered permission, therefore, we retained the band's name, adding "Bluejay" after the Johns Hopkins totemic bird. Audiences and employers reasonably presumed the trumpet-playing leader and negotiator of our contracts to be Jay Scribner, and it pleased him not to bother disabusing them of that error. Soon enough, we sidemen took to calling him by that name, at first in jest, then not. Although he never legally changed names, to our surprise he matriculated at Johns Hopkins as Jay Wordsworth Scribner (adding the middle name to amuse the Department of Writing, Speech, and Drama and to distinguish him from his predecessor in the university) and somehow managed to register his driver's license and bank account in that name. He felt no kinship whatever, he declared to me one evening on the pier at Betterton Beach, with the East Cambridge brawlbrat. But I never ceased to see in Jay Wordsworth Scribner a translation of Jerome Schreiber of Henry Street and Coraxion Hill — in which, as in most translations, something of the original was lost, but by no means all. And from time to time, as shall in time be sung, my counterself reverted to his brawlbrat name.

I had the gratifying sense of being a truly semi-professional musician.

It was Jay, once he had matriculated as a journalism major and duly signed on with the Hopkins *News-Letter,* who pointed out to me the unprofessionality of our department's program in that line and the particular meaninglessness of my majoring therein, as I evidently had no taste for newspaper work. It was another instance, in his opinion, of the same dreamishness-without-reality-checks that had led me up to Juilliard: a kind of *quijotismo.** Since such dreamishness appeared to be my nature, and since we were required to take a certain number of courses within the department, why didn't I try my hand at writing fiction, in the introductory workshop? He himself meant to do so, and poetry as well, as soon as his freshman requirements were out of the way; not because he felt any particular aptitude for those arts, but for the sake of the additional monitored writing practice those workshops afforded and the perspective such practice might give him on the study of literature — just as working jazzmen like ourselves could appreciate Stan Kenton, say, in a way that non-players could not.

Some such conversation must have taken place, for along with my second-year installments of those splendid survey courses, my obligatory makeup of Political Economy 101, and whatever else, I enrolled in the entry-level fiction workshop, presided over by a gentle, deep-Southern Marine Corps combat veteran and Faulkner fan completing his doctoral dissertation on Edgar Poe. As he had no writing aspirations himself and was gratified to have been pressed into teaching-assistantship by our shorthanded, under-budgeted department (whose reasoning must have been that inasmuch as Edgar Poe first codified the "modern" short story, as distinct from the pre-modern tale, a Poe scholar ought to be able to manage a short-story-writing course), he was politely respectful of those of us who presumed to such aspirations. We were encour-

---

* Jay, too, was reading Cervantes with Pedro Salinas — and, on his own, Salinas's love poetry as well, which I had been too lazy to check out. Our professor happened to be, my friend informed me, perhaps the finest Spanish poet of his generation, after Federico García Lorca — whom also I had not read, but Jay had.

aged to call him Bob, and we savored the transmutation, on his
Dixie tongue, of "writing" into "rotting." He recommended contemporary rotters to our novice attention — especially Faulkner,
Eudora Welty, Robert Penn Warren, and other Southerners — and
requested from us a short story every two weeks for (as it turned
out in my case) the next two years. If he could not teach us the art
of rotting fiction, he most certainly helped innocents like me to
learn the art of reading it, how to criticize and take criticism, and,
by the way, how to format and copyedit our manuscripts into
reasonable presentability — no small accomplishments. And he
graded as gently as he spoke.

Thus I was able to raise my freshman C's and D's and F's to
sophomore B's and C's, and — although I had everything to learn
about the craft of fiction, and spent my first year's apprenticeship
writing every sort of genre-junk out of my system — to imagine
that I felt the first stirrings of . . . Vocation. Blessed innocence!
While the rough outlines of western cultural history were beginning to swim into my focus, I was still ignorant enough of the
corpus of literature, and of myself, to find more inspiring than
intimidating the vast alcoves of my predecessors through which I
daily plodded with my bookfiling cart — reading and absorbing in
snatches, as I filed them, Urquhart's Rabelais, Marguerite of
Angoulême's *Heptameron*, Ovid's *Metamorphoses*, the *Panchatantra*, *Gil Blas*, Petronius's *Satyricon*, Somadeva's *Ocean of
Story*, Lucan's *Golden Ass*, Le Sage's *Asmodeus, or, The Devil on
Two Sticks.* . . . Jay, on the other hand, with his superior education, study habits, and self-perspective, scored A's and B's in all his
freshman courses, and on his first try would write for Bob more
accomplished apprentice fiction than I was writing after a year of
one-story-per-fortnight; but he could not withstand his relentlessly
accurate self-criticism, and he eventually withdrew from the workshops (and from journalism) in order to apply himself to the writing of criticism itself. His critiques of *my* efforts, however, while
total and detailed, partook oddly of the same ground-respect as
Coach Bob's: a knowledgeable outsider pleased to help enlighten
a primitive . . . *natural*.

Natural?

Jay it was who first invoked, in that connection, my raconteur father, who compensated for his ninth-grade education by reading several newspapers daily, and for his deafness (Jay had been reading Edmund Wilson's *The Wound and the Bow*) by holding forth as a teller of witty anecdotes. I was doing likewise, he opined, with my Le Sage and Basile and Straparola and Somadeva ("the massive eclecticism of the autodidact," Jay called it) and my always-ready story-per-fortnight: groping, erratic, all over the literary-aesthetical map, but unfailingly on time and never without some minim of originality. I was a sponge, Jay declared, soaking up influences — Where in the world had that Rosh Hashanah poem come from, and another on Themistocles, and another on Andrew Jackson's Federal Reserve policy, of all subjects? — and recombining and expressing those influences not with the flair of a capable dilettante (like himself, in his view), but with the awkward determination of one who has the gift but not yet any proper handle on it.

This flattering appraisal was confirmed for him by the closing passage of the final story I churned out for Bob that year: a presumptuous bit of melodramatic twaddle about the postwar adjustment problems of, of all human types, a Marine combat veteran. Balderdash, Jay let me know — derivative from Hemingway's "Soldier's Home" without Hemingway's authentic knowledge of his material, not to mention his literary skills — yet deserving nevertheless of publication in the ephemeral student magazine in which it appeared (and which Jay helped edit), because the closing passage managed to ascend from bogus realism to a purple stream of consciousness that, while also derivative, bogus, and overwritten to boot, was nevertheless not without some rhetorical force. I was, he suspected, just possibly beginning to find a voice.

Bob thought so, too; he encouraged me to re-enroll in his workshop for a second year (my third of undergraduate study), when I would be the experienced hand and Jay the beginner. I was also invited to sit in on the weekly plenary meetings of the fiction and poetry graduate seminars, to get some sense of more advanced

apprentice work, its authors, and their coaches. That encourage-
ment was enough, I believe in retrospect, to orient my new ambition. There was no epiphanic moment, no "Eureka!" But as I
turned nineteen between my sophomore and junior years, and
especially through the course of that latter, by degrees I began seriously to regard myself as an apprentice writer of fiction.

More "dreamishness without reality checks"? Less so, surely,
than those previous instances that Jay cited, for now I had critics
and teachers to counter any illusions about my competence, if not
about my vocation: not only my fellow amateur apprentices and
my more knowledgeable though scarcely less amateur coaches, but
the great moderns against whose writings I measured mine and
found mine still wretched (without, however, feeling thereby
defeated) and the great ancients, whom I could learn from and be
inspired by without feeling the need to measure my fumblings
against their monuments of excellence. The middle ground
between old and new — especially, as Jay pointed out to me, the
rich nineteenth century — remained largely terra incognita except
for Flaubert, Dostoevsky, and a few others. Dickens, Melville,
Gogol, Chekhov, Twain, from all of whom I might have learned
much of value in apprentice years, came late to me; I remain to
this day largely ignorant of and indifferent to the eminent Victo-
rians and Edwardians and their non-British contemporaries. I
went to school with Fielding and Sterne and Smollett, Scheherazade and Boccaccio, instead of with Tolstoy and Thomas Hardy,
the Bröntes and Trollope, George Eliot and Henry James (William,
however, I read with pleasure). My reality checks, Jay might have
observed, were short on realism.

Too, I was getting laid. Indeed, since my belated de-prepucing
had rendered me fully functional, I was well "ahead" of my counterself on the sexual front, in the respect that while Jay was still
dating casually (in a decade when casual dates among undergraduates seldom led to sex), my new girlfriend and I were humping
away at every opportunity and bending our efforts to increase
those opportunities. There was no golden Betterton Beach job that
second summer; even as the new Bay bridge, still under construc-

tion, promised to open up Maryland's ocean resorts to Baltimore and Washington, the old Bay resorts languished. Our Bluejays band played weekend dances in the city and on the Shore, but Jay and I labored through the sweaty weeks for a Baltimore stonemason, building flagstone patios and walkways in the fast-expanding suburbs; we lived in the vacated row house of a Hopkins social fraternity, where rent was cheap and house rules were all but nonexistent in the summer season. My girlfriend having finished her two-year degree at that Eastern Shore state college, we moved her into a furnished room in the Hopkins neighborhood and found her some temporary job to pay her rent until she entered a downtown secretarial school in the fall to learn office skills. Her ambitions, like my sister's, did not exceed those typical of young American women before the 1960s: some marketable competency like schoolteaching, nursing, or stenography to tide them over until marriage and motherhood and then to "fall back on," as necessary or desirable, when the children were older. As soon as her parents had deposited her in the city and turned back toward the Shore, we eagerly initiated her rooming-house bed — and we slept together thereafter virtually every night for the next seventy-five hundred.

"Another way to put it," Jay observed on the porch of Birkwood Place four summers later, as we reviewed our Baltimore Studentsleben days on my last of them, "is that your experience of women is deeper but narrower than mine — only one in your life thus far, really, and no others in the foreseeable future. Mine is maybe shallower than yours, but a good deal wider." For indeed, in addition to his casual dates he had by that time enjoyed several more or less extended romances and sexual affairs — a high-society Goucher girl, a Polish-American pianist at Peabody, and currently a nursing student at the Hopkins medical complex — and even a brief, tempestuous adultery with the wife of a fellow doctoral candidate in our interdepartmental Aesthetics of Literature program: "the immoral equivalent of war," Jay called that last liaison (he had approved of President Truman's "police action" in Korea), and he soon argued himself out of it on those grounds, as he had earlier argued us out of our petty shoplifting. But he was pleased to have had the edifying experience of moral self-repugnance; to have been briefly an Alcibiades, seeing the better way but following the worse. "Which of our histories will better serve a writer?" he asked or challenged me now.* "For that matter, which'll better serve a husband and father? You'll be the writer, if either of us is," he went on to concede; "but not as good a one as you'd be if you had my experience, or as I'd be if I had your vocation. As for married life, no question: You and your friend are in for trouble down the road, because neither of you has had enough experience of alternatives to know who you are yet, and therefore who your partner is. When the bloom is off, you're both going to find that you don't have much in common besides your kids and your life together."

"Oh, man," I amiably countered: "You are so full of crap."

But he wasn't.

The next three of our student years one would have thought marked *my* ascendancy, not Jay's, despite a few small setbacks. To name one: In the winter of '49/'50, my girlfriend's parents — strict rural Methodist-ministerial types — rifled their daughter's mail from me during her Christmas visit home, inferred therefrom our cohabitation, and insisted we marry at once. No calamity, that — we were anyhow by that time planning marriage, after my graduation — except that I was only nineteen and still partially dependent through the academic season on a small monthly subsidy from my parents, which I feared they might withdraw in well-justified disapproval of my marrying so prematurely. "Why not wait?" they would reasonably ask if we announced our intention, and I would be embarrassed into some cockamamie story. We therefore did the deed secretly, grudging the hand-forcing but not the commitment, with Jay and his incumbent girlfriend standing witness — but a sharp-eyed aunt espied the license-application routinely listed in the Baltimore *Sun* and blew the whistle. The easygoing folks at 301 Aurora did indeed disapprove — of the pre-

---

*June '53, porch of Birkwood Place, Baltimore.

cipitateness, not the bride — but, agreeably surprised to hear that it was not pregnancy that had impelled us (I made up some cockamamie story), they generously continued my allowance for the four remaining months of that academic year. Thereafter, all hands agreed, my wife would be employable, and we could support ourselves on our joint earnings.

Thus that small cloud passed; we more or less forgave my inlaws their high-handedness, and to our innocent eyes every other prospect was sunny. In the era of the GI Bill, to be a married undergraduate was not so unusual as it is nowadays. The university owned an apartment building near campus to house married students, by no means all of whom were advanced-degree candidates — though I was perhaps the only non-veteran and surely the youngest of those young husbands. No matter: My social and sexual life now stabilized and vigorous, my sense of calling reinforced by Bob's and Jay's encouragements, I flowered in my final two undergraduate years. No more C's and D's, not to mention F's; straight A's and H-for-Honors's, now that my "distribution" requirements were behind me. Without forsaking the ancients, I immersed myself more deeply than ever in the Modernists. A group of us read from *Finnegans Wake*, aloud, in rotation, every Tuesday night for two years at our Joyce professor's house, rebeginning the text immediately when we reached the end, with a little celebration like a Simchas Torah. When all signs indicated, correctly, that my baccalaureate was going to be awarded to an expectant father, for two or three worried weeks I all but ceased going to class, holed up in our apartment with Marcel Proust, and read nonstop the seven novels of *Remembrance of Things Past* — salubrious experiences both. I was still writing junk, but more literarily knowledgeable junk. By the standards of the so-called advanced undergraduate workshops that I myself would preside over at Johns Hopkins twenty years later, it was B work at best — gimmicky, thin on substance and genuine texture — but by generous Bob and Company it was well received. I took my B.A. in 1951 with departmental honors, pregnant with our first child and with plans for the M.A.-thesis novel that I would write in the graduate program the following year.

How, then, *Jay's* ascendancy, when I was the rising star, more or less, of what we had dubbed the Department of Writhing, Screech, and Trauma, while Jay had come to abandon "creative writing" for scholarship as he had earlier abandoned journalism for the writing of fiction and verse?

For one thing, as afore-established, while the apprentices in poetry had bona fide masters, we budding fictioneers had only lay coaches: "The blind leading the blind," as Jay put it, "except that they've been blind longer than we have, and know their way around." Instead, therefore, of saying to us authoritatively, "Hey, this is garbage, you know? Ingenious garbage; not untalented garbage; but garbage. What you need to do is save *this* from page two, build on *that* from page four, but cut this and this and this and this, all which are unworthy of the high standard you set with this really professional-grade observation made en passant in paragraph three, page nine," etc. — what they said, in effect, was "Really impressive, man; keep at it." And I did, sans genuine subject matter or bona fide voice; perhaps not standing on thin air as at Juilliard, but building bogus castles in that medium. Had my coaches been publishing writers of undeniable merit, and had they laid on me the constructive criticism I needed, would I have been silenced, or better expedited through my apprenticeship? Impossible to say,* and what evidence there is is indeterminate: Of the two unimpeachable professionals who heard me read (in that pre-Xeroxographic period, poetry manuscripts were mimeographed, but fiction was generally read aloud; all critical response except the coach's was therefore top-of-the-head, and only the coach did any line editing), one — young William Styron, fresh from winning the National Book Award for *Lie Down in Darkness* — politely praised the turgid fake-Faulkner sequence I presented in seminar, whereas the other — Victoria Lincoln, a book-of-the-month novelist wed to one of our philosophy professors — heard me out with ill-concealed impatience and then candidly advised

---

*Jay's advice, to himself and his fellow apprentices, was "If you can't survive, don't."

me to look around for some other line of work. Her put-down quite silenced me — for a month.

"Vicki was right to pole-ax that piece," Jay declared later, on the porch of Birkwood Place. "It was garbage, you know? Ingenious garbage. Literarily knowledgeable garbage. But garbage. You don't have a subject yet. You still don't have a voice, much less a worldview. But you *will* have; there the bitch is mistaken, and one day she'll apologize. What you need to do is quit making babies and get the hell out of Baltimore — by yourself, if necessary. Take a leave of absence from family life. Go down to Louisiana or out to Minnesota and camp on Robert Penn Warren's doorstep until he agrees to line-edit your stuff for a year. If that doesn't do it, go back to Cambridge and jerk sodas for Whitey until you get your act together. Leave the academy to us academics."

Perhaps I should have followed that advice. Had there been some bother-free alternative, perhaps I would have. But my wife had found an okay job in the dietetics office of the nearby hospital in which our daughter had been born; we were among friends on familiar turf and could get by on her salary plus my musical earnings and summer wages as a night-shift timekeeper in the local Chevrolet factory — where I had little to do but read through the entire Harvard Classics volume by volume, in order. I had been promised a teaching assistantship for the fall, and in every spare moment I was too busy making love and English sentences, both with the enthusiasm of ongoing discovery, to consider any interruption of either. That association of sex and storytelling, established then and emblemized for me later by the figure of Scheherazade, persists for better or worse to this day; when I first learned (from Jay, surely) the etymological connection of *pen* and *penis*, my reaction was a mild Voilà. In any case, this second implicit slighting of my first marriage did not escape me, although I made no issue of it at the time. I was busy writing.

How, then, *Jay's* ascendancy, who admitted to being impressed by my simpleminded undiscourageableness and my "not un-Christ-

like insouciance" (Jay's term) about the morrow, at a time when
he and Nurse Beth, his now-fiancée, were proceeding with prudent
caution in the way of birth control and marriage deferral until
Jay's dissertation plans and Korean War draft status were clearer.
In that latter matter, as things turned out, his caution kept him
one step behind me, as he had been one year behind in our early
undergraduate days, and would eventually force him to a short-
term Army enlistment in order to avoid conscription for a longer
period. On the very heels of my semi-shotgun marriage, General
Hershey canceled draft deferments for single college men; just
after my first parenthood, he began drafting married-but-childless
college men — and so I fared better, draft-boardwise, with my
imprudence than Jay did with his foresight. How, then, *his*
ascendancy?

It became clear in our second year (my last) of graduate work.
Johns Hopkins's short-lived "Bronk Plan," named for the university president who inaugurated it in the early Fifties, permitted
exceptionally qualified undergraduates, upon nomination by their
departments, to commence original research as early as their advis-
ers saw fit; even to bypass the bachelor's and master's degrees and
aim directly for the doctorate, which might be conferred when
all appropriate examinations had been passed and dissertation
requirements fulfilled. Thus we had among the upper-level undergraduates a few early-teenage mathematical prodigies, and thus
Jay Wordsworth Scribner (once he outgrew his journalistic and
creative-writing aspirations and settled into literary scholarship)
was enabled to skip the baccalaureate and take his M.A. in
Writhing, Screech, and Trauma the same year I took mine — in
his case, four years out of high school. He would have skipped
that degree as well, had it not been the highest offered by our
department; as was, we entered together a new doctoral program
in literary aesthetics cobbled up (by George Boas of Philosophy,
the eminent Leo Spitzer of Romance Philology, and our poet-
scholar-chairman Elliott Coleman) for the benefit of "writing"
M.A.'s with a strong academic string to their bows who wanted a
no-nonsense Ph.D. in a broader field than any covered by the con-

ventional departments individually.* But whereas I entered the
program faute de mieux — with a fair amount of unsystematic
reading under my belt, but no solid scholarly-critical training or
aptitude, no real foreign-language competency, no historical
grounding in literature and philosophy beyond those introductory
surveys, and no general interest in literary aesthetics — my classmate Jay had already written brilliant papers for Boas and Spitzer;
he could read French and German and Spanish readily and was
working up his Italian, Latin, and Greek; he had dutifully "covered" the sundry periods of English literary and European philosophical history, was deep into Marx and Freud, and had proposed
as his doctoral thesis topic — This in 1952/53! — "The end of
Modernism: Quo vadimus?"

He was, justifiably, the pride of that new doctoral program, all
the more because he resisted the encouragements of his several
mentors to make a career in philosophy, in comparative literature,
whatever. Jay thought he might, postdoctorally, follow Gertrude
Stein's path over to our medical school, not with an eye to the
M.D., but in a Renaissance spirit of learning more about a subject
wherein his fiancée's profession had interested him, just as his mate
(unlike mine, for example) was busily studying literature, not to
be excluded from his concerns. Or he might spend a year or two
down at our School of Advanced International Studies in Washington, to see how his literary-philosophical training rubbed up
against Realpolitik. Or both. Or he might beat the draft by enlist-
ing, and learn Chinese in the Army's celebrated language school
out in Monterey, the better to understand both Ezra Pound's *Can-
tos* and the state of California.

*Of such caliber was the scholarship of this program, I will note here, that of the
several dozen degree candidates in its brief history, virtually every one who completed the doctorate became principally a scholar-critic rather than a working
poet or fictionist. The few of us who became "professional" writers and incidental (even if full-time) academics were, almost without exception, dropouts from
that excellent course of study, which was terminated upon Spitzer's and Boas's
retirement.

But what's your *long-term* goal, Hieronymus? I once asked him, on the porch of Birkwood Place.

"Don't have one," Jay replied. "Don't want one." But then he bethought himself, rubbing the lip of his bock-beer bottleneck against his scarred embouchure. "My long-term goal," he decided, "is the successful completion of all my short-term goals."

Music he abruptly put behind him, except for the Baroque recorder, which he induced me to learn as well. I still played dance music for money; having disbanded his Bluejays, Jay would no longer even listen to jazz, and on our recorders (which taught me to relish Telemann, Handel, Bach) he was impatient with anything later than the Renaissance. "By the seventeenth century it's all coming unglued," he declared, on the porch of Birkwood Place.

Much taken with French existentialism and inclined to anatomize his own motives meticulously, he deplored the relative mindlessness of my life, while at the same time vindicating it more articulately than I myself could have done — variously as an ongoing *acte gratuit*, as the mark of an artistic temper more instinctual than rational ("Get out of the university, man!"), and as the hedgehog's knowing One Big Thing compared to the fox's Many Littles.

Be that as might, my one big thing was getting me nowhere apparent. My M.A. novel (that tidewater Yoknapatawphery that Ms. Lincoln had roundly trashed) I had sent with high hopes to a former fellow writher/screecher/traumer by that time reading manuscripts for McGraw-Hill up in New York while awaiting success. He rejected it, but kindly passed it along to his own literary agent, a fugitive Alabaman who responded favorably to my shoplifting from Faulkner and passed the script on to a fair number of publishers, every one of whom unequivocally said no. I consoled myself that at least I now had an official New York agent, who — rather surprisingly, as I look back on it — attempted as well, and with equal unsuccess, to market the installments of my next grand project as they issued forth over the following several years: those "Boccaccian" *Dorchester Tales* aforementioned, which it embarrasses me to re-mention.

I was, in short, energetically treading water, while a respectable fraction of my graduate-schoolmates were getting into the professional swim: One published a swashbuckling historical romance, with an advance on royalties several times larger than our TA stipend; others published good poems in good quarterlies. My McGraw-Hill ally, mainly a poet, scored a novel *on the side*, placed by the agent who could not place mine. Others yet, though less brilliantly than Jay, were hedging their bets on the muse with solid progress toward their doctorates and the assistant professorships waiting for them therebeyond. By midyear, however, it was clear even to me that I was out of my depth and like to drown: The literary-aesthetics doctoral program was Juilliard all over again, as the M.A. writing program had not been. I had not produced one bona fide academic term paper (I got by on "creative" succedanea that ought to have bounced back to me as did my fiction from New York), and I knew I never would, if only because I was too busy writing my pseudo-Boccaccian tales to do proper research. In Birkwood Place there were *two* babies now, the pretty fruits of ardent impulse — conceived despite their parents' plans to postpone parenthood until I had at least a regular job, if not a profession, and welcomed into our world despite the increased expense and decreased income, as their mother was now out of economic action except for piecework thesis-typing at home.

And yet . . . somehow . . . I don't recall our *worrying* gravely about the future, economic or otherwise, as we surely ought to have done — not even the inverted worrying of a Mr. Micawber convinced that "something will turn up" — whereas Jay inclined to worry increasingly, about his own life-choices and mine, whether they were "authentic" or mauvaise-foi. "What are you guys *doing*?" he demanded of me, on the porch of Birkwood Place, when I remarked in passing that all signs indicated a third pregnancy in just about as many years. "Are you out of your fucking *minds*?"

Beth Duer, who was there too — and whom I liked a lot, and who seemed to like me, and who often gently chided Jay for his aggressive rationalism, and who in time would inspire, but not be the model for, doomed and hapless Rennie Morgan in *The End of the Road* — said, "Jay."

Damned if I know, I replied, and probably shrugged, and probably added that I was too busy writing to think about that.

But I was not too busy scratching out those hundred tales (whereof, in the event, I completed fifty, and sent each to my agent as I finished it, and in time got every one back) to apply for some entry-level college teaching job for the fall, having seen the handwriting on the wall in Spitzer's Methods of Modern Literary Scholarship seminar. As I had only two items in my bibliography, both of them in campus publications, and was unqualified to teach literature or any other interesting thing, I confined my applications to instructorships in freshman composition — the floating base on which many a state-college English department rests. By my lights, I made a responsible job-seeking effort: five or six applications. Jay thought I ought to make at least twice that number; I learned later that one of the other instructors hired along with me that year by the Pennsylvania State College's Department of English Composition had papered the landscape with five or six *dozen* job applications, since, like me, he had a wife and two children to support. I mailed off my handful, telling myself vaguely that if none panned out I could after all go back to Cambridge and, oh, maybe get work with the local newspaper. Or whatever.

Meanwhile, on with the stories! And with the innocent, enthusiastic making of love.

Time-out aria: Two-Step

Time out from this long broken-field end-run rerun; time for a two-step aria: A-one; a-two:

A.

1.

From the exposed low ceiling joists before the bandstand in the old Betterton Casino of happy memory, there hung in 1948 a broken electric sign from an earlier era: in a corroding metal frame, four side-by-side rectangular white glass panes lettered, in order, Two-Step, Waltz, Fox Trot, Intermission (or, viewed from the other side, Intermission, Fox Trot, Waltz, Two-Step: The double-sided sign ran perpendicular to the bandstand and the long axis of the hall, to be viewable by dancers both on our right and on our left). Once upon a time, one supposes, those must have been the dancers' and the orchestra's options — Their only options? — and the serial components of every "set." For the benefit of the rhythmically impaired, one is obliged to imagine, the bandleader must helpfully have flipped a switch before each number to signal what was up.

The sizable "book" of the Jay Scribner Bluejay Orchestra included two or three waltzes — "Anniversary Waltz," "Tennessee Waltz" — which we played on request only, tongue in cheek, in a saccharine Guy Lombardo style. Had we been asked by some homesick Australian, we could even have faked a passable "Waltzing Matilda" (which I only now notice is not a waltz at all, but a march in two/four or four/four time). Stan Kenton, of whose "progressive jazz" we stood in awe, had demonstrated that three/four time, if strongly scored, could swing; and out on our event horizon, Dave Brubeck was working not only in jazz threes but in exotic fives and sevens (as in the groundbreaking album *Time Out*). We Bluejays took respectful note of these innovations; our stock-in-trade, however, was slow "ballads" in four/four, to which the customers "slow-danced," and up-tempo four/four "jumps" to which they jitterbugged. We also played polkas, rhumbas, sambas, beguines, congas, the odd tango, and the Mexican Hat Dance, all likewise four to the bar (bossa nova and mambo hadn't reached us yet), and the short-lived boogie-woogie, scored in four but accented in eight ("Beat Me, Daddy, Eight to the Bar," etc.). But I remember no stock arrangement in our library marked Two-Step or Fox Trot: dance fads from our parents' generation,* we sup-

---

*The two decades between world wars, let's say: after the coming of electricity to rural towns like Betterton, but prior to VJ-Day, by when fox trots and two-steps were passé (we supposed), at least in name. And the absence, from that electric sign, of Charleston, Cakewalk, or Black Bottom, for example, suggests the somber 1930s, not the Roaring Twenties. Had any of us enjoyed the privilege of dancing school, however, we might have learned the fox trot at least as late as the 1950s, as Annie Dillard reports in her 1987 memoir, *An American Childhood*.

posed, and already by 1948 as mysterious to us as the schottisches and mazurkas of nineteenth-century fiction.* None of us (and though a quartet on weekdays, on the weekends we grew to nine or ten) could say for sure what a fox trot or a two-step was, but the whimsical among us, especially in the weekend rhythm section, entertained ourselves with speculations as we shuffled through the leisurely "ballads." The fox is a quadruped; ergo, its vulpine trot must be four to the bar. He/she is "hot to trot," as current bar slang put it; "hot as a fox" — ergo, the trot must be a frisky four/ four, not a slow dance. And as the animal cannot reasonably be imagined to trot with syncopation or an afterbeat ("Lessn he been lamed by a houndawg," our country *trom*bonist offered during a saxophone chorus), the four beats must be, or have been, evenly accented, in the manner more of "swing" than of Dixieland and other sorts of jazz. The fox trot, then, we were satisfied to conclude, was uptempo Depression-era white jazz, some polite precursor of Benny Goodman's swing. We bet Paul Whiteman played fox trots.†

2.

And the two-step? "1. A ballroom dance in 2/4 time and characterized by long, sliding steps," declares *The American Heritage*, and "2. The music to which such a dance is done" — quite as we on the bandstand inferred, knowing the waltz and having reasoned out the fox trot. Give us a *one*, man; give us a *two*: We'll fake you a two-step, commencing with the double birth of Jill and Jack and two-stepping its way to the one-two punch that ended Jay Scribner's second ascendancy.

---

*"Save me the mazurka," a Tolstoy or Turgenev hero will request of the heroine. When mazurka-time comes, however, instead of dancing they step out on the balcony and advance the plot. Analogously, sort of, the owner of the Betterton Casino encouraged us to close each set with a particularly up-tempo "jump," which his patrons would sit out (and order more beer) or dance up a sweat to (and order more beer), in either case advancing his profits.

†*The American Heritage Dictionary* defines *fox trot*, not very helpfully, as "a) a ballroom dance in 2/4 or 4/4 time composed of a variety of slow and fast steps"; and "b) the music for this dance."

B.

I.

Out of one comes two, declare most cosmogonies; out of two, many. The Holy One (Blessed be He!), in order to create, first created a creatrix. For that reason, the Cabala argues, *B*, not *A* (in Hebrew, *beth*, not *aleph*) is the letter of creation, mother of the alphabet and thus, since in the beginning was the Word, of the world. Jill, one could say, by going primo through the birth canal, delivered Jack, anyhow paved his way; our twinned JackandJillery then made our world, until some third — Brother Bill, who named us; naughty nursery rhymes that shamed us; brawlbrat serpent who defamed us in the scrappy garden of East Cambridge — broke that world open with a one-two punch ("Oatmeal" was Jerry Schreiber's *two*, to his lavatory-taunting *one*). The boy who had taught me, with so much else, the essential afterbeat ("Accent on the *two*, man, not the one"), and in his first ascendancy had had his way with my first sort-of-girlfriend ("She didn't two-time you, man," he pointed out to me, correctly, " 'cause there wasn't any *one*-time, right?"), achieved his second in two steps, outstripping me first musically and then scholastically.

I have made clear, I hope, that I begrudged Jay/Jerry none of this, not even his summer fling with No-Names-Please. En route to our A.B.'s (B.A.'s in American, which anglicizes the Latin academic degrees up to but not including the Ph.D. that I never managed but Jay did) — indeed, through the whole period of his second ascendancy — we were closest friends, unsentimental counterselves, of whose connection I was by far the chief beneficiary. Little as I may know the world and myself even now, astray in Time's funhouse at our century's end, I would know them far less without Jay's early tutelage in a thousand things, from French wines* to the drawing of permanently useful distinctions.†

---

*"Burgundies are slope-shouldered, Oatmeal; drinkm up. Bordeauxs are hump-shouldered; laym down. Anytime some wine bore starts smarting off that all reds need to *breathe* before they're drunk, you one-up him by saying 'Not Châteauneuf du Pape.' Where *was* the pope's new house, by the way, dyou think? Avignon?"
†"The opposite of reason isn't emotion, man; it's unreason. And the opposite of emotion isn't reason; it's frigidity. Rationality can be *impassioned*, you know? And the strongest emotion can be rational."

I was his debtor, come to that, for my bride, although he had fidgeted at the marriage even while standing witness to the wedding ("All I said on that bandstand was 'Howja like to *slip your hands*, et cetera") and could come to terms with our subsequent reckless baby-making only as "some kind of existential statement, right?" Yet the *two* of that one-two was his frank suggestion (which I hot-facedly opposed; which he shrug-shoulderedly did not pursue) that the match was after all a mismatch, in for trouble down the road. I would show him, I said to myself — and lo, for twelve or fifteen years I did.

As I was two steps, Jay predicted at some point during that last spring in Baltimore, from winding up my apprenticeship to the fictive muse and beginning a genuine writerly career, such as he too had once aspired to but did no longer. *Only* two steps, I pressed? Or *still* two steps? Both, he supposed: The steps were only two, but neither was small, and both were more or less out of my hands. First (though Jay held the order to be unimportant), I needed to harness my influences and both ride and drive them, the way a good drummer both rides the beat and drives it, rather than being driven and ridden by it, pulled this way and that: Scheherazade and Boccaccio over here, Joyce and Faulkner over there, and their issue those cockamamie Dorchester Tales, little more than narrative attitudinizings. And second, I needed to *wake up*, somehow, or be woken up, in my life: *to* my life; to myself, other people, the world at large. I was . . . How to put it? . . . self-mesmerized, somnambulizing, and while in one respect that might be a writerly asset, even a crucial one, that he himself lacked, it was also an obstacle to . . . *authenticity*.

You're lapsing into French, I complained. We were on our way to a special evening session of the Writing Seminars to hear John Dos Passos, whose *Manhattan Transfer* had been a high-school revelation to me; whose *U.S.A.* trilogy we both much admired despite its technical borrowings from Joyce's *Ulysses* ("Quality shoplifting," in Jay's phrase); whose latter-day right-wingery we proper liberals all deplored — and who, as it happened, lived just then on the tidal Potomac and often visited friends in Baltimore.

Our interest in viewing and auditing the celebrated writer "live" was, if partly zoological or actuarial, nonetheless real: Although a number of heavy-caliber poets had given readings at Johns Hopkins during our studency — W. H. Auden, e. e. cummings, Dylan Thomas — campus "appearances" by famous writers were still something of a novelty in those days, and aside from the reticent young Styron aforecited, no big-name fictionist had visited our seminar.

In the event, it was a depressing evening. Since the 1930s, Dos Passos had written no fiction that impressed us. His literary reputation had much declined, and the rise of McCarthyism — a sore matter at Johns Hopkins on account of the senator's pillorying of our alumnus Alger Hiss and our professor Owen Lattimore — had given an ugly coloration to Dos Passos's ever more conservative political opinions. Whether by nature or in consequence of these circumstances, he proved to be a reticent, all but inarticulate guest ("speaker" would be a misnomer). Athletically handsome in his youth, he had devolved into a bald, beefy middle-aged gent with steel-rimmed spectacles, a glass eye to replace one lost in the auto accident that had killed his first wife, and a perspiratory presence. He would neither read from his fiction, nor lecture, nor "give a talk," only respond to our questions — he was there at all mainly as a courtesy to our department chairman, who had befriended him — and his responses, while cordial enough and candid, were difficult for him and therefore for us. At some point, I mustered courage to ask him whether he was, on balance, pleased to be and to have been a writer. Dos Passos considered (or struggled with articulation) for some moments, wincing at me through those small round lenses, and then said "No." We seminarians were all duly startled. After a pained pause, he told us that in his Harvard years he had been half tempted to study architecture. Now, in his middle fifties (!),* he rather regretted not having pursued that ambition.

---

*Ariast's parenthetical exclamation mark, turning sixty-two and still making sentences, sentences, having never, up to and including this *Once Upon a Time*, reconsidered his calling.

As Jay and I strolled homeward, chastened, across North Charles Street and past the Cambridge Arms Apartments (where F. Scott Fitzgerald had holed up to write "The Crack-Up" while Zelda dried out in Hopkins's Phipps Clinic), my friend remarked wryly, "Tough town for writers, man: Edgar Allan in the gutter, Scott and Zelda on the rocks, Gertrude a med-school dropout, and old Dos Passos just about *dos pasos* from the grave. Good thing for you you're going north to clear your throat."

Two steps in the right direction, I agreed — too surprised at my never having registered till then the sense of the novelist's surname, despite my several years of Spanish, to go on being sobered by his bleak assessment of his calling. As was my habit with Jay Scribner, I made no secret of this little ignorance. Under a streetlamp on the corner where our ways forked, he stopped and shook his head.

"I swear. What is it makes you think you *have* it, man?"

It was an honest question, not an interrogative criticism. I guess I don't think anything, Jay; I just put one damn word after another and the next one after that.

Hands in his hip pockets, elbows winged out, he regarded me. Have I mentioned that this was a delicious Baltimore late-April night, glistening from a warm rain shower, azaleas just opening but dogwoods and tulip magnolias in full bloom? It now was. I shrugged and smiled; I shrug and smile.

2.

As things turned out, I "went north" in two slow steps — to central Pennsylvania for the next dozen years, to upstate New York for the seven after that — before recycling myself (also in two steps, via Boston and remarriage) back to Baltimore, the venue of my two-stage apprenticeship, whereof, in this recounting, I am about to commence the desperate second with . . .

a) a send-off row on the row-house porch of homely Birkwood Place, with my counterself, and

b) a regrettable faux pas de deux, eye-opening, not long after, with B/Beta/Beth Duer, fictitious wife of that fictitious fellow. Fact or fiction, however — factitious, too, and factious, fractious, frictious — it opened my eyes indeed, pulled down vanity, divided self

from counterself, gave me a taste of serpenthood in another's garden who had more or less serpented mine (one taste proved
enough), and catalyzed but did not constitute my first pair of published novels. It is that *b* (likewise that *a*) that this end run is
around — as is this time-out two-step aria, its time now run.

Two. One.

Back to the rerun:

"Cunt-shy, definitely, one way or another," my make-believe
friend tried to make me believe back on that Birkwood Place front
porch some forty Junes past. "That's what's behind this frantic
fucking and baby-making. It *is* an existential statement, but not
the authentic kind I'd hoped it was."

"Jay," Beth mildly scolded from the chair beside mine, and
rested her hand on the bare ankle of my crossed leg.

Man, I said, unamiably, you are so full of crap.

Our row ensued, coolly analytical on Jay's part as usual
(although he had put away as many warm-weather bocks as I —
too many), hot-expostulatory on mine. His wife — they'd married, but Beth had kept her maiden name, an extraordinary step
back then — came to my defense until, as usual, Jay's reasoning
demolished hers. Mine, I'm going to say, sensibly exited the scene
to go change a baby. I counterattacked: called Jay Wordsworth
Scribner a bullying rationalist Pygmalion bent on deconstructing
his good wife (but we didn't have that trendy word in the Eisenhower era) and refashioning her in his image; a creative eunuch,
moreover, become a carping, carpet-slippered critic (an allusion to
Yeats's poem "The Scholars") because he couldn't get it up with
the muse.

"Shame on you for saying that," Beth Duer scolded me, less
mildly, and unhanded my ankle, but didn't exactly deny my
charges against her spouse — charges that Jay himself appeared
almost to relish.

"If I'm making a Pyg of myself," he retorted, "my Gal's well
worth it. But I'm not cunt-shy."

Scolded Beth: "Jay!"

"As for the muse," he went on cheerfully, "chances are you'll get no farther with her than with your doctorate. Not everybody's pants are easy to slip into."

Beth: "*Jay!*"

"Eyes open yet, Oatmeal?"

Et cetera: a first-rate graduate-student row, better than anything like it that actually happened, but the effect was the same. Next day, I drove my young family over the Alleghenies in our bucktoothed Buick Special to State College PA, where we happily commenced the next stage of our life together, second and last of my apprenticeship. At one point in it, Beth Duer visited; we had all chosen to regard our row-house row as a salubrious air-clearing, no hard feelings, and declared ourselves still fast friends despite it. Doctor Jay was out west scouting assistant professorships in interesting places while I toiled at my endless thousands of freshman themes, longhand-written and lengthwise-folded, and my own sentences, sentences, sentences — and it came to light that my "Pygmalion" charge, made wildly out of stung feelings, had hit home, despite Galatea's being, by and large, her sculptor's willing subject. Whatever ensued ensued: Punch One, though not consciously aimed as such. All hands worked through it, imperfectly. After a brief military enlistment (during which, in fact, he studied Chinese), Jay landed a jim-dandy tenure-tracked job teaching jim-dandy literature courses on a jim-dandy campus thousands of miles from central Pennsylvania, and began publishing solid scholarly articles in well-respected professional journals; the Scribner-Duers, too, then, at orderly intervals, generated babies. My instructorship, on the other hand, was dead-end: a year-to-year contract at rock-bottom pay, teaching freshman composition and remedial English six days a week, with no job security whatever and no prospect of either merit raises or promotion until I either completed a doctorate or published a book.

Fair enough, it seemed to me then and seems still in retrospect. Indeed, except for our annually increasing financial desperation — professional desperation, too, on my part, as my *Dorchester Tales* got nowhere — we were quite happy with our no-frills life in our low-rent faculty housing unit on the sprawling Penn State campus. We were rich in new friends, youth, energy, high spirits, and innocence — in that last, perhaps, rather less each season, but with plenty yet to spare. Our third child was born before our first's third birthday. As birth-control pills weren't yet generally available, and abortion on demand was still illegal, and our track record with contraceptive devices was unimpressive, and our libido remained undiminished despite certain new strains in our relation, and we were happy with our thriving three but decidedly wanted no fourth, we resolved upon simple surgery as the surest route to capping our production. We wheeled our babies through the university's prize livestock barns and picnicked in the bucolic countryside with our fellow PYTs — Promising Young Transients, as we un-Ph.D.'d and unpublished English Compers called ourselves. To eke out my meager salary, I played drums on weekends with a half-jazz/half-country dance band in the fire halls of neighboring Allegheny communities. Even occasional baby-sitters were beyond our budget, not to mention regular day care, but we looked forward to my wife's being able soon to get part-time office work if I could jiggle my teaching schedule to fit. Meanwhile, she was handy with a sewing machine as well as with a typewriter, able to make our window curtains and some of the children's clothes and her own as well as to type dissertations. Thanks to my high-school "shop" course, I was reasonably handy with tools, able within limits to repair, service, and even build things for us. I brewed my own beer. We took no vacations except holiday visits to our parents. A movie (with our duplex neighbor-friend checking the kids) was a rare extravagance.

Strapped for money as we were, however, I resisted the pressure to teach in the summer session or do any other moonlighting than those dance-band jobs, for even with a twenty-four-year-old's energy I was unable during the school year to find more than a couple of hours a day, maybe three or four on Sundays — amid my teaching and paper-grading and parenting and dance jobs and housework — to tuck in my Flents ear stoples and address the tale-in-progress in my already-battered old Johns Hopkins loose-leaf binder. Those precious summer months were my only opportunity to go at writing full-time, like a regular writer, and with my family's forbearance I did. More Dorchester Tales — not right, not right, not one of them publishable, something essential missing: a handle, a spirit, a true center of narrative gravity — but something there, too, surely, something rather different and, maybe, still promising. Discouragingly, if I had been discourageable, one of my fellow composition instructors, a war veteran, not only "placed" his first novel (and was straightway promoted to assistant professor) but had previously placed fiction in James Laughlin's *New Directions* annual anthology and elsewhere; he acknowledged that while he had submitted only two or three manuscripts for publication thus far in his career, he had *never been rejected*. The clock was running. My contract was renewed for a second year, with a cost-of-living raise from $3,300 per annum to $3,600, and I had some reason to expect that it might be renewed for a third, inasmuch as the student population was expanding yearly. Thereafter, however, up or out was the Penn State policy; if I had not published fairly substantially by 1956, I would have either to borrow money (Where?) and return to Johns Hopkins for a doctorate that I had no confidence I could complete, or find some other way to make a living, god knows at what — setting aside in either case my writerly ambitions, as I had earlier set aside my musical.

While real, my desperation was neither as great nor as realistic as it ought to have been, given my prospects, three fast-growing children, and a partner whose office skills would soon valuably contribute to our support but could not be expected to manage it alone. I fantasized some Walden-like life in the Allegheny woods, where we could live even more cheaply than we were living already, so that I could write, write, write.

Other than invincible innocence or self-mesmerization, as Jay had called it, together with a heartfelt absence of alternatives, what accounted for that stubborn persistence, of a sort that I have recognized since in a certain number of my Hopkins "coachees"? The fact is that something was happening, changing, clarifying, though still not quite crystallizing. A mostly undramatic but nonetheless seismic ground-shift was reordering my sensibility: a shift compounded of accumulated narrative experience and reading, plus that really rather scarifying moral wring-out with the Scribner/Duers around which I've made a broken-field end run, plus a consequent more or less harrowing re-examination of myself and my "belief environment" — and the serendipitous extension of my *Dorchester Tales* research to nineteenth-century blackface minstrel shows in general and, in particular, to a Chesapeake showboat or floating theater from the early decades of the twentieth, which I remembered having seen, in my childhood, tied up at Long Wharf in Cambridge. The James Adams Floating Theatre, it was called — sometimes billed (and respelled) as The Original Floating Theater. I had come to think of myself, positively, as a naive nihilist: a cheerful, responsible, breadwinning paterfamilial nihilist. Staring at an Aubrey Bodine photograph of "Captain" Adams's Original Floating Theater (and suddenly homesick for Chesapeake country, which I had not visited for more than a year), I conceived the notion of an avant-garde Dorchester Tale in the form of a philosophical minstrel show; perhaps even a *novel* in that form, playing on the showboat's innocently portentous name. Tambo, Bones, Mister Interlocutor — a literal black comedy, so to speak (the term Black Humor hadn't yet been coined). I had read with great interest Albert Camus on suicide; for all my prevailing stoical good cheer, in a couple of particularly dark intervals I had even contemplated that prospect myself ("I should hope so!" J. W. Scribner quoted J.-P. Sartre as replying to an intense young man who had confided the same to him) and had come to certain conclusions.

In the event, the minstrel-show format didn't work, but the dark comic-allegoric conceit wouldn't let go. Perhaps it could serve as the thematic center of a "regular" novel — better yet, of a *not*-so-regular novel, like the extraordinary turn-of-the-century Brazilian one that Jay Scribner had just urged upon me: Joaquim Machado de Assis's *Epitaph of a Small Winner*. Already it was December '54, my second contract-year half run. Perhaps I could turn James Adams's floating theater into "Adam's Original Floating Opera." I imagined a gentlemanly bachelor lawyer back in Cambridge, Maryland: a fellow the same age as the century, with a heart problem as apocalyptic as our doomsday-weaponed times (Nurse Beth, I bet, could supply me with an appropriate diagnosis); maybe with a prostate problem as well, for one symbolical reason or another. A cheerful, civilized-but-folksy down-homer, a touch eccentric but well regarded in his tidewater community, who carries certain historical/biographical scars with stoical good humor but is, in his (ailing) heart, a shrug-shouldered "nihilist" capable not only of suicide on philosophical principle but of blowing up the whole shebang: the entire . . . Floating Opera.

Narrative aria: "Wunderjahr"

Coined by the folks who more or less invented Romanticism, *Wunderjahr* is the German term for a phenomenon associated with the Romantic conception of Genius: the supernoval flare of an until then perhaps quiescent talent into a burst of brilliant productivity; the breakthrough wonder-year in which a Keats (1819) writes nearly all of his major odes, an Einstein (1905) publishes five papers that change forever mankind's view of the physical universe. No Keats or Einstein I, in the mainly tranquil floating opera of my life, 1955 was what will serve as a lower-case wunderjahr. In the world at large, not a great deal happened of historic note: The Warsaw Pact was signed, to counterbalance NATO; West Germany became a sovereign state; the U.S. Supreme Court reaffirmed its historic school-desegregation ruling of the year before. But as my remedial-English students graded one another's spelling tests and punctuation drills,* on one side of a three-by-five card on my lectern in a single January class period I outlined the plot of a novel already entitled *The Floating Opera*, and in the four months between that morning and my twenty-fifth birthday I drafted the novel itself with a confidence, ease, and sense of authority such as I had never thitherto known. The characters and plot are far from autobiographical; the phrase "drawing from life" has always had in my ears the sound of some particularly barbaric capital punishment. But at twenty-four I knew my fifty-four-year-old Todd Andrews's pleasures, whims, and dark soul-nights as if they had been mine; his eccentric, equivocal sensibility, together

---

*English Zip, we Promising Young Transients called that course: our favorite, as there were no compositions to grade and among our students were many of the famous Nittany Lion football players.

with the showboat conceit and the plot mainspring (his resolve
to end his life on a certain fine day in June of 1937), afforded
me a perspective on my tidewater material and some aspects
of my own life-experience such as none of those Dorchester Tales
had done. Whatever the fate of this manuscript, I knew to the
exhilarated bone that my apprenticeship was ended, my authorship begun.

That summer, in a kind of sustained euphoria, I subleased our
faculty housing unit and found us a small ground-floor apartment
facing the waterfront park and boat basin on the corner of High
and Water streets in Cambridge, in very view of the wharf where
Adams's Floating Theater used to tie up on its tidewater circuit.
While my wife (with a little help from her husband) oversaw our
one- and two- and three-year-olds, I revised and polished my new-
born fifty-four-year-old, shipped him and his unconventional floating opera up to my patient New York agent — who, after three
years of trying, had yet to make a nickel from my writing. I drew
a breath, caught a basket of hardcrabs, and before summer's end
conceived not only a companion-piece to the *Opera** but also,
more dimly, a third novel, to complete a sort of "nihilist" trilogy:
the same or analogous material orchestrated in turn as comedy, as
tragedy (as catastrophe, anyhow), and as . . . well, I didn't know
yet — *extravaganza*, whatever; I would cross that bridge when I
came to it. Meanwhile, I imagined a fellow of my then age — but
unmarried, childless, emotionally unconnected — who simply
runs out of motives the way a car runs out of fuel and finds himself
effectively *paralyzed*, smack in the middle of a train-station con-
course, say, unable for one reason and another to decide to do
anything — until he's found there by a sort of guru capital-D
Doctor who runs a half-quack Remobilization Farm out in the
corn-and-cantaloupe boondocks of Maryland's Eastern Shore,
and who prescribes for this affectless bozo, by way of therapy, the

---

**What to Do Until the Doctor Comes*, I called it; it would be published as *The
End of the Road*.

teaching of prescriptive grammar, dear old English Zip itself —
not in a big state university, but in some local teachers-college sort
of place, not unlike the one my wife had attended when I used to
hitch over from Johns Hopkins to "date" her. What if (I asked my
imagination) this moral vacuum of a protagonist, this ontological
Black Hole (back then we didn't have *that* term, either, worse
luck), should become imbroglio'd with a colleague whose moral
intensity and impassioned rationalism are of the order of Jay Scribner's, though of course not otherwise resembling Jay at all except
maybe in some exaggeration of my friend's Pygmalion aspect
(muse forbid any drawing from life) . . . ?

A splendid summer. We swatted mosquitoes, perspired in the
air-conditionless tidewater humidity, and dunked our babies in the
great Choptank, virtually at our rented doorstep. One heavily subtropical August forenoon we saw the old three-masted schooner
Levin J. Marvel set out from Long Wharf in the face of hurricane
warnings to stand downriver toward Cooks Point and the Bay.
That evening, in sober enthrallment, we watched over our sleeping
children in our blacked-out flat as Hurricane Connie roared up the
Chesapeake hour after hour, sinking the *Marvel* with fourteen
passengers and crew, taking out trees and power lines in the
municipal park, and storm-surging the Choptank literally to our
doorsill, so that come morning the park and Water Street and even
our front yard were quite submerged. Rowboats maneuvered
among flooded cars (more prudent than the *Marvel*'s skipper, I had
moved our bucktoothed Buick to the higher ground of 301
Aurora), and to the children's awed delight an unbroken sheet of
water extended from our very threshold across to Talbot county,
two miles away. We mopped and bailed and took the kids wading
among hydrangeas and crepe myrtles, and I wrote and wrote and
wrote.

Back in Pennsylvania, too, after Labor Day, my contract re-
renewed for its up-or-out year and my salary adjusted to perhaps
four thousand dollars, I wrote and wrote and wrote with that same
newfound certainty, despite the usual four-course, six-day teaching
load and the familiar avalanche of freshman theme papers to be

conscientiously critiqued.* Narrative problems posed themselves, as always; I solved them with authority. The imaginary characters of *What to Do*, so different from the equally imaginary ones of *Opera*, I felt I knew no less intimately in their lethal adulterous triangle. So inevitable seemed to me the steps of the bleak black plot, I'm tempted to declare romantically that the novel wrote itself between Labor Day and Christmas. But I wrote it, all right, just as I write this, word after word and sentence by sentence in this old binder with the predecessor of this old pen, relishing the myriad "executive decisions" that every such project requires and making those decisions with ease or difficulty but always with authority. The story's very blackness and minimality were cathartic; by the time I had killed its hapless heroine in a botched abortion, left her hyper-rationalist husband devastated, and packed her terminal, self-abdicating lover off to the Remobilization Farm for keeps, I felt altogether purged, invigorated, ready to plunge at once, with entire confidence, into something new and huge and altogether different — something extravagant, sprawling, farcical, intricated, and brimming with the narrative energy wherewith I brimmed. Already by New Year's Eve (which no doubt I spent a-drumming in John Shay's "combo" in the Undine Fire Hall of Bellefonte PA, resisting ever-more-frequent audience requests for the new rock-and-roll music instead of "that same old Forties shit") I had a fair idea of what that novel project might be.

A wunderbar wunderjahr indeed, 1955 of happy memory.

Unwashed Freudian smegma-flake arietta: "Aha"
    "Aha."
    I know what you're thinking, Jay Wordsworth Scribner,

---

*Theodore Roethke, local folklore had it, used to let them pile up in drifts for a month or so, then fortify himself with a quart of bourbon and grade them non-stop. He did not linger long in Happy Valley; I missed being his colleague by a year or two, as I would later just miss being the poet Charles Olson's at SUNY/Buffalo. In both instances, the large absence of a large poet was still largely present. Jay Scribner called my attention to a passage in William Carlos Williams's autobiography describing the author's visit to Roethke in State College PA and praising him as "the best steak chef since Brancusi."

perched yonder in your denim drowning-duds right now* on the very same state park picnic table beside the little lake up at Whipple Dam, in the Allegheny ridges above Penn State, where you perched in May '56 among the flowering mountain laurel and wild rhododendron and made me your You-Win-Oatmeal speech, yet to be delivered in this chronicling. You're thinking of that cunt-shy drum solo that opened this second opera-act and wondering why it didn't include the double-paradiddle datum of that "simple surgery" aforementioned, along with phimosis, duty-doing, belated circumcision, and subsequent ardent compensation for prior constraint. You're wondering whether there mightn't be some Deep Connection between the constricted foreskin of my early sexual apprenticeship and my chafing, so to speak, through my *literary* apprenticeship, at the constraints of the classic-modern short-story mode. You're even going so far as to speculate that the coincidence of my jim-dandy wunderjahr's following so close upon the simple surgery that ended our personal baby boom might after all be no coincidence: serial impregnations thenceforward of the muse, rather than of one's mate — in short, the sublimation of biological into literary fertility. Really, Jay, I am obliged to declare that in my considered opinion only an unwashed Freudian smegma flake would say Aha at that conjecture.

"Mm."

Punch Two: "You win, Oatmeal. Buon viaggio." Bon voyage
The cloud upon this sunny wunderjahr was that, newfound authority and ongoing creative euphoria notwithstanding, the news from New York continued negative as ever, and the calendar was running. Off in his academic Elysium, my counterself was

---

*When's that? I write "right now" at Langford Creek in May 1992, coming up on age sixty-two. But I'm addressing the open-flied ghost of drowned Jay Scribner, my lost Palinurus, just after his Columbus Quincentenary mishap five months later — and I'm imagining us back in Pennsylvania, conversing as I write, just as I earlier imagined us back on that Baltimore row-house porch, rehearsing our old graduate-school quarrel. Perhaps Time's astray in *my* funhouse, as well as I in its? Not really: The solitary setting down of words is always also a conversation, whether before or after the one set down.

publishing solid (though by his own acknowledgment uninspired) critical articles; he was winding up a book-length study of a tough-minded elder American Modernist poet rather like Jay himself in certain respects, and when some old-line university press contracted to bring out that book, as would surely come to pass, its author would likely be promoted to associate professor with tenure — whether at his present university or some other — before he turned thirty.

I nowise begrudged him his success. Jay was a serious, hard-working academic, building steadily if (after all) not quite brilliantly on a firm intellectual foundation. Although our quarrel had distanced us more than the geographical miles between us, we still regarded each other, warily, as "severest friends and best critics." We exchanged long letters (in which our exhaustively dissected moral wring-out was no longer mentioned), and looked forward to reunion in the spring, when he and Beth and their children planned a job-interview tour of several East Coast universities, perhaps including Penn State. Moreover, I did not envy him his researches and publications as such, much as I envied their academic rewards; his articles I found unexceptionable but pedestrian, with none of the panache of his former musicianship and no appeal except to specialists. What ever happened, I wondered, to his adventurous notion of studying medicine and/or foreign affairs after his doctorate in literary aesthetics? For that matter, what ever happened to his provocative dissertation topic, the winding up (or down) of Modernism?

Jay, on the other hand, quite accepted and warmly applauded my reports of a "breakthrough" with the muse, despite his not having seen its fruits. I had stopped sending my Dorchester Tales for his critical response, because he found the whole project "inauthentic," as he had found its fake-Faulknerian predecessor: "Necessary, maybe, to get where you're going; but in itself, false." I worried too that he might misapprehend and take offense at the ménage à trois of sorts in *The Floating Opera*, not to mention the hyper-rationalist Pygmalion/Galatea marriage of Joe and Rennie Morgan in *What to Do Until the Doctor Comes*, which novel I was all but finished final-drafting.

But *Opera* had been going the rounds of New York trade houses for months already, and nothing good was happening to it. Publisher after publisher turned it down: "Not for us"; "Too *experimental.*" My agent, bless him — that displaced Alabama gentleman and Faulkner fan — persevered, although he, too, reasonably wished that I would make his job easier by eschewing "avant-garde" effects. An ardent wild-game hunter by avocation, he kindly offered to ship me six hundred pounds of frozen moose from a recent Canadian safari to tide the household over until *The Floating Opera* found a berth. But he saw no point in trying to launch its grim little sister-ship until and unless the Opera either floated or went down.

A fourth publisher rejected it. A fifth.

My enthusiasm for the *new* fiction-project, therefore — *The Sot-Weed Factor*, I was calling it, after that earliest-known American satire first brought to my attention back at Hopkins by Jay Scribner — was maddeningly constrained by economic necessity and paterfamilial responsibility. I asked my department chairman, quite seriously, please to fire and rehire me between semesters, so that my few hundred dollarsworth of accumulated pension deductions would revert to me. Not done, he said — amused, however, by the desperate ingenuity of my proposal. Teeth clenched, I actually applied to the Hopkins philosophy department, faute de mieux, for Ph.D. candidacy with tuition waiver and graduate-student stipend. My application was accepted (perhaps out of relief that I was changing fields) by the kindly husband of that best-selling novelist who had rightly but hurtfully trashed my bogus Faulkner.

But how could we imaginably survive on *less* than our meager present income? And how could I manage rigorous technical philosophy, when I hadn't managed the more flexible literary aesthetics program? And how could I possibly *stop writing fiction*, as I would absolutely have to do for several years in any serious doctoral program, at a time when things were going at such a clip musewise that I felt as Richard Wagner reported sometimes feeling, that my pen could scarcely keep pace with my invention? I withheld from my Penn State chairman this news from Hopkins, lest it prompt a decision that he must make in any case come spring and contract time. I buried myself in my mountain of student papers and in the multivolume Archives of Colonial Maryland, which I had discovered in the stacks of Penn State's Pattee Library, and yet somehow found time to play with my children, the dear three of them bunked still in a single small Faculty Housing bedroom. There have been artists aplenty, I knew, so driven as to abandon their families in pursuit of their muse. The Romantic tradition, especially, valorizes such single-mindedness, but I was determined not to let the two become an either/or. If on balance I was no better than a B-minus father, I accept that grade, relieved to have managed no worse.

And I mesmerized myself with sentence-making about Lord Baltimore's virgin laureate of the province of Maryland, who must lose his Cooks Point "estate" along with his innocence in order to find in himself a much-chastened but bona fide poetic voice. Upon his protean, Mephistophelian mentor, Henry Burlingame, I bestowed a few exaggerated attributes of my counterself: Jay Scribner's sometimes aggressive knowledgeability; his distaste for innocence, which he tended to regard as dangerously arrested development. "After a certain age," Jay liked to say, "innocence is guilty."

A sixth publisher rejected my *Opera*. A seventh.

Or was it the seventh who, in early March, wrote to Lurton Blassingame (he of the incongruous Birmingham accent, the abundant faith and moose meat) that while he "could not believe that anyone with so obvious a zest for life as [the protagonist] Todd Andrews would attempt suicide, much less the blowing up of his mistress, his possible daughter, his friends and townspeople, and the whole Floating Opera," he and his colleagues at Appleton-Century-Crofts were sufficiently taken with the story as a whole to offer a $750 advance on royalties if I would agree to revise the novel's ending in the directions of plausibility and palatability.

"Anyhow, it's time you and I met," Blassingame added after telephoning me these tidings. "Why not come up for lunch and have a talk with the fellow?"

If the fellow doesn't understand that a fellow can be a nice fellow, I replied — even a *loving* fellow in some ways — and smile and smile and still blow up the whole show, then the fellow doesn't understand the book.

But my heart buzzed.

"I told him I didn't expect you'd take to the idea. It wouldn't hurt to talk to him, though, before we try somebody else."

I read that as meaning, in polite Alabaman, that if I expected my agent to keep on making efforts in my behalf, I probably ought to make this modest one in his. And so I put on my only suit, kissed my family good-bye for the day, and took the Pennsy train from Lewistown to New York.

In the twilight of the Mississippi showboat era, I had read, some of the newer vessels were equipped with double sets of stage- and houselights: electrical for landings with available power, acetylene for those without. The James Adams Floating Theatre (aboard which Edna Ferber had spent a Chesapeake season home-working her novel *Showboat*) was in historical fact electrified only, with its own diesel generators, but I had fitted my version of it with acetylene backups so that my homespun nihilist hero (who knows the vessel's layout), could slip below-stage at the show's climax at Long Wharf in Cambridge in June 1937 (and the novel's climax in June 1954), turn on all the main gas valves, return to his seat in the audience, and watch the blackface minstrels cavort while he waits for the Opera to blow. It does not (the physics of gases are not in my man's favor), and a muted denouement ensues. En route to Manhattan at this crux of Act Two of my personal opera, I considered alternatives, imagining the derision Jay Scribner would greet them with if he knew the story. Todd Andrews turns on the gas, hears a baby in the audience crying, and bethinks him that his own possible daughter by his ex-mistress is out there with her mother; he relents, turns the gas off, and . . . ? Or he turns on the gas, returns to his seat, hears baby cry, relents, and . . . hollers "Fire!" in a crowded theater? Turns on house-gas, hears baby cry, turns house-gas off and galley-gas on (the Opera's galley was understage), thus scaling down the apocalypse from general to personal, and . . . ?

The proffered $750 ($675 after LB's well-deserved commission) would in itself be but a welcome little bonus: about two months-worth of my instructorial salary, or the equivalent of those non-vested pension funds that I had tried in vain to lay hands upon. But a bona fide book contract, whatever its terms, should assure my promotion from year-to-year instructor to tenure-tracked assistant professor, with a salary raise to as much as five thousand per annum, an almost unimaginable bounty. My position assured, I could politely tell dear dreaded Hopkins to offer my doctoral fellowship to some more qualified applicant. We could think seriously about borrowing to buy some little three-bedroom do-it-yourselfer out in the Penn State countryside. I might score an occasional course more interesting to teach than English o and Composition 1; perhaps be saddled with fewer 8 A.M. and Saturday classes. Most important, even if the Opera fared no better than most first novels by unknown writers, I would be an officially published novelist, not just another aspiring apprentice. Publication of #1 should ease the path for #2 (I would have a publisher, an editor, an option clause), and in #3 I felt I really might be laying hold of something new, different, and considerable. A bucolic green future stretched beyond poor terminal-nihilist Todd Andrews, his damned acetylene, and the blackface minstrels' rendition-in-progress onstage of "The Terrible & Terrific Explosion of the Steamboat *James B. Taylor*, Which Tragedy Occurred at Natchez-Under-the-Hill, Mississippi, on February 19, 1892."

After Newark, as the train crossed the Hackensack marshes (soothing to my spirit despite the junked cars and gull-swarmed landfills) and the Empire State Building hove into view across the Hudson, I imagined a now entirely sympathetic Jay Wordsworth Scribner advising me thus: "Five years from now, Oatmeal, either this novel of yours will be dead and forgotten, like most first novels — in which case your jiggered ending won't have mattered a fart one way or the other — or else it will have been well enough received despite its jiggered ending for some paperback house to want to reprint it, in which case you stick the right ending back on. If the reprint house wants to keep the jiggered ending, you

two-step along till the next chorus after that, by when either
you've sunk into obscurity or else you're well enough established
for your early novels to be reissued — and *then* you restore the
Original and Unparalleled Floating Ending, with a dry little
explanatory foreword to the new edition. If you stick to your
Olympian guns, on the other hand, it's back to Baltimore and East
Cambridge with your tail between your legs, excuse the mixed
metaphor. Think how many people have arrived in Manhattan
with less appealing options: 'Drop your drawers if you want an
audition,' et cetera. What's the problem?"

The problem, I would have replied (other than the principle of
hanging for one's own literary shortcomings rather than another's), is that a jiggered ending, false to the spirit of the novel, could
be the very thing that *sinks* the Opera, and then I'll never know
but what it might have floated in its original design and proved
the Appleton people wrong.

"But if you don't jigger it to suit, there won't *be* anything afloat
out there to prove the Appleton people wrong. The other half-
dozen publishers didn't even nibble."

True. There are, of course, yet further trade fiction houses in
town.

"Assuming that your agent stays interested after seven rejections despite your uncooperativeness and all his efforts with your
earlier pair of losers. The calendar's running, Oats O'Rino, and
here we are in the Hudson tubes already. I say jigger the sumbitch,
unless it turns out you hate Mister Appleton absolutely."

"The power of the press," Lurton Blassingame mock-marveled
as we bade cordial au revoir three hours later to the agreeable
young Appleton editor, whose name and face and office are lost to
my memory. At once half stunned and overstimulated by my first
revisit to New York since Juilliard, I had had some difficulty locat-
ing the Blassingame Agency, tucked up in the Chemical Corn
Exchange Bank on West Forty-seventh Street. I had found the suite
of offices a surprising touch seedy ("old-line bookish" would be a
kinder term), its furnishings secondhand looking, books and
manuscripts piled on every horizontal surface, Lurton's worn

swivel-chair lame and listing — not the slick, high-overhead operation I had somehow fancied. The man himself, whose Dixie drawl had telephoned disappointing news to me several times per season for the past three years, proved a jowly, low-keyed, avuncular gentleman about Todd Andrews's age but more sanguine, who nicely balanced his Southern roots, the high-culture pleasures of Manhattan, and his passion for the hunting of moose and goose (from which latter he was well acquainted with tidewater Maryland). I have had perhaps more "muscular" and professionally savvy agents since — tough women, generally — but none more courteously civilized, or whose interests I could trust to coincide more closely with my own, whether or not he squeezed all the best possible terms out of a contract negotiation. I liked the chap okay indeed; was all the more impressed, now that I had met him and seen the shelves of his published clients, at his having "carried" me for so long with no return whatever. We taxied to a restaurant somewhere small, French, and publishy in the West Fifties: William Faulkner's favorite in New York, LB remarked, and pointed out the great man's favorite table. Reviewing the menu and reflecting that it would be all the more cavalier now for me to stonewall it with Appleton-Century-Crofts, I thought: Here goes most of my agent's modest prospective commission. We toasted Faulkner with dry martinis. Lurton declared his abiding confidence, even at that remove, that considerable rewriting could yet salvage my earlier pseudo-Faulknerian opus into marketability. I demurred — but recognized in that remark, too, a gentle strategy: All right, *don't* completely rework your M.A.-thesis novel; but at least agree to a bit of fiddling with the Opera's stern, and we have *a contract in hand*. Anyhow, let's go say hello to the Appleton chap, shall we?

We did, after a splendid lunch (through which I reflected with a passing pang upon our simple instructor's-budget home fare) and the best white wine I had ever tasted in my life till then. A quick Manhattan walk or short taxi ride (if Blassingame's voice remained Alabaman, his stride was pure New York, and available cabs appeared at his slightest signal) fetched us to my first trade publisher's office, where I was introduced to intelligent young Mr.

Whatsisname. Book-jacket blowups in the receptionist's area and along the hallways; office shelves lined with the Appleton backlist and other tomes; novel-size typescripts stacked more neatly than in Lurton's lair. Appleton-Century-Crofts (Editor Whoever explained to me) was smallish by industry standards even since its conglomeration from three yet-smaller houses. Although most of their profit came from their text- and reference-book divisions, they maintained a modest fiction list and published a number of new titles each season, including one or two first novels. He would be pleased to see mine on their summer list: the best time, in his view, to do a "non-commercial" first novel by an unknown author, as the competition for review space is less intense then than in the peak spring and fall seasons. If I would agree to revise the story's ending toward something less . . . well, *nihilistic* . . . we could make a contract within the week. If all then went satisfactorily, the novel could appear in August, even late July, in time to be reviewed before the post–Labor Day crush. He was not, after all, demanding stem-to-stern revision; a few paragraphs could do the trick, under the showboat's stage at climax-time — he pointed out the paragraphs in my typescript, exactly the ones I had anticipated — after which the denouement and wrap-up could stand pretty much as they were. An afternoon's work, in his opinion.

In my writing life to date, I have had seven several editors at five several New York publishing houses and have admired all of them — men and women, youngish and oldish, with various backgrounds, temperaments, and editorial styles, but invariably civilized, intelligent, sophisticated, hardworking, agreeable people, balancing their literary enthusiasms with their need to keep the company solvent — a difficult enough job even back when the houses were independent of parent corporations. By big-business standards, book publishing is small potatoes, and the fiction trade is its second least profitable department, after poetry. Trade editors enjoy nothing like academic tenure; they move up or on or out with considerable frequency. The company may die under their feet (Appleton will, a few years after this scene); they themselves may die (Edward Aswell did — my second editor, at Doubleday, my second publisher — after publishing my second novel, *What to Do Until the Doctor Comes*, as *The End of the Road*) or leave the business (Timothy Seldes did — my third editor, at my second publisher — presently to become a literary agent, after publishing my third novel, *The Sot-Weed Factor*), or switch for one reason or another to some other house (Anne Freedgood did — my fourth editor, at my second publisher — after publishing my fourth novel, *Giles Goat-Boy*, and the story-series *Lost in the Funhouse*), perhaps taking a few of "their" writers with them (thus I moved with Freedgood from Doubleday to Random House, my third publisher, who brought out the novella-triad *Chimera*). Or one's agent may decide to go for a better contract, at another house, than one's "old" publisher is willing to offer — thus my second agent, Lynn Nesbit, then of ICM (whom the late Donald Barthelme liked to call "the Mother of Postmodernism" because at one time she represented Barth, Barthelme, William Gass, and John Hawkes, among others), moved me to my fifth editor, Peter Israel, at my fourth publisher, Putnam, for my fifth novel, *LETTERS*; and my third agent, Andrew Wylie, moved me to my fifth publisher, Little, Brown, and my seventh editor, Patricia Mulcahy, for my eighth novel, *The Last Voyage of Somebody the Sailor*, after Peter Israel had shifted positions in the Putnam group and shifted me to my sixth editor, Faith Sale, who brought out my sixth novel, *Sabbatical*, as well as the essay-collection *The Friday Book* and my seventh novel, *The Tidewater Tales*. And this present *Once Upon a Time*, my twelfth book and ninth more-or-less novel, will likely be contracted by my fourth agent (Deborah Karl), at my third agency (Wylie, Aitken & Stone), to some eighth editor (Ms. Mulcahy having left Little, Brown for another house), whether at my fifth publisher or some sixth. As in academia, where one's loyalty is typically first to one's field and one's position in it and only second to any particular academic institution, so too along Publishers Row and among the unstable "stable" of any publisher's writers — Devil take any of whom whose own first loyalty is not to the muse.

As was mine, I still stoutly maintain, that March post-noon

when I shortly agreed with agreeable Mr. First Agreeable Editor —
whom I was never to lay eyes upon again; whose publishing company folded not long after the *Opera* sank (a commercial failure,
like most first novels, but a modest critical success despite reviewers' quibbles about its sentimentalized climax), and did not
resurface as did *Opera* nine years later* — to follow Good Jay
Scribner's counsel and jigger the story's climax for the sake of a
contract and a stay of execution, so to speak, for my literary
future. Not to have done so, in my then pass, would have been to
face a professional suicide much likelier than Todd Andrews's literal gas-valving understage of Adam's Original Floating Opera —
which opened valve, in two sentimental paragraphs, I jiggered
shut.

"The power of the press," Lurton Blassingame mock-marveled
at the brass rail of The Brass Rail, where we toasted my change of
heart with bourbon and soda before I caught the evening train
back to Happy Valley. And as we sipped he wondered aloud, in
passing — vis-à-vis *Opera*'s sexual triangle and its darker replay
in *What to Do* — "Only a few far-out academic types go in for
that sort of thing, don't you think? Wife-swapping and such?"

"So," declared Jay Scribner two months later, perched on a picnic-
table top up at Whipple Dam, where we two couples and our four
point five several children were celebrating my twenty-sixth birthday: "You win this round, Oatmeal. Bon voyage to your jiggered
Opera." He raised in toast a decanted glass of my yeasty home
brew, the only alcohol we could afford until my upcoming promotion and pay raise; raised it only half-high, as booze was verboten in the state park and Jay's toast was not unqualified. "It

---

*To be republished in a mass-market paperback edition, then in a new hardcover
edition with the original and correct ending, and with that ending in all subsequent mass-market and trade paperback editions and sundry translations down
to the penning of this sentence, when the second Doubleday Anchor trade paperback edition remains briskly in print and the first Romanian hardcover edition
(the novel's dozenth-or-so translation) recently arrived by diplomatic pouch from
Bucharest. I nod itward: Hello there, ghost of 1955.

really looks as if you're on your way. You've got your act together and a contract in your pocket. Here's to all that."

We sipped, and sucked our cigarettes — I guardedly, for I knew this "friendchip" mode of Jay's. Our four born children played on the brown sand beach of the little lake: a large pond, really, backed up behind a dammed mountain stream, its water still cold as snowmelt. Beth Duer was ruddily once more pregnant. Their visit had been abbreviated and unavoidably less than easy, given the blowout among us that I have end-ran. Moreover and unexpectedly, Jay's job-interview tour had borne no fruit. His best-case scenario had been a bid from the Ivy League, with which he could at least have improved substantially his position "back west"; but those eminent departments had found his critical work as unexceptional as it was unexceptionable. Only our ivyless Penn State appeared genuinely interested in recruiting him, for the enlarged graduate program we anticipated upon our upcoming escalation from College to University. Quite aside from the problematics of our foursome's dwelling under the same academic roof, however, the fact was that a land-grant institution, still heavily weighted toward agriculture, forestry, the mineral industries, engineering, and "education," offered no advantage over Jay's present base. All the same, we four had managed a tentative rapprochement, and because the Scribner/Duers were leaving directly from our picnic to begin a homeward cross-country camping trip, the intramural pressure had been off all day. We had even agreed that a reciprocal visit was in order. To Jay's mild appall, my firsthand world, and my household's, remained bounded on the east by the Atlantic surf off Ocean City, on the north by uptown Manhattan, on the south by Roanoke, Virginia, and on the west by the Alleghenies wherein we were picnicking. There was more, Beth and Jay assured us.

My mate withdrew beachward, to "check the kids." Watching her go, Jay knuckled his eyeglasses back up onto the bridge of his nose, his long-habitual gesture even when they hadn't slipped down. "You've *needed* me, man," he went on, speaking as if to my retreating spouse. "Since first grade I've been your moral coach and critic, right? Your gadfly. I would even say I've been your frigging *counterself* — although that's not the job description I had in mind back on Henry Street. But you don't need me anymore."

Beth brightly guessed she'd go help check the kids. "You do that," her husband said, and lit another cigarette.

"You being you," he went on then to me, "you're going to need moral coaching and criticking all your life. But you don't need me *around* anymore, in the flesh or on the phone or in letters, because you've internalized me. I'm onto you and into you, Oatmeal."

I decided to say nothing at all, for as long as possible.

"My job now is to toddle off and disappear out west, like some hybrid of Helper and *Spielman* in the Ur-myth. Your capital-T Trials aren't over with, by a long shot, but you've gotten the hang of your magic weapon, and you've cleared the first hurdles. Your Wunderjahr is under your belt, and soon enough you'll be ready for your Wanderjahr. You have good personal and academic friends. Presently you'll be having literary friends, too: established writers and poets, accepting you as a peer. I envy you that. Your book in the works could be a *real* breakthrough, I think: more so than these first two, as you've described them. I even made up a word last night for what I think you and some of your contemporaries are doing: *Postmodernism*."

I only tipped my cigarette ash in acknowledgment. Jay's praise could be heady indeed, but I had learned to be wary of it. He regarded me steadily.

"My prediction is that by the end of the century, old Penn State English Compers will be telling new instructors that both you and Ted Roethke did time in English Zip and Comp One, right here in Happy Valley. You're off and running, is my point, and with luck it'll be a good long run."

Home brew must be decanted, for the reason that when one siphons it from crock to bottles for capping and final fermentation, the yeast settles bottomward while converting the last of the sugar into alcohol and carbon dioxide. When the bottle is later uncapped and the fermentation pressure released, the CO_2 bubbling out of solution stirs up those sediments and beclouds the beer unless all but the last inch or so is quickly and adroitly poured off into a glass. The home-brewing tradition, including the art of decanting and in some instances even prized yeast cultures, had been passed down through thirsty generations of Penn State graduate students and entry-level instructors, certainly since Prohibition and probably since the college's founding in 1855. Keeping an eye out for potential rule-enforcers, I discreetly poured myself another home brew.

"*My* career, on the other hand," Jay said, as if addressing now the hemlock woods beyond the lake, "which got off to a much better start than yours, isn't panning out, and my gut feeling has become that it isn't going to. I was a much better musician than you were, but not better enough to blow my life through a horn. Back in Bob's old workshop, my fiction was better than yours; but you're turning out to've had the calling and maybe even the talent, and I didn't have either. My scholarship is solid, and so's the range of information behind it; I know ten times more stuff than you do, man, about ten times more things. But it won't really fly, you know? I get off the runway all right, but I want to *soar*, and I'm not going to, so screw it. Should I try poetry, dyou think? Revolution, maybe? Italy?" He flipped his cigarette away. "Lung cancer?"

These startling questions were not of an interrogative character. I sipped my adroitly decanted home brew.

"I have this feeling . . ." Jay said, twitching his nose, and left the statement suspended.

One's long-term goal, I could not resist echoing him from the row-house porch of Birkwood Place, may defensibly be the successful completion of all of one's short-term goals.

My friend turned upon me his levelest gaze and, as if at what he saw, slowly shook his head. "There was a time not so long ago," he said, "when I seriously considered *killing* you, man, because it seemed to me that, figuratively speaking, you'd killed me. That moment passed, and now I wish you well. But it's lucky for you I'm a fictional character, Oatmeal, because *I don't take things back*. I've rubbed your nose in yourself like a puppy dog's in its own poop and maybe put a dent in your invincible innocence. Ciao now, and buon viaggio. You're done with me, but not me with you; in one form or another, as they say in the Ur-myth, I'll

be back. Have a nice career meanwhile. Have a nice life. Don't
take any wooden nickels."

He turned back toward the pond beach, from where our
women were returning with our children, and in a different tone
concluded, "Speaking of which, as I may have mentioned, if I were
you I'd find myself a different shipmate, kids or no kids. But *I'm
not you*." He grinned his sunniest, most befreckled brawlbrat
grin. "Any questions, before you rassle me for insulting your
marriage?"

I ought to have asked what he meant by the startling assertion
that he was a fictional character. Instead, I asked merely What's
this *Ur-myth* business?

"Jesus, Oatmeal. Look it up. Time to bail out of here, Beth-
babe."

Bon voyage, then, I suppose. You have indeed insulted us,
Jeronimo. I hope we won't be seeing or hearing from you for a
long time.

"Likewise, man. But look it up, okay? U R hyphen M et cetera:
Ur-myth."

Okay: On with Act 2

I *did* look it up, Jay/Jerry/Hieronymus/Jeronimo — that Ur-
myth business — four years later, in 1960, when *The Sot-Weed
Factor* appeared and at least one of its reviewers noted that its
author had clearly been influenced by the Ur-myth in general, and
in particular by Otto Rank's treatise on the myth of the birth of
the ritual wandering hero.* I had not in fact yet read Otto Rank
(or Carl Jung, Lord Raglan, Joseph Campbell, and the other myth-
meisters); did not know what exactly a "ritual wandering hero"
was; had quite forgotten your having mentioned something called
the U R hyphen M et cetera at Whipple Dam State Park, Pennsylvania, on 27 May 1956, just before aspersing my first marriage all
but unpardonably, until that book reviewer put me in mind of it.

---

*See the aforesung aria "This is a story I've told before."

For in the busy interim, much water had gone over yonder spillway.

"*For in the busy interim*," my counterself mocks, not uncordially, perched as before (but in his drowning-denims) on that state park picnic table right now.* Nobody else in sight. "Career?" Jay prompts.

Career? Well, in brief, since you ask: the original *Opera* launched in August '56, promptly to submerge with scarcely a ripple except, surprisingly, nomination as aforefootnoted for that year's National Book Award in fiction. *The End of the Road* ditto in '58 (not-bad reviews, no nominations) — both novels to resurface in the Sixties and commence their ongoing reprint voyage. *Sot-Weed* finished in time for publication not long after my thirtieth birthday, by when *Giles Goat-Boy* was a-planning and awaiting, for its crystallization, only my look-up of those Ur-mythologers, plus some immersion in the teachings of the Buddha. Promotion to assistant professor of English at PSU. Promotion to associate professor upcoming. In a word, okay. Yours?

"Mine!" Jay fists his specs, as back in Eisenhower days. "Certain short-term goals satisfactorily attained, let's say: thanks a lot. Houses? Cars? We Yanks measure progress by such items."

We do. First house bought, a little do-it-ourselfer in a rural village outside State College. Pleasures of petty-bourgeois homeownership first savored: lawn mowed, grapes raised, wine vinted as well as home brew brewed, tomatoes cultivated, partitions sawed through, kids played with in own yard. Violation of sovereign airspace by overflying planes frowned at. Volume of personally owned Earth calculated by projecting small rectangular lot to center of planet and applying Law of Prisms to allow for taper to point. Mild disappointment registered at small total cubic mileage thereby arrived at, offset by pleasure in relative numeracy. Nego-

---

*27 May 1992, my sixty-second birthday — One-minute birthday? — is when I pen these words, my Parker *ree*mote having once more given Time some spin-within-a-spin, as we've yet on that date even to *embark* on the overture-cruise to this latest floating opera. Perpend that datum, head-scratching reader of this bottom-bottled note. My minute's up: Time in.

tiations begun for somewhat roomier "ranch-style" house on larger ridgeside lot sloping up toward Whipple Dam. Green buck-toothed Buick Special traded in on brand-new cream-and-coral Pontiac wagon, how I prized it, for cheapo camping vacations with kids — now nine, eight, and six years old.

"Friends?"

Friends. Warmest personal and professional friendships of my life before or since, I believe, since you ask — always excepting my special connection with the self-styled fictional character "Jay Wordsworth Scribner" and my total one with the shipmate that this opera had better be floating me back to, sentence by sentence. *Where is she*, Jay? Where are we?

"You know I can't answer that, man, except in dumb images. Hyperspace? The Ur-myth, et cetera. *Happy Valley friendships*, you were saying."

Not the sort you were envying me in prospect — William Carlos Williams meets Theodore Roethke, and like that. Just colleagues and pals, mostly. But I had the gift of friendship in those days, and hospitableness.

"Music."

Music?

"*Music*."

Music. No more paying gigs; rock and roll put us out of business after 1960. But the university was recruiting good senior people, and our new Chaucer man happened to play a fine gut-bucket trombone, and our new Hemingway man blew an earnest jazz piano; so we kept our hand in at one another's parties. We all gave parties back then. *Threw* parties, I believe the verb was.

"Other recreations?"

Come off it, Scrib.

"Other recreations."

Tennis again, which I hadn't played since high school; this time I learned the game. Lots of backyard badminton, now that I had a backyard. Football catches, baseball catches. Camping I mentioned already, with the kids; we picked that up from you and Beth.

"Leave Beth out of this."

Beach-camping, too, with close friends and their kids. Field archery and bow hunting, though I never killed anything. Stalking the Allegheny forests in October was so beautiful! Gardening. Parenting. House projects. Reading. Brewing. Et cetera.

"Philosophy."

Jesus, Jay.

"*Philosophy*, Oatmeal."

Philosophy, philosophy: Teaching Plato and Aristotle and Hume and Schopenhauer in the undergraduate Humanities survey courses — and writing *The Sot-Weed Factor* — taught me that what I had mistaken in my first two novels for existentialist nihilism was radical innocence in disguise. I was still an atheist, a moral relativist, and a Happy Valley existentialist of sorts, but I had William James under my belt on the subject of mysticism, and I was reading Alan Watts and D. T. Suzuki on Zen Buddhism and nodding my head *yes*. Then I saw that book reviewer's comment on *Sot-Weed*'s obvious influences and remembered your Whipple Dam mention of the Ur-myth, so I piled into Jung and Raglan and company to find out what I was driving under the influence of. I found out I'd been *teaching* the damn thing without recognizing it — in the *Odyssey*, the Oedipus plays, the *Aeneid*, the *Divine Comedy*. Teaching it and living it, too. My gut feeling was that I understood unitary mysticism and the myth of the wandering hero about as well as a rational skeptic can. While I was playing Dixieland jazz and pruning tomato vines and chugging home brew and grading student papers and building bookshelves and refereeing kiddie quarrels and stalking deer and writing sentences in this old binder, I worked out to my satisfaction a tentative tragicomic view of mysticism, et voilà: Giles the goat-boy, for better or worse, lacking only the element you supplied me in Rome in 1963 — the "strong" relation between Mystery and Tragedy. Did you and I never speak of this before?

"Other drugs."

Beg pardon?

"We have the home-brewed alcohol. We have the Zen and the

Tentative Tragicomic View of Mysticism. What other Controlled Dangerous Substances, or uncontrolled?"

Ah, well. Dexedrine, in point of fact, for quite a while there, daily on workdays from about 1958 — halfway through *Sot-Weed*, when the workload of teaching and writing and parenting got so heavy that I was literally falling asleep at the writing desk, head down on this old binder. But even at low milligramages I hated the rush of amphetamines, the push. So my Hemingway-piano pal put me onto Parnate when it first came out: an MAO inhibitor and psychic energizer —

"I know the pharmacopoeia, Oatmeal. Parnate's potent stuff."

Little red uppers, how I loved you: the smooth and sustained psychic lift, without Dex's twitchy push. I would happily have stayed with Parnate for the rest of my natural life, the way I've stayed with this old pen and this old binder — but a certain number of spoilsport users began dropping dead of cardiac arrest or freaking out when they ate Brie cheese, and the manufacturer pulled Parnate off the market. It's available again these days, I believe, but the list of no-nos is so long and scary that I'm astonished at how I used it for years with no restrictions whatever on what I ate and drank, and no side effects at all. Absent Parnate, after *Giles* I switched to Dexamil for the next half-dozen years or so: one per day on workday mornings, as I filled my pen and opened my binder. It's another amphetamine, not as gentle as Parnate, but gentler than straight Dex because the Miltown damps down the motor push.

"Spare me the *Physicians' Desk Reference*, man; I was married to a nurse once upon a time. Busy little pill-popper back there, weren't you."

The Sixties — though the counterculture didn't reach Happy Valley until after I left it for Buffalo in '65. Even though the dosages were low and seem to've left no scars, I shake my head now at such prolonged chemical insult to my peasant constitution. Was never otherwise "into" "drugs," but will not deny that up in the Queen City, between marriages, I experimented recreationally (never scriptorially) with marijuana and hashish. Sort of enjoyed the hash, but was off cigarettes by that time and didn't like smoking anything. Never dropped acid or snorted coke. Have been off all such chemistry for twenty-plus years now, except vitamin C and beta-carotene daily at breakfast, one aspirin per even-numbered day for heart-attack prevention, coffee through the morning, table wine with dinner, and a beer nightcap, since you asked. Want to try a pharmacological analysis of my oeuvre, old smegma flake?

"Aha. No thanks — though I can imagine some apprentice critic's comparing the formal intrications of your fiction in that Parnate/Dexamil period with those Aldous Huxley Doors-of-Perception shots of the webs that spiders build when they're experimentally stoned."

I wasn't stoned, man; just wider awake than usual. Nature and habit take care of that for me these days, more or less. That's it?

"Three more items, actually. Marriage?"

Nunnayerbeeswax. What else?

"Marriage."

No soap. Hey, Scribling, where did "no soap" come from? Never mind. Out there in the world, the 1950s have reached '62: We haven't even mentioned the H-bomb tests and Strontium 90 in our children's milk, the Rosenberg executions, Khrushchev pounding the UN desk with his shoe, the French loss of Vietnam, the Hungarian revolt, the Six-Day War, ICBMs and Sputnik, jet airliners, Castro's revolution, the Eichmann trial, John Kennedy's election and Marilyn Monroe's suicide, men in space, the Cuban missile crisis, and you want to talk about —

"Skip the file footage. Marriage."

No soap.

From his jeans side pocket, Jay retrieves my watch. He consults it, rotates left-handedly its bezel, raises his eyebrows, shakes it, puts it to his ear. "Little sucker seems to've stopped, just when we were moving into the Sixties." He repockets it. "The ball's in your court, lad; I've got all the time in the world these days. Who wants to go sailing, anyhow?"

Then I'll choose my words with care and hope for the best — my line of work, after all. The half-dozen years in question — '56 to '62/'63, I guess — were a time of considerable burdens, explorations, and problems, addressed by the couple in question with energy, persistence, optimism, hard work, and steadily eroding innocence but really quite formidable productivity, plus plenty of fun and satisfaction along with growing pains (accent those last two words either way). Self-preservation, I add in passing, was by no means the driving force behind all those pages of prose fiction, but it was among their welcome by-products. Separately and together, the couple managed their difficulties as best they could within their capabilities: the usual problems and emergencies of parenthood; the expectable abrasions of a dozen years' intimacy after little prior experience, as also of growing into one's thirties in less than perfect synch. In the hiking shoes of marriage — as you yourself may have noticed, Jeronimo — some rough edges wear smooth, some make calluses, and some raise blisters that can end the trek.

"In short, I was right about you two."

You were right, Smegma Flake — but not in short. Even here in '62, with twelve rewarding though certainly not untroubled married years behind us, and Khrushchev and Kennedy head-to-head on the brink of apocalypse, and we spouses-errant coming onto the famous mezzo del cammin de nostra vita, it's going to take another eight years, with plenty of good things in them, to wind up the pas de deux that started under that Two-Step sign in the Betterton Beach Casino in the summer of '48. I'd call that bonding.

"I'd call it innocence."

Long live innocence, then.

"Long-lived it was. Ur-myth, Oatmeal."

What?

"Next-to-last item, man: U R hyphen et cetera. Do your duty."

Duty-do aria: "The Ur-myth, yes"

The Ur-myth, yes. Doo dee doo, dum dee dum.

Once Jay Scribner had mentioned it vis-à-vis *The Sot-Weed Factor*, and I had gotten around as aforerecited to checking it out, the thing possessed my imagination for nearly a decade: the century's Sixties and my thirties, when I was, in James Joyce's words, still "jung and easily freudened" enough to be thus possessed. Passé now, a quaint late instance of the nineteenth-century passion for global syntheses, the cyclical pattern of ritualized heroic adventure (a.k.a. the Ur-myth) seemed to me then profoundly illuminative, a melody capable of infinite reorchestration.

Lecture time: Comparative mythologists in the nineteenth century (that is to say, philologists, cultural anthropologists, and comparative religionists, notably Max Müller and J. G. Frazer) had noted striking general similarities among the résumés of mythical wandering heroes the world over, and had attempted to explain the common features of those heroes' careers as allegories variously of the solar cycle (diurnal or seasonal), the associated rhythms of agriculture, the stages of human life and the succession of generations, the rise and fall of civilizations — virtually whatever involves literal or figurative maturation, achievement, decline, dispossession, death, and rebirth or the promise thereof. In the first third of the present century, Sigmund Freud famously applied features of particular myths, most often classical Greek or Hebrew, to psychoanalysis, and vice versa (the "Oedipus complex," *Moses and Monotheism*, etc.); his breakaway protégé Carl Jung more expansively deployed mythic archetypes to explain both normal and abnormal human psychological development, and, coaxially, accounted for the myths as common human psychodrama writ large, cultural expressions of the "collective unconscious." Lesser figures such as Lord Raglan itemized in considerable detail the biographical similarities of mythic and quasi-mythic heroes from widely disparate cultures, without presuming to explain the isomorphy.*

---

*In Chapter XVI of *The Hero* (1936), Raglan lists 22 salient features of the monomythic "pattern" and then measures against this template 21 several ritual heroes, from Oedipus and Joseph through Watu Gunung and Nyikang to Siegfried and Robin Hood, giving each a score. The items, in Raglan's words, are these: "1) The hero's mother is a royal virgin; 2) His father is a king, and 3) Often a near relative of his mother, but 4) The circumstances of his conception are unusual, and 5) He is also reputed to be the son of a god. 6) At birth an attempt is made, usually by his father or his maternal grandfather, to kill him, but 7) He is spirited away, and 8) Reared by foster parents in a far country. 9) We are told

These pioneering studies much influenced the old masters of literary Modernism, especially T. S. Eliot and James Joyce, and by mid-century their work in turn had inspired a veritable industry of "myth-criticism," among whose notable practitioners were the eminent Canadian Northrop Frye, my Penn State Hemingway-piano friend, Philip Young (see whose beautiful essays on Rip Van Winkle, Pocahontas, and other classical American myths), and my later Buffalo colleague/friend Leslie Fiedler. Jay Wordsworth Scribner did not deign to dabble in the mode. "I want to *be* a mythic hero, man," he will declare to me in Rome in the spring of 1963, strolling with me in light April rain through the Villa Ada tourist campground. "And if I can't be one, I'd want to be the Magister Ludi in that field, like Joseph Campbell. You've read *The Hero with a Thousand Faces?*"

Nope.

"*Jesus*, Oatmeal!" He stopped us in our path, not far from the red-and-beige Volkswagen Microbus that I was living and touring Europe in with my young family. "You're trying to write that goat-boy novel without reading Campbell? No wonder the damn thing's stuck!" For so it was, or threatened to become, partly from the distraction of living and working for the first time in a foreign country (we had wintered in Andalusia) and partly from unresolved thematic problems.

---

nothing of his childhood, but 10) On reaching manhood he returns or goes to his future kingdom. 11) After a victory over the king and/or a giant, dragon, or wild beast, 12) He marries a princess, often the daughter of his predecessor, and 13) Becomes king. 14) For a time he reigns uneventfully, and 15) Prescribes laws, but 16) Later he loses favor with the gods and/or his subjects, and 17) Is driven from the throne and city, after which 18) He meets with a mysterious death, 19) Often at the top of a hill. 20) His children, if any, do not succeed him. 21) His body is not buried, but nevertheless 22) He has one or more holy sepulchres."

Among the heroes rated, Oedipus scores highest, with 21 points (he is not remembered as a lawgiver). Jesus, whom Raglan tactfully omits from his ratings (the argument of *The Hero* being that these chaps are mythical, not historical), would come in at 19 or 20, comparable to Theseus, Moses, and King Arthur. My sot-weed factor, Ebenezer Cooke, does less well as a solo act; taken in conjunction with his cosmophilist mentor, Henry Burlingame, however, he is in the league of Bellerophon and the Welsh hero Llew Llawgyffes.

I've read *around* him, I replied. I have some idea of Campbell's handle: an ex-Joycean hooked on Jung and the Ur-myth. . . .

"'Some idea' . . ." With the heel of his left hand, Jay batted his left temple. "Do both of us a favor, okay? Stop everything else you're doing. Let your bunkmate take the kids to the zoo for a day or two; there's a nice one in this town. I'll lead you by the hand to a first-rate English-language bookstore that carries the Bollingen series, and I'll buy you Campbell's *Faces* out of my Fulbright allowance, and you'll sit yourself down on the nearest Roman park bench and read it from cover to cover."

It's that good?

"Who said it was good? In my opinion, the whole business is a quaint late instance of the nineteenth-century rage for global synthesizing, like Freud's psychology and Einstein's Unified Field Theory. They're in the spirit of Darwin and Marx, fifty years too late for that sort of thing. When you guys finish inventing Postmodernism, people will appreciate what George Boas used to tell us: that those global generalizations are reached only by ignoring enough particularity. I myself happen to think that the *differences* between Oedipus and Jesus, or even between Perseus and Bellerophon, are at least as important as their similarities — but that's middling old me: Saint Hieronymus the Cross, patron of nitpickers. Campbell's handle on the myths might turn out to be exactly what you and your goat-boy need right now, the way you needed Machado ten years ago to get your *Opera* together; that's why I mentioned the Ur-myth up at Whipple Dam, when you were describing *Sot-Weed*. Who cares if the guy's a crank? Pliny's natural history is full of holes, but Shakespeare found it useful."

Et cetera: "Jay's" familiar, friendchippy mix of ego-deflation and heady praise (but in Rome that year, separated from Beth Duer, he had reverted to being Jerry Schreiber, the brawlbrat redux, and insisted I call him by his East Cambridge name). It was the second time — in ten years! — that I had heard from him the term "Postmodern," which Jay/Jerome claimed to have picked up from somewhere in Arnold Toynbee's multivolume *A Study of History* ("One more twentieth-century regression to nineteenth-century synthesizing") and put a different spin upon. I filed it away in my erratic memory and promptly forgot it for the next seven years.

Now, then (that colloquial contradiction suits the hybrid time of this aria, an effect of using my Pumblechook Parker simultaneously as *ree*mote and as pen): At the time I sing of — my Wanderjahr, not yet narrated, with its pause in "the -rome of St. Jerome" — Jay Scribner was still non grata in my house on account of his several criticisms of my marriage.* Now that his own was in an apparent crisis (from which, in the event, it would recover), whereas mine was in an apparent net good health that would prove, alas, more merely apparent than I knew, upon learning that my old counterself was doing a solo Fulbright lectureship in Rome, I set aside my grudge enough to propose and arrange a wary path-crossing when our family's Spanish winter residency was finished and our "VW" itinerary ("Volkswagenischer Wanderjahr") fetched us to the Eternal City. His terse letters from Italy to Spain had been addressed to me only, and signed *Schreib.* My "bunkmate," who had divined Jay Scribner's reservations about her, wanted no further commerce with the fellow and was understandably affronted that I did.

In the matter of the Roman reunion, however, I prevailed. After the Whipple Dam picnic in 1956, the break between Jay and me had left me without my most candid critic and general aid to navigation, and while I had indeed, as Jay prophesied, to some degree "internalized" him, I felt a need to check my internally guided course against an outside fix. My tentative "tragic view of consciousness," for example, and "tragicomic view of mysticism" wanted filtering through Jay's critical intelligence. And there were more personal and private concerns that I could use his advice on, at least his reaction to, if our discussion of those impersonal ones went satisfactorily.

---

*"So I insulted your first marriage," Jay will tell me, sometime into my second: "You all but *scuttled* mine, Oatmeal, unintentionally, with that Pygmalion/Galatea crack and what it led to. Want to swap culpabilities?"

Therefore the Rome meeting was arranged, by when we-all would have camped through Portugal and back across Spain, through the south of France, and down the Italian Riviera. Jay/ Jerry's would be the first familiar face — almost the first American face — we had seen since leaving home the previous autumn; that ought to ease the strain, I thought. All the same, in the interest of family peace I abbreviated the reunion and confined it to a virtual tête-à-tête: this long stroll together through the Villa Ada park after the briefest of hellos to my family. For the same reason, I now declined his bookstore-visit proposal, but promised to find and read Campbell on the Ur-myth first thing when I got back home.

"Too late," Jerry Schreiber said: "Your birthday's coming up next month, just at the end of your Grand Tour, and you're going back from Southampton to New York *by ship.* Are you with me?"

Nope.

"*Thirty-three,* man. *Westbound. Night-sea journey.*"

Come again?

"Don't say 'Come again'; I hate those fake-folksy expressions." He thumbed his eyeglasses up. "Give me the plot of *Giles Goat-Boy* in one sentence."

Um. The world is one big University, divided by cold war politics into rival campus blocs. The hero is sired somehow by the West Campus mainframe computer on a virginal librarian no longer in her first youth. To hide the scandal, the baby is put out with the prize goats on one of the University's remote experimental livestock farms, and through his kidship he's raised by the goats as one of themselves, watched over by a maverick old genius named Max Spielman.

"Spielman."

Right. Max is persuaded that this kid, George Giles the goat-boy, may be the mythical Grand Tutor destined to reform the Curriculum and redeem the University from error. So he coaches the kid in the CVs of all his predecessors, introduces him to the human side of his nature, provides him with a program for Grand-Tutor-hood, more or less, and sees him off with a set of riddling tasks that the lad has to perform on the Main Campus. The first time out, Giles takes the language of the tasks literally, and fails them all. On his second go-round he reconceives the tasks in metaphorical terms, and flunks them just as miserably in some opposite way. That's about where I am now in the plot outline. On the third try, with a little applied Zen, he'll *transcend* the tasks somehow — at least the terms of their setting — and "pass" in some paradoxical way that rises above the Pass/Fail categories. After that, your guess is as good as mine.

Schreib shook his head. "My guess is *better* than yours, Oatmeal. That's the plot in one sentence?"

In one syllable, I wish I had had the wit to say: the first — *Um*, close enough to *Om*. But Jer was already drawing me a picture, commencing with that mystic syllable's capital initial: a large O penned with my black-and-gold old Sheaffer (not yet cracked in Hamlet's castle) on the blank back of a campground map, both of which items he had peremptorily borrowed from my shirt pocket in mid-plot-summary.

"Campbell turns Raglan's linear catalogue into a counterclockwise circle, or cycle," he declared, "because the hero's mysterious termination echoes his mysterious origination, and there's the suggestion that he may return. It turns out too that various points in his trajectory have their reciprocals on the opposite side of the circle."

He drew a vertical axis through the diagram:

"The sacred grove, or World-Navel, for instance, here at the top, where he's conceived and finally apotheosized, is the counterpole of the *Axis Mundi* here at the bottom, where he consummates his sacred union, fathoms the great mysteries, transcends categories, steals the precious Elixir — all that crapola."

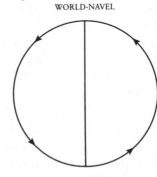

WORLD-NAVEL

AXIS MUNDI

He drew a second, horizontal axis, quadrating the circle:
"He crosses a capital-T
Threshold here to begin his
adventures in the twilight
zone — his westward Night-Sea
Journey and the rest — and then
he has to *re*cross it over here to
bring his illumination back to
the daylight world and do work
with it, William Jameswise. Up
here in the northwest quadrant,
he gets the summons to
adventure, and he may have to
be *re*summoned down here in
the southeast quadrant, the
heart of the mystery,

WORLD-NAVEL

SUMMONS

THRESHOLD
OF ADVENTURE

SUMMONS

AXIS MUNDI

where he's shacked up with the ogre's beautiful daughter or aton-
ing with God. Et cetera: All that's in Campbell. Now, then: Assuming that your cockamamie campus allegory is really just a manner
of speaking — programmatically *sophomoric*, as befits the University conceit — what you need to add to Campbell's schematic
is something like this. . . ."

Vertically down the left-hand hemicircle (the quadrants of
Departure and *Initiation*) my friend lettered in block capitals the
word *MYSTERY*, its central *T* neatly crossing the circle's east-west
"Threshold" axis. Vertically up the right-hand quadrants (*Return*
and *Reign & Death*) he lettered the word *TRAGEDY*, its *G* the
reciprocal of *MYSTERY*'s *T*, and then annotated the circle's whole
perimeter:

"The hero's apprenticeship," Schreib pointed out with the butt
of my pen, "is a penetration into capital-M Mystery. He has to
shed identity-tokens — articles of clothing, maybe even his name
and his physical body, the way Joyce's Stephen Dedalus sheds his
family, his girlfriend, his religion, his country, even his language.
You know all that, even though you yourself are trying to hang

on to as much as possible. The culmination is his unitive experience, literal or figurative, at the *Axis Mundi*: *Cal*houn's backseat gone to heaven, you might say. All that's in Campbell and your plot synopsis: very Zen Buddhist, with a dash of

Plato and the Christian mystics. Over *here*'s what interests me."

He poked the word *TRAGEDY*. "Here's where old Sophocles has his say, and West meets East, or parts company with it. Neither Campbell nor the other myth-meisters nor even William James pays enough attention to this side of the coin. They all acknowledge that the mystical experience is as ineffable as it's noumenal and enabling; they all remark that after the hero returns transfigured and routs the pretenders and founds his city and establishes laws, he unaccountably falls from favor and leaves his kingdom to close the circle, and that his children don't inherit the throne. But they don't confront the tragic aspect of that ineffability: that the message *inevitably* gets distorted in transmission, the spirit in the letter, the noumenal in the phenomenal — and that this discrepancy is both unavoidable and ultimately fatal to the message as well as to the messenger. Depending on how you look at it, this is either the tragic view of mysticism or the mystical view of tragedy, or both. In any case, it's the human heart of the matter, Oatmeal, and in J. W. Schreiber's Henry Street opinion, Sophocles has a better handle on it than the Buddhists do. *Colonus* is your goat-boy's final destination — but unlike Oedipus, he knows that fact from

Square One. If that's your particular spin on the Ur-myth, it sounds almost worth doing."

He returned my Sheaffer and the campground map. Twitched his freckled nose. Grinned, arms akimbo, thumbs hooked in jeans side pockets under the Villa Ada cypresses. "You're welcome."

Yeah, hey, thank you there, Jer, for sure and then some. Look: About some things that've happened between us . . . I'm sorry, needless to say.

"Maybe not so needless. On with your story, man — in which we come now to the Helper's Departure episode, right about here. . . ." He touched the nine o'clock end of the Threshold axis on his anticlockwise diagram. "But sometimes here. . . ." He touched three o'clock, the far side of the Threshold. "Typically an affecting scene. Let's cut it short, okay?"

You've helped me indeed, I told my counterself. More than I quite realize yet, probably.

"Probably. Noise in the signal, und so weiter."

For one thing, I believe I understand now what you meant by my upcoming Night-Sea Journey. There's more to that than *you* quite realize.

"Yeah?" He seemed as pleased as I was sobered. "Buon viaggio, then. Have a good Ordeal, man. Maybe I'll see you on the far side of it."

May that be.

He regarded me. "It's no picnic, Oatsarino, that second quadrant. But at least you'll have a handle on what's hitting you. You'll know the script."

Right.

"The *paradigm*."

Paradigm, right.

"Buon viaggio."

The same to you, Jay.

"Name's *Jerome*. Like the saint?"

Right.

Back to that picnic table: Wanderjahr

As you warned, I say to Jay Scribner now,* it was no picnic, that westbound night-sea journey and the rest. Hoo, boy.

"I sympathize, Oats. Ordealwise, I was already half a lap ahead of you back in the Rome of Saint Jerome. Bethless. And I'm still half a lap ahead."

The goat-boy book got written. When *don't* the books get written?

"When the night-sea journeyer is me."

But the *cost*, Jay . . .

"Yes, well. It was you who told *me* about the original of the Sanskrit *Ocean of Story*, written in the poet's own blood."

Give me Sheaffer's Skrip, any day.

"We bleed in any case, no? At least you got your pages written. *Pay the price, but don't count the cost.* Whose line is that?"

Mine, mit Blut geschrieben — mine too, but not only mine, alas. In your Henry Street opinion, old accomplice, when did the 1950s end?

"Whose Nineteen-Fifties? *Yours* ended in the spring of Sixty-Three, in my opinion, on the ramparts of Elsinore, not long after our little chat in the Villa Ada campground."

Right enough. What an obstacle course, one's twenties! What a proving ground, one's thirties! The heroic cycle really is our lowercase lives writ large.

"In blood — also sweat and tears, the proportions varying from case to case."

And/or in homely Skrip or Quink, with many a fine Ah between the Ouches. It just now occurs to me, by the way, that through the years of my black-and-gold Sheaffer, my ink was always Parker's Quink, as if foreshadowing the pen to come; and that through the years of this burgundy-and-brushed-aluminum Parker, my ink has always been Sheaffer's Skrip, as if reprising the pen that was.

---

*Whipple Dam PA, more or less, I guess, round about Independence Day '92, penman and partner having just returned to Langford Creek from their annual two-week spring/summer sailing cruise on Chesapeake Bay — our last of any length until the fateful fictive fall one aforeovertured. Time's funhouse, etc.

"Mirabile."

What's more, for readers and writers alike, I've always thought, the first and final narrative question is not "What happened?" but "Who am I?"

"You've always thought that, Oatmeal?"

Ever since it occurred to me, just now. Right enough, Jay Wordsworth Scribner: My personal 1950s began in 1949, at age nineteen, when the muses called and I married prematurely but by no means unhappily or unproductively. They ended in the late spring of 1963, at age thirty-three-and-a-little-bit, when I made a mismove in Hamlet's castle and cracked the predecessor of this present *ree*mote. A long decade.

"Soviet missiles removed from Cuba. Black civil-rights demonstrations in Cambridge, Maryland, among other American places. JFK assassinated . . ."

Background footage, Q.E.D. In the foreground, *MYSTERY* says Buongiorno to *TRAGEDY* in heroic majuscules, while in my lower-case wanderjahr, muddlement meets misery, of a sort. That pen . . .

"Aforesung."

And now reprised. Gift of my first-life partner, I've decided to believe though am not entirely certain. Used and used through college for every written thing, and likewise through my first ten teaching years —

"Aforesung."

I used and used and used and used that pen, and here and there abused it. In Maryland and Pennsylvania and Andalusia, that pen wrote everything up to and including the first half-draft of the goat-boy novel, and then the journal of my low-budget tour through Spain and Portugal, France and Italy, Austria and Germany, and Denmark as far as Helsingör. In the Rome of St. Jerome, you borrowed that pen to draw me a road map to the magical Elixir, or the Dragon's treasure trove. In a manner of speaking, however, that pen *was* the Elixir. As one might say —

"That the key to the treasure *is* the treasure?"

Words to that effect. In Hamlet's castle, that key cracked.

"Elixir all down your shirtfront! But hey, no omelets without breaking eggs. Cracked like a code, let's say, not like Jack's down-hill crown."

Who knew that then? Your "map" and my own researches had alerted me to such cues, of course, like the goat-boy with his Grand-Tutorial script: the Golden Bough here lost, which must be re-found for safe passage through the otherworld, et cet. I knew how old I was, if not quite who it was who was that age. But "Shit" was all I said when the Sheaffer cracked: "There goes my pen." We were at the northmost, farthest point of our Grand Tour. Just as, at Gibraltar, we had looked south at Africa across the Strait and sighed *Someday*, so now on that Danish battlement we looked east across to Sweden, imagining beyond it Finland, Russia, endless Asia, and thought *Someday*. Then we turned our Yankee faces westward, homeward — and a casual mismove cracked my pen. Bemused by the correspondences but unalarmed (for I'm no mythic hero, and *Giles* is meant to be a *comic* novel), I VW'd my family down through Holland and Belgium and over to England. Where I picked up, in Rochester, in "Mr. Pumblechook's premises" —

"A long way from Hamlet's castle. But Shakespeare and Dickens speak the same language."

— this pen, of which the other turns out to have been the mere anticipation, but who knew that then? This pen, of which I've been more careful and caring in the use, at least up to Columbus Day '92. This pen, Jeronissimo, *which must get me back to* US. Where am I, for pity's sake?

"The question, I believe you said, was *who*."

First and finally! But we're stuck in the middle somewhere, and I want out. Give me back my watch, Jay. Cut the crap.

"Ah ah . . ."

If you're drowned, I'm sorry. I'll miss you again, as I've missed you before when you and I've been on the outs. I hope Beth's okay. Enough of this *once upon a time*, now; get me out of here.

He winces. "If I'm drowned, you're sorry. You hope Beth's okay. Christamighty, Oatmeal!"

Overwhelmed, I fling this instrument at the face as ambivalently familiar to me as my own. Anyhow I *mean* to do so — Par-

ker shmarker, *ree*mote shmeemote, just now I don't care if it's
fucking Excalibur; I want *out*, and back to normal old *US*, and on
with sweet everyday Act Three (of three) before the curtain closes,
if that's where we were when that tropical depression hit the fan.
But the pen hasn't left my hand; that befreckled face doesn't even
blink; all I've done is write *Overwhelmed, I fling* etc.

"Now write this, old buddy," Jay instructs me calmly:

Sigh: I've written it.

"Read me the dialogue tag."

Jay instructs me calmly. Okay, I get it.

"Never a quick study, our Three Oh One Aurora, but a persistent one. Listen to what you're telling yourself now, man, whoever
that might be and whenever *now* is: that you and I are indeed
somewhere in the middle of something, astray in Time's you-
know-what, from which the only way out is what fetched you in,
scribble scribble scratch, one word after another. No shortcuts
through the labyrinth."

Suddenly sure of my ground, I tell him *There you're wrong.*

"So I'm wrong." Jay shrugs and smiles, but I know this aspect
of him well; he's interested, all right. "So show me."

With a few quick penstrokes — strokes both literal and figurative, of this both actual and virtual pen — I do.

Ur-myth wrap-up aria: "'Straight through the maze,'" almost

"Straight through the maze," this pen wrote in the hectic American high 1960s, in an essay called "The Literature of Exhaustion."
Having invoked the figure of Theseus threading through the Cre-
tan labyrinth, that essay concludes:

> The commonalty, alas, will *always* lose their way and their soul; it
> is the . . . virtuoso, the Thesean *hero* who, confronted with baroque
> reality, baroque history, the baroque state of his art, need *not*
> rehearse its possibilities to exhaustion. . . . He need only be aware
> of them, their existence or possibility, acknowledge them, and with
> the aid of very special gifts — as extraordinary as saint- or hero-
> hood . . . — go straight through the maze to the accomplishment of
> his work.

Rereading this brave conclusion a quarter-century later, I reflect to myself: Yes, well. *Almost* straight through the maze, let's say.

A difference between my old comrade Jay Wordsworth Scribner, for example, and for example the scribbler both of those labyrinth-lines and of these — a difference that, since our college days at least, my counterself has never been unmindful of, although I myself lose sight of it from time to time — is this: that like the aforesung hedgehog who knows his one big thing, I keep on making sentences. Life bangs and buffets, delights and disappoints (that's Life's job); the books get written regardless, or almost regardless. Neither better nor worse than they are, there anyhow they are. Praised here, damned there, here prized, there ignored or misapprehended, there nevertheless they are, following one another through my decades as coherently and inevitably (so it appears to me in retrospect) as those decades themselves: successive chapters of an ongoing story, yet each as unaware of the next to come as the successive arias and recitatives of this opera-in-progress. My spirit regards them and, in boastless affirmation, nods its head. Fortune's celebrated slings and arrows have neither passed their penner by nor on the other hand singled him out like St. Sebastian for riddling. Like most North American writers, I've been spared persecution, censorship, political exile. The physical infirmity, mental instability, and self-destructive compulsions that have plagued many a fine fellow fictioner have not plagued me. Such life-trials as I happen to have undergone have been real enough, but unremarkable: the aforenoted routine alarms and occasional heartbreaks of parenting; assorted family emergencies; a scarifying divorce after twenty years of first marriage; certain painful nose-rubs in my several human shortcomings — nothing so ordealish (thus far, thus far*) as, e.g., the visitation of dreadful affliction or devastating trauma upon child or spouse or self. Spared and more than spared: on balance, blessed.

In sum, for better or worse a pretty ordinary, in most respects most fortuned threescore years, lived pretty ordinarily by an

---

*Mid-July, 1992, Langford Creek writing room, grown-up children and growing grandchildren a-visit from here and there.

unheroic fellow with no extraordinary qualifications for tenoring this Ur-myth wrap-up aria, not to mention an entire floating once-upon-an-opera, except . . .

That *the sentences get written* — as Jay's do not, who knows so many things more; who penetrates, comprehends, connects, remembers, *does* (and has done) so many things more, through so considerably more various a history. These sentences get written (as Jay's do not), and like molecules into complex organic compounds, they aggregate into narrative passages, paragraphs, pages, chapters, books books books, which hang together like the acts and stages of a meaningful life and are in fact mine's meaning, anyhow its most tangible expression.

Jay Wordsworth Scribner, on the other hand, knows who he is, so it seems to me, as "I" do not; has always known, from East Cambridge Jerry Schreiber brawlbrat days through now, despite changes of name and address, condition and appearance, passions and priorities. Quite as his long-term goal has been the successful completion of his short-term goals, so Jay's Ur-identity has been the being of his successive selves — foulmouthed brawlbrat, gifted semi-pro jazz trumpeter, star late-starting student, meticulous but impatient scholar-critic-philosopher, adventurous voyager-in-reverse, relentless examiner of his own life and the lives of others, both of which generally come out wanting. That's my Hieronymus, plain as day to me despite whatever complexities and apparent contradictions. I know the chap as well as he knows himself, and rather better than I know me.

Notwithstanding which, he's *lost*, my steersman and trailblazer; has somehow always been. It is the sum of Jay's fate, almost, to be, though not a loser, lost. What's the sum of mine?

The sentences get written, the books, the books. Don't ask *me* who their author is; I just work here, pushing this Parker. That's who I am, you might say, almost; you might almost say that I know who I am after all: penner of this and that and this, although they may bear titles like *Lost in the Funhouse* and *The Last Voyage of Somebody the Sailor*, and their Ur-theme (equally their "subtext") might be said to be their penner's quest for just that item of knowledge: who in the fluxing world he is. "How can I tell what I think," asks E. M. Forster, "till I see what I say?" As for me, till I see what I say I can't tell *who I am*. Therefore (unlike my penless counterself here penned) I say and say, and see and see . . . and come to know, whether or not I tell.

From all which ariaizing it would seem to follow, almost, that the analogy holds after all between those uppercase derring-doers of the Ur-myth — Theseus, Perseus, Oedipus, Odysseus, Aeneas, Watu Gunung, Siegfried, Dante's Dante — and such lowercase preoccupants therewith as yours truly. What for so long possessed my imagination, my imagination reciprocally possessed, and was enabled by. Theseus enough in the workaday labyrinth of life, with the myth itself as my Ariadne-thread I threaded it, thread it still; not to the end of slaying some Minotaur (for the realest Minotaur is the labyrinth itself: labyrinthine life-in-the-world; our labyrinthine selves), but to the end of broidering forth that maze into scripted speech. No adversary, this labyrinth, but a resplendent arabesque, a chaos most artfully structured.* Not the intricated hazard-path to some treasure, but itself the treasure.

That being the at least imaginable case, and this *Once Upon a Time* a maze as strait as ever me amazed, why might I not — by the great myth enabled, with my trusty pen equipped — not only follow the thread straight through it to the accomplishment of my work (the regainment, love, of *US*), but straight-line that scripted thread myself, shortcut it through this ariabesque from where I am to where I was and would be? Uppercase or lower-, isn't that what herohood is *for*? What the myth's *about*? Let Jay stray, per his fate; by mere heroical Parkered fiat, love, here I come! Straight through the maze!

Almost.

Not, however, quite; not quite at all. If I'm odysseus minusculed, I've been fetched by this Ur-myth wrap-up aria not a-dream to the shores of home but to that offing wherefrom one sights on the flanks of Ithaca the very shepherd-fires — So near! So far! —

---

*In Friedrich von Schlegel's memorable phrase, the mode of the Arabesque is "ein gebildetes, künstliches Chaos."

just before the Aeolian winds are loosed and one is blown farther
off than ever. Where I've sung myself, I now see — so far from
"straight through the maze" to you, to *US*, to welcome denouement — is into sobering recognition that just as the key to the treasure may *be* the treasure, so the path through the labyrinth *is* the
labyrinth. What may seem a ramble may turn out to be efficiency
itself; the only shortcut is the rightly taken long way home.

In sum (almost), I learn by going where I have to go: on, on,
on with the ongoing story.

On with the Sixties: a self-guided solo tour

When singer and family moved norther yet in 1965 — from
State College, Pennsylvania, up to Buffalo, New York — they
bought a large, comfortable old house in the city's once rather
grand Central Park neighborhood, abounding just then in
downward-mobile American elms afflicted with the Dutch disease
and upward-mobile professorial families newly recruited by the
fast-expanding State University of New York. They made a down
payment and financed the balance with a twenty-five-year mortgage loan, shaking their heads in merry disbelief at its impossibly
distant pay-out date: *1990!* By when both mortgagors, then thirty-
five, would be sixty years old, and their youngest child thirty-six!

Now* this soloing tour guide is threescore-plus, that youngest
child thirty-eight. Still shaking my head (but no longer in disbelief), from the perspective of my sixties I regard my Sixties: America's, as I lived and worked through them on the Niagara Frontier,
at the edge of our troubled republic:

The calendar decade was half run before I encountered its coun-
tercultural aspect. My then marriage (our literal night-sea journey
behind us, from Southampton west to home at age thirty-three and

---

*6 August 1992, just returned to dear subtropical Langford Creek and this float-
ing opera from a splendid, strenuous week of hiking, mountain-biking, and
white-water rafting in the high, dry, beautiful Colorado Rockies, our aging bodies
(antecedent not to be confused with that of "they," above) gratifyingly trim and
fit, ready for the hurricane season — and perhaps a bit of sailboat cruising in
October.

a third, but the figurative one scarcely in mid-course) was in a crisis that this change of venue was hoped to ease: a full professorship, with a substantial salary increase and my initial semester free to complete *Giles Goat-Boy*; money for that larger house, a second car, and private-school tuitions for the children as they moved into adolescence, not untouched by parental Sturm und Drang — a fresh start. The nation, too, was turbling, though not yet critically: After our Tonkin Gulf Resolution of 1964, things were escalating in Vietnam; the black civil-rights movement was tending from nonviolence toward incendiarism; my Buffalo colleague-to-be Leslie Fiedler had already remarked America's change from a whiskey to a drug culture (just when I was beginning to learn *wine*); such Beat Generation gurus as Timothy Leary and Allen Ginsberg were showing the way; rock music was turning acidic; pop art was popping; men's hair-styles were lengthening, women's skirts shortening.

Penn State and environs, however, in academic 1964/65 remained bucolic, 1950ish (they would not for long). Pompommed and bobbysoxed cheerleaders cheered the Nittany Lions on football weekends as they had done for decades. Half a hundred social fraternities beer-bashed on Saturday nights and pawed "coeds" in "make-out rooms." The crewcut Reserve Officers Training Corps was a major campus operation. We professors lectured in tweed jackets and narrow neckties, shaved daily, and graded strictly. If in Happy Valley there were hippies, communes, druggies, anti-war demonstrations (as presently there would be), I don't recall them.

I myself, while politically passive by temperament, was altogether dovish on the matter of the war. For a congenital rational-skeptic, I was, as aforetestified, fairly deep into Zen Buddhism. And my protagonist-in-progress was shaggy Giles, a dropout from birth who attempts to drop back into the "University"; who fails, rejects, and finally transcends his "Assignment" and ultimately meets his tragimysticomical consummation in a novel that would be much read by High Sixties Americans: the only book of mine ever to achieve the *New York Times* best-seller list, although most of its readers then were college students (as they are today — in many instances the children of the first edition, so to speak). But I wore my collars buttoned down, my neckties thin, my hair (already tonsured by baldness) clipped close, my sideburns short. I took no drugs more exotic than my workadaily Dexamil and the evening home brew that I still brewed in the basement of our country-village, edge-of-the-forest home. I comported myself very like the tenured academic and petit bourgeois paterfamilias that I mainly was, earnestly striving — with my spouse and within my limitations, for the sake of our still-young children and the dozen-plus years of a connection we had once thought exemplary — to bridge the ever-widening gap between us. Through one post-Wanderjahr semester, I even sought "professional help": (solo) marriage counseling from a clinical psychologist at the university. I found him to be, alas, a benignantly passive, unhelpful chap, the best I can say for whom is that his fee for doing nothing was not exorbitant, and that I can't imagine quite how *anyone* might have been of genuine assistance.

Situation too banal to dwell upon. Yet it was the most pro-longedly distressful of my life to date: once-happily-wed partners grown out of love and out of synch, but not out of their Three Rs: responsibilities, resentments, and regrets. Inasmuch as a share of our soreness had inevitably come to be associated with aspects of our long Penn State residency, when out of the blue an offer came for a very considerable change of scene — urban, expansive, ram-bunctious, energetically self-inventing, and by our standards hand-somely remunerative — we accepted it straightway, sorry to have to leave the place where we had lost much innocence, but eager to believe (perhaps in what remained of that innocence) that the move might after all make the difference; that a shift to the city might lead us out of the woods. We shall learn, of course, that just as naive travelers bound (say) for Spain expect to find Spain but instead find themselves-in-Spain, so our strained connection will merely shift mise-en-scènes, our sore differences be the same, ever sorer.

Notwithstanding which, even in hindsight the move seems to

me to have been in all ways for the best. The novelty will distract, refresh, and for a time reinvigorate us: money to spend, new friends and colleagues with the camaraderie of the freshly recruited (80 percent of SUNY/Buffalo's large English department had been hired within the previous three years, all as additions to existing staff; we called ourselves the Ellis Island of Academia), a prevailing air of bustling avant-gardism in the museums, the concert halls, and the liberal-arts departments of the university — and conspicuous, even flamboyant, contingents of the counterculture, particularly on and around a campus called in some quarters "the Berkeley of the East." So much novelty, so much distraction, cultural/intellectual effervescence, political fervor (all, for me at least, stimulating input) will indeed extend the marriage another four years, by no means all domestically unhappy, though plenty troubled — at the end of which, our "middlescence" largely behind us, our children finishing high school and entering college, our financial situation importantly bettered by my Buffalo salary and a gratifying upturn in my lecture-and-royalty income, and our congenital unsophistication at least a little polished in such lively company, we shall be in altogether better position to effect what will nevertheless prove, alas, an acrimonious and scarifying split: "irreconcilable differences," by mutual agreement.

All that to come! Meanwhile, back in Hapless Valley, I wind up my twelfth and final year's classes.* We sell the hillside house — into which we have put so much work; under whose roof we have so loved and quarreled — take our children out of their country schools, faretheewell good friends of so long standing, and in the

---

*Among my undergraduate students wherein, mirabile dictu, is a lively and attractive "coed" who, by reason of her achieving the highest grade-point average in the university's 110-year history, will that spring be designated Penn State's official 100,000th graduate, and who five years later — How preposterously unimaginable we each would have found the idea at the time! — will become she to whom this floating opera is in every sense dedicated. As the 1950s — *my* 1950s — went from Wunderjahr to Wanderjahr, this self-guided Sixties tour solos from her to her. So must this opera, you to you. So near and yet so far, this footnote's glimpse of you — hand raised and answer ready as always in the classroom, as close as . . . Ithaca to Odysseus, before the fell *What if* winds blew.

summer drive lump-throated out of Allegheny country up into Great Lakes country, Niagara Frontier, edge-of-the-country country — where a modest private "streetcar college," the quiet old University of Buffalo, lately annexed by New York's ambitious state university system and given virtual carte blanche by Governor Nelson Rockefeller, aspires to become an academic leading edge: in the language of its mandate from Albany, "a great university center."

I had first visited the place only that spring, sidetripping across the Peace Bridge from a literary festival in Ontario (where I read from *Goat-Boy*-in-progress), and had been favorably enough impressed to revisit for interviewing later that season, sidetripping from another SUNY operation in the Finger Lakes region (where I lectured on Mystery and Tragedy: The Twin Motions of Ritual Heroism). Somewhere along the way, my first-life partner must have had a look at the place too, though I can't remember the occasion and believe her to have been prepared to make the move sight unseen. What I do remember, clearly, is camping with the children in a state park on the bluffs of Lake Erie a few miles below the city, driving in to meet a realtor with whom we had been put in touch — his specialty had become the sale of large, comfortable old Central Park houses to newly recruited senior faculty — and in just a couple of hours selecting and arranging to purchase the dwelling that I would live in for the next four years, my co-mortgagor for the next five, of my seven-year professorship at Buffalo: the house in whose dandy sunporch study, under Beard Avenue's dying elms, I would finish *Giles*, write the story-series *Lost in the Funhouse* and the essay "The Literature of Exhaustion," and begin the novella-triad *Chimera*.

We were immensely pleased: a fresh start, we truly hoped and more than half believed, whose freshness in prospect was beclouded only by the circumstance (learned, fortunately, too late for us to factor it into our decision) that among the several other new departmental appointees that academic year was Associate Professor of Comparative Literature Jerome Schreiber.

"Oh *shit*!" we exclaimed unanimously, upon my learning and

reporting this news and with some difficulty exonerating myself of
having known it earlier. It must have been clear, however, that I
was as sincerely consternated as was my mate by this unwelcome
souvenir of Birkwood Place front porch, of Whipple Dam picnic
table, and of —

"The Rome of Saint Jerome": expository catch-up aria
   "The Rome of Saint Jerome," Jerry Schreiber had quipped in
course of our Villa Ada campground stroll in the spring of '63, "is
arrived at by removing first the *saint* and then the *je*."
   The Rome of -rome? I waited for him to elucidate — we had
so little time to talk, after so prolonged a breach; there was so
much that I wanted his response to; neither as brawlbrat nor as
"Jay Wordsworth Scribner" had my counterself inclined to gnomic
utterance — but some other matter pressed, most likely from my
side of our peripatetic tête-à-tête. The subject changed, perhaps to
Ur-myth, night-sea journeying. . . .
   Now* he elucidated:
   "When Beth and I married, you may remember, we pledged
each other total honesty in our connection, and our unspoken
assumption was that total honesty implied total fidelity, physical
and emotional. *Programmatic* fidelity, I believe you once called it,
not altogether admiringly: the only program worth subscribing to,
in our then opinion. *Your* marriage, like most, was a heartfelt
emotional/intellectual muddle (I'm astonished that it still persists;
you guys must think with your limbic systems); ours was a pas-
sionately rational secular sacrament, intensely thought through

---

*A mid-October evening in 1966, in a modest Chinese-Canadian restaurant in
Fort Erie, Ontario, just across the Niagara River from Buffalo, whence both
"Jerome Schreiber" and the composer/conductor Lukas Foss elected to commute
over the Peace Bridge to their American employment — Jay, at least, for political
reasons. A nip of winter-to-come already in the early fall air whistling down from
Lake Superior and points north. But I foot this note on the ides of August '92,
sultriest dog-day time at Langford Creek, waiting like a tenpin at the far end of
Mother Nature's alley for the season's hurricanes to bowl over and up from
Africa. May she roll gutterballs — after which, we expect, there'll be good fall
cruising through Halloween: perhaps down to "the *-rome* of St. Jerome Creek,"
perhaps even beyond.

and clear-sightedly contracted after a sufficiency of prior experience and general maturation.

"So we believed, Oatmeal. That Pygmalion/Galatea rap you laid on us is a bummer, by the way: Beth Duer and I have always been a match. I know more stuff, and I reason more forcefully, but she's stronger and wiser in most ways, and spiritually quicker. I can't imaging loving anybody else; I can scarcely take an *interest* in anybody else, male or female. Sartre and de Beauvoir's example to the contrary notwithstanding,* it seemed clear to us that anything less than programmatic fidelity was mauvais foi, as we used to say."

He took a bite of Chinese-Canadian egg roll and shrugged his shoulders, down to which his hair now curled. And his sideburns were earlobe-long, his trousers bell-bottomed, his eyeglass lenses circular in steel-wire frames.

"So we believed, Oatmeal, until Life, let's say, showed us how much we were fooling ourselves. In my programmatic way, then, I flipsided the program. Not to feel morally one-up on Beth, I opened our marriage all the way. Spouse-swapping, group sex, AC/DC — we tried 'em all, at my insistence. When we had disgusted ourselves enough, which didn't take long, we binged on abstinence — I did, anyhow, to teach myself how much I could do without.

"That's more or less where I was when you saw me under the pines in Rome, or were they cypresses? I had gotten rid of the saint, and with a little help from your friend the Buddha, I was working on the *je*. Since all roads lead to Rome, I went to the end of the road imagining I'd find Rome, and found myself-in-Rome instead. Has that been said already? So then I *lost* myself-in-Rome by losing myself in Rome, so to speak — all to the end of finding my way back to Beth and the boys.

"She, meanwhile, was not sitting on her hands. She'd given up professional nursing to nurse our sons; by the time they were

---

*The "open" relationship of Jean-Paul Sartre and Simone de Beauvoir was as admired by many wannabe-existentialists in the 1960s as it is retrospectively contemned e.g. by present-day feminists.

weaned, she found that *she* was, too, from full-time physical caregiving and from me. When Saint Jerome went off to find himself in Rome, Beth Duer took up with a black civil-rights activist in Baltimore who inspired her to do a law degree — all the rage in those days of rage. The antiwar movement brought us back together and up to Peace Bridge country. Beth, as you may have heard, is counseling draft resisters and flag burners. I'm here because she's here and because this new university of ours seems hospitable to Post-Neoterics like you and me and Jorge Luis Borges."

He upped his eyeglasses.

"This hot-and-sour soup is neither nor."

Post-Neoterics?

After the unsettling news reached Beard Avenue that my old comrade was among my new colleagues, I made no move to look him up. On the contrary. I was on academic leave, remember, busily setting up housekeeping, exploring our new environs, final-editing *Giles* for its publisher, and assimilating as best I could my discovery of the extraordinary *ficciones* of the Argentine writer Jorge Luis Borges, to whose art I had been led by a cryptic picture postcard from Jerome Schreiber the year before, mailed from Baltimore to my Penn State office — my only communication from him since Rome. On the verso of a view of Johns Hopkins's Gilman Hall, its message consisted of a large block-capital *B* initialing a column of proper names, thus:

B : uffalo
orges
altimore
(rawlbrat)

Two provincial U.S. cities bracketing a little-known Latino writer and bracketed in turn by my surnominal initial and Schreib's sobriquet: I puzzled over it for a time, shrugged, and presently mislaid but did not forget it. Of Buffalo I had heard

ACT 2 333

interesting reports: The maverick critic and culture-watcher Leslie
Fiedler, who had written favorably of *The Floating Opera* and *The
Sot-Weed Factor*, had joined the booming new SUNY operation
up there and spoken of it warmly to me on a recent lecture-junket
of his to Penn State. I had never visited the place, but in the coming
lecture-season I was scheduled to recross paths with Fiedler at a
Canadian university nearby, and at his suggestion was considering
a side-trip to inspect his new home base. Of Borges I had read the
sort of literary mention that leads one's muse to murmur "Better
check this hombre out," but I had not yet gotten around to doing
so. Baltimore is where the card came from, in both senses: Jay/
Jerry might have moved back there after Rome (I had heard uncertainly from mutual friends that he had "gone hippie" since his
marital separation and had more or less dropped out of academic
life), or he might simply have been visiting family and alma mater.
But I could not imagine what the sense of the message was: what
connection old Scrib, a chap not given historically to gnomic utterance, perceived among all those *B*s. Had brooding over his break
with Beth, I wondered, blown the poor bugger bonkers?

Now here I was in -uffalo, reading -orges in my bright Beard
Avenue study with such entire absorption that my all-but-finished
huge new manuscript (a stack of typed pages more than a foot
high), its author, his marriage, new domicile, city, and professional
situation all lost themselves in the miniature labyrinths of the
Argentine's vast, meticulous imagination — or would have done,
but that I kept remembering Jay's cryptic card. *Buffalo*, I now
understood, he had himself applied to, or at least set his sights
upon, back when he posted it, and was perhaps recommending
that I do likewise. *Borges* he was no doubt urging upon me as he
had erst so consequentially urged Joaquim Machado de Assis,
Ebenezer Cooke, and Joseph Campbell. Wherefore *Baltimore*?
Had he not gotten the historical sequence arsy-turvy (and unaccountably left Happy Valley out of it), if such a sequence was what
he had in mind?

I was mildly curious, but much more concerned with assimilating this newfound, extraordinary writer, whose work so forcefully
spoke to me that I felt my own could scarcely proceed until I had

come to terms with his — not an unusual state of affairs for a fledgling in any art, but disconcerting to a full-feathered mid-careerist. And I was in no hurry to risk disturbing the tentative new détente at home, on which I was betting my marriage, by resuming a connection almost certain to open old wounds. On the other hand, my counterself was now my colleague; although our department (which more or less comprised Comparative Literature as well as "English") was almost as large and at least as various as Penn State's, and our residential/social scene much larger, he and I — they and we — could not avoid each other forever. The Empire State's Queen City had its attractions — the Albright-Knox Museum in handsome Delaware Park, a fine symphony orchestra under Lukas Foss's direction, gracious residential neighborhoods, a number of good restaurants — but it was not Rome or Paris or Manhattan or San Francisco; most of us new recruits had been recruited by the appeal of our job description and our academic department, not because we had spun the globe and chosen the city of Buffalo as our favorite spot thereupon. In consequence — and also because so many of us *were* newly arrived — there was among us a high degree of collegiality, much socializing at one another's large, comfortable old Central Park houses. At these cocktail or dinner or after-dinner gatherings, "Jerry Schreiber's" name came not infrequently into the conversation. He and I were generally known to have the same alma mater and to be old acquaintances, less generally to have once been intensest friends. As Jay/Jerome was regarded (and benignly accepted by our unbuckled department) as a bit eccentric — his alternative names, his middlescent conversion to hippiehood, his kicking over the academic traces to become a left-handed perpetrator of "concrete verse," a devotee of William Blake, Charles Olson, and Allen Ginsberg, and a no-longer-much-publishing professor of such esoterica as angelology and comparative shamanism — while I was regarded (correctly, and with equal benignity accepted) as a straight and predominantly conservative fellow except at the writing table, our apparent coolness to each other raised no eyebrows.

"We have all sorts of constituencies," a departmental vice-chairman remarked to me. "Schreiber represents the hippie-druggie-anarchist precincts for us."

My friend the hyper-rationalist! At departmental meetings and official university receptions (which I attended, to get the lay of the land, despite my being officially on leave), I would catch sight of him across a room — tieless and jacketless these days, perhaps wearing a Mexican coarse-woven shirt with his bell-bottomed jeans, no longer smoking cigarettes as all the rest of us still did in '65, nor, at parties, drinking alcohol. Gin and tonic in one hand, Parliament filter tip in the other, I would nod shortly; knowingly, Jay would smile, hands in pockets.

What finally bridged that chiasmus, as it has done several times already in this opera, was music. Schreib I understood to have gone back seriously to playing jazz ("Gone *forward*," he'll correct me when I first respeak him). Our Provost of Social Sciences — a silver-haired psychologist who had once played tenor sax in Tex Beneke's postwar "Glenn Miller Orchestra" — reported that Jerry Schreiber had become a sort of white Miles Davis, blowing a truculent, "far out" jazz mostly with black musicians in a downtown club; that, together with a piano-man from my department, he had persuaded the ex-saxophonist to unpack his horn, which hadn't been out of its case in years, for an evening of jazz at the provost's large, comfortable old Central Park house, just around the block from ours; that the experiment had gone well but for the catching up that my neighbor felt he had to do to get from Tex Beneke through Coleman Hawkins and Charlie Parker to Stan Getz and the present — and but for the want of bass and drums to drive things along. As a member ex officio of the Appointments and Tenure Committee, the provost happened to know that an incoming associate professor of American Studies was an able jazz bassist and author of a study of "urban blues"; and he understood that I not only played drums but had brought my gear with me to Buffalo. Perhaps the four or five of us could find common musical ground and from time to time entertain ourselves in one another's large and comfortable old et ceteras?

With some misgivings, I agreed. Jay I knew to be, the saxophonist and pianist I correctly surmised to be, more accomplished and sophisticated musicians than was I, who for years had played only down-home Dixieland and "old standards" with my Penn State comrades — ever less frequently since my Wanderjahr and subsequent marital "night-sea journey," which I hopefully imagined might be about done with. Precisely in light of that hope, my larger apprehension was reconnection with my counterself.

In the event, things went quite easily. Schreib was late arriving at the appointed get-together; I set up my Slingerlands beside the provost's piano while he tuned and warmed up his horn and bantered with the pianist — another devotee, indeed a protégé, of the "projective verse," "deep image" poet Charles Olson, late of our department, whose large and charismatic presence had evidently left as large an absence at SUNY/Buffalo as had Theodore Roethke's* at Penn State. The pianist took the measure of his instrument in a style compounded nicely of Bill Evans and Thelonious Monk, a pleasure to accompany. The psychologist/provost had already begun his "catching up" homework; his technique was clearly of professional caliber, but he laughed at his impressive imitations of John Coltrane's "sheets of sound." I made no bones about my musical limitations; they pooh-poohed them, and in fact were such agreeable musical company, after my considerable absence from playing, that I was not unhappy with my brush- and stick-work.

By the time our trumpeter appeared, we were in mid-"Green Dolphin Street" and gravitating toward the "cool jazz" idiom of Evans, Getz, and Gerry Mulligan as our common ground, from which in the months and years to come we would make excursions backward, forward, and sideways: the last jazz group I was ever to play in, and the best. Although I was its weakest regular member, from the fall of 1965 until the summer of 1973 — when I packed up my gear for the move back to Baltimore — I never played better.

In the manner of musicians at work, we acknowledged the late arrival with nods and carried on. My counterself unpacked and

* Aforefootnoted.

muted his horn, quietly warmed up in an adjoining room, and then moved into the margins of Dolphin Street with discreet fills and obbligati to the saxophone lead. While Piano took the next chorus, host greeted new guest, new guest final-tuned his horn against host's, and the two then so wittily traded off lead and harmony on the eight-bar bridge that we all hey-heyed their smooth improvisation.

Next chorus was Jay's. While he stood before me (turning his back to the "audience," as in those days Miles sometimes did) and played as if *at* me a muted but spiky solo — at once restrained and aggressive, chafing at the limits of the tune's rhythm and harmony — I was able amid smiles and nods of approval to look my changed friend over for the first time since Rome. Changed he was, not only in dress, hairstyle, and eyeglasses. That solo summed him up: muted but spiky. Piano groaned *Ni-i-ce!* Sax and Drums agreed. Not quite through the final four bars, Schreib simply stopped (Miles did that, too, on occasion) and let the accompanied silence resolve his truncated improvisation, if only by underscoring its truncation: the palpable presence of absence. Sax and Piano knew better than to "fill in"; we chuckled together at the rude effect while Schreib smiled Buddhalike at me, nodding his head slightly on the afterbeat, his trumpet mouthpiece poised two inches from his scarred embouchure, his eyes a-twinkle behind their round lenses.

Okay!

Sax took the next chorus. Through its first eight, my counterself smiled and nodded on, while with raised eyebrows and tight lips I returned his unsettling contemplation. On the second eight, to my relief, he turned to the others and did sultry fills between Sax's phrases, then played the bridge absolutely straight (an amusing, even inspired nonimprovisation) before handing the lead back for Sax to close out, with Trumpet in tight harmony on the final four.

Yeah.

We broke then for drinks and smokes and mutual encouragements — all of us except Jay/Jerry, who intermittently noodled on beside the piano, as if to himself. We would definitely get together again soon, we all agreed, maybe weekly or biweekly, maybe alternating between Sax's large, comfortable old Central Park house and mine (Piano lived in a smallish apartment; Trumpet had no piano in his Fort Erie digs; Mr. and Mrs. Drums, however, had moved their modest upright from Pennsylvania to New York for the sake of our daughter's continuing lessons and my ever less frequent occasional use, and our "club basement" was comfortably sound-insulated from our Beard Avenue neighbors). The chat was of these matters and of music: our separate professional or semi-pro backgrounds (it was acknowledged that "Jay Scribner" and I had shared bandstands in Baltimore and Betterton Beach), our current tastes in jazz. Schreib said nearly nothing, but was entirely amiable; it was accepted that such was his style. Mostly we made music, and on the horn my counterself was eloquent indeed in his muted, spiky new way — a far cry from the open-belled, gold-throated warmth of Prom Night 1947.

Next Sunday evening, then. Chez moi. Does anybody know a bassist? Done and done and (Jay cocked me one quizzical smile before nodding) done, and Piano knew a fellow not great not bad who he believed could blow bass with us till our urban blueser came on line. "Hey, I got your card," I remarked aside to Jay as I packed my gear for the many-thousandth time. He nodded, regarding me amiably, and nodded on, as if still strolling Green Dolphin Street. "I'm into Borges," I said. "But I don't think I understand *Baltimore*."

He beamed. "I'm not sure you ever did, man."

Our nearest approach that night to conversation.

The provost's wife, I reported to mine, had appeared twice or thrice through the evening to listen for a while or join our intermission chat, but had mainly gone about her own business, as had the couple's children. The other players' mates, as I had rather expected, had not come along; it was a jazz session, not a party. Especially inasmuch as next Sunday's reprise of it would be in our basement rather than a living room, there would be nothing socially amiss in Mrs. Drums's not appearing at all, if she wanted to avoid Associate Professor Schreiber. Alternatively, she could pop in on us once or twice to bring down the hors d'oeuvres and meet my new musician-friends; or she was welcome to hostess the evening, if she chose. Scrib looked to be no problem: cordial enough, but aloof and taciturn these days, with everybody. A touch spiky, perhaps, but muted. Had not even mentioned Beth Duer; had mentioned nothing, really; I wondered whether dope had rewired his circuits. It appeared to me that his marginal presence, in so ample and various a scene as our department and the Greater Buffalo Metropolitan Area, was going to pose no difficulties after all, and that our new musical connection, so far from encouraging further relations between the two couples, would effectively take the place of such relations — to which Scrib had seemed, gratifyingly, no more inclined than I.

"Mm."

Perhaps I ought to have left well enough alone, particularly as the group's first session in our house — and Jay's first visit under a roof of ours in nearly a decade — went smoothly and agreeably: bare-minimal social exchange between hostess and Trumpet (and, for that matter, between host and Trumpet, except musically); a clearly reciprocal stance of benign incuriosity, facilitated by Jay's quasi-stoned, smiling taciturnity. And I did, in fact, through that first Buffalo academic year and the summer following, pretty much leave things be, counterselfwise. The household weathered our first Buffalo winter, shoveling the countless lake-effect snowfalls off driveway and sidewalks and admiring how city and citizens coped efficiently with anything short of double-barreled blizzards. Penn State friends came up to visit, found us evidently pleased with our move, and reported that the counterculture was turning Happy into Hippie Valley. No new close friendships, but we enjoyed an active social life and the collegiality of our neighborhood. Our now fourteen-year-old daughter, for example, met the high-schoolmate — a neighbor-colleague's son — whom years later she would reconnect with and marry; our sons, thirteen and eleven, seemed satisfied, on the whole, to have exchanged rural for urban life. My travels facilitated by a full-fledged airport, I gave readings that year round about the country. In January I took up my teaching duties at SUNY/Buffalo, including the direction of my (and the university's) maiden graduate seminar in fiction-writing. My royalty income was still meager, but all three of the novels were back in reprint editions and picking up foreign contracts; there was a serious film option on *The End of the Road*; and while my publisher's advance on *Giles Goat-Boy* had been modest indeed, all indications were that they meant to publish it more vigorously in the season to come than they had published *The Sot-Weed Factor*. Perhaps we would take up skiing, for outdoor exercise through the next long winter. If *Giles* did well, perhaps we could afford to think about a modest weekend-and-summer retreat in the nearby hills, such as several of our new acquaintances enjoyed.

Meanwhile, I was hard at assimilating Borges in my sunporch workroom under the failing elms on the avenue that was a variant of my name, and beginning to envision an unorthodox volume of short fiction: not a conventional collection of discrete stories, but some sort of . . . nonlinear series, maybe, certain items of which might be designed not expressly for print but for live authorial voice (a medium that my public readings had interested me in), or specifically for monophonic or stereophonic tape, or some combination of those media — a more or less high-tech reorchestration of the oral storytelling tradition. I had published only a handful of short stories over the years, in *Esquire* and a few literary quarterlies; now I began to fancy linkages among them, and resonations between their mainly realistic material and the realms of myth and fantasy in which my imagination had dwelt since 1960.

Indeed, I had come to feel that "that Ur-myth business," to which Jay Scribner had first directed my attention, was no longer so much under my belt as on my back, like Sindbad's Old Man of the Sea. Partly to unseat or exorcise it, partly to discharge or exorcise some more personal preoccupations, partly to come to terms with Sr. Borges, partly to try a voice and explore one theme of the project I was beginning to have glimpses of, sometime that winter I wrote the first story expressly meant for the new book: The monologue of an exhausted and disillusioned spermatozoon in unwitting mid-reenactment of the cycle of ritual mythic heroism, it was called "Night-Sea Journey." *Esquire* ran it in their June '66 number, on the newsstands just in time for my thirty-sixth birthday. My classes were finished, but the children's weren't, and I luxuriated in our first upstate springtime in our large, comfortable old Central Park house: rehabilitating a screened patio off the garage and planting wine-grapes on its associated trellises, exploring the Erie lakeshore and province of Ontario across the way, revising those earlier stories with an eye to their place in the new project, making notes toward new ones, and (for reasons I could scarcely have articulated, but I trusted my hunches) casually researching the entire corpus of frametale literature: stories-within-stories from every culture and century that I could find them in.

Once upon a time, I told the children at dinner sometime that spring, your father got lost in a funhouse.

"Was it the one in Ocean City?" they wanted to know: the only one they'd seen. "How old were you? Were you scared?"

I had been twelve or thirteen, about the same age as my elder son just then. The place ought to have been Ocean City, Maryland, in World-War-Twotime, when German U-boats prowled the coast, and shore-resort streetlights were "browned out," and the beach was sometimes fouled with tarry oil from torpedoed ships (so we were told, though it may have been the discharge of passing tankers flushing their bilges en route from Delaware River refineries), and boys my then age were expert airplane-spotters half hoping for an enemy attack. In fact, however, it was some New Jersey shore resort that Aunt Roon and Uncle Doc had driven us visiting twins to for the day: Asbury Park, maybe, or Ocean Grove. It was dark in there; I managed somehow to take a wrong turn, got separated from Jill, made voice-contact with another stray, and soon enough found with him the proper path. We weren't "lost" for more than a few minutes, and hadn't been truly frightened, just a bit tense. Upon our exiting, it was revealed that my amiable companion-in-the-labyrinth was a young Negro, as we called them back then, and this circumstance occasioned some good-natured teasing from all hands en route back to Springfield, New Jersey, in my aunt and uncle's big Nash or Packard, for such were the times.

I had been impressed that the boy hadn't *talked* like a Negro, just a regular person; and that in the pitch-darkness together it had been as if . . .

In Maryland in those days, I reminded the children, no blacks would have been *admitted* into the funhouse, or into any other establishment in the Free State where they could not be segregated.

Boyoboy, they agreed, stout liberals like their parents. But in fact we were unhappy about reports of ghetto-black "rough stuff" at our daughter's urban public high school (I remembered the white delinquents, bullies, and brawlbrats of East Cambridge). With less than easy social consciences, but the consent of all concerned, we were transferring her to a highly regarded suburban private day school for the coming year, our older son to a fast-track semi-boarding school in the city, from which he would come home on weekends, and our younger to a nearby suburban public school, 90 percent white and middle-class, which charged such urban "white-flighters" a modest tuition. Most of our neighbors had similar arrangements with good private and parochial schools; a minority felt it important that their children be "exposed" to "urban reality." Life, I reckoned, would soon enough take care of that; small loss if it happened not to; meanwhile, let's get our kids well and safely educated. Appropriately, perhaps, for one turning thirty-six, I discovered myself to be more "conservative" on this and other matters (e.g., the tempestuous campus sit-ins, strikes, and trashings associated with the growing antiwar movement) than I was used to thinking of myself as being. I was an off-the-shelf stock liberal, not a radical, and by temperament an observer, not an activist. As my fiction tended ever more toward the "experimental," its author came more and more to respect the conventional, the "centric," without which the unconventional and eccentric lose effect, even intelligibility. Anyhow, from the perspective of Buffalo I was an ex-Southerner, no doubt less purged of racism than I thought myself to be.

When I stopped by my university office sometime in that birthday week to pick up my mail, I found Jerry Schreiber standing in the mail room, reading the current *Esquire*. At sight of me he

beamed, nodded, knuckled up his specs, and displayed the Night-
Sea Journey story.

"Good show, Oatmeal. Let's talk sometime."

Post-Neoteric?

"Right brain left brain, man," he said now — mid-following-
October, in that undistinguished Chinese-Canadian eatery aforefootnoted,* not far from his and Beth's "pad" in Fort Erie,
Ontario. He sipped from a clear plastic tumbler of iceless tapwater. In the decades whereof I sing, the North American fondness
for peppery Szechuan and Hunan dishes had not yet established
itself; the prevailing cuisine in our Chinese restaurants was still
bland Cantonese: lo mein, chow mein, moo goo gai pan, sweet-
and-sour everything, heavy on the cornstarch. We were sharing
two such items, I mainly enjoying Molson's Stock Ale (no Tsing
Tao yet in such places) while Associate Professor Schreiber sipped
his water. I was there for at least three proximate reasons:

— Jay had amiably repeated, at our first fall jazz get-together,
his springtime mail-room proposal, that he and I have a talk sometime: a proposal that I had uneasily set aside for the summer.

— Beth Duer had even telephoned, in July or August, crisply
but cordially to expand that invitation to dinner for the four of us
at their place. We had made lame excuses, which she readily
accepted without pressing for further catch-up conversation. The
woman had seemed an altogether different Beth: self-possessed,
articulate, "in charge" — Galatea ascendant. Her legal defense of

---

*But I foot *this* note shortly after Labor Day '92, the season's maiden Atlantic
hurricane having lately devastated first Bahamian Eleuthera, where singer and
spouse had made December vacation reservations; then south Florida, where we
had thought to spend part of the coming winter; and finally part of Louisiana's
Gulf Coast, which we happened to be going to lecture-visit next month, not long
after the Columbus Day frame-action of this floating opera. For us, the disappointing inconvenience of a one-two-three punch to our travel plans; for a
quarter-million Bahamians, Floridians, and Louisianians, a flat-out catastrophe;
for the United States, the most expensive natural disaster in its history, compounded just a few days later by Typhoon Omar in Guam and Hurricane Iniki
in Hawaii. Here on the Langford Creek floodplain, we foot these notes and monitor the weather reports for Hurricane Andrew's alphabetical successors.

the draft evaders and resisters — and, more recently, of certain of my friends and colleagues arrested for joining in the campus strikes and sit-ins broken up by the National Guard — had made her a hero of the local antiwar movement, a combination Florence Nightingale and Clarence Darrow. A prominent liberal Buffalo law firm had taken her on as an associate, specializing in such cases.

— *Giles Goat-Boy* was doing gratifyingly well. Although Jay Scribner allowed to having large reservations about that novel, and I myself would eventually come to take less pleasure in it than in any other of my books, it was enjoying both critical and commercial success on a scale new to my experience. For some weeks it floated on the *Times* best-seller list, rising to #5 before its hardcover sales tapered off. For the first time, my royalty income for the year bade to exceed my university salary, and inasmuch as my tax lawyer* had written a limitation-of-earnings clause into my publisher's contract for the purpose of keeping me in a moderate income-tax bracket, I was assured of that approximate parity for some half-dozen years to come. In the event, that circumstance would make divorce economically manageable, even with three children entering private colleges in quick succession — the most expensive years in the life of middle-class American parents. Just now, the unaccustomed affluence (film options on both *The Floating Opera* and *The End of the Road* were being periodically renewed, too, and foreign royalties were trickling in, and my lecture-junket schedule had begun to exceed my nominal limit of one overnight per month) allowed us to begin saving for the children's college tuitions and to scout in earnest for a country retreat somewhere south of the city. But what my colleague proposed was a quiet Chinese-Canadian dinner, just the two of us, to celebrate Giles's dropping *off* the best-seller list and to discuss what seemed to him the altogether more promising project of which I had

---

*I had a tax lawyer! A partner in Beth Duer's firm, which three years later would supply my divorce lawyer as well.

remarked that my spermatozoic "Night-Sea Journey" was to be a part: fiction for print, tape, and live voice.*

And so over the Peace Bridge to Ontario I went, not without misgivings and despite apprehensive grumblings at home. For from whom if not my counterself, howevermuch altered, was I to hear the term *Post-Neoteric* and learn its meaning, wherewith to solo myself through the Sixties into the third act of this opera and thence, no longer solo, even unto *my* sixties? We met at the appointed place and hour. Jay was waiting for me in the restaurant parking lot, leaning against his car and smoking a marijuana cigarette butt, held in a "roach clip," which he offered to share, when I drove up in one or the other of ours.†

No thanks, Scrib. I'm into Canadian ales these days.

Despite or because of the crisp fall air, my colleague was in no hurry to go inside. The MSG used in Chinese cooking, he declared (I couldn't judge how seriously), "regressed" him to the fellow he had been before "the Rome of Saint Jerome": the fellow I had known in Baltimore and — What was that little park called, near Penn State? Whipple Dam, right, where he believed he had first mentioned the Ur-myth. That's why he had chosen this restaurant: mediocre Cantonese, but heavy on monosodium glutamate for retrospective exposition. Meanwhile, we really ought to groove on this foretaste of winter in the air, which he had learned was called

---

*Not transcribed into this recitative, but made clear in course of the Chinese-Canadian meal to follow, is Jay Scribner's presumption that that spermatozoon narrator's rational-skeptic companion ("among the first to drown") had been modeled upon himself. "Sometimes," remarks the disillusioned narrator toward the story's end, "I think I am my drownéd friend."

†Owing to the demands of American adolescent-parenting, and thanks to the goat-boy's prospering, we had lately become a two-car family. The vehicle here will have been either the tailfinned white Buick station wagon (the only car I've ever owned that I disliked from day of purchase to day of sale) for which we had traded in our red-and-beige Microbus in Pennsylvania after our fateful Wanderjahr, or else the secondhand black VW that we had recently picked up in Buffalo — the classic old Beetle with a kick-in fuel reserve in lieu of visual gauge. As aforeobserved by J. W. Scribner, we Americans measure our progress — anyhow our life-transit — by such indices.

by Canadian meteorologists *sec Supérieure*, as if it were a fine dry table wine. So I wasn't yet doing dope?

Nope. I'll just have a pre-parley Parliament with you, to be sociable.

"*The independent life of objects*, Oats O'Rino. That's what pot and hash teach us to appreciate. You've no idea."

Maybe I do.

Jay inhaled, shook his head, exhaled. "I really doubt it, man, till you've been there. It's why a head can stare for half an hour at his own left hand, or at a lemon on a plate. The freaks think they see the secret of the universe there — and I suppose they're right, in the Tennyson way: *Flower in the crannied wall* and like that.* But what they're no-shit seeing is the truth of left hands, you dig? The independent life of lemons. It's worth seeing."

Another time, maybe, Jeronimo. I've got U.S. Customs to pass through.

"Quaint old U.S. customs. We get a fresh perspective on 'em from over here. Vietnam ain't the same on CBC."

Shall we try the local MSG?

He twitched his nose. "Wham bam thank-you-ma'am, is it? Let me kill this roach, then, and you're on." He did so, and upped his wire-rims. "Bear in mind, though, Oat-boy, when the time comes, that whereas with alcohol you think you can drive safely when you can't, with grass and hash you can feel too stoned to get through a fucking *doorway* and actually be quite capable of nego-tiating a toll booth and driving down the Thomas E. Dewey Thru-way. Not that I recommend it."

I promised to bear in mind both the proposition and the non-recommendation — and before decade's end would find the for-

---

*Jay's reference is to the lyric often cited by his mentor, George Boas, to exemplify the "Seamless Web Weltanschauung":

> *Flower in the crannied wall,*
> *I pluck you out of the crannies,*
> *I hold you here, root and all, in my hand,*
> *Little flower — but if I could understand*
> *What you are, root and all, and all in all,*
> *I should know what God and man is.*

mer in fact true, the latter nonetheless sound. We went inside, started off with egg rolls, hot-nor-sour soup, iceless tapwater, Molson's Stock Ale, and (my suggestion, once Jay had had his hit of Chinese-Canadian MSG) what I believed he had called "the Rome of Saint Jerome"? There followed his Wordy aria on same, a reversion indeed — I wouldn't call it a regression — from muted, spiky Miles D. Schreiber to the Jay Scribner of Whipple Dam picnic table, Birkwood Place front porch, and suchlike disquisitory mise-en-scènes. Did this suddenly sustained articulateness imply that his prevailing current "head" mode was (to use an old-Jay term) inauthentic? Mauvaise foi?

"Right brain left brain, man," he said now,* and not only introduced me to the bicameral theory of human brain functioning (the analytical, cogitative, linearly inclined left brain and the intuitive, contemplative, gestaltic right, each controlling the opposite "hand"; he invoked rigorously the memorable title of a forgettable 1947 novel by one Nancy Wilson Ross: *The Left Hand Is the Dreamer*), but applied it metaphorically to what might else be mistaken for a schizoid splitting of himself into Jay Wordsworth Scribner the left-brained hyper-rationalist and Jerome Schreiber the Zen-Buddhist former brawlbrat.

"They're both there, man; always were. Takes two wings to fly, and like that? Only the emphasis changes, and sometimes we fly in circles. Anyhow, I'm left-handed, as you may have noticed: That jiggles the old yarrow sticks. Are you into McLuhan?"

I confessed that I had yet to get around to reading the guru of nearby Toronto, whose *Gutenberg Galaxy* was scripture among certain of our graduate students and colleagues.

---

*I.e., then. Here at page-foot it's the ides of September '92; I'm back in Baltimore, back at Johns Hopkins, back in my Gilman Hall weekly seminar room with our current crop of graduate-student apprentices, and writing these sentences in the mornings before reading theirs in the evenings, but — that seminar being my sole academic responsibility these emeritus days, and my ship-and-spiritmate being on academic leave this year — spending more of each week at Langford Creek than is our autumn custom. Hurricanes permitting, perhaps we'll take the opportunity, sometime between now and haul-out, to do some longer-than-overnight fall cruising, perhaps even down into the "Chesapeake Triangle."

Jerry Schreiber of Byrn and Henry Streets, East Cambridge, Maryland, shook his head at my remissness. We were both smiling; ever since I had lent him *The Book of Knowledge* in second or third grade, I complained, he had been telling me what I needed to know.

"And you generally learn it, sooner or later," he granted. "You even put it to use, unlike some." That compliment paid, or perhaps difference acknowledged, he declared that *linearity*, more than rationality or intellectuality, was the operative distinction between, one might say, the "Baltimore" of Jay Wordsworth Scribner and "the Rome of St. Jerome." On the one hand, Wallace Stevens's gray jar on a hillside in Tennessee; on the other, W. C. Williams's red wheelbarrow in the rain, on which so much depended.*

Hey, Jay?

"Borges, for sure. But also Allen Ginsberg's Tibetan finger-cymbals."

I'll just have me another Molson's Stock Ale, I guess. You want to mainline some more MSG, so we can talk the same language?

What he meant, it turned out over moo shoo pork, was that just as he found his allegiance divided (in jazz and other life-departments) between the self-conscious and the spontaneous, the sophisticated and the naive, the rigorous and the relaxed-improvisatory, the history-accepting and the history-repudiating, so he had learned equally to admire, but not yet successfully to reconcile, the linear and the gestaltic or otherwise nonlinear, particularly in his own makeup.

Jay-babe?

"The trouble with McLuhan, you'll see right away, is that he leaves you feeling that linearity is *wicked*, when in fact it's simply not the whole story. Lots of things in life aren't linear, but plenty of things *are*. The trouble with *Giles* — one trouble, anyhow — is that it's this interminably linear salute to nonlinearity. Your goatboy scores by transcending the linear, but the novel never does. You dig?"

---

*Explicatory footnote waived; sense of allusions clarified in what follows above.

Maybe. Why not call it a successful linear approximation of nonlinearity, like *Remembrance of Things Past* and *Finnegans Wake?*

Jay only smiled.

Okay, I acknowledged: I'm no Proust or Joyce. But I swear by all the Molson's Ale in Canada that a hymn to nonlinearity needn't be nonlinear. It need only be hymnic.

"Now we're talking." My counterself beamed approval. "Maybe I'll just have me some of that poison, too."

We sipped ale and talked books, I reported to Beard Avenue next morning — for the house had been dark and all hands asleep, or pretending to be, when I made my way back to the United States of America 'round midnight. Books, ideas — like that. No Beth Duer, no you and me, no past history. It was like back in Baltimore over Gunther's bock, except it had a one-shot feel to it. More like a coda than an overture.

"Mmp."

Concerning his cryptic postcard, Jay had remarked only that, as to *Borges*, he had just lately learned that that hombre was to be next year's Charles Eliot Norton Lecturer at Harvard. Maybe if I rang him up early, we could get him to Buffalo. And as to *Baltimore* — well, I had done a recent reading down at the old stand and had no doubt observed for myself the fallen state of our once-vigorous Hopkins Writing Seminars: little more than a holding action these days, under adverse administrative weather. It had occurred to Jay — he seemed even to have discussed the idea with the program's founder, now aging and frail of health — that if my then-forthcoming book or the one after it happened to "famous me up" enough to impress President Milton Eisenhower, and/or if some major change in my life-situation should incline me to leave SUNY/Buffalo as I had recently left Penn State, then perhaps et cetera. But mainly he had just been musing upon the letter *B*, his then-estranged wife's initial and the Hebrew letter of creation: a bit of *vers concret*. Speaking of which, did I know George Herbert's Renaissance "pattern poems"? Did I remember Rabelais's flask-shaped ode "O bouteille" in Book Five of *Gargantua and Pantagruel?* And Lewis Carroll's tail-shaped Mouse's Tale in *Alice*

in Wonderland? Left brain right brain: There was still enough
Johns Hopkins in my counterself — "enough residual Geistesge-
schichte," is how Jay put it over Molson's Stock Ale — for him to
savor the cultural-historical provenance of the apparently avant-
garde. Dealing with a historyless hippie grad student who declared
that all history is bullshit, Professor Schreiber would incline pro-
visionally to agree — and then walk that student rigorously
through the long history of that attitude: Henry Ford's "History is
bunk," Karl Marx's "History is the propaganda of the winners,"
and the rest, maybe back to iconoclastic Alcibiades. What Jay
most admired in Allen Ginsberg were the reverbs of Walt Whitman: the Good Gray Poet come out of the closet, very much in the
American grain. Likewise Richard Brautigan as a stoned early
Hemingway or Haight-Ashbury Jack London, fueled by cannabis
instead of whiskey.

Who's Richard Brautigan? I had asked.

And when Beckett and Borges wrote what might be thought of
as a literature of exhaustion (by which term Jay meant the exhaustion of certain literary conventions, not — *pace* Marshall
McLuhan — the petering out of printed literature itself), it pleased
the left-brain side of Jay Wordsworth Scribner to recall the anxiety
of the Romantic poets a century and a half earlier: their concern
that their eminent forebears were an impossible act to follow; their
Hobson's choice, as they sometimes perceived it, between a tame,
epigonic neo-classicism and a programmatic, perhaps strained and
inauthentic "originality." This anxiety or felt ultimacy Jay would
then trace back (with Walter Jackson Bate of Harvard) four thousand years, to the Egyptian Middle Kingdom scribe Khakheper-
resenb, whose fragmentary papyrus of circa 2000 B.C.E. — one of
the earliest extant literary texts — is a poignantly phrased complaint that its author has arrived on the scene too late: that "the
poets of old" have already exhausted the best effects of the
language.

It had occurred to me over our moo shoo to wonder whether
Scribe Whatsisname mightn't have been working, in 2000 B.C.E.,
an already-established Middle Kingdom literary genre — let's call
it the Literature of Complaint — resolved to write a last-ditch

death-of-art poem that would blow away all the other such apocalyptic complaints in the corpus. Jay liked that; he recalled how
George Boas used to tease us that Homer must have had an easier
time of it with his "wine-dark sea" and "rosy-fingered Dawn" than
we apprentices were going to have, three thousand years later in
the history of metaphors. "That was back when we both believed
we were going to be writers."

If he could still imagine that he was one, Jay had declared near
our amiable evening's end, he would take for his literary navigation stars not the likes of Borges (whom however he still urged
upon me, as "the appropriate corrective after *Giles Goat-Boy*"),
but certain of the Alexandrian and Roman "Neoterics" of the first
century B.C.E., with which he felt our historical moment to share
some important aspects. Most especially, he had come to admire
the poet Catullus. Indeed, the Rome of Jerry Schreiber/Jay Scribner was not finally the Rome of St. Jerome, but the Rome of the
Neoterics.

Neoterics.

"'Moderns.' Proto-Modernists, really, but without the artist-as-
hero hang-up of our big Modernists. No big-deal epics for Catullus and his pals: passionate, but skeptical; playful, but rigorous
and sophisticated; subjective, but formalist. Like saying *Screw
you, Oatmeal*, as exquisitely as a Bach fugue."

Is that what you're saying, Jay?

He blew a low note on his Molson's bottle, regarding me the
while, then smiled. "The hour grows late, man, and my MSG's
about to crash. Borges is your neo-Neoteric, but without Catullus's wonderful ferocity and elegant vulgarity. My point is, your
job is not to follow Joyce and company, but to follow people like
Borges and Beckett who've already done that. You've got to be a
post-Neoteric, you dig? Post post post."

Hence the postcard?

Two-part disharmony, Splitsville unduet, story too banal to tell:
"Mmp"

"Mmp" is how I rather imagine the foregoing account's being
acknowledged over the breakfast table of that large, comfortable

old house on Beard Avenue, in that once rather grand and still not ungracious Central Park neighborhood of Buffalo, New York, under those moribund American elms. Truth to tell (briefly, restrainedly), life was ever less harmonious at that address. Nobody's fault, everybody's, from hers and his to Lyndon Johnson's and Jorge Luis Borges's, and not excepting all hands' progenitors and progeny, but let it be mainly on two heads that were once unanimous but lately found themselves facing in ever more opposed directions, each polarizing the other; both parties distressed, frightened, and resentful at what was happening in their large, once-comfortable old et cetera: a domestic unduet as steadily escalating, divisive, and sickeningly irreversible as our government's tarbabyish involvement in Southeast Asia. On tranquil Langford Creek,* I review my writings from that troubled time and shake my head at their ill-camouflaged desperation; more fairly and painfully, at their desperate attempts at affirmation. "Love! Love! Love!" cries the disenchanted spermatozoon of "Night-Sea Journey," just before he takes the final plunge. The "absurd, unending possibility of love" is what cuckold Menelaus celebrates (in "Menelaiad," 1967), back home in Sparta with wife Helen after the Trojan War. There is "a positive artistic morality in the literature of exhaustion," hoped the essay of that title (also 1967). The stories published that year and the next are bleaker yet: "Title," "Autobiography," "Petition" — all links in the Möbius-strip series *Lost in the Funhouse: Fiction for Print, Tape, Live Voice*, brought out in the fall of 1968.

"He wishes he had never entered the funhouse," declares the narrator of that book's title story, speaking of his thirteen-year-old self. "But he has. Then he wishes he were dead. But he's not. Therefore he will construct funhouses for others and be their secret oper-

---

*Where we note with relief that Hurricane Bonnie has turned north off Bermuda just before the fall equinox and blown itself out at sea; and that Tropical Storm Charlie has fizzled before reaching hurricane strength; and that T. S. Danielle (as I pen this post-equinoctial parenthesis) has stalled just off Cape Hatteras and is not expected to make a landfall. The brisk late-September air beckons us a-sailing.

ator, though he would rather be among the lovers for whom fun-houses are designed."

Yes, well: soon enough. Meanwhile, the couple strove — for each other, against each other, their differences potentiating (and potentiated by) their children's more or less tempestuous teens, and not helped at all by that alarming period of American history, with which their domestic turmoil is indelibly associated in this singer's memory and imagination: surely the nation's most trou-bled period in the second half of this century, and its most divisive since the Civil War. Money, at least, was coming in: The pair bought a furnished cottage for weekends and summers on Chau-tauqua Lake, across from the old Chautauqua Institution, where they diverted themselves with concerts, plays, and operas. The place came equipped with a smaller guest cottage, a dock, and a swimfloat; the new owners added a canoe, an old outboard run-about for waterskiing, and — the fulfillment of a minor but life-long ambition of this Splitsville ariast's — a small secondhand daysailer, in which he taught himself the art from a how-to book. Two seasonsworth of lakeside family barbecues under the fine tall ash trees and great black willows on the seawalled lawn; of explor-atory sailing voyages down Chautauqua's sixteen-mile length from Mayville to Jamestown; of gargantuan winter snowdrifts, iceboats on the frozen lake, ski-lessons on the nearby slopes for outdoor exercise in the heroic winters, snowbound weekends around the fireplace in blizzards howling off the Great Lakes onto their smaller one — all of these punctuated, alas, with tempests non-meteorological, memories of another sort.

The sentences got written. *Lost in the Funhouse* came together in the year when America all but came apart — Martin Luther King, Jr., assassinated (from airliners junketing me to off-campus lectures, I saw smoke towering from one inner city after another, as in a World War Two flick); Robert Kennedy assassinated; Lyn-don Johnson brought down by the war; "peace" riots violently suppressed outside the Democratic National Convention in Chi-cago; Richard Nixon narrowly elected by the "silent majority" on his "law and order" platform; my home campus and half of those

I visited besieged from time to time by riot police or National Guardsmen with tear-gas grenades; my colleague Fiedler arrested for "maintaining a premises" where marijuana was smoked (he kept the lawn mowed, he confessed, and made the mortgage payments on his large, comfortable old house in Buffalo's Central Park neighborhood, under those elms); my counterself, comparativist Jerome Schreiber, arrested with "the Buffalo Seven" for their protest-occupation of the university's central administration building — and our marriage came unglued with the republic. In 1969, husband and wife legally separated: She got the elm-shaded Beard Avenue LCOH, custody of the children, alimony/child support to maintain all hands' accustomed living standards, and a new car in which to drive our daughter off to college. He got the lakeside cottage as his year-round residence, the sturdy green Pontiac wagon that had latterly replaced the hated white Buick, and most of the house library. Lump-throated, she turned her back on their first Summer Place, which they had hoped might "help," and in which she had had so brief a pleasure. Lump-throated, he turned his on the city house that they had early agreed was the best thing about their move to Buffalo, though by then he would have ranked things otherwise. That same year, he was awarded his first honorary doctorate, from the University of Maryland; he used the occasion to revisit his native town, regather with his family, and apprise them of the change in his circumstances. In 1970, not at all amicably (both parting partners had aggressive lawyers), the divorce became final, just as the marriage it ended turned twenty and the parties thereto forty.

So banal a story. At that time, one in four American marriages went the way of theirs here unduetted; today* the rate is one in two. But this was *their* once-so-felicitous union; those were *their* children, just two years shy of being all three off to college and

---

*25 September '92, Tropical Storm Danielle now banging away at Delmarva and pushing up the tides on Langford Creek, where we've just winter-covered our pool and hauled and stored our old canoe, outboard runabout, and Sunfish sailboat, leaving only the original sturdy *US* for us to keep a weather eye on as wind and water rise.

more or less on their own (ariast had made a pitch for Mom and
Dad's staying together through those two more years, and had
only reluctantly agreed, without quite believing it, that on balance
the children would be better off without their folks' ever-sorer
joint residence); those were *their* Theirses now legally divided into
Hers and His.

That period, especially the year 1969, remains in many ways
the low point of my threescore-plus, mainly but not solely on
account of the divorce hassle. One child's adolescence had become
an acute problem. I was the defendant in an auto-accident suit for
damages far exceeding my insurance coverage (Innocent, Your
Honor, I still swear! But Plaintiff was a pedestrian, and the venue
was his home town, Brooklyn, where judges look more kindly
upon local pedestrians than upon out-of-town motorists. We settled). A single man again, isolated and lonely in that Chautauqua
cottage and a scruffy little Buffalo pied-à-terre, my closest company my loyal hippie graduate students and their wives and girlfriends (and, more and more, my counterself), I went through too
much Molson's Stock Ale in the evenings and drove too fast
through blinding weather down the Thomas E. Dewey Thruway
from Buffalo to Chautauqua (No connection with that accident,
Your Honor; just off campus, *that* was, before cocktail time, fetching my daughter home from high school at thirty-five mph). More
dutifully than pleasurably, I experimented at Jay's suggestion with
hashish and marijuana and, at the suggestion of my lonely hormones, with what by legal definition was still adultery.

That much said — and ah, relief, to have its saying done
with! — there were most certainly compensations, and, before
long, light at what would prove to be tunnel's end. The sentences,
for one thing, got written. I asked Jay Wordsworth Scribner, rhetorically, When do they not? and as was his wont with rhetorical
questions, he carefully replied. Purged of the Ur-myth (and of fiction for tape and live voice) but not of classical Greek mythology,
I began a comic novella about Perseus, Andromeda, and Medusa,
in its refracted way more autobiographical, for better or worse,
than anything of mine before or since till this. Charmed by that

narrative space, but still a book man,* I made notes for a second, related novella about Perseus's less distinguished cousin Bellerophon: he who bestrode the winged horse Pegasus and slew the tripartite Chimera; who in my version aspires to become a mythic hero by imitating perfectly Lord Raglan's model of mythic heroism, and becomes instead a perfect imitation of a mythic hero. . . . The image of that particular fabulous monster, Bellerophon's quarry, suggested a ground-metaphor for an imaginable next book: three interrelated novellas, as different from one another as lion, goat, and serpent, yet fused by theme and structure into a fire-breathing single entity.

Jerome Schreiber approved, and Jay Scribner filled my ear with Golden Ratios, Golden Rectangles, logarithmic spirals, Fibonacci numbers, "to rigorize it up, man, so it won't turn into your *Song of Myself*, you know? Some sappy ode to middlescence" — for he knew of certain other things happening in my unaccustomed bachelor life. He suggested that the third novella reorchestrate (his term) some entirely other melody than those of the Greeks and Romans, inasmuch as a serpent is more different from goat and lion than are goat and lion from each other. And when he noted that *Bellerophoniad* in typescript was longer than *Perseid* by a certain amount, he suggested that I make the third piece longer than the second by the same proportion, so as to equal the combined length of *P* and *B* — or, better yet (life being short), make it proportionately *shorter* than *P* and lead off the series with it, so that *X* plus *P* would equal or at least approximate *B*.

"Phi, man: the Golden Ratio. Post-Neoteric."

Furthermore, I should hook the tail of #3 (*Bellerophoniad*, by his rearrangement) back toward the head of this as yet unimagined, much less written #1 so as to suggest neither a simple loop like *Finnegans Wake* nor a circle-with-a-twist like *Funhouse* but a logarithmically opening spiral, "like, you know, old M33

---

*Who quickly learned to define *novella* as "a narrative fiction too long to sell to a magazine and too short to sell to a book publisher."

up there in Andromeda, or the next go-round of your life, if you don't blow it."

And I should give at least some thought to providing the whole shebang with an exit door or escape hatch out of the Fabulous altogether, the Long Ago and Far Away and Never Was, back to the Here and Now and Newspaper-Real, to allow myself ideological maneuvering room down the road. Options open, et cetera — as he hoped I was keeping them in my personal affairs.

Yes, well. I'll think about it, Scrib, for sure.

"You do that, Oatmeal. Beth, by the way, says hello."

Beth does, does Beth? My warm regards, then, to that formidable female, your wife the Duer, and a toast from me to your flexible and unconventional but evidently perdurable and no doubt *authentic* marriage. In some way that I resisted analyzing, however, it seemed to me even in prospect a mistake, a betrayal of something, even a minor perversity, to reestablish or even revisit the closeness I had once enjoyed with Mrs. Jay and with the Scribner/Duers as a couple. I put off their subsequent dinner invitations; kept them, as a couple, at cordial arm's length, although I continued and valued my musical connection with "Jerry Schreiber" (still spiky, muted, Buddha-smiling, a departmental enigma) and valued even more the reestablishment — over off-campus delicatessen lunches and in unscheduled office drop-ins — of my feedback link with Jay Wordsworth Scribner, my counterself, who approved of what was happening to my life, but was sympathetic to the pain of it.

"Where on the diagram are you now, Oat-boy?" he would ask me — smiling in my office doorway at the cyclical mythic-heroic schema that I had enlarged from his Roman sketch, annotated, framed, and hung for a time on one cinderblock wall.

Still lost in the funhouse, Jay.

"Have fun, then, man."

I quoted the opening line of that series's title story: "For whom is the funhouse fun?"

Inveterate answerer of rhetorical questions, Jay quoted back the narrator's reply:

"Perhaps for lovers." End-of-1960s aria:

Yes. Well. Even before light at tunnel's end, certain consolations in and of the dark.

Should the time arrive (which Zeus forfend) when any of this singer's offspring — in their teens back then, thus fortyish now* — comes marriagewise to Splitsville as did their dad, I wish that child at least such here-and-there encouragements as were my good fortune, not to mention (yet) light, light, light down the line, at tunnel's end. In the dark, meanwhile, e.g.:

— The sentences, as aforewritten, got written. In tempest-time, praise be to *work*; that homeliest, sturdiest, and most reliable of Personal Flotation Devices. Any meaningful, attention-demanding work well done will do, but especially the *making* of things (or, I should think, the doing of good, such as teaching or healing; merely "doing well" will prove hollow consolation, children, except insofar as it eases the burden of alimony payments, double lawyers' fees, triple college tuitions), and most especially the making of things favorably received, by and large, by one's peers. If my fictioneering career had happened to slump in synchrony with my marriage, that latter life-convulsion would have been more than painful. As was, the sentences not only got written but were, praise be, gratifyingly (though by no means universally) well received.

— Their author began taking better care of himself. The '68 jacket photo on *Lost in the Funhouse* shows him, cigarette in one hand, coffee cup in the other, relaxing between sessions in a sound-studio before a bank of Ampex tape recorders. His shirt is white, his tie narrow, his fringe of hair clipped short, as are his sideburns. Of those trappings, by 1969 only the morning coffee remained: I

---

*First day of October '92, unseasonably cool at Langford Creek, where the geese moving down from Canada have brought Niagara Frontier weather with them — too near-frosty, alas, just now, for sailboat cruising. As the hurricane season welcomely winds down, the Quincentenary Columbus Day fast approaches, and with it my middle child's fortieth birthday: his married sister forty-one, his married brother thirty-eight. Tropical Storm Earl wanders the ocean off Bermuda, curving erratically north*east*ward now, away from us. We begin to uncross our fingers and look forward to fall sailing.

quit smoking (and put Ampexes behind me, too), did more skiing, played tennis indoors and out four seasons a year, reined in (but did not forgo) my dinner wine and evening ale consumption, and obeyed vehicular speed limits — all to my physical and psychological benefit. For better or worse, like nearly all my male colleagues I took to teaching in clothes less formal than suits and ties. I let what hair remained to me grow just long enough to become *curly* again for the first time since JackandJill babyhood, and wore sideburns down to my earlobes. My body, never unhealthy, felt more consistently fit than it had for years.

— But if my appearance became more casual, like a nineteenth-century British officer posted to the tropics I did not permit myself to "go native" in my bachelor housekeeping and general habits. "Every artist is as bohemian as the deuce inside!" exclaims Thomas Mann's Tonio Kröger. "Let him at least behave outwardly like a respectable being." Tidy by temperament, I hired a once-a-week country housekeeper to keep the Chautauqua premises clean and the laundry laundered, did all the maintenance and grounds-keeping chores conscientiously myself, and prepared all my meals, with reasonable attention to variety and a healthy diet. No stand-up breakfasts or TV dinners. For that matter, virtually no TV.

— In this and analagous areas, from clothes-shopping and furniture selection to bookkeeping and business decisions, where I was long accustomed to depending upon, sharing with, or at least consulting my spouse, I came to take satisfaction in my new independence and self-reliance. Much as I missed family and family life after so many years of immersion in them, I found it refreshing, if often lonesome and sometimes a touch scary, to be "on my own": answerable only to my conscience and the law; free within those bounds to do as I damn pleased; to dispose of my time and any surplus resources as I saw fit. Platitudinous to say, invigorating to feel: The responsibilities and strictures of middle-class family life, however willingly assumed and profoundly rewarding, are, undeniably, strictures. Shedding them — however reluctantly, sorrowfully, and far from completely — has its liberating aspects, even for a fairly cautious creature of habit.

— Thus there came to be, presently, lovers, and, before very long, love. Those stumbling commas mime my hesitations, even trepidations, as to the doing then, likewise the telling now. As of this hour, I happen never to have bedded a woman with whom I wasn't at least half in love. By busy sexual-revolutionary standards, therefore, the catalogue is short; its quality I declare enviable, its aftertaste sweet; good women, all few of them; good friends, good lovers. Of the most important except for the Most Important, this aria (neither Guess Who nor Kiss and Tell) will sing only that if I thought I knew already what were depth of heart and moral passion, she showed me that I did not — and by the way instructed me in the art of eating artichokes. Pumblechooking these lines, I summon clearly to my nostrils over a near quarter-century's distance the fragrance of her favorite skin cream, its name . . .

Nunnayerbeeswax.

And this blessing, children, tendered in mid-tunnel, *before* light at end of same, though not before the fortuitous, serendipitous reappearance in the wings of this opera, headed for stage center, the smiling bearer of that light. Soon enough — as the Sixties flamed on from the riots in Chicago and Paris, the Chinese Cultural Revolution and the Soviet crushing of the Prague Spring, toward our bombing of Cambodia, the last convulsions of our Vietnamese misadventure, the Yom Kippur War and the Arab oil embargo — it became my unspeakable good fortune and new problem — but what a rich one! — to be obliged to choose between two excellent women; presently to find the question of choice resolving lightly of itself, though less lightly and of-itself-ishly the delicate matter of implementing that resolution.

May there be for you, dear my children, no If and When; but may the like good luck be yours, if and when!

End of 1960s. End of tunnel, but not of road. End of aria; of solo self-guided tour; of Act Two of *Once Upon a Time,*

Almost.

Loose ends to be tucked up:

When will this scary decade end? I asked Jay Scribner/Jerry Schreiber one pallid Buffalo afternoon late in 1969. My counterself leaned against my office doorjamb, smiling and smiling at the sore fact of my marital separation and at some guarded tidings that he had just received, from me, of my subsequent private life. The query was prompted by the usual public uncertainty about whether 1970, for example, should be regarded as the closing year of the 1960s, as is the arithmetical case, or the opening of the 1970s, as common sense prefers. Inasmuch as the question was at least half rhetorical, my half-colleague half-answered:

"When its loose ends are all tucked up."

Ah, so. The Moratorium demonstrations, e.g.? Woodstock and the Weathermen? Nixon/Kissinger? *Hair*?

"Mere file footage. Tuck away, man. Beth says hi, by the way. Also good luck."

That loose end I've tucked already, Jer. I won't be seeing you guys again until and unless it's couple to couple, and I'm not a couple these days.

He nodded. "We can wait. Don't hurry. Tuck. Enjoy."

Loose ends, let's see. I still drove my trusty-rusty green Pontiac wagon. . . . Ah, and I had been named to a new endowed chair at the university, the Edward H. Butler Professorship. Its endowment included a generous annual-expense allowance for which I had no proper use, it being intended to fund scholarly research (not my line), associated travel (my lecture schedule kept me as traveled as I cared to be), and book purchases (I am a book lover, but not a collector; I bought a set of the old eleventh-edition *Brittanica* and the seventeen out-of-print volumes of Burton's *The Book of a Thousand Nights and a Night*, and wanted nothing further). At the end of the first budget year, therefore, most of the ten or twelve thousand annual-expense dollars remained unspent. The money could not be drawn as salary; my conscience wouldn't let me squander it, as some suggested, on phony "research travel" to Paris or the Caribbean. I considered establishing with it an Edward H. Butler Lecture Series to bring writers to the campus for public readings and seminar sessions with our apprentices, but in those expansive days we had already so ample a departmental budget for visitors that I was kept busy writing introductions and making social arrangements for them: Donald Barthelme, Jorge Luis

Borges, Richard Brautigan, Anthony Burgess, John Hawkes, Joseph Heller, Doris Lessing, Norman Mailer, I. B. Singer, and many another. What then legitimately to do with Mr. Butler's largesse? I was approaching forty and had been teaching full-time, almost without respite, for nearly twenty years. What I really craved in the academic way was more released prime-time for reading and writing. It therefore occurred to me to propose that that jim-dandy expense account be allowed to accumulate untouched and then be used, every third semester, to hire a visiting writer in my stead at no cost to the department. I rather expected this proposal to be dismissed with an uneasy chuckle, as had been several I'd made to my tax lawyer.* After some months of collective head-scratching, however, the Empire State's accountants saw fit to approve my two-thirds-serious plan, effective 1/1/70. I would therefore be on paid leave for the spring semester of 1971 and the fall semester of 1972, to look no farther: a relevant end that I deliberately here leave loose for tucking when the time arrives.

"Aha."

That about does it, old Smegma Flake. On the literary-aesthetic front, I had little use for the Beats — Kerouac, Ginsberg, and company — although like my counterself here addressed, I appreciated their being very much in the American grain (*one* American grain, anyhow). And when my comrade Fiedler declared publicly that the American novel was currently polarized between the examples of "redskin" Norman Mailer on the one hand and "paleface" Saul Bellow on the other, my reaction was "I hope not," for though I respected both, I was no major fan of either. My living literary heroes were Nabokov, Beckett, Borges, and Calvino (Gabriel García Márquez would not come to our gringo attention until the decade's turn); there was no fifth, unless perhaps some amalgam of what would come to be called the American Postmodernists — Barthelme/Coover/Gass/Hawkes/Paley/Pynchon — an amalgam in which I was pleased to find myself sometimes included.

---

*E.g., that writers, like oil wells, be given depletion allowances (I had done actuarial calculations, semi-numerate, on the average productivity of twentieth-century American novelists); that a novelist's whole life be deductible as business expense, since all of it is potential grist for the mill.

"Mm hm."

Loose ends, loose ends. What was *I*, Wordy Scrib, just then, if not an ongoing loose end? Between lives (But who knew for sure?), between wives (ditto), between decades both calendric and life-historical, at emotional sixes and sevens, trying simultaneously to steer my children through their adolescence and myself through my middle-, yet learning after all to savor what was savorable in all this betwixtness and loose-endhood. And always, by the way — Or was it the rest of life that was by the way, and this central? — making up and setting down, one after the other, sentences about Perseus, Bellerophon, and in time Scheherazade and her kid sister, Dunyazade: the sentences of the book *Chimera*.

"A decade ends," Jay Scribner declared, "when the next commences. *Your* next won't commence until your scene changes. Looks like I left one *B* off that postcard, between Buffalo and Baltimore."

Betweensville?

"Maybe. Got to split now, man."

One last loose end, old friend, my first of this dialogue: What's 1970, decadewise? End or beginning?

Jay shrugged, and in East Cambridge French replied, "Entr'-acte, peut-être?"

Comment?

He glanced at his wristwatch. Waggled his fingers. "Au revoir, Oatmeal. Don't hurry, okay?"

BETWEEN ACTS
Light

⟨ ⟩

OKAY. Jay took my timepiece; I'll take my time in this suspended passage between Acts Two and Three (of three). Neither guide nor guided here, out of happy habit or mere professional momentum I ply my *ree*mote across the lines of my battered binder, marking time, watchful for what this black Skrip brings to light. Time's arrow on the butted cap points pointward, to where the ongoing present's nib resistlessly pasts the future, elucidating all three. Were the pearl-gray stone a-cap that cap a penlight, it would beam just abaft the penman's shoulder and illuminate whoever looks thereover at these sentences a-making.

Are you there?

Light. Between the decades sung and those now* to sing, a bright suspension of *B*s — blizzard/Boston/Barbados/blizzard — bridges the brawlbrat *B*-card's Buffalo-to-Baltimore. On a pearl-gray end-of-February day in the Sixties' last year (by common-sense calendrics), I flew from Buffalo to my lectorial once-a-monther, this one at Boston College. Landed late at Logan Airport in a Beantown blizzard; barely made it across town with my Jesuit host in time to hurry straight onstage for my eight-o'clock number — which,

---

*Act Two's first-draft curtain-close penned on 9 October 1992, a rainy mild Friday at Langford Creek. Forecast uncertain for the weekend ahead, now past. On the Monday following, houselights darken and stage lights rise (Harvest Moon, too, over our creek's east fork) for this second entr'acte. Perpend this note, reader.

that season, was a strenuous ninety-minute reading of the story
"Menelaiad" from *Lost in the Funhouse*: seven concentrically
imbedded tales within tales, their sequence tracked for the audience with numeric flip-cards (1-2-3-4-5-6-7-6-5-4-3-2-1) and a
handheld series of incremental quotes within quotes — climaxing,
in the inmost tale, with the Delphic oracle's response to Menelaus's
anguished cry: *Who am I?** My stomach empty (we had missed
the routine pre-lecture dinner), my adrenals still pumping from the
close connection, my whole attention concentrated on timing,
delivery, and the orderly sequencing of those visuals lest I lose
myself indeed in my own funhouse, I was grateful that the auditorium lights were down, the audience invisible but not unfeelable,
everything focused like a pen-nib on the unfolding and then refold-
ing narrative. However comedized and transmogrified into fiction,
Helen's husband's essential question was undeniably much mine,
as was his distress: acknowledgeable and addressable only by artful indirection. The "absurd, unending possibility of love,"
invoked at the story's close, is what had carried both him and me
through its sore and growing complications — together with, in
my case if not in Menelaus's, the considerable good fortune that
"of of what one can't make sense, one may make art."

"... *the absurd, unending possibility of love,*" he and I presently concluded — the latter of us in a happy, exhausted sweat,
my spirit re-purged by empathetic laughter and the unending possibilities... of language, anyhow. House lights came up; Language and I nodded grateful acknowledgment to our audience. I
looked forward to the quick late drink-and-dinner that my host
had promised to supply in lieu of the formal one we'd missed, and
then to bed, for this particular reading-program truly left me
spent. First, however, the customary brief audience-mingle and
book-signing in the auditorium lobby — and after that, if I didn't
object, a smaller pro forma reception in a room just above. No

---

*" " "" " "" " " "" ' ", replies the story, its live author holding aloft those quote-
strings port and starboard of himself. In conformity with British usage, all U.K.
editions of *Lost in the Funhouse* patiently reverse those double and single quotes.

need to stay long, but this latter was an invitees-only affair tradi-
tionally associated with the college's visiting-lecture series.

Well, all right. These folks had, after all, hauled through a
snowstorm to hear me, and had attended Menelaus's tale for a full
hour and a half. I could certainly sip a glass of wine and nibble a
canapé with them — both promised at Reception Two, invitees
only. Of Reception One, a mere entr'acte, we would make quick
work.

But a small side-pleasure of these reading junkets, I had come
to know and enjoy, is that from time to time a former student,
colleague, or other past acquaintance turns up to say hello, having
migrated, as Americans do, from where last known. In Nebraska
or Indiana, a strayed Dorchester Countian; in California or Wyo-
ming, a Johns Hopkins undergraduate classmate; in Baton Rouge
or Boston . . .

Among the well-wishers and autographees, bearing nothing to
be inscribed, but luminescent in light-beige boots, fashionable
orange wool minidress, and megawatt smile that I remembered at
once as having lighted the Penn State classroom where, some five
years since, I had led her and her classmates in Humanities 1
(*Truth, Goodness, and Beauty*) through Sophocles, Plato, Aristotle, Lucretius, Job, Dante, Hume, Keats, Dostoevsky, Mann,
Joyce, Camus — her hand beaconing with eager question or
ready answer — there stood the Pennsylvania State University's
100,000th graduate.

"Hi."

Head cocked, winter coat folded over folded arms, hand neither up nor out but face alight, waiting to see whether and how
quickly I would remember her. . . .

Hi indeed. I did remember — quickly for me, whose name-
retrieval prowess in out-of-context situations is not formidable —
for although she and I had not been close (more by temperament
than by policy, I've never been "close" even to my graduate
students except during the entr'acte between my marriages,
aforenoted but not here quite yet begun), she had been close
indeed to one or two of my colleague-friends, at whose recom-

mendation she had signed up for Truth Goodness and Beauty with me. Not heard from or of since we had gone our separate ways from Happy Valley in '65; my uncertain memory was that with several good graduate-school fellowships to choose from among, she had elected Chicago's prestigious Committee on Social Thought: Saul Bellow/Hannah Arendt country. How came she to be here in blizzard-bound Boston, shlepping through the snow to say hi to her old teach? Was she Ph.D.'d? Professoring somewhere hereabouts?

"A long story."

So tell! How was Chicago? How (and for that matter *what*, exactly) was Social Thought? How goes it with Truth Goodness and Beauty these days? Long stories are my long suit!

But Reception One, clearly, was unreceptive to extended story-swapping. Other lobby-folk stood by, unsigned books in hand; my gentle Jesuit was already at my elbow, Virgiling me elevatorward to Reception Two — invitees only. What a pity, when there, inarguably, stood Beauty (arms still folded, head still cocked), no doubt Goodness as well and, for all I knew, Truth to boot: beige-booted, miniskirted, tale untold. A proper pity, I truly felt — suddenly-surprisingly-*strongly* felt, and plainly said: We haven't even spoken yet e.g. of Happy Valley, have we? But there's this *other* reception upstairs, see — invitees only, I'm afraid — that I'm a touch late for already. We'll really have to catch up at some less distracted, less bespoken time. (How? Where? I'm c/o SUNY/Buffalo these days; in whose care are you?)

To Friar Virgil, hustling me elevatorward with a clutch of invitees, I explained: Prize Penn Stater, first-rate student, lit up the whole classroom; it occurs to me now that I really ought to've imposed a bit on you and the invitees and —

The doors of the near-full elevator were ready to close like opera-house curtains, may already have begun closing when she — quicker-witted than I, as she would prove ever to be — nick-of-timely handed me back the initiative I had failed to take, and our future.

"May I come along?"

That smile itself would have stopped automatic doors from closing, had not Friar V or one of the invited — or perhaps the orange wool minidress and beige boots — done us that service. By disposition and long habit slow on the uptake (Menelaus-weary, too, just then), I was not, however, brain- or hormone-dead. Of *course* come along, I said at once, and soon enough over stand-up wine and canapés I got the basics clear: that with more than enough credits for her degree (from Norman Maclean's Committee on the Humanities, by the way, not Social Thought) she had left Chicago; that she was just now teaching high school in a Boston suburb and sharing an apartment with several other single young women; that she had noted in *Boston After Dark* my scheduled visit to B.C. and had braved the blizzard crosstown from Brookline to say hi. Having now done same — and quite enjoyed the show, by the way, she allowed: funny, sad, in places moving — she would leave me to my obligations to the invited.

Obligations, I agreed, were duly to be honored. Duly honoring these, however, would be short work, and I was hungry, likewise thirsty, for more substantial fare and conversation. Would she join my steadfast cleric Virgil and me for a small late dinner, somewhere that she and he could decide upon while I mingled with the invited? A place convenient, preferably, to wherever I was billeted (Consult Friar V on that), for it had been a long day; a place, ideally, where even at this late-by-Yankee-standards dinner hour one might find oysters and champagne to toast . . . Truth, let's say; also Goodness. Et cetera?

She would. All of that came to pass — Heart-constricting idiom, Time's ever-past-tensing point! My obligations to the invited fully honored with a right good will (for I was suddenly re-energized), my host kindly drove me and led her (in her silver-blue Impala convertible) a short, snowplowed way to an agreed-upon seafoodery out on Route 9: Tollino's, not far from the Charterhouse Motel, where I was to lodge but had yet to check into. A round of halfshell oysters and champagne indeed, then, and polite general conversation in the near-empty restaurant. Bluepoints, we three agreed that those bivalves doubtless were, from Long Island Sound

or points north, but I here imagine them to have been Chinco-
teagues or Chesapeakes, a salty foretaste of Act Three; and I was
pleased to recall for our host that it had been a Jesuit missionary
among Lord Baltimore's first colonizers (Father Andrew White,
S.J.) whose 1634 *A Relation of the successful beginnings of the
Lord Baltimore's plantation in Maryland* inaugurated the literature of my native ground. After which pleasantries, it being clear
enough at that late hour that his own obligations to the invited
were honorably discharged upon the young lady's volunteering to
Impala me off to the nearby Charterhouse en route home to
Brookline, and that she and I had catch-up talk yet to talk — my
good Society-of-Jesus Virgil gracefully yielded guideship to . . .

My sharp young Beatrice-in-the-works, though neither of us
knows *that* yet, do we, smiling over second-round oysters and
refilled flutes, free now finally to begin to speak at leisure (not,
however, undistractedly: that knockout dress, the dark-walnut
hair and eyes, the luminously open smile and forthright way of
talking — and had I really heard Virgil murmur, in parting, that
he would be there to fetch me to the airport after breakfast, as
arranged, *if I needed a ride?*) of her closeness to our Penn State
Hemingway/piano mutual pal; of how she had talked her way into
Saul Bellow's Chicago seminar and found the fellow peacock-vain
but comparably brilliant; of life-corners turned out there in Windy
City by passion grand and heartbreak yet unmended, which, out
of a moral clarity and courage-cum-vulnerability that I would
come to love, had driven her from that place and her well-earned
degree to refuge with a friend in Boston and to an earlier-than-
intended start on what anyhow had been her lifelong ambition:
not college-professoring,* but *teaching* — plain old unglamorous,
unprestigious, unremunerative high-school teaching, her never-
doubted vocation since, oh, first grade.

---

*Much as she had admired a number of her professors, present company candidly
included, and had even enjoyed "crushes" on one or two of them, present company not. I had been so *stiff* back then, so standoffish! Did I remember a certain
awkward conference in my Penn State office . . . ? I did indeed.

In short — for the full tale was by no means told — a bit older
and a good deal more seasoned since Happy Valley; heart-scarred
still, but on the mend; doing nicely, thanks; much enjoying the
lively Boston/Cambridge scene, and (I gathered) "dating" again,
but not currently attached.

"And you?"

Ah, well. The sentences get written, anyhow.

She had noticed. And?

And *I* had noticed that the staff of our all-but-empty restaurant
pretty obviously wished we would bottoms-up our bubbly and go
on with our stories elsewhere. Perhaps my motel has an attached
bar/lounge; let's Impala ourselves thereto, I proposed, check me
in, and see what Truth looks like over a nightcap in that lounge.

Done: Initiative Three of my four that evening, she having
taken the two prior crucial ones of coming to hear Menelaus's epic
plaint and of inviting herself into that reception-elevator, I of validating that self-invitation and of proposing dinner with me and
Virgil. Nifty convertible: her first car, bought secondhand. Nifty
driver. Nifty snowbanked Boston night through which to negotiate the few blocks from Tollino's to the Charterhouse. Back in
Hum 1, we two had never presumed past bright "Miss R——"
and cordial-but-standoffish "Professor B——"; by now we were
at ease with each other's first names, the American equivalent of
French tutoyer, and within respectful bounds were being fairly
candid in the questions-and-confidences way. There turned out to
be, indeed, in the Charterhouse, a quiet, in fact vacant lounge,
where she ordered us something-or-other — two TG&Bs straight
up? — while I signed in at the reception desk.

"So l'Chaim." Beige boots tucked up, orange hem tugged down,
lounge-lighting smile. "Where were we?"

Have we established that the color-word *chartreuse* means
"charterhouse," more or less, from the color of the liqueur made
in Chartreuse, France, by monks of the Carthusian order (Latin
for "Chartreusian"), whose abbeys came to be called *chartreuses*
wherever located — as in Stendhal's *La Chartreuse de Parme*,
whereto his hero Fabrizio del Dongo repairs at the novel's end to
do penance for his tragic affair with the Marchesa Clelia?

"Probably."

Then where are we indeed, bright former student and nifty newfound friend, so enjoyably sharing a common wavelength despite our several differences? Eighteen years after this nightcap-night in the Charterhouse of Boston, in midst of an essay called "Teacher," my Parker will pen *And in the motel's all-but-empty lounge I was told at last* [her] *long story and some shorter ones, and I told mine and some shorter ones, and presently I took initiative Four*, here reprised in

An arietta resung: "Plato has Socrates teach"

"Plato has Socrates teach in *The Symposium* that the apprehension of Very Beauty, as distinct from any beautiful thing or class of things, is arrived at by commencing with the love of, even the lust for, some particular beautiful object or person. Thence one may proceed to loving beautiful objects and persons in general, the shared quality that transcends their individual differences — may learn even to love that shared quality without lusting after it: 'Platonic love.' Thereby one may learn to love the beauty of nonmaterial things as well: beautiful actions, beautiful ideas. . . . Whence the initiate, the elect, the platonically invited, may take the ultimate elevator to Beauty Bare: the quality abstracted even from beautiful abstractions. This is the celebrated 'ladder of love,' as I understood and taught it in Humanities 1 at Penn State, Miss R's hand raised at every rung. Our relationship began at the top of that ladder, with those lofty abstractions: Truth, Goodness, Beauty. Now my (former) student taught her (former) teacher that that process is reversible, anyhow coaxial; that ladder a two-way street; that ultimate elevator — May I come along? — a not-bad place to begin."

On with the lights.

One if by land, two if by sea; how many if by *ree*mote? Through that blizzard of *B*s she beacons me to a tunnel's-endish feast of lights. From snowy Boston back to snowy Buffalo, I smiled. When our paths crossed next (two lecture dates later, by arrangement, in springtime Pittsburgh), my news was that my life's first half looked to be coterminating with the decade — or had already so done, depending on one's calendrics. Thirty-nine in '69, I was officially "separating"; would be living thenceforth year-round in what had been meant to be (pardon the plural dispossessive) "our" vacation cottage. No reconciliation expected.

She sympathized.

Thereafter, we kept more frequently in touch — by letter and telephone, now and then by literal touch (the odd weekender at Chautauqua, another lecture date in New England) — and found that our Charterhouse conversation was by no means done. I was not, however, my Boston belle's sole conversant, nor (as aforesung) was she yet mine; we were only, with each reconnection, each other's ever-more-significant. That summer, while I boarded one teenager, hosted the other two and their friends, dealt with divorce- and accident-lawyers, and somehow wrote the *Perseid* novella, she cheered me with postcards from Greece and Israel, including one of the cliff from which Perseus is said to have rescued Andromeda from the monster Cetus before they all turned into the constellations that inspired my story themabout. For her possible amusement, I added to the myth the young priestess Calyxa, who dwells at the center of a spiral-shaped memorial to Perseus's past exploits and leads him out of it, to his future. Seashells and spirals in general, and in particular spiral seashells, became our totems; a day would come when Italo Calvino would dedicate to us a public reading of his lovely shell-tale, "The Spiral."

A buzz of *B*s: In Buffalo and Boston, at Brown University and in the Big Apple (where we blenched together at a pre-release screening of the vulgar film version of *The End of the Road*) — by year's end (decade's turn), we were seeing to it that our paths intersected at every opportunity. At spring-break time '70 we bopped off on "BeeWee" (British West Indies Airlines) to Barbados and bliss among the bougainvillea: our most time together thence far, that Caribbean holiday, by when our separate decks were clearing, if not yet altogether cleared, of significant others. Amid the welter of my domestic crises and litigations, our busy separate teaching schedules, my parental responsibilities and lectorial travels, our occasional weekends together in her city, mine, or some other, and the inevitable ups/downs/ons/offs of new lovers adjusting (and adjusting to) their differences, we were meeting each other's friends and discussing summer plans. Would she consider cottage-keeping with me at Lake Chautauqua through that season? Weathering storms and power outages, teenage children and graduate-student friends? Would she come sail and swim and water-ski? Tennis-play, opera-go, out-cook? Make love and sentences together?

"Maybe." It was not Greece and Israel, was funky old Chautauqua, nor was it Boston/Rockport/Marblehead/Cape Cod. For her the step was a considerably larger one than for him, who must abide there anyhow among his midlife responsibilities, beleaguerments, and incidental pleasures. Were we that serious?

Yes, off and on; increasingly *on.* But airports and long-distance telephones, letters and lecture dates, weekend trysts and Caribbean vacations, we agreed, were not the best way for potential partners really to get to know each other. Working as well as playing together, housekeeping and daily-lifing together were sounder courtship, we agreed; and courting we surely were by then, courting the future, with appropriate caution — but the court was in intermittent session, the jury still out. So, then: Maybe. Even probably, but *maybe* for sure.

Boston, I would have told Jay Wordsworth Scribner in my fortieth May, may be the *B*-to-be on that B-card of yours, not Baltimore. But my brawlbrat buddy had by then de-Buffaloed; had followed Beth Duer back to Bay country, where she'd joined a D.C. law firm and bought the both of them a bungalow in Bethesda. Jay was gypsying academically in the Baltimore/Washington corridor, writing "street poetry" under the name J. Scribner while teaching as Jerome Schreiber in the Johns Hopkins Evening College (renamed Continuing Education) and various University of Maryland extension programs. In terse, infrequent letters to me, he re-tisked the lean times that our alma mater's once-notable writing program had fallen upon; he duly deplored the Nixon/Kissinger escalations of our national debacle in Southeast Asia, but was himself becoming ever less political, he declared, or at least was redirecting his political attention. The ecology of the Chesapeake estuarine system, he reported, was coming to engage and concern him more than the Cold War machinations of CKI-GAB.* Should history ever let him stop being a peace activist, he intended to become a Greenpeace activist. Had I heard of that outfit?

I had not;† was too busy coping, hoping, and sorting things out (also making sentences) to give war and peace their due. She'll come; she won't come, can't come, shouldn't must might; it was one of those intervals when one's personal future holds its breath more obviously than usual. Then she phoned me her decision, and on midsummersday, the year's longest, as I was arranging things upstairs, I heard a happy crunch of tires on driveway gravel; saw in the broad late-afternoon light her olive Cutlass convertible, successor to that maiden silver-blue Impala, roll to a halt chez moi, packed to the plimsoll; sped downstairs to welcome her chez nous before she changed her mind.

"What am I doing here?"

On with the lights: Your large step taken, long drive driven, "What am I *doing* here?" you reasonably wondered, laughing uncertainly as we embraced in the cottage's rear entry.

Seeing the light, I hoped — when in fact it was I who would need this summer's light to see my way clearly. Among remembered noteworthy sidelights to that light:

— *The late-afternoon sidelit tree-lined lakeshore*, as seen from our old Rebel daysailer, our old Lyman lapstrake wooden runabout, or our not-so-old Old Town canoe — none of those quite "ours" yet — on such days as that solstitial one of rare Chautau-

---

*Pronounced "chickie-gab": Jay's cynical run-together of CIA and KGB, which, like the military superpowers they spied for, each depended on the other for justification, in his opinion.

†Here, as elsewhere, my counterself got wind of things betimes: Greenpeace had been established just the year before. By when the folksinger-environmentalist Pete Seeger sets forth upon the Hudson in the sloop *Clearwater* to campaign for the cleanup of that river, Jay Wordsworth Scribner (bankrolled by lawyer Beth) will have bought and commissioned the old ketch *American Century* to propagandize in like fashion for depollution of the Chesapeake watershed.

qua sunshine (the "lake effect" beclouds those upstate skies two days out of three).

— *Lightning storms* off to westward, out over Lake Erie, whose pyrotechnic approach we admired from dock, patio, or porch till dash-for-cover time, as we admire these days* the Chesapeake blasters barreling down Langford Creek. Then time-out love, by candle- and oil-lamp light, until spoilsport Niagara Power restored our service and time came to reset our clocks.

— *Neighborly bonfires* (a lakeshore tradition); *July Fourth flares* outlining the lake's perimeter (another); *the odd fireplace fire* as late as early June and as early as late August in that nippy, near-Canadian latitude — these lights go without singing. Not so *zilches* — Remember zilches, those echt-late-Sixties navigation lights for space-trippers? Having rigged beforehand a ceiling-high braid of twisted plastic trashbags over a galvanized tub of water, one sat on the floor in the dark with a ring of one's half-stoned friends, lit the thing's tail, and passed the joint or sipped legal beer while admiring the zilch's sinuous slow combustion and the eponymous sound of molten fire-drops zilching into the water. Best zilched outdoors; among conservative neighbors, however, a darkened porch or well-ventilated kitchen served. Zilches, yes.

— *Lake-fly rheostats!* Twice or thrice a summer, those essentially harmless nuisances the size of fat mosquitoes hatch all at once in hordes of an African prodigiousness, battening Chautauqua's fish (and bats) and for a few nights making human outdoor life all but unmanageable. In their short-lived billions they swarm to any light — to any light-colored surface, for that matter — there to perch, poop, and die, presumably having mated and laid eggs somewhere between these acts. One learned to ride out lake-fly nights in the darkened cottage, awed by the mighty outside thrum of all that protein on the wing; otherwise, by morning every night-lit window, even whole exterior white clapboard walls, would be covered with their gluey brown excreta: "lake-fly spots," almost impossible to remove. One learned too — we did, anyhow — not only to mate in the dark as they did on such evenings,

*No date given; time's out in this entr'acte.

but to amuse ourselves between acts with the Lake-Fly Rheostat Effect: So instantaneous and finely tuned is the swarm's response to gradations of luminosity, we discovered that with the dimmer switch of our bedroom light we could "conduct" their massive hum precisely, eliciting gradual or rapid crescendi and diminuendi, high- or low- or mid-volume pulses, and other sonic effects. Arthur Fiedlers of the lake flies, we led our zillion-member orchestra through whole pops programs: Beethoven's Fifth (hum-hum-humm *humm*), Jingle Bells (*hum*-hum-*hum*, *hum*-hum-*hum*, *hum*-hum-*hum*-hum *humm*), and acid-rock "reverb" effects such as the Beatles had lately turned to. John Cage, we imagined, would approve.

— *The Perseid meteors*: In honor of my mythic protagonist and his new friend and guide Calyxa, we inaugurated what would become our mid-August custom, a wee-hours spectation from dock or deck of the annual Perseid meteor shower. There across the upstate sky hung the dramatis personae of my novella, radiating falling stars: old Cepheus and Cassiopeia, the hero's in-laws; his estranged (now ex-) wife, Andromeda; winking Medusa, his adversary-ally, who has loved him all along and who, her head held high in her hero's hand, turns the whole cast into constellations at story's end. In my fiction, Calyxa becomes the famous spiral galaxy M33, a mere spin-off from Andromeda. In fact . . .

O say, can you see . . . ?

"What *am* I doing here?" you must have re-asked yourself at least from time to time through that trial season of love and lake flies, art and athletics, housekeeping and hospitality (Who was houseguesting? My extended-visit teenagers, two-thirds of them en route to college, or their dad's new girlfriend, leaving like them on Labor Day to go back to school?), for not until early August did I belatedly see the light. The *Perseid* novella by then long since done, I was stuck in its sequel or companion piece, about Bellerophon bogged in early middle age, trying unsuccessfully to re-spur Pegasus into flight. Trapped in my own metaphor (I had chosen it half for that reason, to draw the issue and turn the screws on my situation — which, however, those *Chimera* novellas are no more than incidentally "about"), my marital fingers burnt, divorce-scars fresh, parental guilt-trip duly tripping, I was wary of "rebound" commitments; likewise, still, of those differences of age, stage, and derivation that at the same time, given the large overlap of our interests and values, were among the sources of our shared pleasure — not unlike being of opposite sexes while sharing heterosexuality.

Thus was I damagingly dilatory in facing, broaching, and reconciling my mixed feelings about the unasked question that loomed ever larger, lakeside, as the clock of summer ran: What next? Quo vadimus from here? Is this freshwater salty-dog summer to be our grand opera's first act? Our mini-operetta's only? Or a mere entr'acte in our thitherto-and-thenceforth separate scripts?* It was necessary, evidently, for me to all but lose you in order finally to find myself and us: On the August day most conspicuously appropriate for proposing the best answer to summer's question, I painfully and conspicuously did not so do. The sequel very nearly broke off our story, and at that suddenly unthinkable prospect — by dawn's early, red-eyed light, I'm going to bet — the scales fell from my eyes. Not surprisingly, it took some doing to undo my just-done damage; to make as clear to you as it was unequivocally now to me where my real heart lay.

DWGMPMFUP,† 40, with three centrifugal college-age-or-thereabouts children, seeks harmonious female lead for third act of floating-opera-in-progress and partner for second half of life. Has come ardently to prefer one particular SWJF former-student/

---

*We became, in fact, confirmed opera fans at Chautauqua, whose venerable Institution, across- and down-lake from our cottage, boasted a creditable summer-repertory company and half a dozen productions per season. Once, at least, we literally floated thereto and -from, sailing our little sloop over to the opera-house docks in dress-up clothes after dinner as if Lake Chautauqua were Sydney Harbor, and outboard-motoring home in the dark with only a flashlight for navigation-aid.

†Pronounced *Dawgumpumfup*: Divorced White Goyishe Male PostMod-Fictioneering University Prof.

present-schoolteacher, just turned 27, although not one of those specs (*F* excepted) had been a particular prerequisite. Shall we?

. . . . *"Yes!"*

Each of those suspension-points a reasonable and reasoned hesitation — yours, mine, ours — overcome, on our bottom line, by joy. Let meteors zilch down from Perseus & Co.! Let Pegasus lift off for heaven, Bellerophon aboard, and with them my unbogged *Bellerophoniad*! Bid Scheherazade make ready backstage to complete my *Chimera* and launch who knows what sequelae, as this refueled Pumblechook zips frictionless across this old binder's leaves! Turn the lake-fly rheostat on High; roll away those lake-effect clouds and let the sun shine in! Show me your family, I'll show you mine! Let autumn blaze through Buffalo and Boston as we blazon our betrothal, plan a year's-end wedding bash, bop back and forth between our still-separate burgs, also down to our birthplaces to meet our several in-laws-to-be — in the between-times (which is to say, mainly) teaching like crazy and, chez moi, making sentences, sentences. As I'll be beginning our married life on academic leave (there's that left-loose end tucked up), let's honeymoon in the Caribbean and apartmentkeep in Cambridge through the spring semester — *your* Cambridge, not mine and J. Schreiber/Scribner's, whom by the way you haven't met yet, have you? — so that you can finish out your teaching year. Then back to dear Chautauqua for the summer and at least one academic year in Buffalo before we re-abide in Boston for the year thereafter, visiting-professoring at B.U. while we decide where we want to put down roots for this opera's upcoming Act Three. Let another beastly Beantown blizzard bloody near bury my bride-to-be in Brookline on her fly-to-Philadelphia-to-be-weddinged day, but not quite: You'll as bravely bang through it out to Logan as you banged through its foretwin to say hi at Boston College, while I Pontiac my children from Chautauqua to Brotherly-Loveville for the nuptial festivities. Let me buss my bride under the bema and break the bridegroomal wineglass underheel! Between Hanukkah/Christmas and New Year's, we'll dance a horah in Rittenhouse

Square with our buddies assembled;* we'll home from honey-moon to find an unanticipated welcoming committee: my teensters evicted from their large, once-comfortable old Central Park house, the henceforth-custody of all three our surprise wedding gift, shall we say. Bravely you'll embrace it, and them: Welcome home, kids, to Chautauqua/Boston/Buffalo, wherever we hereafter are when you're between college terms or colleges and not yet living on your own. We'll do our darnedest to help them improvise their new lives as we improvise ours; partly in consequence, they'll gravitate New Englandward as we do, and settle in there — at M.I.T., at Boston U., in New London and Hartford — as this entr'acte barrels to a close in the spring of '73. By then, three *B*s bid for us: We can abide in Boston, me at B.U., you back at nearby Wayland High (but you've had your fill, you feel, of the burnout workloads of full-time public-high English teaching, even at such superior schools as that); we can backtrack to Buffalo, me to my SUNY/ Buff Butler chair, you to the Buffalo Seminary, where you've had your baptismal go at private girls'-high teaching, become an ardent convert thereunto, and covered yourself with pedagogical glory in your trial year there. Or — a whole new ball game, sort-of-fore-seen in a certain brawlbrat B-card — we can build our new life in an all-but-brand-new bailiwick for both of us: Edgar Poe/H. L. Mencken country, lately enjoying a bit of a renaissance, we hear; not only Baltimore — where a just-right job at a just-right girls' school beckons you, and the reinvigoration of the Hopkins Writ-ing Seminars beckons me — but the Bay!

Quoth (in a word) the brawlbrat: "Baltimore!" Shall we brave it, bambina mia, or bid him bug off?

But hey, you know all this. Between us, if you're here to hear, it goes without saying. *Are* you, somehow, here, dear dedicatee?

---

*Most of the most important ones except one: Jerome Schreiber/Jay Wordsworth Scribner, who'll be off bareboating in the British Virgins while we're beach-basking in Bird-of-Paradiseland, Tobago. I've told you about Jay Scribner, no? My all-purpose best-buddy/bête-noire? My combination coach, critic, con-science, and confidant, whom I sometimes call my counterself, always a step or two ahead of me except when he's a two-step behind? No?

Push on, Parker; pop the big questions. We're at this 'tween-acts
tunnel's end: Is that light I see ahead, or mere more blank paper?
Knock knock, old *ree*mote: Who's there? By fall '73 (North Vietnamese Tet Offensive, Yom Kippur War and Arab oil embargo)
the Sixties have bidden us bye-bye. More to Pumblechook's point,
during the drafting of this entr'acte our fateful *Columbus Day '92*
has come and gone; is history! Where are we, then, now?* When
is *Once Upon a Time* these days? Where am I? Where is . . . she?

*21 November 1992, just back to Baltimore/Langford Creek from a Boston/
Cambridge lecture-revisit to Harvard — last lectured at, as it happens, in '73.
Reunion with one of those erstwhile-teenster children (almost the age now that I
was then, and living and working in that neighborhood) as well as with sundry
former students and colleagues teaching thereabouts. For bride and bridegroom,
twenty-two years after that so-consequential *Yes!*, a happy re-hello to scenes of
our blizzard-blessed remeeting at B.C. — scenes duly dusted with Boston's first
snowfall of the season.

ACT 3 (OF 2)

〉〈 〉〈

Reprise: "What am I doing here?"

"What am *I* doing *here?*" she reasonably demands to know, rearriving through this opera's back door as welcomely as once she arrived at my Chautauqua cottage, and made it ours. "What's going on? Where *are* we?"

As then, I quickly, joyously put down this pen, more or less — shirt-pocket it, something, anything, I don't know — and hurry to embrace her, relegating all questions to the page-foot.* But like Aeneas's arms through Venus on the battlements of Dido's Carthage, mine pass through her image as through light or language, embracing nothing. One or the other of us (I ought to've known) is incorporeal, a verbal virtuality, a hologram of longing. From this opera's point of view, ineluctably, it's she: a nonplussed, pained, potentially indignant figment.

She looks around us (right through me), at what in the light of her presence we both see to be an airy nothing, though of some magnitude.

"What *is* this?"

I hear hurt and, in hurt's margins, maybe more, but still chiefly puzzlement.

---

*How'd she get here? What time is it now? Where's old *US*? What's she, e.g., wearing? Can't say.

I can explain, I think.

"I hope!" Plainly skeptical, she just as plainly means what she says. When did she ever otherwise? Trusty *reemote*, fail me not, as I here try:

Semi-(but only semi-)sheepish, semi-(ditto-)explanatory semi-aria or -duet: "As best I can"

As best I can in a clutch of mere prose sentences, I synopsize what's more nearly explainable, if at all, in not quite six hundred pagesworth of Parkered looseleaf manuscript, a bit over four hundred of processed printout, maybe three-hundred-odd of bookprint —

"Bookprint!"

— if it gets that far: an overture and two actsworth of floating opera-sentences, plus interlude and opposite-twin entr'actes.

"Explain?"

Right. Back in 1990, see — end of the Eighties or beginning of the Nineties, whichever — when all in the same calendar year I turned six-zero, went emeritus, wound up *The Last Voyage* et cet. —

"I was there, [*pet name*]."

"Right. As I wish you were here, in the literal flesh — or better yet, me wherever your literal flesh is. Anyhow, after the usual postpartum kenosis, maybe a touch more than usual this time because of that string of coincidences, I began what I couldn't and can't resist thinking of as my Last Book. . . .

"Last book!"

Not necessarily (I hasten to add, as much to myself as to her) that there won't be any after it from this good-as-new old pen, but that it's meant to wrap up riffs that I've been noodling for forty years. Like, you know, floating operas, water-messages and night-sea journeys, lost paths and last voyages. . . .

"Last book."

Granted, the whole idea is a touch self-concerned, a touch valedictorian and maybe self-dramatizing, a touch —

"A touch. . . ."

I reach out; she does, too. If only! But one of us is insubstantial, mere light of words. The trouble with *ree*motes . . .

Well: There's this couple, see, like us in some ways? In some ways *actually* us, I suppose —

"*Us!*"

I know, I know: a no-no. But bear with me. On Columbus Day '92 (still two years in the future when I started this story), they set out — *we* set out — on a little end-of-the-season Chesapeake sailing cruise. Their boat — *our* boat, you understand, but not really ours — is called *US* —

"Us!"

Upper-case *U-S*. I know, I know. Anyhow, out they set, more or less in the wake of these sort-of-friends of theirs named Beth Duer and Jay Wordsworth Scribner, who're sailing Columbus's first voyage in reverse, back to Square One and beyond. Jay, anyhow, is doing that, maybe solo, or so he says. Bear with me.

She does, not without difficulty, as she has always done, not always with difficulty, before replying. Those predawn conch-calls from across the creek; fast-eroding "Potamock Island" and the old eco-ketch *American Century*; my suspended passage; "our" impulsive wind-up-the-fall-season sailing cruise. Pickup of empty cask from edge of marsh; loss overboard of pen in Queenstown Creek; sanctuary in "the *-rome* of St. Jerome." Then Tropical Storm Jerry and *US*'s impasse in the Dorchester marshes, or wherever. Our inadvertent separation —

"Separation!"

I should say our inadvertently *becoming separated* —

"*Becoming separated!*"

As best I can, I explain as best I can: those endlessly forking waterways through the tall spartina; that loblolly-pine grove and dry-rotting picnic table, as sharply focused in my imagination as if projected by a camera obscura. "Jill," "Jay," covered-footbridge passage and painful au revoir, return of Parker *ree*mote in exchange for wristwatch. Then Act One, Entr'acte in the Dark, Act Two, Between-Acts Light . . .

" . . . *!*"

No need to say it: So careful of our privacy that she winces at even the tiniest, 'tween-the-liniest personal references in my fiction; wishes I wouldn't even do the handful of interviews that I do once every four years or so, when a new title's out. Keep the fiction fictional and our factual lives private, is her position; mine, too, in principle, although we know good writers who routinely work close to the bone of personal experience. It's not our style — most emphatically not hers, but not mine, either, despite the undeniable circumstance that here and there from time to time et cetera, since after all one's fiction doesn't come from nowhere. Still and all, even this *Once Upon a Time*, after all, is, after all . . . you know. I mean, there's really no *US* —

"No us!"

The boat; their boat. Even the couple: They're certainly not us in the sense that et cetera, even though et cetera, any more than Dante's Dante-and-Beatrice in the *Commedia* are et cetera. Projections; fictions. *Reemotes.* And it's not as if I've been spilling my guts or kiss-and-telling, even though admittedly et cetera. I made up this Jerry Schreiber/Jay Wordsworth Scribner character mainly to goose things along, but also to frame and distance the whole show. Remember those floating reed islands in the Shatt al Arab that the Marsh Arabs live on, generation after generation, adding new layers of spartina to the top as the bottom rots away? What I imagined was three opera acts like marsh islands of time, each about twenty years long, and on each island a different guide or helper to guide the quote/unquote hero — the "tenor," let's say —

"You."

Not *me*, but "me": the small-time Dante character, lost in Time's funhouse. A projected likeness of Sister Jill guides the guy through Island One: womb to college, more or less. Then this Jay Scribner character prods him through Island-Two/Act-Two, except that I solo through the 1960s. As discreetly as I can, needless to say.

"You."

The *I* character. Really, [*pet name*], it's not autobiography: it's a kind of ship's log of the Inside Passage, framed by this fictitious literal voyage. And even though it infracts House Rule Number

One, I have to hope dot dot dot. Because where we are right now . . .

"We."

Us.

"Where *are* quote-we-unquote right now?"

Deep breath. Couple of twists of this *ree*mote, which I've really got the hang of now, and you'll see the whole show: Right now in the playback we're on the threshold of Act Three — of three, I'm presuming. End of 1960s; turn of decade; end of tunnel but not of road. Curtain about to open on our married life, all twenty-two years of it and counting, just as on a certain snowy Boston evening in Feb '69 (Michel de Montaigne's birthday, as it happens) a certain pair of elevator doors was about to close — *were* about to close? — may already have started closing, which if they did — I mean if they *do*, it's that close and contingent — if they do, there goes Act Three: our entire future; our whole life together. Unless, dot dot dot

Rescuaria: "May I . . . ?"

While I thus replay for her in a hurry this opera thus far — holding open, as it were, those fateful elevator doors — she considers. No: She *deliberates*, as she did not between Receptions One and Two on 28 February 1969.

"In that case," she presently responds, and turns on her klieg-light smile, "may I . . . ?"

Allah, Apollo, Jesucristo, YHWH, Zeus — all applicable gods and spirits nameable and unnameable be praised! Welcome aboard this floating elevator, love! Joy to the world!

"On one condition." Serious-faced now. "Maybe more than one."

Write your own ticket! Just get yourself aboard here, into my arms here! Haven't we always kissed in empty elevators since Day One? Ai yi, we can't: One of us is still virtual. So: conditions.

"You bet. To begin with: No Act Three."

No Act Three! Our personal private floating island! Our life together!

386 ONCE UPON A TIME

"Exactly. Draw the curtains on that before they open, s.v.p.: Nobody's business but ours."

No Baltimore and Langford Creek! No travels traveled and writings written! No teaching awards for Her or literaries for Him! No children married, no grandchildren, no sailboat cruising. . . .

"Her finger's on our elevator's STOP button," she warns me: "She means business."

Oy veh is mir, no Act Three. Okay. Okay?

"For starters. Now, then: That make-pretend Jay Whatsisname with his back-and-forth names and his unzipped fly — What's he on the payroll for?"

My brawlbrat vanguard? My counterself?

"That's the problem. I like the guy, actually, as a fictional character — muted but spiky, et cetera. But not only is this whole so-called opera a Song of Thyself; even the sopranos, altos, and baritones are echoes of the lead tenor."

Madame Bovary, c'est moi. . . .

"In a novel, okay. In your more-or-less memoir, okay, even, for Acts One and Two. But not in our real-life private elevator from Nineteen Seventy to now, whenever *now* is these days. Either we get out of his novel or he gets off our lift, right about here — and he takes that Beth Duer person with him, while he's at it, and all that Potamock Island *American Century* stuff, too. Our life together is *real*, [pet name], not virtual, and it's really nobody else's beeswax. I mean it: We kiss in empty elevators only."

Of course she does — mean it, I mean. Whenever didn't she, my true and proper counterself? But hey: The guy's got my watch, for one thing.

"Your *virtual* watch, right? So you do a few virtual tricks with that virtual *reemote*, and allakazam. That's *your* department — and here's our floor: One Nine Seven Zero." She keeps her finger on CLOSE. "No Beatrice-trip for me" is what she's telling me; "no Whatsername — Socrates's chick, that led him up Love's ratlines in the *Symposium* when we read it together back at Penn State? Diotima, right; hell with that. No such patronizing angel-of-mercy, show-mere-mortal-male-hero-the-way crapola for us" is what she's saying: "I'm your *partner*, [*pet name*], not your Better-Half Guiding-Light Muse. No wonder things went haywire down in that marsh! How're you going to get us out of there, so we can touch and hold and get on with it? What time is it, by the way?"

Deep breath: I could say simply . . .

But it's not that simple; time's not ripe yet to say that. I ask, instead, What time *was* it, last time she looked? Time of year, I mean.

"Early-Decemberish, at least. You've been at this *forever*."

'92?

"Of course Ninety-Two! Where've you been?"

. . . So what's new, [*pet name*], please? I mean what *will* be, by the time our times are in synch again? For a while yet, I need to stay put in this suspended passage, tucking up loose ends — maybe not as much longer as I'd feared, now that you've shown me the light, excuse the expression. And I'm hoping you'll stay with me, 'cause I think I'm onto something. I think I might even see . . . But first, the news.

"You mean like Yugoslavia's self-destructing? Somalia's starving to death? Xenophobia's breaking out like zits all over Europe?"

Mm hm. What about the home front?

"New president-elect? Like that?"

Ah, so. And the *home* home front?

She considers: "Well: It's been a cool and gloomy fall for my first real teaching leave. Almost none of the biking we'd planned; even the foliage was dull this year. Good weather for writing, evidently, and paradise compared to Bosnia and Somalia. All the same . . ."

Sailing?

"Scarcely any."

Deep breath. What can you tell me about October 12th?

"Columbus Day?" She considers, warily. "A Monday, wasn't it? Monday, yes, 'cause the first Bush-Clinton debate was on the Sunday night just before it. There was a full moon that Sunday night, but too chilly to be outside and too cloudy to see anything anyhow. Anti-Columbus demonstrations here and there, but nothing ugly. Oh: And NASA began a mission called SERENDIP to listen for extraterrestrial radio signals in our galaxy."

From Sindbad's magic island?

"They're going to scan twenty-eight million frequencies for ten years, if I remember correctly — Are you listening?"

Intently. Meanwhile, back at Langford Creek?

"*Nobody's beeswax but ours.* Don't push me, [*pet name*], or I push OPEN and you're on your virtual own."

I mean just in general. Like for instance —

Ruefully but determinedly, she shakes her head. "Come see for yourself, as soon as you can." Her eyes meet mine, as they say — in a certain way, with a certain look. "It's been no picnic, waiting all alone . . . out there on that virtual sailboat, virtually stuck in a virtual marsh in the middle of virtually nowhere."

Are you telling me . . . ? Do you mean we really . . . ?

"Not really: virtually. Boyoboy, am I tired of *virtually*! Come get us out of there, okay?"

Good as her word, she presses that virtual button — and alas, the lift's all mine.

Calendrical-error-assisted narrative Doppler-Effect aria: "On 12 October 1990"

On 12 October 1990, a Friday, the writer of this sentence first-drafted in this old binder the opening notes of the overture to *Once Upon a Time: A Floating Opera*, to wit:

"Gone."

What?

"*Century.*"

Ah, et cetera.

Reckoning then two Columbus Days down the road, to the Quincentenary, in order to find the day of the week on which this exchange would be exchanged, I made one or the other of two errors, inexplicably (for an amateur sailor/navigator accustomed, despite his innumeracy, to such analogous calculations as time/speed/distance, course and compass corrections, tide times and current sets) but honestly and fortuitously: Either I inadvertently reckoned only one year ahead instead of two, and so arrived at an

US-departure day of *Saturday* 12 October '92, or else — more likely, but still passing strange — I properly reckoned two years ahead (*Sunday* 12 October '92) but then applied the necessary leap-year correction the wrong way, as nonprofessional navigators will sometimes miscorrect for variation between True and Magnetic courses when moving from chart to compass or vice versa — and so arrived not at *Monday* but once again at *Saturday* 12 October 1992, as the timetable of that overture attests. To aid the navigator in correcting for variation and the rest, there are venerable mnemonics;* Who ever supposed one would be needed for leap-year correction in our house, where leap days have a particular significance?†

Felix culpa! Serendipitous fault! Dear old innumeracy! For while I had foreseen, in arias long since sung, that the calendar of my sentence-making would run more swiftly (i.e., the sentences come more slowly) that that of *US*'s voyage into the Chesapeake Triangle, and that therefore a time must come when the time of my tale would be overtaken by the time of its telling, back then I could predict neither when this narrative syzygy would come to pass nor what, when it did, might be its effect. A year went by, and most of another — '90 turned '91 and '92; age sixty followed suit; Overture was succeeded by Interlude, Act One, Entr'acte, Act Two — in the course whereof, as with any landfall, a very roughly approximate Estimated Time of Arrival at that conjunction became calculable, barring major setbacks or set-forwards. By when Hurricane Andrew tore ashore in late August '92, and his lesser siblings — Bonnie, Charlie, Danielle, Earl — blew themselves out offshore in the weeks thereafter, it became possible not

---

*E.g., the elaborate reversible acrostic *TVMDC* (for True, Variation, Magnetic, Deviation, and Compass), to be back-read "Can Dead Men Vote Twice?" when correcting from compass to chart, and, when "uncorrecting" from chart to compass, fore-read "True Virgins May Date Casanovas," or some such — I forget, exactly.

†Because those Boston College elevator doors first opened, closed, and reopened for us on the night of 28 February 1969, and we awoke in La Chartreuse de Boston on the morning of 1 March — an anniversary unfailingly celebrated thereafter in our house with oysters and champagne, e.g. And on leap days . . . but enough said.

only to refine that ETA but, as one sometimes does in literal navigation, to adjust both course and speed (my weather eye ever on
"Tropical Storm Jerry's" approach, my net progress serendipitously assisted, without my knowing it, by that cross-my-heart calendar error, as by a tailwind or an unfactored-in fair tide) to the
end of . . .

The end of this opera, almost. Let me explain:
    Time flies, all right. But imagination, goosed by serendipity, can
fly faster, and not only overtake it but catch thereupto at such a
clip that in a narrative equivalent of C. J. Doppler's celebrated
Effect, the future's red shift is greened. Chronology's passage
becomes suspended, is even rewound a frame or two, or twisted
back upon itself like a Möbius strip reading ONCE UPON A TIME
THERE WAS A STORY THAT BEGAN, et cetera. Time's been out since
Act Two's curtain; *we have not yet begun Act Three.* Indeed, per
musely elevator-order *there will be no such act*: Narrative present-
timewise, we're at the end of this opera, almost — have been, in
virtual fact, since tell-time overtook tale-time on Columbus Day
'92.
    And when was that, exactly? Let me explain. It was not,
Q.E.D., on that misreckoned *Saturday* Columbus Day '92 when
(as I wrote on Friday C.D. '90) three conch-calls waked us to our
overture. Nor was it on some post-Quincentenary Columbus Day
arrived at by full recounting of "our" third-act 1970s and Eighties
up to 12 October '92. Nunnayerbeeswaxville, that particular
floating island: NO TRESPASSING.
    When was it, then, that the telling overtook the tale? See
Between Acts: Light's first footnote, here refooted for readerly
convenience.* We have vertiginously rearrived at Time's time-out,
Columbus Day 1992: our starting place, almost. The end of this
opera, almost.

---

*Act Two's first-draft curtain-close penned on 9 October 1992, a rainy mild Fri-
day at Langford Creek. Forecast uncertain for the weekend ahead, now past. *On
the Monday following*, houselights darken and stage lights rise (Harvest Moon,
too, over our creek's east fork) for this second entr'acte." [*Italics added.*]

But not quite: "Loose ends, Oatmeal"

Quite as I reckoned, that just-sung aria fetches from the wings or overheads my minatory counterself: brawlbrat ex machina, lord of Time's flies. Are you wired, Saint Jay? Old Dopplergänger, do you read me?

"Like a book." My man duly thumbs his eyeglasses, shakes his head. "An *unfinished* book. Loose ends, Oatmeal! This whole non-act you're trying to float is one large loose end: a Doppler Special Effect. Nothing doing."

Salty Charybdis to my revanished muse's Scylla, you and she are dopplerganging up on me! No Act Three she; No Loose Ends you — What's a chap to do?

The question being rhetorical, Jay answers it: "*Tuck up*, man, pronto. Don't miss a trick, or you're stuck in hyperspace for keeps."

My long-term loose-end goal, I assure him, is the successful tuck-up of every shorty: that left-behind dinghy, for instance: oars, fuel can, empty cask —

"And my current short-term goal," he lets me know, "is to monitor your progress toward that longie. Your Nineteen Seventies, your Nighteen Eighties: five booksworth of second life. No cutting corners, Oats, if you want your watch back and the rest. Don't miss a trick — but no trick endings."

Done.

"Done?" My normally untakeabackable pal shows signs of being very nearly so taken. "Whatchamean, *done?*"

All behind us, alas, for one thing: Tempus fugit, in very truth. But tucked up, too, is what I mean. Don't underestimate this handy-dandy *ree*mote, friend!

Some arias back (I explain), when it looked to me as if this floating opera might go down with all hands before re-reaching home port, like a certain Admiral of the Ocean Sea I *casked the log* of that event-rich, twenty-year-and-ongoing discovery-voyage, 1970–199_: Middle age; death of peers and parents, marriage of children and birth of grandkids; exploration under sail of Chesapeake and Caribbean, and (under auspices) of Europe, Hawaii, Alaska, Japan; modest recognition, modest affluence, modest plateaufication; assorted peak-passings and capacity-reducements; sundry modest scaling-backs and -downs as early middle age middles on through mid to late! All virtually Parkered by this *ree*mote (I here declare) into a virtual Act Three, then tucked up in a certain sea-wreathed casklet as tightly as ever water-message was, and by this pen-hand virtually transmitted off our dock into the waters of Langford Creek *on the second Saturday of October* '92, thence to wander erratically on that weekend's winds and tides before homing ashore in our precious marsh-patch, not a dockslength from the dock wherefrom I launched it — and there to be espied and retrieved by tenor and soprano on *Monday*, Columbus Day '92, immediately upon their backing *US* out of slip to commence an open-ended end-of-season sail, if so they do. Done.

"*Done?*"

Emphatically. No corners cut, no tricks missed. We set out on the Quincentenary Columbus Day, which I truly mistook to be that Saturday. Turns out it was the Monday following, and so on that same Saturday we haven't yet set out, and maybe won't. Simple. Virtuality be praised!

Jay eyes me with open disbelief. "Where'd you find that cockamamie cask, then, please, that you now claim to've filled and creeked before page one?"

Where'd I find that cockamamie cask; let's see. I found that cockamamie cask . . . exactly in the muddy crotch of a marshy gut-fork in the middle of nowhere, somewhere south of East Cambridge, Maryland. Tilted toward one tine of the Y, it was, as if to mark somebody's way. Empty, it was, then, that cockamamie cask, and so I tucked it up and reserved it for possible future use. Well I did, too.

"Mm hm. Tell us now just when this fortuitously found object was found, Oatmeal, since you guys haven't started your voyage yet. We're all ears and raised eyebrows."

When found? When found. I could say "Once upon a time," Jay, but time's not ripe yet to say that. No cutting corners! That FFO was by me found sometime between breakfast and lunch on 27 May 1991, my sixty-first, as I penned and then reviewed a certain passage in this opera's marshbound interlude, to wit: *Better this objet trouvé be lost than my motive power; it's nothing but an old empty cask. . . . And who says I'm going to lose it? I am not by nature a loser of things, except in memory,* et cetera — and not always there, Q.E.D. Found, reserved, subsequently stuffed with Act Three of a floating opera in progress (detailed chronicle of composer's replenishment from December 1970 through October Wheneveritwas '92) and with this pen-hand launched into Langford Creek just prior to the opening notes of the overture to *Once Upon a Time.* Good old Christian Johann Doppler.

"Jee-sus. And exactly what were you doing, prithee, in that make-pretend down-county marsh at that make-pretend Place Where Three Ways Meet when you came across this make-pretend empty cask that you now pretend you later filled, though you haven't yet set sail? Tuck up, man; I'm keeping score."

Your métier. Like Theseus his thread or Hansel and Gretel their breadcrumb trail, I was retracing my way out of the woods, across a certain covered footbridge and back through the labyrinth, en route home to a certain *US*, learning by going where I'd been. From a certain dry-rotting picnic table in a loblolly-pine grove, I slogged back across mudflats and other déjà vu marsh scenery toward where I had left a certain dinghy, and fortuitously refound it despite my having neglected in this opera's Interlude to beacon its location with one of its oars. There the dear old thing nestled in the cordgrass, intact and undisturbed, both oars tucked up under its midships seat and my faithful hand-bearing compass high and dry in its stern along with deck moccasins and socks, which I've been without since this opera's floating Interlude. With their aid I first rowed and then outboarded back and back, almost due east, toward one of a number of similar-appearing watercourses leading deeper into the all-but-trackless marsh: a watercourse fortuitously distinguished, however, by a red plastic outboard fuel can lashed head-high to an improvised fasces of cattails just reachable from the dinghy (and by me now reached, unlashed, tucked up under the thwartships seat, and there secured). Back up that watercourse I dinghied — Fork Two, it was (of two), forking from the stem of a certain marshy trivium, or

Place Where Three Ways Meet, one of many such tidewater trivia in my boggy birthland and yours — and arriving or rearriving at the very crotch of that Y, I discovered thereupon and recovered therefrom a jim-dandy casklet, sea-wreathed and barnacled, rusty-hooped but snugly coopered withal, and contentless but for its own bung, which had been irretrievably banged inside it. This cask I fetched from the mother-muck (first noting, for future reference, its inclination), rinsed muckless in the brackish gut, and tucked up under that same thwartseat beside the fuel can; for who could say but what it might one day come to my rescue as I had its and prove the very vessel for casking off some water-message — e.g., the "Act Three" log of my forties and fifties, our American century's Seventies and Eighties? And so indeed it came to do, rebunged so stoutly as to be not only unsinkable but unopenable, on that Dopplered Columbus Day '92 that I had misanticipated to be the Saturday of "our" setting out in "*US*" — when in calendric fact we won't set out until the Monday following (i.e., Columbus Day), if indeed we do at all.

There, then: tucked up! On now back up that aforemarked tine and its own serial dilemmas, right left left — which will be to say right *right* left (right?), as I'll be reversing the reciprocal of my Interlude-course through this marsh-maze — straight back to *US* and, with no further complication, out and on with our story.

Done.

"Done?" About time . . . :

Jay Wordsworth Scribner fists his specs. "Done?"

Done and done, old front man. Anchor aweigh! Damn the torpedoes! Done-diddly-done-diddly-done. My watch, s.v.p.

He shakes his curly head; puts his my-watched left hand behind his back. "Diddled, for sure. But done? *Not* done, lad! All to do! All but all, anyhow."

Not so, Jay.

"So so so! Like Hansel's bird, I've followed and swallowed your tricksy trail of virtualities. You're nowhere!"

Not so. Not so.

"So, man, so! Virtually so, anyhow. Look around you!"

Alas, he's right, my freckled gadfly, my vigilant virtual Virgil: We're suspended still in a verbal hyperspace as empty as CC's cask. I scratch my head; I fiddle my Pumblechook. Some loose end yet untucked, I venture, like the final digit of an access code. Jay pretends to consult my watch.

Swiss army knife!
   "Beg pardon?"
On my left-hand fingertips I tick off the What-if waypoints of our voyage: conch-calls three, waking, *Century* gone, suspended passage, *Let's do it*; departure of *US*, espial of cask in marsh-patch and retrieval of same; first-night anchorage in Queenstown Creek, cask forced at cockpit happy hour and found empty, dinner and bedtime tuck-in; then pocket pen and step up on deck to sip Dunkelbier and check out the nighttime universe; aria "What are we doing here?" and unanswered query *How did I open that bottle of Beck's Dark?*
   Aboardship (I declare triumphantly to Jay), except in bed I'm never without Swiss army knife in pocket — "Tinker" model, to be specific: two blades (one large, one small, both sharp), gimlet, Phillips screwdriver, extractable tweezers and ditto toothpick, combination can-opener/small-slotted-screwdriver, and combination standard-slotted-screwdriver/*cap-lifter*, with which last I lifted the cap of that bottle of Beck's Dark just prior to taking a leeward pee (recommended only with hook down in snug harbor, reckless friend), going forward to bid good night to *US*'s anchor rode, and losing this without-which-nothing Parker overside. My watch, sir.
   He regards me, my foregoer, my clarion-calling counterself. He shakes his curl-haired head; rubs pensively his scarred embouchure with the back of his left hand (I squint in vain to tell the time). He quotes me dryly from some Act Two recitative:* "*If you're drowned, I'm sorry. I'll miss you, as I've missed you before.* Christamighty, Oatmeal!"

---

* *Back to the picnic table: Wanderjahr.*

That I shall, Jeronimo mio. Miss you.

"You can hardly wait for bail-out time."

Be that as may, miss you I shall.

"There's a lot I could say right now," he lets me know, his thumbs hooked in his jeans hind pockets. "Boyoboy. But I'll just quote your *other* friend, from a few pages back: 'Either we get out of his novel or he gets off our lift.' Also, 'a few virtual tricks with that virtual *ree*mote, and allakazam.'" Eyeglasses up. "The root difference between you and me, Oat-boy..."

He pauses; he grins — and that teasing ellipsis clicks the combination. Brandishing Pumblechook like the aegis/golden-bough/godseye/wondertool it is, I write the sentence *The sentences get written* and others after it, e.g.: *Get thee behind me, Brawlbrat!*

Can the drowned sigh dryly? My counterself sighs dryly. "You haven't heard the last of me, Oatmeal."

Who wrote that sentence? Auf Wiedersehen, Jay-babe, and Amen! Time to zip your fly, man. Tuck up.

Right hand on zipper, left extended meward, Jay Wordsworth Scribner smiles. As if answering the biggest rhetorical question of all, he says "About time," and zip: He's gone.

In the nick of we-know-what, I catch my watch. Allakazam.

EPISONG

〰 〰

Aria: "Dante's Dante"

Dante's Dante, in the *Commedia*, sojourns three days in the otherworld, learning by going where he has to go: not the first such lost-and-found weekender, nor the last. Now,* thanks to a certain serendipitous time warp, we're on the predawn cusp of 12 October 1992 (a Monday). Behind us is not only this long operatic weekend, but our score and more of unsung years à deux, their virtual tale water-messaged off in a virtual but well-bunged cask labeled NUNNAYERBEESWAX, to gain even further body and flavor as it floats. Ahead lies a surely eventful, anyhow ineluctable end-of-one-season-beginning-of-another voyage, presently to be embarked upon. Meanwhile we snooze in hypertime, until in our creekside bed — creekbed? — we hear or dream, from out there somewhere amid vague wild-goose-music, a clear conch-call. Then another. Now† a third.

---

*Per calendar, winter solstice '92: a Monday, second day of Hanukkah. Author and mate back at Langford Creek from a week's Caribbean vacation and repacking to begin, with the new year, a different journey, of longer time, perhaps to Columbus's first landfall and beyond — he penning, in the sunstopped interim, this episong.
†Time in. Rebegin.

Reprised duet: "Gone"
   "Gone."
   What?
   ". . . Dream, I guess."
   Ah.
   But this is no dream: I'm I, and (Muse be praised!) you're you.
We're here. We're now.
   "Now?" you wonder, sleepily. "What time is it anyhow? Can
you see your watch?"
   No need, Pet Name: The time is once upon.